THE AUTHOR

Fran Brady was born and schooled in Dundee and is a graduate of St. Andrews University. She spent many years working in community development and charity management.

She began writing fiction in 2006.

Other novels by Fran Brady:
A Good Time for Miracles
Eleanor's Journey
The Ghost of Erraid

Find out more at www.franbrady.com

Published in 2017 by FeedARead.com Publishing   Second Edition
The author has asserted their moral right under the
Copyright, Designs and Patents Act, 1988, to be identified
as the author of this work.

For all those who remember the sixties.
And for those who don't — even if they were there.

ACKNOWLEDGEMENTS

My heartfelt thanks to:
- all those who read, commented, encouraged and were brave enough to be brutally frank
- my old pals from Chattan days who rallied round wonderfully, sent me lots of emails, dredged up lots of memories and put hours of work into advising and criticising
- my husband who puts up with a wife rarely without a laptop on her knee
- St Andrews University and dear old Chattan: they gave me the magical memories that were the inspiration for the book.

Youth's a stuff will not endure
William Shakespeare

3

RED GOWN GIRL

by

Fran Brady

CHAPTER ONE: CAROLINE AND HUGH

A shaft of weak, early February sun was disturbing the sleepy students and distracting attentive ones. Caroline watched the dust motes swirling around the lecturer's gaunt profile. He never looked at his students, preferring to gaze upon the quadrangle outside. Rumour had it that he had once lectured to an empty room without noticing – but this was difficult to prove as, by definition, no-one had been there. A metaphysical conundrum, like the one he was, at this very moment, attempting to outline to a hundred baffled undergraduates.

This three o'clock lecture – Logic and Metaphysics – was Caroline's least favourite. So far, in a term and a half, she had understood virtually nothing the man had said. Her notes defied interpretation and served only as joke material at the after-dinner gatherings in Chattan, her hall of residence. Luckily, the textbooks for the course were simple and quite interesting. She and her friend, Patsy – a mad Irish medic - had sat up till three in the morning recently, arguing whether Descartes could be proved to have actually been a dog, using his own logic.

'Plato seems to be trying to imply that …' Henry Castleton Forsyth, Dean of the Faculty of Arts (Cassie to his friends), jingled the coins in his pocket and weighed his words. They were always likely to come back to haunt him in an assignment or exam paper. It could be daunting to see a mere throwaway remark appearing in black and white. First-year undergrads were especially prone to it, even down to his little witticisms. Not that they understood these, of course. *Casting artificial pearls before real swine* – that was one of his favourites.

The quadrangle was beginning to fill up with red gowns and the occasional black of a lecturer. Quad tower clock began to drone the hour. Plato would have to carry on trying for another day. With relief, he turned from the window and strode across the dais, swept up his papers and books from the lectern and whirled out of the room, black gown billowing behind him. It was always surprising, this sudden burst of life after sixty minutes of near-motionless muttering. His relief was instantly mirrored by his students. Pens were thrown down, fingers flexed, tongues and tonsils exposed in yawns. A hum of conversation broke out and began to swell. A loud burst of laughter from one small group acted like a starter's pistol and the noise erupted.

Caroline looked across the lecture room at the group. The boys were all tall, public-schools types. One of them had a flashy old sports car, in which he roared around town, farting like an old horse – the car, that is, not him. The girls were Mary Quant disciples - very short skirts and strange, asymmetrical haircuts. They countered the chill north-east wind with thick, brightly coloured tights and drooping furry hats.

This was *The Chelsea Set*, as they liked to call themselves, also known behind their backs as 'The Oxbridge Rejects'. Having failed to gain a place at either Oxford or Cambridge, they had reluctantly settled for the third oldest university in Britain. They brought their London manners with them: they thought they were what Caroline's Aberdeen granny called 'nae sma' drink'. Certainly there was nothing small about them: not their allowances from their rich daddies; not their air of doing the other students a favour by slumming it in this backwater.

Like everyone else in Lecture Room One at that moment, Caroline looked across at the group. She found her eyes caught and held by the tallest boy. He was lounging, one buttock propped on the sloping desk, long 'varsity' scarf trailing, a flick of blond hair dangling across his brow. He had been attending to one of the other boys who was doing a caricature of the Dean – the cause of the burst of laughter. But his eye - the one that wasn't obscured by the flick – roved briefly round, met Caroline's cool glance and faltered. He felt pique, curiosity and … something else. A wriggling worm of excitement.

'Tea at my pad?' drawled Cynthia. 'I've got a new toasting fork and some amazing crumpets. And Mummy sent some wonderful anchovy paste in her last mercy parcel.'

Cynthia's pad was the upper flat of a beautifully converted old house by the harbour. It had a spectacular sea view. Daddy was a big shot in The City and Mummy's mercy parcels hailed from Fortnum and Mason. Cynthia's daily help would be stoking the fire at this very moment, ready for a tea party arriving.

The Set murmured approval and began to drift towards the door out to Quad. Hugh Appleby-Bodington hesitated. The lure of Cynthia's roaring fire and savoury crumpets was strong. Out of the corner of his eye, he saw Caroline link her arm in with a small, chubby girl whose long fair plait hung down to her waist. The ill-assorted two - Caroline was tall and slim with a shock of black curly hair – were heading for the other door. On an impulse, he excused himself from The Set.

I say!' he hurried over to the two girls, drawing level just before the door. 'What did you think of that lecture? Isn't old Forsyth an absolute fossil?'

Caroline turned to snub him: she had little time for The Set. Brought up on a farm in rural Scotland, the daughter of sturdy folk and honest toil, she found their airs and graces ridiculous. But the word *fossil*, alliterating with Forsyth, struck her as funny and she could not suppress a grin. He rushed to open the door for them, holding it ajar, bowing low and 'making a leg' like a Shakespeare character.

'Wilt milady take tea? A warm posset? It is passing cold out there.'

Caroline snorted. 'I think not.'

But her friend, Elspeth, simpered towards him. 'Oooh, yes please! Plato always makes me thirsty.'

He was caught between the two of them - Caroline, still in the room, looking scornful, Elspeth outside, as keen as a puppy for a walk. A noisy batch of students took advantage of his door-holding services. Once they had swarmed through, he realised that Caroline had slipped past among them and was now striding out on to North Street, Elspeth panting after her.

'Where's Hugh? We can't go without Hugh ...' The Set had stopped just short of the other door. Hugh shook his head like a dog sloughing off water. *What on earth was he doing?* He strode across the room, weaving through the rows of desks.

'Coming!' he called. 'Just having a bit of sport.'

'Put the serving wenches down,' reproved Colin Carruthers, owner of the flashy, farting sports car. 'You don't know where they've been.'

Smarting from Caroline's dismissal, Hugh joined in the laughter.

Caroline strode along North Street, head bent into the bitter wind, red student gown wrapped tightly round her. Elspeth trotted at her side. When they had to pause at the corner of Greyfriars Gardens to let two cyclists turn in, she grumbled: 'We could have been sitting in the nice warm Union now – and he'd have been paying. He might even have taken us to *Rusack's* for a proper afternoon tea.'

And he would have been squiring them for all the world to see: Elspeth's maidenly heart throbbed at the thought. She was baffled by Caroline's behaviour.

Caroline was a little baffled herself. The boy was ... a ... a ... *popinjay!* Nice Elizabethan word to go with his Elizabethan charade. But he *had* come over to issue the invitation, had actually broken ranks from the bunch of snobs. Perhaps the play-acting, which she had taken as mockery, had been to cover uncertainty, even shyness. Maybe he really had wanted to take her – them – out to tea. And he *was* handsome – a real dish ...

They turned into Chattan. The smell of burnt toast did nothing to cheer either of them up.

'Are you sure it's not burning?'

'I don't think so ... not if I keep the iron moving. It's hard, though, if your hair was longer it'd be easier. Whoops, sorry!'

'Bloody hell, Elspeth, keep the damned thing away from my head! You're supposed to be ironing my hair straight not burning my ears off.'

'It's working, though.'

'Really? Let me see.' Caroline rose from her knees and peered in the spotted mirror above the deep sink in the laundry room. 'Mmm ... yeah. It's definitely straighter at that side.'

'What's that ghastly smell? What's burning?' A large heap of dirty washing walked into the room, supported by a pair of long, shapely legs, clad in thick black stockings. The red mini-skirt which could be glimpsed just below the heap failed to cover the stocking tops and suspenders but, in deference as much to the Scottish winter as to decency, a pair of purple stretchy bloomers, trimmed with black lace, hid bare thighs.

'Burning? Can you really smell burning, Patsy? I'll kill you, Elspeth, if you've burnt my hair.' Caroline turned to glare at Elspeth; then darted forward and snatched the iron out of her friend's hand, lifting it away from the ironing board cover to reveal a smoking brand. 'Thank God for that! I thought it was my hair.'

The dirty clothes were dumped into one side of the double sink and the top half of an attractive girl came into view. Patsy Macnamara met all the current criteria of feminine beauty: she was five foot ten inches tall; she weighed less than eight stones; she had bony shoulders, no bosom, tiny hips and shoulder length, straight, flicked-at-the-ends hair. If she had not been the least pretentious and most entertaining person in the world, small, chubby Elspeth and frizzy-haired Caroline would have hated her.

'What are you bloody Brits up to now?' Patsy came from Northern Ireland. Catholic by birth, agnostic by inclination, she affected a strong spirit of Irish nationalism. For a couple of pints of Guinness, she could always be relied on for a rousing rendition of *The Patriot Game*. She had, only this week, been ejected from a history lecture for passing loud, scathing remarks about Lloyd George's handling of The Irish Question. She had left the lecture room singing cheerfully, and her voice – surprisingly deep for one with so little chest – had floated around Quad: *Six counties are under John Bull's tirr-ann-ee*. She cared little about the expulsion: she had only gatecrashed the lecture to do a bit of Brit-baiting. Her chosen field was medicine.

She shook *Tide* soap powder over the clothes and turned on the tap.

Clouds of steam gushed out. Whatever else might be said about the living conditions at Chattan, no-one could deny the pressure and temperature of the hot water.

'For heavens' sake, turn that damned thing off and add some cold. Quick! The steam will make my hair go curly again.' Caroline put a protective hand over the straightened side.

'The weather'll do that for you, the minute you step outside.' Patsy gestured to the window: thick fog obscured the view of the West Sands. 'Sea-haar! Sea-haar!' She made it sound like the cry of migrating birds, wisely quitting Scottish shores as winter drew on.

'Come *on*, Caroline.' Elspeth rubbed at the burnt ironing-board cover. 'Let's get your other side done. I've got tons of reading to do for Monday's tutorial.' She was thinking of her pile of European History books, obtained that morning from the library.

'What is it this time, O swotty one?' Patsy began to feed the soapy clothes through the wringer between the sinks. 'Are we still on the Spanish Inquisition? Those guys had the right idea, I can tell you. Just torture the buggers till they say they believe in the Pope! Then they'll know what's the true faith.'

'Great logic!!' Caroline knelt and laid her head on the ironing board. 'You should try that on Fossil Forsyth.'

'That's not a bad idea. I can't go back to British Constitutional History, that's for sure. Logs 'n' Metafizz, eh? Three o' clock in Lecture One?'

Caroline's head shot up, almost knocking the iron out of Elspeth's hand. 'Don't you dare even think of it. Old Fossil would kill you if you started any of your carry-on in *his* lecture.'

'Turn me into a fossil, eh?' Patsy began to turn the rusty old wringer. It emitted blood-curdling screeches, precluding any further conversation. By the time she finished, Caroline was making a satisfied *moue* at her hair in the mirror and Elspeth had gone off to the Seven Years War.

'Are you going to the hop in the Younger tonight? Is that what all this self-torture is about? Got your eye on someone?'

'I came up to this illustrious establishment to get a degree not a man.'

'Well, no-one ever said you can't do both. Come on, tell Aunty Patsy all about it. Who is he? Or do I have to torture it out of you, like those Spanish guys?' She advanced, arms outstretched, fingers tickling the air.

Caroline screamed and fled. Monica Baxter, fourth year classics student, Head-of-House in Chattan, met the chase and found her red gown caught and almost pulled off by a hysterical Caroline. Then, as she straightened herself and turned, she met Patsy full-on. Her withering remarks about *foolish first-years who need to grow up* echoed down the

11

corridor.

'You can't be serious, old chap!' Colin Carruthers poured sugar from the glass bottle into the frothy coffee and lit a cigarette.

'It would be fun. Loads of people go. What else have we got to do?'

'Not much. This place is such a dead-and-alive hole. Miranda was just telling me in her last letter about all the fun *she's* having.' Miranda was Colin's twin sister, who had obtained a place at Oxford. He was still smarting under the ignominy of ending up in St Andrews.

'There you are then! *Q. E. D.* We go to the Hop.'

'The girls would never forgive us, Hugh. You know what they say about *those cattle-markets.*'

Cynthia, Dorothea, Belinda and the other Chelsea Set girls had expressed their opinion of the Saturday Student Hop often enough. They preferred to keep their social energies for the Balls. They shone at these formal occasions, modelling the latest creations from London's boutiques and sporting the largest corsages from their escorts. So far, there had been one Ball in the men's residence, St Salvator's, just before Christmas last year – a glittering affair – and a small, select one in January in Abbotsford, one of the three women's residences. They were looking forward to several others before the end of this term. They expected that the boys in The Set would squire them. Colin and Hugh had already done their duty by Cynthia and Belinda, taking a turn of each. They would soon be called upon by other girls in The Set and Hugh felt a creeping boredom at the thought.

He extracted a meerschaum pipe from his pocket and began the tricky business of filling the bowl with shreds of tobacco. Tamping them down took several minutes. At last, he struck a match and, for the next five minutes, frenzied sucking alternated with gasping and choking. The pile of spent matches grew and his face was bright red.

'For God's sake, give up and have a fag!' Hugh had paused for a breather. 'Can't think why you bother with the damned thing anyway.'

Hugh was wondering that too, though he cherished the image of drifting through life leaving a trail of fragrant pipe smoke. Cynthia had swooned the last time he had managed it. Now he conceded defeat and laid the pipe in the ashtray to cool.

Colin suddenly turned his head and sniffed. 'Can you smell that?'

Hugh's olfactory glands were temporarily disabled. 'What?'

'It's food! Real food!' Colin smacked his lips. 'What's on the menu at Sally's tonight?'

'Mince and Tomato.'

The boys eyed each other. Sally's (St Salvator's Residence for Men) did an unfortunate line in watery, grey mince, served with a large cold tomato in the middle of each plate. It also specialised in slimy, transparent cabbage and mashed potato threaded through with uncooked pellets.

'Are you thinking what I'm thinking?' The smell of Joe's legendary fish and chips was filling the café. 'Only thing is, old chap ...' Colin tugged down the corners of his mouth. 'I'm skint! The Pater's allowance doesn't come into the bank till the sixth of the month and that's Tuesday. Three days of penury to go. Pockets to let, old man.' He flapped the pockets of the duffel coat which hung on the back of his chair.

These were full of many things – pens, notebook, a well-thumbed paperback, cigarettes, matches, comb, car keys, room-keys, a ball of string, a dog's lead (left over from his visit home at Christmas), a hairy half-eaten packet of Rollos, and much more. But definitely no money.

'If you spent less on petrol for that old banger and poured less down your throat in *The Cross Keys,* you'd not run out in the fourth week of the month.'

'But these are our salad days – gather ye rosebuds, and all that.' As if on cue, the mellow voice of Andy Williams drifted out of the juke-box, r recalling *The Days of Wine and Roses.*

'But this is the third month in a row you've borrowed off me. Budgeting, old fellow, budgeting – you should try it.'

'Take pity on a poor inferior being.' Colin ogled the counter. 'Who could resist such a sight? *Breathes there a man with soul so dead?*'

'Oh, all right.' There had never actually been any question of Hugh resisting the golden-battered fish and chunky chips, liberally sprinkled with vinegar. Sally's mince-and-tomato had never stood a chance. 'Here's the deal, though ...'

Colin was halfway across the café towards the counter. Hugh caught up and pulled him back. 'Here's the deal,' he repeated. 'I buy the fish and chips and you come to The Hop with me tonight.'

'You drive a hard bargain, sir. You would corrupt my innocence in the fleshpots of Saturday night at the Younger Hall?'

'Fleshpots? Chance would be a fine thing! Do we have a deal?'

The bargain was sealed over two hot, greasy newspaper packages as they wound their way towards Sally's in the freezing fog.

The imposing doorway of the Younger Hall thronged with students queuing to pay the entrance fee to The Hop and have their wrists

13

stamped in purple ink. Caroline, Elspeth and Patsy surrendered their coats – bright red duffle for Patsy, old sheepskin, inherited from an aunt, for Caroline, serviceable grey trenchcoat for Elspeth –at the *Ladies Cloaks* hatch. Cilla Black was demanding why *Anyone who had a Heart* would not simply take her in their arms. The dancing area was delineated by pillars which created a square in the middle of the room: it appeared to be a solid mass of heaving, sweating bodies. The area outside the pillars was not much less crowded.

'Holy Mary, Mother of God,' intoned Patsy in Caroline's ear as they tried to fight their way towards the drinks area where bottles of Coca-Cola and Seven-Up were on offer. 'Are we wise in the head?'

Though the three of them attempted to hang on to each other, they were swept apart like flotsam in a cruel sea. Caroline was already regretting her choice of attire. Having just finished knitting an enormous, knee-length sweater, she had not been able to resist teaming it with stripey tights to produce a fashionable beatnik look. She was already sweating and thinking longingly of the sleeveless cotton tunic she had passed over in favour of the thick ganzy. But she had to persevere: a bottle of coca-cola was the requisite prop for lounging against a pillar whilst waiting to be 'asked up'. The press of bodies gave a sudden heave as the front row, having acquired their drinks, turned to push their way back out. Caroline squealed as a shoe came down on her foot. Then she felt a tiny, electric dart, a surprisingly subtle claim on her attention above the pain in her foot and in among the swell of bodies. She saw the head and shoulders of Hugh Appleby-Bodington above the crowd: he was holding a bottle of coke in each hand. He jerked his head, inviting her to break free and join him in a less congested spot.

Oh Lord, him again. The Set Piece. Fat chance he's got. Rather get my own drink.

The hefty girl who had stood on her foot, turned round and began apologising, her face about three inches away. Her breath was cheesy with a hint of constipation. Caroline made a snap decision: putting her head down, she charged out. She could feel her hair starting to curl on her forehead and her face was running with sweat. A couple of girls, passing arm in arm, gestured with their hands towards their eyes. Caroline knew at once what they meant: the cheap mascara and eyeliner, liberally applied to produce the beatnik look, had been no match for the heat and sweat and her headlong surge through the crowd had smeared them to panda-like effect.

Down the marble stairs she sped, into the bowels of the Younger and through the heavy door whose brass plaque proclaimed it to be reserved for *Women*. The room was empty and icy cold, the windows running with condensation. She treated herself to several minutes respite from the beatnik sweater, letting the damp air soothe her hot skin. She had only a scrap of handkerchief which she soaked in cold water and used to scrub her eyes. The toilet cubicles yielded only small sheets of scratchy paper, useless for drying anything. Her comb snapped on the second tug through her fast-curling hair. She emerged some fifteen minutes later.

Thank God! At last! I was beginning to think I'd have to come in and get you – thought you'd fainted or got locked in.'

Looking up, she saw a pair of long legs dangling through the banister railings: Hugh was sitting on the upper flight of the stair, a coke bottle in each hand, one empty, one full. Aware of her red eyes and frizzing hair, Caroline mounted slowly towards him. He waved the full bottle.

'Bit flat by now, but it's still got your name on it.'

She *was* thirsty. Two or three gulps of tepid water from the drinking fountain in the toilet had not been nearly enough. She grabbed the bottle, tipped back her head and poured the liquid down her grateful throat. 'So? What's a city slicker like you doing slumming it here?'

'Thank you very much, Hugh. That was so kind of you.' Nanny Bodington had often used this method of teaching him manners, saying for him what *he* should have said.

Caroline had never had a nanny and her mother and father had never employed such devious tactics to teach her manners: a clip round the ear from her father or a sharp *tut* from her mother had done the job. She hesitated and he waited, enjoying her discomfort. His patience might have had its reward but for a four-abreast gang of chattering girls coming down the stair. Face flattened against the banister rails as they passed, he did not see Caroline slipping upstairs. He just caught her back view as she hurried away from the top.

'Goddamn it! There's playing hard-to get and there's being a downright pain in the backside. That wench needs to be taught a lesson.' He strode up the stairs and gazed wrathfully around the foyer but she was nowhere to be seen. Had she gone back into the Hop? He groaned: it *was* a cattlemarket, and a hot, sweaty, graceless one at that. Colin emerged, red-faced, panting, but triumphant, with a giggling girl on each arm. He grinned at Hugh and thumbs-upped with both hands, mouthing something unreadable but clearly lascivious. Hugh shook his head and laughed. 'Good luck!'

The happy trio went off into the night. Hugh wondered what on earth Colin was going to do with them since he had no money in his pocket and it was hardly weather for a moonlight stroll along the sands. He was making his way towards the door when two girls came across the foyer from *Cloaks* and fell in behind him. Instinctively employing the courtesy drilled into him at his public school, he held the door open for them to pass through. His attention was caught first by the tall girl but his gaze dropped quickly to the short one when he heard her speak.

'I knew it was a mistake. It's always the same. They should pay us danger money to go in. Why they don't limit the numbers? My feet are crushed and I didn't even do any dancing. Caroline can go on her own next time.'

He might have ignored the whining voice completely but for the word *Caroline*. He had already made enquiries to ascertain the name of the woman who was leading him such a merry dance. Now he recognised Elspeth from the philosophy lecture, though he could not have given *her* a name. The two girls barely acknowledged his presence. They were intent on getting out into the fresh air and putting the horrors of The Hop behind them. He had formed no plan but he found himself following them. He had no skill as a stalker, however. After a few minutes, the taller girl suddenly swung round.

'Are you following us? What the hell for?' She had a dancing Irish accent.

Hugh summoned all his upper-class charm and bowed but he actually had no idea what he was going to say. Glancing around for inspiration, he saw that they were just outside the Star and Garter Hotel. 'I could not help hearing your thoughts on that desperate scene in the Younger. I share your feelings and have also escaped. Shall we partake of a commiserating bevy together?' He waved his arm at the hotel door, which opened to emit a cocktail of steamy warmth, beer fumes and cigarette smoke as a posse of laughing students came out. A blast of icy wind, straight off the North Sea, helped his cause.

'Is he for real?' demanded Patsy, as they allowed themselves to be shepherded into the pub.

'Really gorgeous,' replied Elspeth dreamily as they settled on red velvet seats to wait for Hugh bringing one half of shandy and a pint of Guinness.

'You did what?' Caroline stared at her two friends in the mirror. She was leaning across a wash-basin, one of a row in the bathroom, her hands above her head fixing an enormous plastic roller into her hair.

Patsy hoisted a small buttock on to the adjoining sink and faced her. 'We were never about to turn down the offer of a free drink now, were we?'

16

Elspeth took up position on Caroline's other side. 'He asked us all about you: where you come from, what else you're doing besides Logs 'n' Metafizz, what you like to do, what kind of music you like ...'

'What colour of knickers you're wearing ...'

'Patsy!' The bald facts of life, as witnessed on the farm, held no mysteries for Caroline but such salacious talk was new territory. 'Anyway, I'm not interested in him; so he's wasting his time.'

She finished putting in the six huge rollers which were her nightly companions and tied a chiffon scarf over them. The three wandered out into the corridor.

'Well, *I* think he's lovely, Caroline,' said Elspeth.

'I think his Chelsea-swank manners are just a façade. I think he's quite shy and rather sweet underneath. I bet if you got him away from The Rejects, he'd be quite different.'

'I thought you were reading English and History, not pop psychology.'

'Well, *I* think he's lovely!'

'Anyone for a nightcap?' Strictly against Chattan rules, Patsy kept a wee supply of what she called *the pocheen*, hidden at the back of her wardrobe. She liked to lace their nighttime coca with a little belt of it.

Elspeth pursed her lips. 'I must get up before chapel tomorrow and get started on my Seven Years War essay.'

But her two friends were already in the room, Caroline poking up the dying embers of the fire to create a blaze, Patsy swinging the kettle on its trivet over the flames.

CHAPTER TWO: PETE AND ALICE

'Have you heard from Caroline yet?'

Morag McCafferty served up two bowls of steaming porridge and dumped the heavy black pot back on the stove. She handed the bigger bowl to her younger son and sat down beside him with a sigh. These dark winter mornings did not get any easier.

Pete McCafferty attacked his porridge hungrily. Although it was still pitch dark and bitter cold outside, he had already been up for more than two hours and had completed all his early morning chores on no more than a mug of sweet tea at five o'clock. Now he had twenty minutes to wolf down his breakfast, wash, change and be off on his bike.

That had been the deal, struck three and a half years ago, and he had never defaulted on it: not even when the snow was on the ground; not even when he was fighting a heavy cold last January. When Pete's fifteenth birthday had been looming, Jed McCafferty had assumed that his younger son – like his older brother, James – would leave school and settle down to a life on the farm. Jed had worked hard to expand and modernise the farm he had inherited from his father and there was plenty of work for the three of them now.

But Pete had other ideas. Ever since he could remember, he had been fascinated by mechanised transport. Growing up, he had been an avid collector of pictures and articles from magazines and newspapers: anything which featured cars, buses, lorries, trains - anything with wheels and an engine. He had haunted railway and bus stations, watching in fascination, happily breathing in petrol and diesel fumes and recording reams of mysterious numbers in small notebooks.

As a little boy he had talked of becoming a train driver; then, when a little older, of driving a huge articulated lorry. As he progressed through Forfar Academy and it became clear that he was 'a clever laddie', his teachers began to fill his head with greater ambitions. By the time he was heading towards school leaving age, they had convinced him that he should 'stay on' and take his Highers with a view to going to college.

Jed was incredulous. 'A mechanic, you mean? You want to become a mechanic?' he said when Pete first explained his hopes. 'You want to spend all day in a dark wee pit staring up the backside of some greasy old car when you could be out in the fields in God's good fresh air?'

Pete forbore to remark that his father spent a fair bit of *his* time in a dark, smelly cowshed staring up the backside of a bellowing, calving cow - and explained that there was a bit more to his future plans than that.

'But what about the farm? You're needed here, you ken that. You've no

18

need to be looking for any other job. Your place is here with your brother and me.'

The battle raged for several months. Morag tiptoed round the two protagonists. Secretly, she was excited at the thought of one of her sons breaking the mould. She came from a farming family herself and her three brothers had all followed their father into the family farm, whilst she had done the expected and married a neighbouring young farmer. Pete's ideas and ambitions seemed like a breath of fresh air to her. But she had to support her husband, of course, so she only encouraged Pete in private. Not that he had needed it: he stood his ground.

And so a bargain was struck. Seeing that his son was as stubborn as himself, Jed reluctantly accepted the inevitable – but with a proviso. Pete could only go off to school when he had completed a list of early morning tasks around the farm; and he could only bury himself in homework in the evenings and weekends once another similar list had been completed. Pete groaned at first when he saw the lists.

'It's the best we can do, son,' Morag said. 'Let's have an end to all this argy-bargying. I'm worn out with it.'

Now, three and half years on, he was so used to the punishing routine that he barely noticed it. It had made him extremely fit and kept him focused on his schoolwork: there was little time for sport or social life. In his fifth year, as predicted by his delighted teachers, he gained A passes in Maths, Physics, Chemistry and Technical Drawing. Only one fly marred the ointment: like every establishment of further learning, Dundee Technical College demanded Higher English for entry to its courses, especially the ones that would result in letters after one's name.

The principle of Archimedes, calculus, trigonometry, logarithms, chemical formulae: none of these presented any difficulty to him. But Shakespeare's *Macbeth*, Milton's *Lycidas*, Tennyson's *Morte D'Arthur*, Dickens *Copperfield* ... these were all like Double Dutch. He had no interest in stories, whether based in history or fantasy; he took no pleasure from the language or the narrative, though would have sympathised with the Dickensian character who extolled *facts, nothing but facts*. And so, the start of his sixth year at school found him trying again to get the dreaded Higher English, which he had failed first time round.

This was how the friendship with Caroline began. They had been classmates for years without paying each other any attention as they grew through the spotty, sweaty years of adolescence. Now they were both young adults in their eighteenth year. She came across him, sitting in the bike shed, sighing over another failed attempt at analysing Macbeth's fatal character flaw and relating it to that famous thane's downfall.

Somehow they got chatting and it ended in her offering to help him.

So began months of long, slow walks on fair weather days and, when it rained, long, spun-out cups of coffee in the café near school, discussing books, plays and poems. Homework assignments were talked over before being tackled and checked before being handed in for marking. It had been this checking process that first brought Caroline to Pete's house. He phoned her one Sunday afternoon, having spent hours on a critical appreciation of the dagger scene and a character study of Lady Macbeth, but still feeling desperately unsure of them. With his father pacing the hall behind him, muttering about the cost of unnecessary phone calls, he was unable to talk out his worries properly and she offered to cycle over.

This was the first of many such visits. The two would sit in the parlour. Morag lit the fire as soon as she heard Caroline was coming. A tray of tea and freshly baked scones would be provided. Jed scoffed at such 'pandering and pampering' but Morag knew what was what in farming circles and she had no intention of giving Caroline the chance to say she had not been properly treated as a guest should be. Besides, Morag liked Caroline: perhaps she saw in her something of the lively, imaginative girl she had been herself before the straightjacket of the farmer's daughter's destiny had closed around her twenty-odd years ago.

James, Pete's older brother, sniggered and made lewd suggestions about what the two got up to over the tea-and-scones-in-the-parlour. Their classmates made assumptions and teased them. But they had all been wrong. The friendship between them had blossomed demurely, and had always been the servant of their studies. They rarely spent time talking about anything that was not directly relevant to the book he was reading or the essay he was writing. Mutual attraction, however, can be just as effectively nurtured in the confines of formal discussion as in explicit declaration. Jane Austen knew that.

Once the exam had been sat and there was no more to do but wait for the results, they never even discussed whether or not they would keep seeing each other: Caroline was by this time such a regular visitor to Fintry Farm that she no longer waited to be admitted at the kitchen door, simply coming straight in, calling: 'Hi! It's me!' and helping herself to any home-baking that might be cooling on the kitchen table, just as Jed and the boys did. With high summer upon them, they spent the time still talking but now, instead of studying, they were cycling and rambling, climbing the hills, paddling in the icy burns and playing tennis on the weedy village court.

He scraped a C pass and their jubilation was as great as if he had matched the A's in his other subjects. They celebrated with an all-day picnic in Freuchie Den, lingering and ignoring, for once, the call of his evening farm tasks. And it was in the warm evening, with the scents and sounds of summer teasing their senses, that they shared a first kiss: not planned; not expert; but not regretted or apologised for. They were about to mount their bikes and head for home, when she caught her foot in a creeping tangle of willow bay herb and stumbled, would have fallen on top of the bike, if he had not caught her. The sudden proximity hastened the inevitable and it seemed as comfortable and natural as all the developments in their relationship over the past year. When they broke apart, they grinned delightedly at one another. Then they mounted their bikes and cycled home, their companionship as easy and unembarrassed as always.

As the summer drifted by, their growing fondness for each other reflected the same unhurried pace. They still did a great deal more talking and laughing than kissing and cuddling. They were virginal innocents, schooled to propriety by parents, teachers and ministers: their knowledge of passion between the sexes confined on her side to romantic poetry and on his to biology. They were happy in their comfortable, undemanding relationship and in its comfortable, undemanding pace.

When she went off to St Andrews University in the first week of October, he was already two weeks into his course at Dundee Tech. and her leaving was barely noticed by him, dazzled as he was by the excitement of college, exhausted by having to rise an hour earlier to complete his chores before the fifty-minute cycle into Dundee every morning. She would be home for weekends often, she assured him. They parted the day before she was due to leave, laughing and joking as ever, promising to write often.

But she did not come home for more than one weekend, early in the first term. Her letters, as promised, were frequent, full of funny observations of people and circumstances but, as the weeks went by, they became incomprehensible, laced with Latin tags and literary jokes. His replies were short and stilted.

When she came home at Christmas, they had their first-ever quarrel: he was boring, unimaginative, provincial; she was affected, snobbish, pretentious; he could talk of nothing but technical design and engineering theories; she could talk of nothing but ancient manuscripts and enlightened philosophers; he was excited by new technology, the coming age of the computer; she was captivated by metaphysical theories and medieval poetry. The more they tried to recapture the old camaraderie, the more strained their relationship became. By the time she went back in mid-January to *her precious St. Andrews,* all that was left for either of them was a baffled sense of loss and irritation. Since then, no more letters, just a brief note on a picture postcard of the Castle Sands: *Back in my ivory tower. Maybe I'll let down my hair for you one of these days – C.* Not knowing the tale of Rapunzel, he shrugged and tossed it behind the clock on the mantelpiece from whence Morag rescued it and also puzzled over it.

Now, he rose and tossed his spoon into the well-scraped bowl.

'No, mam, no news of Miss High-and-Mighty Caroline. She's too grand for the likes of me now.' He hurried off upstairs to the steamy bathroom: Morag always ran a deep hot bath for him before he ate his breakfast so that he could get rid of the smell of the pigsty before setting off for college. He had perfected the technique of jumping in and out of the water and dressing in just ten minutes flat.

'I'd no' have thought it of her,' sighed Morag as she cleared their bowls and stoked the fire with the logs that Pete chopped every weekend. 'She's no' the lass I took her for.'

Jed eased off mud-encrusted wellie-boots and, feet clad only in thick socks, entered a kitchen fragrant with frying bacon and fresh toast. Without a word to his wife's back as she stood at the stove, he fell upon the steaming bowl of porridge on the table, splashing creamy milk and sprinkling white sugar liberally on it, then wolfing it down in six enormous mouthfuls. Before his spoon had settled in the empty bowl, Morag had replaced it with a plate of sizzling bacon and two fried eggs, yolks firm but not hard, as he liked them, with two thickly buttered slices of toasted home-made bread.

She poured him a big mug of tea-with-two-sugars then busied herself clearing up but, once his plate was empty, she poured herself a cup and sat down opposite him for their customary *wee natter*. He spread her home-made marmalade on a third slice of toast and sipped his second mug of tea in a more leisurely fashion. She had taken Caroline's postcard from behind the clock.

'*Back in my ivory tower. Maybe I'll let down my hair for you one of these days,*' she read. 'What do you think it means, Jed?'

He did not reply, partly because his mouth was full of toast and marmalade, partly because he had very little interest in the subject. He was not immune to Caroline's girlish charms and enjoyed having a bonnie young lass around the place as a change from his sons but he had little interest in the relationship between the girl and Pete. If the lad would not be a farmer, then anything he did was a matter of indifference to his father.

22

'I think I know what the ivory tower bit means,' pursued Morag. She was well aware of his studied indifference to Pete and simply ignored it. 'I mind I read that once: *the ivory towers of academies.* So she must be talking about all the school buildings at St Andrews where they go for their lessons – though how towers made out of ivory would survive the winters there ... There's aye that snell sea-haar.'

Jed laughed. He had had a better education than his wife and he frequently had to help her out. 'It's not *academies*, it's *academia*.'

'What's that?'

'It means the world of higher education and learning – universities, I suppose.'

'Well, there you are ... and I still don't see what good towers made out of ivory would be.'

'It's just a metaphor ... a ... .an expression. It means that the folk in universities are away in a world of their own, studying a whole lot of stuff that no-one else understands – or probably needs anyway. They're not part of the real world.'

'Do you think that's what Caroline's doing? I can hardly believe it of her; she aye seemed such a sensible lass.'

'Well, perhaps she's changed. Maybe going somewhere like that has changed her.'

'But in such a short time? It's no' even been six months since she started there.'

Jed shrugged, losing interest, and began to rise.

'But what's all this about letting down her hair? She doesn't even have long hair, just that daft curly mop o' hers.'

Jed was filling his pipe prior to retiring with it to the 'old cludgie' at the back of the farmhouse. He was glad of the modern indoor facilities upstairs if his bladder made demands in the middle of a winter's night but, by and large, he preferred the outside hut which had served the farmhouse folk for some sixty years, especially for what he always referred to as 'the serious business'. He paused on his way out.

'It's one o' those old fairy tales, love. I mind Alison had a picture book with that story in it.'

Alison had been Jed's younger sister, bright, golden-haired, full of singing, and suddenly struck down with meningitis at the age of seventeen. She had been dead within the week, only a few months after Jed and Morag's wedding. He could still surprise himself with the ferocity of his angry grief, even after all these years: how quickly his teeth clenched and his throat closed.

'What was it about?' Her voice was quiet. She had loved the girl too.

23

Jed's voice had a rough edge. 'I canna mind much about it. I think it was the usual beautiful-princess-and-prince-charming stuff. She was locked up in some high tower and he came an' stood at the bottom of it. He kept asking her to let down her long hair so he could climb up it and into her tower.'

'That sounds painful. He'd have tugged her hair out by the roots.'

'Well, it *was* a fairy story.'

'So, do you think it means Caroline wants Pete to go though and see her in St. Andrews and …'

'Climb up her hair? Like a head-beastie! Are you calling your son a louse?'

'Jed! Get off wi' ye! You ken fine what I mean.' Laughing, she pretended to chase him out the kitchen door with the broom that stood at its side.

She listened to him shucking into his boots again then tramping purposefully off to 'commune with nature' as he described his morning session in the cludgie. Within a few minutes a curl of pipe smoke could be seen escaping from the holes in the thatched roof of the old hut.

Morag stood irresolute in the middle of the kitchen floor, the postcard still in her hand. She had watched and approved the developing relationship between this girl and her son, the spontaneous enjoyment of each other's company, the effortless companionship. She had long ago come to the conclusion that such was the bedrock of a lasting, happy marriage. Passion, sexual fulfillment – if it came – might wax and wane but just loving spending time together, talking, laughing, sharing life: that was the good stuff, as rare and precious as gold. She had it in her own marriage and thanked God daily. And she was sure she had recognised it in Caroline and Pete, young as they were. To see it thrown away so lightly by them both made her feel sick with the sense of waste. *I won't let them*, she thought. *It would be a crying shame. I can't stand by and watch it and do nothing* … Thoughtfully, she replaced the postcard behind the clock on the mantelpiece. Then she collected the hen-mash bucket and made her way out of the kitchen and across the yard to the chicken-coop.

James McCafferty dropped the metal hasp on the barn door down into its cradle, closing in the herd of contented, newly milked cows. For the tenth time, he surveyed the landscape. Beyond the circle of the farmyard lights, the countryside was in darkness with only scattered pinpoints of yellow light from a few cottages. No sign of a lonely bicycle lamp.

Where is the wee bugger? he thought irritably, for the fortieth time in the last hour. In truth, his brother was head and shoulders above him in height: James was short, stocky, beefy-chested, a bulldog of a lad; Pete was tall, rangy, full of running, like a prize greyhound. But James always thought of Pete as *wee,* partly because he was younger but mainly because he had always been treated as the baby of the family, indulged by his mother and excused by his father. Or so it had seemed to James who had never quite got over the jealous shock of seeing his parents withdraw their attention from him and focus it on a mewling baby who had arrived on the scene without – as far as he was concerned – warning or welcome. James had benefited from the rift between Pete and Jed these past three years, encouraging Jed's intransigence with regard to Pete's farm-chores and his scorn of Pete's ambitions, basking in Jed's approval as the son who was doing the expected thing.

It was almost six o'clock now. Pete's last lecture or tutorial always finished at four. Knowing the cows would be bellowing, udders throbbing, by half past, he always sat near the door and slipped out as soon as the tutor stopped talking, down the marble stairs, straight to the bike shed. He would be on his way by five past, pedals spinning, legs pumping, rearing up from the saddle to tackle the steep challenge of Victoria Road, then racing out on to the Forfar Road. He was not unaware that the other students lingered to chat about current assignments, looming exams and – with more verve –the kaleidoscope of girl-boy activity in the town's student scene. Dundee was still a mere satellite of St Andrews but it was scheduled to become an independent university in three years time and 'the split' was eagerly awaited. Already the student population was growing and the scene livening up.

Pete's classmates, unburdened by bellowing cows, would drift down to *The Ref* – the town's imposing Reference Library with its sweeping stone staircase and enormous revolving doors – where they would make a great show of settling into one of the long tables, spreading out an impressive range of textbooks, then leaving these to go and stand outside, looking down towards the Caird Hall, taking in the bustle of the city centre, puffing on Bristol or Strand cigarettes. They might repair to a tearoom on Reform Street, to put off still more time before returning to their forlorn study tables. Pete had heard them talking about these after-class activities, had been reminded of them when Caroline had been chattering on about *coffee in the union after lectures.* But he knew such pursuits were not for him. It had been possible to fit in the after-school walks and coffee-bars times with her before evening milking when he had had only a ten minute cycle ride home from Forfar. But now, with the journey from Dundee, such dalliance was out of the question.

It had not been too hard at the start in September when it was still light till six and the weather was mild. By the end of October, the clocks had reverted to Greenwich Mean Time and the early evenings to fast-falling darkness. The weather played its winter tricks and he was wet and cold by the time he struggled home. The steamy, smelly warmth of the cowshed was very welcome. Jed and James never spoke to him when he arrived: the noise of the milking machine precluded conversation. But they acknowledged his arrival, Jed with a wave of his hand and James with a wink and a grin. Though they never admitted it to him or to each other, they had a sneaking admiration for his tenacity. Only once had he been later than ten to five – his target time - when snow had forced him to dismount and carry the bike up the farm track. Jed had made no comment but the track had been cleared the next day.

Once milking was done, Pete would hurry through the farm kitchen, collecting the two large, freshly-baked, thickly-buttered scones which Morag always left on the table for him, cramming these into his mouth as he raced upstairs to strip off his college clothes and don an enormous wool ganzy which his mother had knitted for him, and a pair of his father's old dungarees, which were too short for his long legs but were wide enough to accommodate the ganzy. Thick wool socks – more of Morag's handiwork – covered the shortfall of the dungarees. Then he would race downstairs, pull on his wellie-boots and head off back to the cowshed to clean it out. He did not forget to slip his little *tranny* into one of the pockets of the dungarees and the cows enjoyed half an hour of Del Shannon, Cliff Richard, The Batchelors and, increasingly, the hot new group from Liverpool, The Beatles. Cowshed done, he would head over to the pigsty to freshen up their straw. A few other small tasks would complete the list before he hurried back to wash and change for the evening meal at seven. This left him the rest of the evening for his studies and his disappearance upstairs, with a shovel of hot coals from the kitchen range to put in the tiny fireplace in his room, was now an accepted part of his routine.

Tonight, however, ten-to-five had come and gone; the milking had taken them, short-handed, till nearly six o'clock. Neither had commented on the glaring lack of the third member of the milking team; Jed had simply stumped off leaving James to turn off the machine and close the barn. Now James scanned the empty countryside one last time – no sign of a homecoming cyclist. He felt a little worm of unease thread its way into his disgruntlement: *What if something had happened to him? An accident?* He thought of Pete's practice of tucking in behind a bus or lorry to benefit from the pull of its slipstream. *What if the bus or lorry had braked suddenly and Pete had crashed into the back of it? What if …?* But James was not

26

given to flights of fancy and his imagination ran out.

In his turn, he also stumped towards the kitchen door. 'Bloody wee skiver!' he exclaimed aloud. He startled one of the farm's Jack Russell ratters who was prowling hopefully outside the kitchen door, hoping for the ham bone from the soup he could smell cooking.

Pete ran doggedly up the rise, breathing deeply in through his nose and blowing out through his mouth. He was looking forward to cresting the hill and coasting down to the dip before turning up the farm track. It was the longest run he had done for many months but, once he had got into his stride, he had rather enjoyed it, even forgetting for a while his father's impending wrath and his brother's probable taunts at this failure to be home in time for milking.

He had been making good time after a slight hold-up in getting out of college – they had been doing a practical engineering experiment and he had had to clear up the equipment once the tutor had left. But he pedalled furiously, topped Victoria Road and passed the impressive old school building of *The Morgan* by twenty-past four and was cruising along, whistling *Please, Please Me*, heading for the Kingsway roundabout and open countryside, when disaster struck. He was on the shards of smashed lemonade bottle lying at the side of the road before he had time to avoid them. He managed to jerk his front wheel clear but his back wheel had never stood a chance. Dismounting, he stared in dismay at the tyre, knowing at a glance that the small puncture kit in his saddlebag would not look at it: it was slashed beyond repair. This, in itself, was not a problem: one of the sheds at the farm was full of old bikes with tyres which could easily be prized off and recycled.

I'll just have to push it home as fast as I can was his first thought but, by the time he had rattled it past the roundabout and a few yards up the long road towards home, he knew that it was not going to work. The tyre was so damaged that the metal wheel rim was bearing the weight of the bike and would soon be too twisted and battered to take a new tyre. He realised that he needed to find somewhere to leave the bike safely until he could run home and borrow the farm's Landrover. Both he and James had learned to drive on the farm at an early age. He could easily drive back this evening and fetch the bike, fix it up with a new tyre and have it on the road in time for tomorrow morning. Of course, doing all that as well as catching up with cowshed and pigsty duties would take most of the evening: he would be up till past midnight writing up the notes from this afternoon's practical and preparing for tomorrow's tutorial. *It'll be hardly worth my while going to bed,* he thought as he thankfully crested the top of the rise and began to trot down to the dip.

He had realised that he needed to find a place of sanctuary for his maimed machine and quickly decided that he needed to turn back and throw himself on the mercy of one of the smart bungalows that ran along the side of the Kingsway, the city's dual-carriageway ring-road. Looking along the row of well-kept detached houses, his eye fell on one with lights glowing at its uncurtained bay window, a pale grey Hillman Minx car in its drive, but, best of all, a bicycle leaning against its garage door. *A fellow-biker'll understand* he thought.

He left the bike just inside the gate, not wishing to seem presumptuous. A tentative touch of the white button on the front door had produced a melodious snatch of *Fur Elise*. Then the door was opened briskly by a well-groomed lady whose perfume reached out to engulf him as she stepped forward into the doorway. She wore an immaculate tartan pleated skirt and a pale green fine-knit twin-set with a string of pearls at her throat, matching pearl studs in her ears. He was momentarily disconcerted by her elegance until his eyes had travelled down to her feet. She was wearing a pair of comfortable, rather battered slippers, exactly like his mother's 'baffies' into which she slipped her tired feet of an evening, prior to fading through to the tiny room off the kitchen, which she called *my snug,* for 'some peace and quiet'.

'Yes? What do you want? 'The woman's voice was cultured and a little suspicious.

The baffies gave him courage: 'I'm sorry to disturb you. I need help. I'm a student in Dundee and I was cycling home – I live on a farm …' He gestured vaguely north-east behind him. 'I ran into some broken glass and my back tyre is slashed. I need somewhere safe to leave the bike for a couple of hours – I'll drive down and collect it tonight. Could I leave it in your drive?' He gestured towards the other bike, already propped up against the garage door, noticing for the first time that it was a ladies' model. Obscurely, he felt that its presence lent weight to his request.

'Who is it, mum?' A voice floated out into the hall behind the woman. She did not answer, continuing to appraise Pete as he stood in the glow of the ornate carriage lamp that hung over the front door. Another figure appeared behind her, a smaller replica: neat, shapely, managing, he saw as it came forward, to invest the Morgan school uniform with dainty elegance. Mother and daughter regarded Pete for a moment then mother laughed.

'I think we have the converse of a damsel in distress requiring the services of a gallant knight, Alice. Here we have a knight in distress throwing himself on the mercy of two damsels!'

The girl stepped into the light and Pete saw that, although her figure and deportment were her mother's, her countenance and colouring were certainly not. The mother was crispy blond curls, blue eyes and creamy complexion; the girl was sleek dark hair caught up a high pony-tail, dark eyes and olive skin. She looked, Pete thought, rather *foreign,* having what his grandfather would have called *a touch of the tar brush.* Her voice was low and deep.

'For heaven's sake, mum! You'll have to stop reading those Arthurian legends. This is Dundee not Camelot.' She turned to Pete. 'What's the problem?' She had a brisk, no-nonsense air that immediately made Pete feel better and hopeful. He explained again his plight and his need.

'But, of course,' the girl said. She stepped out on to the doorstep beside him and gestured to the garage door. 'Just prop it up beside mine. I was about to put it away in the garage. I'll put them both in there and you can come and get it whenever you like this evening.'

He demurred, insisting on opening the garage up-and-over door whilst she wheeled in her bike. He brought his own vehicle and positioned it behind hers. Then he closed down the heavy door, locked it and handed her the key.

'Will your father be able to get his car in all right?' he asked, anxious not to cause a problem.

She eyed him with a gleam of amusement. 'There's only my mother. That's *her* car in the drive. She's going out again this evening. That's why she's left it in the drive. You'll have collected your bike by the time she's garaging the car. She's always late home after one of her evening classes.' *Alice,* he thought now as he began to jog his way up the uneven track to the farmhouse. He remembered the name on the front door: *Band – Alice Band!* Obviously her parents had had a sense of humour at her christening. But who were her parents? Where was her father? *There's only my mother,* she had said. And *who* was her father? Not Scottish, that was for sure.

An interesting girl, cool, self-possessed, different. He was rather looking forward to collecting his bike from her later this evening.

CHAPTER THREE: DOROTHEA AND HUGH

As the echoes of sung Latin grace died away, Augusta Goldsmith, Warden of Chattan, tinkled her soup spoon against her water glass and rose to address the House. Black gown waited for chattering red gowns to subside into silence as those near the top table turned to *sshhh* those at the back of the long basement dining-room. She was not a tall woman but her pugnacious, squat figure and strongly featured face commanded attention. A lecturer in forensic medicine in the Dundee wing of the university, she was accustomed to taming unruly students. She had been one of a select band of *lady students* who had graduated from St Andrews in the thirties, daughters of wealthy, enlightened families – her own mother was a Bloomsbury Set bluestocking – who had blazed the trail for the hordes of girls now pouring into universities all over the country.

'I have an announcement, ladies. Our annual ball will be postponed by one week.' A ripple of surprise ran round the room. 'I know we set the date last term for the sixteenth of this month but I am afraid I have to be at a conference in London that weekend and it begins on that Friday night. I know you would not wish to have your Ball without me.'

The expressions on quite a few faces contradicted this assertion but, if she noticed them, she ignored them. 'So, I have checked with the other residences and there are no other balls scheduled for the following Friday, the twenty-third. I have also contacted the band and consulted the kitchen staff: both are kindly willing to oblige me with this change of date. We shall therefore go ahead with it.' She twinkled at them. 'It will give you all another week to complete the wonderful artistic efforts which I know are going into decorating your room parties.' She sat down and gave a nod to the white-aproned staff waiting to serve the top table, indicating that the meal might begin.

As the two girls whose turn it was to serve their table rose and made their way over to join the queue at the serving hatch, Patsy addressed Elspeth, Caroline and the others, all residents of their half of C floor.

'So, have us lot decided what we're doing?' Patsy had a grand disdain for English grammar in the spoken word although she was quite capable of writing a textbook specimen. The other seven girls looked doubtful. Speculation and dissent rumbled up and down the ten-seat table:

'What about Charlie Brown and Snoopy? – I love that stuff!'

'Didn't we agree on Arthurian Legends for our theme?'

'I still think Alice in Wonderland would be a good'

The other two girls began to bring plates, each with a fish covered in bright orange breadcrumbs and twisted into a contorted curl. The fish skittered about on the plates as they were passed down the table.

'Geez, you'd think they'd kill the buggers before we have to eat them!' Patsy exclaimed as she tried to spear hers – the orange crust resisted her fork and the fish shot off her plate and landed in her lap. 'God, it's making me feel like a murderer,' she moaned. 'Sitting on my knee like a pussycat.' The table erupted into gales of laughter as platters of yellow sprouts and grey potatoes were set in the middle.

A nearby table of third and fourth years tutted and even the top table on its raised dais broke its splendid isolation and glanced reprovingly at *those bejantines*. (St. Andrews' word for women freshers.) The discussion meandered up and down the table between mouthfuls of the unappetising food. A nearby table of second years became noisy then suddenly hushed and looked smug and secretive, glancing patronisingly at the bejantines' table. They were well satisfied with their own room-party plans and able to spare some pity for others less inspired.

'Hell!' Patsy suddenly exclaimed.

'Indeed,' agreed Caroline, smarting under the second years' superiority. 'Hell's teeth, in fact.'

'No, I mean, what about *hell* as our theme? We can have flickering flames with red and orange crepe paper, and decorate the walls with drawings of famous wicked people – Henry the Eighth, Hitler, Stalin, Attila the Hun, Lady Macbeth, Mr Hyde - all being consumed in the flames.'

'And some naughty ones as well: Lady Godiva, Lady Chatterley, Mae West, Bardot, Casanova ...'

'We'll need a few wee devils with horns and tails and forks.'

'And make punch with lots of spice in it and call it *hell-fire hooch.*'

'What about cardboard crazy paving leading up the corridor with *good intentions* written on it? You know, the road to hell is paved ...'

The idea caught the group's imagination and the suggestions came thick and fast. Jennifer, whose room was the chosen venue, being the biggest, was artist-in-residence – her talents as caricaturist were well known. By the time the bowls of watery custard and glutinous jam had been scraped clean, they were all champing at the bit to get back to her room and begin serious planning.

At last the room fell silent as *The Gusset* rose – the nickname was partly a play on her name and partly due to Augusta Goldsmith's splayed-footed walk which Doctor Patsy had diagnosed as a bad case of the double gusset. She bowed her thanks to her dining companions, who all bowed formally back to her before processing behind her, down from

31

the dais through the dining-room and out the door. Before the last acolyte had bolted through the swing-doors like a worried rabbit, Patsy was on her feet:

'Come on! There's work to be done while the muse is upon us.' Ignoring the sour looks of the superior second years and disapproving third and fourth years, she surged towards the door.

'It's your turn to clear table, Patsy Macnamara.' This came from Anne, a girl with a strong Methodist background. She found Patsy's language shocking and her personality unsettling. Patsy's predictable response – a colourful oath - did nothing to revise this opinion.

'I'll do your rota, Patsy. It's your idea – you need to be in on things right at the beginning.' Elspeth began to collect plates and tumblers. Anne looked disapproving but the others were already bearing Patsy off.

'If I don't go to bed soon, I shall lie down right here and sleep.' Assenting groans and yawns greeted Caroline's prediction.

'Yeah, if I don't lie down, I'll fall down.' Even Patsy was flagging. It was almost two o'clock in the morning and Jennifer's room was littered with sheets of paper covered in drawings. Copious amounts of coffee had been consumed; ashtrays full of cigarette butts were scattered among the drawings all over the floor, furniture and bed. They had importuned the domestic bursar, a twittery, persuadable lady, to ransack Chattan's cellars and find them rolls of old wallpaper. Jennifer had plenty of chalk in a range of colours and her talents had been in heavy demand for the past five hours. Now her wrist was aching, her knees were sore and her eyes behind upswept spectacles were red and bleary. But her suffering was not in vain: they were well on the way to a spectacular room party with a brilliant theme and fabulous decorations. Stretching and yawning, the girls began to drift off, most of them thoughtlessly leaving Jennifer to survey the debris and clutter in dismay. Anne and Elspeth fell to and briskly cleared up the mess. Neither of them had been able to contribute much to the creativity that had resulted in the piles of drawings but they did understand the need to leave Jennifer with a bed to sleep in and a floor to walk on.

Elspeth caught up with Caroline and Patsy outside her own bedroom door. 'Of course, we've still the thorniest problem of all to sort out: who are we going to ask to be our escorts? Though, I suppose *you* don't have that problem, Caroline …'

'Ah yes! The glorious Hugh Apple-pie-bed-ington.' Patsy looked pleased at this flash of wit so late in the night.

'If you think I'd ask that stuck-up, pretentious, affected …' Caroline's list petered out in a yawn.

'Well, if you don't want him, we'll toss for him. What do you say, Elspeth?'

'I think Caroline protests too much,' said Elspeth and skipped into her room, closing the door on Caroline's outraged face

Dorothea licked her fingers and sighed happily. 'Delicious!'

The other six people sitting on the floor of her spacious A floor room in Chattan murmured sleepy agreement. It was three o'clock on a Wednesday afternoon: no lectures or tutorials on the traditional half-day and one of the two afternoons a week that Chattan opened its doors to gentlemen callers for a decorous two-hour period. The three boys and four girls had been consuming a large Pound Cake from America, sent all the way from Virginia by Dorothea's aunt. The fire flickered cheerfully and a replete silence settled on the group. Dorothea slipped across the landing to the chilly bathroom and returned thankfully to the soporific warmth. But, before she could sink to the floor, her eye caught the view from the west-facing window: icy, brilliant sunshine; miles of golden sand; horizon of navy-blue sea; creaming white horses tossing on bucketing waves. She felt suddenly restless.

'Let's go for a walk along the beach!' Groans greeted this suggestion and no-one moved. Then Hugh rose and came to join her at the window.

'You're right, Dorothea. It's much too good an afternoon to waste *frowsting* by the fire.' He surveyed the slumped group but was met by unashamed rebuttal.

'We prefer to wallow in our happy mire. Leave us to frowst in peace.' Colin stretched his long legs on the hearth-rug and lit another cigarette.

Dorothea was delighted to have Hugh to herself. She had set her sights on Hugh as her escort for Chattan Ball in three weeks time and was working up to asking him. As the two made their way along the corridor of A floor towards the staircase, she rehearsed her invitation speech. She was a little in awe of Hugh and this would be her first Ball. Only Colin and Hugh were Sally's residents and they had chosen Belinda and Cynthia respectively for partners for that Ball; then Belinda had asked Hugh as her partner to the Abbotsford one, where she was resident, and had smuggled Cynthia and Colin into her room party as well. Dorothea was longing to catch up with them: wear her glittering, swirling evening dress; pin on the corsage delivered before the Ball commenced; and be escorted by a handsome young man in formal evening dress. She was the only member of The Set resident in Chattan – her A floor room, with its amazing view, would normally have been reserved for a final year magistrand or graduate research student, but her father had been at Rugby with The Gusset's brother and old-school-tie strings had been pulled. Chattan ball was one of the biggest of the year and invitations much sought after.

Hugh strode along the corridor. He had his own agenda for this walk and it also featured the Ball. He had been mulling over in his head for days now how he could persuade Caroline to invite him to be her escort. He didn't even know if she already had one lined up. He needed to talk to those two friends of hers again. Then he needed to engineer another opportunity to talk to her. Being in Dorothea's room in Chattan had focused his thoughts and he felt the need to have a good, long think about the situation. A brisk walk along the shore would be just the thing – pity Dorothea would no doubt be chattering away by his side, but he would endeavour to tune her out, placate her with a few grunts and lose himself in his own thoughts. He bounded down the first flight to B floor with Dorothea panting behind. As he began on the next flight, she managed to catch up with him and crook her arm into his.

'Hang on. My little pins can't keep up with a daddy-long-legs like you.'

He felt a rush of irritation followed by guilt born of well-drilled manners. 'Sorry, Dorrie. I'm just dying to get out in the fresh air.' He patted the fingers that lay on his arm, then impulsively, with a cry of 'Hang on to your hat! Here we go!', he threw his arm round her waist, lifting her almost off her feet as he pelted down the stair, carrying her with him. They fetched up giggling and breathless on the landing of C floor. Their momentum carried them forward and they cannoned into Patsy who had just climbed the stair from D floor below.

'Whoa! Are ye trying to knock me over? And me a mere will-o-the-wisp!' In fact, Patsy, though stick-thin and fragile in appearance, was *tough as old boots* – her own description – having grown up with two horse-playing brothers. She presented a ramrod defence and held her ground.

'Sorry! Sorry!' Hugh and Dorothea chorused in unison. Then Hugh exclaimed: 'Hello! It's Patsy, isn't it?'

This could be a stroke of luck, he thought, Dorothea temporarily forgotten. *She'll know which room is Caroline's. Maybe I can just hang about a bit and sort-of bump into her before we get chucked out at four o'clock.*

'I'm just grand, thank you, kind sir.' She twinkled at him and Hugh had an uncomfortable conviction that she was reading his mind. 'But I can't stop here chatting to you, delightful as it is. I'm due at *Caroline's* for tea.'

She let her voice trail along the three syllables of the name, her glance flicking from him to Dorothea, who was boggling at this exchange. Hugh felt an urge to begin excusing himself, explaining Dorothea's presence and their relationship – or lack of it. But Patsy had marched away along the corridor with a cheery wave. She paused outside a door and allowed herself a quick glance to confirm that he was watching. *Slaver-on, my little apple-pie,* she murmured as she opened Caroline's door and disappeared into the room.

'Oh, come *on*, Hugh.' Dorothea stamped her foot. 'What on earth are you doing staring after that Irish trollop? It'll be getting dark soon. Are we having this walk or not?'

His reply was not encouraging. She was forced once again to trot after him as he strode off at an uncompromising pace and, though he slackened his pace, heavy footed, on the wet sand and thawed into some small talk after a few hundred yards, he did not enlarge on his acquaintance with Patsy and Dorothea did not pluck up the courage to issue the Ball invitation after all.

'Drat!' exclaimed Caroline through a mouthful of lumpy porridge. She had picked up a letter out of her pigeonhole on the way into breakfast and was now reading it, brow furrowed. 'I'll have to go home this weekend – in fact, I'll have to go for a long weekend. Friday and Monday as well.'

'What for? I thought you said you weren't going home at all this term.' Patsy dumped down a plate of rubbery scrambled eggs.

'I wasn't. I don't really want to. Everything's changed. It doesn't feel like home any more.'

'It's you who's done the changing,' said Patsy sagely, wolfing down the eggs and scraping margarine on to a piece of rock-hard toast. 'So, why go, then?'

Caroline continued reading to the end of the letter then laid it down, with a sigh. 'I'll have to go.'

'Is something wrong? Not bad news?'

'Nothing serious, but horrible for poor mum. She had a fall on the cellar stairs - we've been needing a decent light down there for yoinks – and she's broken one wrist and sprained the other.'

'Ouch! Your poor mammy!'

'Yeah … well, thing is … she can't manage to do much with her hands at the moment so Dad and the boys are having to do pretty well everything. She even had to get Dad to write this letter. She says they're managing OK so far, but Dad's got to go away to some big farmer's convention – something to do with Britain maybe joining the Common Market.'

'I might have known. That'll be the cause of all our ills from now on. I said it right from the start.'

Caroline ignored this burst on Patsy's anti-European banjo. 'Mum says she needs help with personal things - you know, washing, dressing and so forth - and with Dad away from Friday to Monday ... The boys can do the farm work and help with housework but she draws the line at asking them to fasten her bra-strap!'

'She said that?' Patsy was impressed. Her own mother sucked in her breath and made the sign of the cross if anyone mentioned intimate things like underwear in front of men. She had even pursed her lips and cut off a label from one of her skirts because it claimed to be 100% *virgin* wool: in her eyes that word was only ever to be used in its proper context – when referring to the *Blessed* Virgin, Mary, Mother of God.

'Well, no, not quite,' laughed Caroline. 'But I can read between the lines. I'll have to skip lectures on Friday and Monday. Elspeth will let me copy her notes from Mod. and Med. Hist. and Anne's always good for English Lit. I'll set off after Logic and Metafizz on Thursday and be back by Monday evening. It doesn't matter if I miss a couple of those – old Fossil will never notice and his lectures are rubbish anyway.'

'I expect he speaks very highly of you as well.' Patsy rose and wrapped her red gown round her thin frame. She glanced out the window. 'Brrr! What a country! What weather! I must be off, Got a nine o'clock at the Path. lab. Cheer up, it's only one weekend. Mind, you'll miss all the fun starting to get the room-party decs ready.'

'I know.' Caroline was the picture of gloomy martyrdom; then she rallied. 'You should speak about miserable weather, coming from that rain-sodden bog you call home!'

'For that,' said Patsy severely, 'I may just snatch Mr.Apple Pie from under your sneering nose and ask him to the Ball - that's if that snobby tart I saw him with last Saturday hasn't snapped him up already.'

'Help yourself. I've no use for him.'

'You'd better hurry up, though, there'll only be four days left to the Ball when you get back – all the best men will have gone. Better get on with it this week. Who else have you got to ask?'

Caroline waved an airy hand as Elspeth appeared, porridge bowl in hand. 'Elspeth and I have already made our plans, haven't we?'

Her dumpy friend goggled. 'We have?'

'Mmmm....' Caroline did some quick thinking. 'It's quite lucky I'm going home actually. I'll be able to ask them in person.'

'Ask who?' chorused Patsy and Elspeth.

'Oh, just a couple of doting swains from back home who are dying to sample a bit of the high life in this Mecca of sophistication.

Patsy cast an eye round the dining-room and wrinkled her nose as much at the room and its occupants as at the smell of slightly burnt porridge and very burnt toast. 'Mecca of sophistication is it? What swains? You never mentioned them before?'

'Ah, but we don't tell *you* everything, do we, Elspeth?'

Patsy made to descend upon her then caught sight of the clock on the wall. 'Eeek! I must go! I can't be late again – They're threatening to lock me out if I don't start coming on time. Bloody Brits!'

Caroline and Elspeth returned to their breakfast and ate in silence for a while. As they finished their breakfast and rose together, Elspeth ventured: 'Do you really have two boys at home who'll come through for the Ball? That would be great! Patsy's been crowing all week about having three men dangling after her and will-she-won't-she choose one of them – *or* one of the hundred others she's got tucked up her sleeve.'

'Miaow, green-eyed pussycat! But, you're right. She does need taking down a peg or two.' The pressure to find an escort for the night was aggravated by the ease with which Patsy could choose from a gaggle of hopefuls. Her fashionable looks, fascinating accent and the fact that she normally disdained all advances made her a sought-after prize. So far, Caroline and Elspeth had failed to catch the eye of any man, except, of course, the despised Apple-Pie.

'Oh, there are always guys down on the farm desperate for a bit of city life.' She wished she felt as confident as she sounded. 'Don't worry, Elspeth, it's in the bag!'

CHAPTER FOUR: CAROLINE AND PETE

As she swooped down to the dip on her old *Raleigh* bike, Caroline ran the plan through her head for the umpteenth time. Over the past three days, she had mulled over how she could redeem her promise to Elspeth and return with two fellows 'in the bag' for the Ball. She had sorted through the boys she knew at home, rejecting most of them as either unimpressive or unavailable, several being away at universities themselves now around the country. In the end, she had come back to her first idea: time was running out; she would be on the way back to Chattan and an expectant Elspeth – not to mention a taunting Patsy – tomorrow afternoon. She dismounted to wheel her bike up the farm track. It was pitted with puddles and she did not want to arrive splattered with mud. She tapped on the kitchen door and pushed it open tentatively: the old days of breezing in seemed a long time ago. A wonderful smell made her mouth water; Sunday dinner was cooking.

Morag was bending over an open oven, presenting an ample rump clad in bright royal blue. She was basting a saddle of lamb which was overlaid with a thatch of rosemary twigs. 'Is that you, Janette?' she called over her shoulder, continuing to baste the sizzling roast. 'Just put those things on the table. I'll see to them later.'

'It's me!' Caroline attempted an echo of her old insouciance. 'Hope you don't mind me just coming in.'

Morag whirled round, kicking the oven door shut expertly with her heel. 'Caroline! It's fair grand to see you, dearie. I didn't know you were home this weekend. Pete'll be pleased … Sorry, I thought you were a woman from the church with some magazines.'

'I'm just home to help mum out. She's got a broken wrist and Dad's away …' She explained her mission of mercy. Morag tutted in sympathy and promised to get Jed to run her over to see Caroline's mother soon. Home baking would no doubt be in short supply with the woman of the house *hors de combat*. This was a gift from the gods, she thought. She had been wondering how she could progress her meddlesome intentions.

'I'm glad to get you on your own, Mrs. McCafferty. I have something I want to … Well, I'm not quite sure how to … Maybe you could help me to …' *Crumbs, metaphysics is easier than this. Blast the damned Ball!*

Morag beamed. 'And I've something I've been hoping to talk to you about, dear. And it could be they're no' a million miles apart! Let's get ourselves a cuppa.'

'Have you time?'

'The lamb'll be another hour and I always get the tatties and sprouts ready on a Saturday night. With the Kirk in the morning, there's never time to think about cooking till we get back.' She took off her voluminous apron to reveal her Sunday best, a smart royal blue skirt and cardigan with white ruffle-neck blouse. She began to lay a tray. 'The fire's on in the parlour. We'll go through there. Jed and the lads have gone to see to a couple o' daft ewes-in-lamb that have got themselves stuck on a ledge up the hill. There's a bit o' a storm forecast later and they're worried the daft beasts'll panic if the wind gets up. We'll get peace in the parlour if they come back in.'

This suited Caroline: she had been hoping to get a chance to talk to Morag without any of the men around. She carried the tray through to the room she remembered so well from last winter when she and Pete had been flogging through the Higher English curriculum. She could almost hear the rustle of pages, their murmured discussions, the rattle as he threw the hod of coal at the fire; smell the ink from his pen, the fresh, hot scones, the clean soapiness of his hair; see the card table set up in the corner with the firelight flickering on the stack of books.

'And how are you liking the university?'

Caroline felt a grin spread across her face. 'I love it!' *It was* true, she thought, in surprise. *I do love it.* In the first term, she had struggled with the alien culture. But now … She had never had a close relationship with another girl of her own age. At school, she had been so far academically above all the rest that she had never felt part of the crowd. She had been the only girl in her year to go to university. Striking up a friendship with Elspeth and Patsy, her neighbours in Chattan, had been a revelation to her. And she had come to love the traditional formality of it all: what had at first seemed bewildering was now comfortable routine.

'What's it like?' Morag felt a surge of envy, sensing the girl's absorption in a strange, exciting world. So Caroline described it: the magic of the ancient town, the grey, old buildings of Quad brightened with red-gowned students; the formal meals in Chattan with the sung Latin grace and late-comers bowing to the top table; the late-night huddles round room-fires; the dusty lecture rooms and even dustier lecturers; the age-old traditions like Raisin Monday, when first-year students had to give a bag of raisins – or, nowadays, more often a bottle of wine – to their Senior Men or Senior Women, who had 'adopted' them. The Seniors would then give them 'raisin receipts' in Latin which had to be carried around for the whole day and produced on the demand of any other Seniors. These were often written on the most outrageous things: one poor lad had had to lug round the sail from a boat for the whole day; others had found their receipts written on pyjamas and frilly nighties which had to be worn, on chamber pots, rolls of toilet paper, hats, boots, banners, cricket bats, rugby balls – the list was endless. If the Latin was found to be faulty, the bejant or bejantine was required to sing three verses of *Gaudeamus Igitur* – the 'Gaudie' – there and then, wherever they found themselves. If caught in Quad itself with an erroneous receipt, they would be made to stand up on the ancient stone bench in the chapel cloister and serenade other students as they swarmed around between lectures. 'It's just crazy!' Caroline's eyes were shining as she recalled it.

'And what was your receipt on?'

'It was on an old potato sack. My senior woman thought it would suit me, coming from a farm. She had painted the words on it but some of the paint flaked off so I got caught and told that some of the words were wrong. I tried to explain that it was because some of the paint had fallen off but it didn't make any difference. I still had to sing!'

'In Quad? Up on the bench in cloisters?' Morag had caught the parlance.

'No, I was spared that. I got caught in the Union coffee bar and luckily it was so noisy that hardly anyone heard my awful singing. But Patsy, my Irish friend …'

She broke off at the sound of boots tramping into the porch off the kitchen, men's voices over the sound of a tap running. The women looked at each other in alarm. They had not even begun on the meat of the matter.

'Bugger!' Caroline blushed. 'I mean … Sorry, Mrs M!'

'Drat! Never mind. Wait a minute.' Morag bustled off and Caroline heard her light voice over the deep tones of the three men. Then she came back in leaving the parlour door open.

'I told them I wanted peace to listen to *The Archers*,' she said. The familiar signature tune blared out and she let it drift through to the kitchen, before shutting the door and turning the wireless down.

'Now, my dear, interesting as all your tales of' - she recalled her conversation with Jed – 'of *academia* are, I think we've other matters on our minds. We've twenty minutes while the lads get themselves tidied up and the tatties cook.' The girl was silent, looking down at her winter boots intently. 'You first, love.'

'It's right nice to have Caroline round for Sunday lunch again, isn't it?' Morag spoke to no-one in particular as she doled out the last bowl of steaming soup. There came no answer save the sound of Jed blowing on his spoon and James slurping cautiously. After a further moment's silence, catching her hostess's eye, Caroline ventured:

'This is wonderful soup, Mrs McC. I really appreciate it. You should see the stuff we get in Chattan. It's like dirty dishwater.'

'Perhaps it *is* dishwater.' Pete did not look up, his expression did not change and his voice was monotone. Under the table, however, the toe of his old slipper lightly touched the toe of Caroline's suede ankle boot.

She gave no acknowledgement of this. 'It would be economical, certainly.'

'You could call it *re-cycling*.'

'We'll get there faster if we cycle, I suppose.'

'Though walking is good for you, too.'

'Especially in the countryside.'

'But bad for the cows if you leave the gates open.'

'Five-barred ones are my favourites.'

The exchange continued for a minute and a half, neither speaker looking at the other. It wandered around and arrived at a place of total disconnection from its starting point; then it began to backtrack through earlier topics, through tenuous links, finally returning to base.

'Sundays should be days of rest, of course.'

'But Mondays are always best for doing the washing.'

'Even for washing dishes, would you say?'

At last the heads came up and eyes met in a sizzle of connection. Jed and James were turning their necks from side to side like Wimbledon spectators.

'Oh, yes, *and* for making soup.'

'Out of the dirty dishwater, of course.'

'Of course!'

Both Pete and Caroline were wearing ear-to-ear grins. It was a game they had played often over the course of last winter. She had started it to encourage him to let his mind roam and associate words freely. 'Your mind is logical and literal,' she had explained. 'That's fine for algebra and geometry but poetry and creative writing are different. They thrive on flights of fancy and figures of speech.' And she had introduced the game, *Free-Think*, she called it, where one of them, at any time could suddenly take the conversation off in an unforeseen direction. They would then both build on it with more and more thinly related responses, often reaching a hilarious conclusion. Pete had introduced the refinement of having to work backwards to the starting point. Even after the exam was over, they had kept it up. Sometimes they could take as much as fifteen minutes to complete the full circle, with one of them starting to lead back but the other branching off in yet another direction.

Jed cleared his throat. 'Is there any more soup, mother? I'd take another wee drop.'

Morag surfaced: she had been floating in the pool of light that seemed to be lying on the table between Pete and Caroline. 'Gather up the bowls,' she said vaguely as she moved over to the stove. *I was right! I knew it! A blind man with a white stick could see they're made for each other.* She lifted the lamb roast on its platter and set it down in front of Jed.

'But I said I wanted more ...' Jed gave up as the carving knife was placed in his hand and his wife turned to see to the potatoes. Besides, the smell of the rosemary-seasoned lamb was driving out all interest in second helpings of soup. As she drained the King Edwards into the sink, Morag saw Caroline through a cloud of steam, mouthing something to her. Careless of her Sunday-morning hair, washed and set the night before, she leaned across and cocked her ear.

Caroline set down the stack of dirty soup-bowls. 'Job done, I think,' she murmured. 'A wee walk after lunch should clinch it.'

Morag turned her back on the three men at the table as she tipped the steaming contents of the colander into a serving dish. 'What about the other one?' Then, seeing Caroline's confident look falter, 'Och, leave him to me. I've always known how to handle Master James. You get Pete organised and just tell him James'll be right keen to come with him.'

'Deal!' Caroline threw a sprinkling of salt over the tatties. 'All right, all right. Coming!' She winked at Pete who beamed and winked back.

The February fields were brown and bare and the wind was keen but there was a snatch of winter sunshine and the horizon had not yet begun to darken. The boy and girl walked side by side along the muddy track bordering the desolate field that would be waving with golden corn, come the summer.

Large helpings of Morag's apple crumble and custard after the lamb roast had kept them all lingering round the table, sipping at cups of strong tea. James produced *The Sunday Post* quiz and declared himself quizmaster, proposing 'girls against boys'. It was neck in neck up to question eighteen, with Jed and Pete majoring on questions political, technical and geographical and Morag and Caroline romping away with those literary, historical or culinary. Question nineteen dealt with a medical matter that looked set to stump all four of them. To everyone's surprise, including her own, Caroline suddenly came up with the correct answer, recalling one of Patsy's diatribes. Question twenty was easy - they all answered it instantly - which meant the girls won by a whisker.

Caroline declared she really must go home. The quick phone call to her mother had promised she would be back home mid-afternoon. Then catching Morag's eye, she remembered the burden of her visit. How to get time with Pete on his own?

He solved the problem himself by offering to keep her company and cycle home with her. Seizing the opportunity, she said: 'Actually, what I really fancy is walking home over the fields. I'm still so full of dinner that I think my bike would buckle under me. And it's a nice afternoon for a walk …'

The fitful sun conspired, sending a sudden ray through the kitchen window. Pete assented at once and went off to pull on his boots. Morag winked encouragingly at Caroline, but Jed glanced doubtfully at her feet.

'Ye're no' thinking of tramping the fields at this time o' year in those?' He indicated her smart suede boots. Needing the confidence of looking her best, she had dressed in a black, calf-length skirt and red ribbed jumper with matching red stockings. The dainty ankle boots complemented her ensemble perfectly but would be hopeless for water-logged fields and muddy paths. Morag swept to the rescue, however, and now Caroline's feet were encased in a pair of old Wellington boots which had belonged to James in primary school and the suede boots were in a borrowed shopping bag.

'And what about yer bike?' Jed seemed determined to place obstacles in the path of true love and ensure its traditional rocky ride.

'Oh, I can leave it just now, if you don't mind,' Caroline replied. 'I'll come back for it tomorrow.' In her heart she was thinking anxiously of the list of tasks she had to complete tomorrow morning before her father bore her off to catch the bus from Forfar to the station in Dundee. The last train to St. A's was at four o'clock so it was a tight schedule. Hearing the doubt in her voice, Morag hurried in:

'No need for that, dear. If you don't need it again this visit, we'll get it over to your place soon. I'll be going over some time this week to see how your poor mother is managing and Jed can take me in the Landrover - we'll get your bike in the back of it.' She beamed at Caroline and glared at her husband who seemed about to find yet another objection.

And so, now, obstacles – and Jed – overcome, they were alone together for the hour it would take to walk the three-and-a-half miles to Caroline's home. As they sloshed along a muddy track towards a five-bar gate, Pete said: 'One of your favourites, isn't it?' recalling their *Free-Think* at the dinner table.

'Sure is.' She began to climb it as nimbly as long skirt trailing onto Wellington tops would allow. He put a hand on the gatepost and vaulted over it. Then he held out both hands to help her descend.

'Thanks.' She was glad of his help as a boot heel caught the hem and she almost tumbled to the ground.

'You must be going soft at that fancy university of yours. I've seen the day you would have jumped it as well.'

'And I still would. I still can. But not in this skirt!'

'A poor excuse!'

'I'd like to see *you* try it then.' They both burst into giggles. He might look terrific in his Highland Dress kilt – Morag and Jed had given both their sons the full regalia for their eighteenth birthdays - but he would look a bonny sight in a long skirt.

They tramped on in companionable silence. Then Pete looked over the fields and, lowering his voice into an old Forfar farmer's accent, he said: 'The grund's fair bare the noo, Bill. But it'll like be sowin' time afore we ken it. Hae ye got yer seed ready?'

Caroline likewise lowered her voice and adopted the accent. 'Ach, Ben, Ah'm thinkin' Dame Winter's got a wee trick or twa up her sleeve yet. Ah've only jist sterted lookin' at the seed catalogues. Fit like dae ye think the lambs'll be dae'in this year?'

They were off into quarter of an hour's impromptu dialogue which ranged over: Bill's arthritis and Ben's chesty cough; a range of cures or palliatives; Bill's wife's extravagance – a shop-bought holly wreath last Christmas when the hedgerows were full of the damned stuff; Ben's wife's bad decision to spice up their mince and tatties with a pinch of curry powder after a visit to Dundee's first Chinese restaurant; the disgraceful actions and expectations of young folk today; and so on. This was another of the games Caroline had instituted last year to help Pete understand how character can reveal itself through dialogue and hence how to extract a character study from a play. Bill and Ben were only one set of characters; there were several others and, as with the Free-Think game, Pete had been hesitant and sceptical at first but had grown into it and become as good as Caroline at it. It too was a game that had outlasted its original use and become part of their relationship. That they had dropped so happily and easily back into both games, after the constraint of Christmas, made him feel like hugging her as if she were a long-lost, very dear friend. He seized her hand and swung it gaily. 'And how is life in the great St A's?'

Morag's admonition drummed in her head: *And don't be goin' on about all the fun you're having at St Andrews. It's no' fair on him. He hasn't had a chance to make friends or have any fun. He's always to be home for the milking and Jed keeps him too busy at weekends for him to get back into Dundee for any o' their dances or parties.*

'It's fine. What about you? Is the course all you hoped it would be? Are you enjoying the lectures? What are the classes like?'

He responded willingly, describing lectures, tutorials and practicals. Fresh from their Bill and Ben sketch, he mimicked one of his tutors, making her laugh and call up a comparison with The Fossil. She thought fleetingly of the boy who had coined the nickname for Old Forsyth: Hugh's townie manners seemed a very long way from this familiar rural setting and comfortable companionship. Pete launched into detail, losing her in a welter of technical language, as they crested a small hill and saw Caroline's farmhouse home in the lee of another hill in the distance. They were more than halfway there. *I've got to get on with it. It's now or never!*

He felt, almost at once, her disengagement and left off enthusing about developments in diesel technology. She was frowning, kicking at stones on the ground and rubbing her nose with her gloved hand. He stopped and turned her towards him.

'What's up, Caro? No, don't deny it. You've got something on your mind. Come on. Tell Uncle Peter.'

Here goes! 'I've got something to ask you, Pete.'

'I knew it! Kicking stones and rubbing noses. I can always tell.'

'It's Chattan Ball this week, on Friday. I was wondering if you would come to it - as my partner?'

He was taken aback. He had never been to a Ball. James had tried to persuade him to give his kilt outfit a second airing – it had only been worn once to a family wedding – at the annual Young Farmers dinner-dance but he had declined. He had seen the state James rolled home in and had heard his boastful tales. James' description of the long-suffering lassies who spent the evening watching their escorts descend into inebriated buffoonery did nothing to change his mind. But none of that resonated with the cultured lifestyle Caroline had portrayed in St Andrews.

'Of course, if you don't want to … It doesn't matter. It was just an idea.'

He shook his head. 'I didn't say I didn't want to. I mean, what sort of thing is it?'

'It's just a dance, and there's a dinner, and we have room parties. We're having a smashing one in Jennifer's room – she's one of the girls on my wing – and we've got a great theme, with terrific decorations, and there's drinks in the rooms – we're allowed some alcohol – and everyone dresses up. Oh, do come! I know you'd enjoy it!'

'But why me? Surely, you've plenty smart St Andrews fellows dying to go with you?'

'Of course.' She did not disabuse him of this notion. It was an alluring, if fictitious, idea. 'But, I thought you'd like to come and see where I'm living and meet my friends. And,' - she had an inspiration - ' I would love to show *you* off to them. My handsome man-from-back-home! Let them see that we are not just country bumpkins where I come from.'

He was flattered, energised by the challenge. 'Well, if you think I'd be …' He felt a rush of reckless happiness. 'Ach, why not? Go on, then. Tell me when I have to come and what I have to do. And what do I wear?'

The next twenty minutes were spent happily discussing the details: his Highland Dress outfit would be perfect; he needed to make sure he sent her a corsage – she would arrange it from one of the florists in St. A's and get the bill sent to him; she would book him into a bed-and-breakfast for the night; and he must be there by seven o' clock.

'But, how can I get away in time?' he groaned. 'There's the milking and my chores. And how will I get there?'

'Your mother's on our side. She and I have discussed it. She'll sort your father out about the farm chores and she'll talk him into loaning you his car for the night.'

'Are you sure? But James will moan his head off at being left with it all to do.'

'No, no! He's going to come as well. I have a friend at St A's who needs an escort to the Ball. Your mother is telling James right now. I'll book you *both* into The Ardgowan Hotel for the night – it's just across the road from Chattan - and I'll order *two* corsages from the florist.'

Pete whistled. W*omen! We men are no match for them.* They had reached the path up to Caroline's house; she stopped and reached up to kiss his cold cheek. 'I'll be fine from here, Pete. You get off home before dark. Thanks for walking me home. I'll see you when you're better dressed - in St. Andrews on Friday. Go and book in to the hotel first then come across. It actually says *Mackintosh Hall* over the door but everyone calls it Chattan. There will be maids in the front hall taking messages up to tell us when our escorts arrive. I hope you recognise me when I come down in my posh evening frock!'

'But where is it?'

She put her hand into the pocket of her winter coat and drew out a sheet of paper. 'Directions. Very easy. You can't miss it. Don't be late.

And wear the full thing – sporran, *sgian dubh*, the lot. Put those English fops in their penguin suits in the shade!'

She was gone, striding up the farm track, and he was left to make his slow way home, head spinning, heart singing. It wasn't until he was almost home that he remembered he had had other plans for this coming Friday: when he had picked up his bike from the Bands' house some two weeks ago, he had spent a delightful half-hour chatting to Alice, which had almost culminated in asking her out. She had side-stepped, saying she 'did not do dates.' However, she *had* made it clear that she could be found most Friday nights at *The Hap,* a café throbbing with juke-box music and lively teenagers. He had never been to it but knew its reputation as a dating-and-mating market. The last two Fridays had proved impossible because of college work, but he had resolved to go there this week and look for her. Unused to such dilemmas of the heart, he trudged home, boyish face clouded with doubt.

'Now, what's wrong with *his* face?' Morag watched him pass through the kitchen on his way to change into his farm-chores gear. She was feeling very pleased with herself: James, after a wee word from her, was delighted at the prospect of 'gate-crashing' Chattan Ball. In vain, Morag explained he would be the legitimate escort of Elspeth, Caroline's friend. As far as he was concerned, coming from a farm in rural Angus into such a rarefied environment ranked as gate-crashing and the idea thrilled him. He liked Caroline and was amused by his little brother's antics with her but he did not take her university career seriously. At least Pete was learning something with obvious practical application. As far as James could make out, St Andrews was full of freeloaders, spending their time studying a lot of rubbish, subsidised by hard-working tax-payers. For all that – though he would have denied it – he sensed the glamour and was excited about getting the chance to be part of it for a night. He and Morag had spent a happy hour planning how to talk Jed into loaning them his 'town car', a big Ford Zodiac, and how to persuade him to find ways round the absence of both his sons for an evening and a morning. Jed was, in fact, always generous with extra money and the use of his car for the boys to enjoy themselves – provided the enjoyment took place outwith farm work hours. But it was going to be impossible to get all the evening chores done before they had to set off on Friday and they would not be back till ... *probably well into the afternoon on Saturday*, James said hopefully, envisaging a late night and a decadent, hung-over long lie in the morning.

'We'll need to get help this time, that's all there is to it. There's no reason why not. It's time we had another pair of hands anyway. Pete's *never* going to be a farmer and, the sooner you and Jed accept that and let him get on with his own life, the better.' Listening to Caroline, Morag had felt shame at the comparison between her freedom in St Andrews and Pete's shackles. Then, as James shrugged: 'I ken fine you've enjoyed being the blue-eyed boy these past four years and letting Pete suffer for having other ambitions besides the farm. But, do you not think it's high time we put an end to the game? You're no' wee boys fighting over who's going to get the most attention from your father any more. You're grown men. Pete's never complained, no' even to me. But I'm fed up watching him racing around trying to fit everything in. He'll be having an accident on that bike of his, one of these days, tearing home for the milking, especially on these dark winter nights.'

James remembered his own fears when Pete had been late home because of the lemonade bottle incident. 'But who can we get at such short notice?'

'Well, I've had an idea. See what you think ...' Ranging over all the possibilities, she had come full-circle, her own bit of *Free-Think*. Caroline had three brothers, two older and one younger than her. They were all still at home, working alongside their father to make the most of the opportunities that new machinery and wider markets were bringing to farmers. She would be going over to Inshaig Farm this week to see Caroline's mother: surely the two of them could persuade one of these strapping lads to help out at Fintry on Friday night and Saturday morning.

'Do you think I should offer to pay him? I mean I wouldn't want to insult them but I wouldn't want to seem like I was sponging off them.'

James had not been much help, having little understanding of etiquette, farming or otherwise. He knew the Inshaig brothers from encounters at YF meetings but had certainly never put his mind to considering their – or anyone else's - susceptibility to insult. Such sensitivities did not feature much in YF society.

'You could find out, though, Jimmy lad, couldn't you? Ask around at the YF meeting tomorrow night? This kind of thing must happen from time to time – if farmers get sick, or maybe even have a *holiday*.' The McCaffertys had never had such a thing but she had heard that one or two farming families had even begun to go *abroad*.' Then I could leave off going to Inshaig till Tuesday and I'd know what was best to say to them. What do you think?'

Before James could answer, Pete came back in, dressed in mucking-out gear. 'What's this about Inshaig?'

She explained her plans but he did not seem as pleased with her fairy-godmother efforts to get him to the Ball as she expected. Recalling the shining, tangible connection between the two old schoolmates earlier on, she was puzzled. She had expected some misgivings about how he might fit in at Chattan and some worries about how to escape from his chores, but his lukewarm reaction bewildered her. Had they quarrelled again on the way back to Caroline's home?

James had no such qualms. 'It's going to be a great lark!' he declared, slapping Pete on the back. 'Imagine us, eh, Brer? Swanking it with the toffs at the 'Varsity! We'll show them how real men enjoy themselves.' He went off whistling jauntily.

Morag and Pete exchanged glances. 'Is that what's worrying you, son? I'm sure he'll behave himself when he gets there. He's like a one o' those funny animals that change colour depending on where they are - a *camelot*, is it? He behaves like a lout with those YFs, I ken, but he has been brought up proper, same as yourself, and he kens how to behave himself in proper company. He'll no' let you down.'

'What? Oh, no. I'm sure he'll be OK. It's not that. Oh, Mam! Why does life have to be so complicated?' He moved towards the outside door and grimaced when he saw that the predicted bad weather had arrived and sheets of rain were sweeping across the farmyard. The light had almost gone, hastened on its way by leaden-grey clouds, and the wind was howling like a demented soul. 'Good job we got those ewes in this morning.' He struggled into waterproof trousers and boots, cursing under his breath, turning the everyday process into a grudging effort. Finally, with a last irritable snort, he was ready.

'Ach, women! Who needs them?' was his parting shot, leaving Morag to wonder what on earth had got into him.

CHAPTER FIVE: MARJORY AND THE BLACK BOY

Seventy-seven, seventy-eight ... Alice swept the hairbrush through her long black hair, the rhythm aiding her concentration as she regarded herself in the dressing-table mirror. Years ago, she had read about a Victorian girl who never missed giving her tresses one hundred strokes every day. The description of waist-length, shimmering locks had fired her imagination and filled her with a zeal that had become habit. The five minutes this exercise took was also her reflection time. As a child, she had used it to imagine herself living in the latest book she was reading; in early teens to fantasise about film stars and pop singers – Cliff Richard a big favourite; and now, with her eighteenth birthday looming and all the pressure of gaining university entrance, it was her escape time. Worries about class-work, homework, essays or assignments did not intrude upon hair-brushing time: it was the only time in her day that *was* free of them

She thought now of the boy-on-the-bike: Farmer Pete. Two Fridays had gone by since that Monday evening when he had come back for his bike and they had stood in the garage chatting. He had been attracted to her, had seized the chance, as soon as she said how much she liked James Bond, to ask if she would like to go to the pictures and see *From Russia with Love*, currently showing at *The Gaumont* in Dundee. Not for the first time since last September, Alice cursed the promise she had made to her mother that she would not date any boys this year but would concentrate solely on her studies. Marjory Band had been very disappointed when her daughter had failed to pass all five Highers in fifth year. Three out of five, only one with an A pass and one with an ignominious C pass, were not good enough. Alice must do better. Marjory blamed herself, as she always did. She had not been strict enough, allowing Alice to spend most of her evenings at 'The Ref', pretending to study, posing on the balcony outside, open to invitations to Green's coffee bar on the Nethergate, a mere ten minutes walk away, spending as much time there as at her table in the library. There were a few very clever girls and boys who seemed able to behave like this and still land amazing marks – or perhaps, more likely, they secretly worked at home and preserved a front. Alice was neither clever enough to need so little study or devious enough to carry out such a deception.

This year, she was under a very different regime: no more evenings at The Ref; no more Saturday night dates or dances. Marjory conceded one respite in the housebound evenings and weekends: Alice might go on a Friday evening to *The Hap* cafe, meet her friends, play a little juke-box music, have a little fun. There were several other feckless ex-patrons of The Ref and Green's, whose parents had got together last summer when the disastrous results had come out, to devise the strategy and strike a pact to enforce it. They stood shoulder-to-shoulder when their offspring protested, trying on the age-old 'everybody-else-gets-to'. Some of her fellow sufferers-under-the-lash had resorted to deception and she had been asked a few times to provide a false alibi. The one time she had reluctantly lied outright to a friend's mother, a quick phone call from this suspicious lady to her own mother had soon rooted out the conspiracy. Any ideas Alice had entertained about subterfuge had withered away under Marjory's scathing 'even *you* must have known such childish behaviour would soon be found out'. Do you have any brains at all?'

So, she could not accept Pete's – or any other boy's - invitation. She had devised another response which she hoped would preserve her dignity and enhance her attraction: Now, when 'asked-out', she simply said, 'I don't *do* dates', hoping it sounded like Garbo's *I-vant-to-be-alone*, and employed a middle-distance stare, as if glimpsing some faraway world or time-zone with much more alluring prospects than a Saturday night snuggle at the pictures with a mere earthling. She now had a string of would-be swains vying to be first to breach her defences. Pete was the latest enthralled recruit, even glancing over his shoulder for a sighting of her distant siren. But she was too much attracted to leave him – or herself – without hope: 'I can be found most Fridays at *The Hap*, though - do you know it?'

What teenager in the Dundee area did not? For Pete, it was just one of many places that he cycled past but never sampled. He hesitated, flicking through his Friday night commitments: milking, cowshed, pigsty, chopping logs and hosing down the tractors; then writing up all the notes from the week's lectures and practicals so that he had the weekend clear for assignments and reading ahead. How could he fit in cycling into Dundee again and spending an hour or two in a café?

Alice misread his hesitation. She shrugged and turned to go back into her house with a throwaway, 'See you around, maybe.' He ran after her, starting to explain, but at that moment the headlights of her mother's car swept in, illuminating the pair in the drive. He had time only to call, 'I'll try and get there some Friday this month. Promise!' before Marjory Band was upon him, jingling her car-keys and acknowledging his '*Thank you so much - I'll be off then,*' with a dismissive nod.

But now two Fridays had come and gone without a sign of him. Ninety one, ninety two … *I'll give him one more chance*. She recalled an R.E. lesson about Jacob in the bible: *I'll put out a fleece. If he's not there this week, I'll give up on him and not think about him again.* Ninety-five, ninety-six …

'Alice! Telephone!' her mother's voice drifted up from the foot of the stairs where the telephone table stood. Alice finished the last three strokes quickly and hurried down the stairs. *Maybe he's looked up our number in the telephone directory!*

A moment later she was listening to Millie Morton, mother of three, begging her to babysit on Friday evening. An unexpected dinner invitation; important for Tom's career. Sorry such short notice. She'd pay Alice more than usual.

Alice might have refused but Millie had already explained to Marjory her reason for phoning. Her mother's watchful stare put paid to any fleecy plans. Alice assured Millie that she would be happy to babysit and 'No, absolutely not', she had no plans for this Friday night. It would be a pleasure and no need for the extra money, Millie was already more than generous …'

Marjory watched her daughter drag her feet up the stairs; then, she went back to doing her makeup before setting off for her Shakespeare class.

Damn! Damn! Damn!' Alice threw her school books on to the desk in her bedroom. 'Damn Millie and her brats!'

She watched her mother's car roll out of the drive into the Kingsway traffic then she turned back to the pile of homework. She had already done the easier stuff for her Higher History class: her B higher pass last year had been in Geography and she enjoyed learning the history attached to places around the world. But she was also attempting to upgrade her sad C pass in Higher English; and to redeem failures in Maths and French. She was *not* enjoying any of these. Her one A pass had been in Domestic Science, which she loved but which her mother dismissed as 'not a proper school subject at all'. Given her way, Alice would have gone off to Domestic Science college this year but Marjory's derisory *Oh, for heaven's sake, Alice, not Dough School!* had smothered her dreams.

She stacked books and jotters in three piles, closed her eyes and drummed a finger over them: *eeny, meeny, miny, mo* … The childish rhyme ended and she opened her eyes to see her finger resting on Euclid's Geometry. With a resigned sigh, she pulled the book and jotter towards her. Half an hour later, her head a jangle of exotic words for dull concepts – isosceles. hypotenuse, quadrilateral – and her jotter page a muddle of scored out, rubbed out and overwritten figures and diagrams, she closed Euclid with a snap, close to tears. The French prose fared little better. By the time she reached Palgrave's Golden Treasury of English Verse, she felt like a wanderer in a maze without a map. A third rewrite of a comparison of Milton's *L'Allegro* and *Il Penseroso*, based on the copious red-pencil notes covering her last attempt, was the *coup de grace*.

Finished at last, in search of comfort, she found herself in the kitchen assembling bowls, utensils and ingredients before she realised what she was doing. Within minutes she was immersed in reading recipes and adapting them to available ingredients, a light tune bubbling from her pursed lips. By the time Marjory returned, the house was filled with a mouthwatering aroma. Her daughter was in the kitchen, in her element, spooning lemon drizzle over a warm cherry and almond cake; two mugs of freshly percolated coffee, laced with vanilla and topped with whipped cream stood beside it. She greeted her mother: 'Well, Shylock! How's your quality of mercy?'

Marjory checked her usual opening question - *have you done your homework?* – and responded gaily: 'Signor Antonio, many a time and oft on the Rialto, you have ... Then she took a gulp of the delicious coffee and sank her teeth into a slice of cake.

'Well?' Alice was nibbling her own slice and sipping from her cup thoughtfully. 'What do you think? Too much vanilla? Do you think lime drizzle or maybe orange would be better? I'm not sure if lemon and almonds work together.

'Oh, Alice, it's fine. It's only food. Now tell me what you had for homework tonight and how you got on with it. Let me see the results.'

Later, clearing up the baking detritus and washing their cups and plates, Alice found herself wondering how it was for Farmer Pete. She knew from the enthusiasm with which he had talked of his course at The Tech that he was pursuing the career of his choice. Had it been plain sailing for him with the full backing of his parents? Had he also plain-sailed through all the required Highers for college entry? Would she ever see him again?

Marjory applied Ponds Vanishing Cream to her face and neck with firm upward strokes. Like Alice's hair-brushing time, these minutes in front of her mirror were her reflection time. And she had much to think about.

Tonight, at their *Appreciating Shakespeare* evening class, the tutor had dangled before her the prospect of becoming serious about her studies and even, eventually, gaining a degree – though that would be many years down the line since she had had so little formal schooling. But universities were being encouraged to take 'mature students' and there was even talk of creating a *University of the Air*, using radio and television broadcasts, telephone tutorials and postal assignments. Marjory's head was ringing with her tutor's: 'Oh, yes, Mrs Band, you are definitely the kind of student they are looking for. I think we're going to have a new Labour government before the year is out, one keen to tap into the potential of under-achievers like yourself.'

Under-achievers? Well, she was certainly that. The only child of a missionary father and a long-suffering mother, brought up in a series of remote villages in Africa, she had been casually home-schooled till the age of twelve by her mother, and then inadequately tutored by a stream of short-stay, enthusiastic, but largely untrained, young teachers in an American missionary school near Nairobi, where she lived during the week in the compound and went home to the current village at weekends.

In the summer of her sixteenth birthday, she had gone back to the village, bored and restless, anticipating the usual dreary round of prayer meetings, domestic tasks, dragged-out days in intense heat, evenings reading on the verandah with her parents and sweaty nights under mosquito nets. Her mother worked hard to ensure that her precious daughter grew up a lady and mixed as little as possible with the natives: she might endorse her husband's attempts to improve the lives, both temporal and eternal, of 'the black babies' but she drew the line at allowing Marjory to fraternise with them. She disliked the Americanisms that Marjory had brought back from school and a lot of holiday time was spent ironing these out of her daughter's behaviour and vocabulary.

But this summer, it was all different. Mother was ill: her first bout of malaria. Her father, busy with outreach work and regularly away from the village for long stretches of time, hastily engaged a companion–governess for Marjory, a flighty French girl of nineteen, the daughter of a doctor, recently arrived at Kijabe Hospital. Amélie and Marjory had themselves a glorious, carefree summer, exploring and picnicking round the countryside, camping out under the stars, chatting up the locals, making up all sorts of games and fantasies. Marjory's French became laced with Provençal patois and Amélie's English with American slang. It was Marjory's one experience of 'teenage' fun and she still, despite its catastrophic ending, thought of it with nostalgic affection.

Innocent, excited by the freedom, entranced by Amélie's sophistication, she never really stood a chance of surviving that summer. There were huts full of young black lads watching the two pretty white girls romping around unchaperoned. The one who got lucky with Marjory came upon them one late evening, sitting beside a campfire they had lit. He fed them a sweet herbal drink which he told them his mother made as a tonic. Both girls became langorous and loose-tongued as they drank, Amélie fell asleep and Marjory found herself in the boy's arms, being kissed and caressed, wonderful new sensations flooding her body as his fingers explored bits of her anatomy she scarcely knew she had. The legs that he pushed apart felt like floating logs detached from her body and his weight on her simply part of a descending cloud coming to claim her senses. The sudden bolt of pain through the lower half of her body briefly recalled her to reality but the mouth she opened to call out was immediately covered by large wet lips that seemed suck the breath out of her. She lost consciousness.

The biting of insects woke them a few hours later and they staggered home, propping each other up, Amélie cursing colourfully in her native tongue. When they finally surfaced the next afternoon, bleary-eyed, blotched with insect bites, lips cracked with thirst, it was to find that Rev. Band had returned home that morning. One sight of the two girls confirmed the rumours he had heard from neighbouring missionaries as he had come nearer and nearer home. The two reprobates were separated immediately and not allowed to speak to each other again. The next day, they were despatched: Amélie back to Kijabe, Marjory taken by her tight-lipped father to stay with another missionary family thirty miles away. There, the middle-aged mother agreed to act as duenna, a part she had already played with some skill for her own two daughters, now grown-up and safely married.

The rest of the holidays passed in familiar boredom tinged with embarrassment before the disapproving eye of her hostess. Marjory retained very little of her last evening with Amélie. Sometimes she let her mind probe the hazy memory of the black boy's attentions and would feel a flicker of those strange, wonderful sensations. But her father's face would be immediately before her, his 'behaving like that when your poor mother is lying at death's door' ringing in her ears; and the sensations would wither. By the time she went back to school a month later, she had reduced the memory to a shameful dream.

Then, the nausea began; then, the actual vomiting before breakfast; then, the sick headaches each afternoon and the all-day tiredness. Both she and the matron at the hostel where she boarded during the week assumed she was unwell, that it would pass. After two weeks, matron called in a doctor. When, in answer to his question 'Have you noticed any other symptoms or changes in your health?', she reflected that she had not had any monthly bleeding for some eight or nine weeks, his eyebrows shot up into his hairline.

The following weekend, Matron came back home with her, saying she wished to talk to Marjory's parents about their daughter's health. Marjory, convinced she had some mysterious terminal illness, was alternately full of foreboding and filled with a sense of romantic importance. Exhausted and nauseous, a languishing invalid, she waited sorrowfully on the verandah, expecting her convalescent mother to rush out of the study, where the three adults were closeted, and scoop her up in a tearful embrace before solicitously tucking a rug round her knees. Instead, her father opened the door of the study and thundered: 'Marjory! Come in here at once!'

Her mother had indeed been tearful – floods of tears, in fact – but there had been no embrace. When she heard the scandalous, scandalised word, *pregnant*, Marjory almost fainted. Then she felt the familiar rush of vomit in her throat and turned to throw up into the nearest receptacle - an unlucky waste paper basket. By the time their native servant had been called to clean up the mess, Matron had departed, shaking her head sadly, ignoring Marjory who sat weeping on the floor of the study.

She did not return to school and the next two weeks were spent trying to respond to her parents' questions and take in the horrific news. Such an eventuality had never crossed her mind. She had only the sketchiest notion of how babies are made and born; her mother had never talked of it, simply explaining the onset of menstruation as a woman's curse which passes in time. Even if she had had a clear memory of all that had happened round the campfire she would probably not have known its significance or potential consequence. Worldly-wise Amelie could have put her straight but the girls had been parted before any discussion between them of the night's events. And, rack her brain as she did, she could not conjure up the boy's face. It had been dark and the flickering campfire had distorted everything; she had been so quickly reduced by the sweet drink to an almost hallucinatory state; and, anyway … Finally losing her temper, she shouted: 'All those bloody black boys look the same to me!' Her father's look of disappointed disgust deepened.

He was for questioning all the village boys and conducting a full investigation but her mother begged him to consider their reputation in the tight-knit missionary community and his position in the tight-laced organisation which employed him. Once she had spent three days weeping and wringing her hands, Mrs Band's fear of being discovered as the mother of a daughter who had 'gone off the rails' brought her to her senses.

By the time Marjory was in her fourth month, she had ceased feeling ill, which was just as well because by that time she was on a rather rough voyage to Great Britain. Mrs Band was not well enough to travel – the shock and stress of the past weeks had jeopardised her recovery.

56

Marjory's holiday duenna was glad of the opportunity for an extra visit home, with her fare paid for the price of her silence as to Marjory's condition. For those who asked, the girl was going to Britain to finish her schooling. Mrs Band had thrown herself on the mercy of a maiden aunt in Scotland, who had recently been released from twenty years of caring for her ailing parents, Marjory's great-grandparents. Aunt Mavis responded quite cheerfully to Mrs Band's desperate letter: it would make a nice change, she said, to be dealing with dirty nappies, broken nights and endless washing at the *other* end of the life cycle. Marjory's arrival and situation would certainly cause comment and gossip but Aunt Mavis was willing to take her on as a poor sinner in need of redemption and to provide not only a home for her and the baby but an environment that would ensure such a thing never happened again. Mavis saw it as her Christian duty and no less than a call from God.

Thus, Marjory ended up in Aunt Mavis' big, old tenement flat in Dundee, settling into the room that had not long ago housed her dying great-grandmother and still bore traces of this in its furnishings and lingering slight smell. True to her word, Aunt Mavis placed her under a benevolent house arrest, providing for her basic needs kindly, but not allowing her any social life other than church on Sunday morning. Even there, Mavis' beady eye was upon her, hustling her away from any contact with the opposite sex, though quite what kind of man would have been attracted to the sallow-skinned, hollow-eyed, pregnant schoolgirl was unclear.

Still in shock, homesick for Africa and all the life she had ever known, Marjory moped her way through her pregnancy and shivered through her first Scottish winter, uninterested in her new surroundings, filled with a sense of having thrown her life away and of being such a disappointment and a failure that she was best kept hidden from the rest of the world. The minister at Mavis' church listened to the explanation of who this girl was and what had happened to her; he shook his head and endorsed Mavis' vocation to provide present sanctuary and future protection; and he smoothed the path for the girl's acceptance into his congregation. It was never clear whether he meant to insinuate that Marjory was – in common Dundee parlance *–a wee bit elevenpence in the shillin'* or whether someone inferred this and set the rumour circulating. Whatever its genesis, it proved a comfortable fiction that helped the good folk in the Dundee kirk to accept and pity, rather than judge and condemn. Marjory's withdrawn expression and passive behaviour confirmed the belief that she was *simple* and had been sadly *taken advantage of* by some native in the jungle. She was pitied and patronised, regarded as their resident good cause: the women knitted bootees and shawls; the men made a cot and reconditioned a pram. They spoke slowly to her, patting her like a stray dog.

The baby girl was born in March in a discreet nursing home in the nearby village of Newtyle: she was spared the stares and speculation of a maternity ward full of married women and curious nurses. The Rev Band's detailed directions saw to that. After nine months of bewildered misery, Marjory smiled for the first time since that fateful night in the African bush. She looked at the tiny puckered face, grasped a minute fist and prized it open to slip her own pinkie inside, nuzzled the fluffy down on the baby's head and burst into happy chuckles, tears pouring down her cheeks.

The next ten years were devoted to caring for her child. With no other outlet for her young mind, she devoted herself to finding out all she could about babies, toddlers and growing children. She read all she could find on the subject of feeding, weaning, teething, tantrums and child development. Embarrassed by her youth and single status, she stood apart at the school gates, not making eye-contact with the confident, twenty-something, married mothers, confirming the rumour that she was *strange, not quite all there.*

But she did encourage Alice to make friends, having read about the importance of developing social skills early in life. Mavis, who doted on the child, relaxed her guard to allow children's parties and weekend visits from schoolfriends. The other parents were happy in the knowledge that the *adult* in the house was a middle-aged, respectable pillar of the church and not the odd, scandalously young mother, about whom there clung a seedy whiff of past scandal – *Well, you only have to look at the child, quite beautiful, of course, but definitely a half-cast … and they say her father is a missionary … She was only sixteen … that auntie is a saint, taking her in like that.*

Marjory's mother died, her heart desperately weakened by the third bout of malaria in two years. Alice was only six months old, still breast-feeding, too young to be left and much too young to undertake the long voyage to Africa. In any event, as is the way there, the funeral and burial took place within forty-eight hours. Her father came home for three months furlough shortly after. He spent an uncomfortable three weeks of this with Mavis and Marjory, torn between acceptance of his grandchild and condemnation of his daughter. He did not say it outright, but it was plain that he blamed Marjory for his wife's death and believed that the shock and stress, when she was just beginning to recover from the first illness, had weakened her irreparably.

Mourning a mother she had left in such miserable circumstances and would never see again, racked with guilt, Marjory drew still further into the shell that she would inhabit for the next ten years. Reverend Band set sail for another benighted village in Africa leaving Mavis with strict instructions. His regular letters thereafter always reinforced these wishes, with scriptural quotes to justify them, and ended with assurance of relentless prayer for his daughter's sadly stained soul.

During the next ten years, Marjory, from time to time, thought to get a job: not from financial need as her father's allowance to Mavis was generous, but because she longed for company, friends, stimulation – what she thought wistfully of as *LIFE*. But she lacked even a decent basic education, barely able to write without spelling and grammatical errors, unable to type or keep financial records. She had no hope of getting an office job; even shop jobs – except for some seedy corner shop – were beyond her reach. In any event, Mavis did not think any job that entailed meeting the public would meet with Rev Band's approval and that ruled out pretty well everything that she might be able to do.

'We have to be so careful, my dear. Your father does not want you in the public eye at all. He is anxious to keep your disgrace as little known as possible.' Mavis lovingly smoothed the glossy dark hair of the little girl on her knee – the much-loved 'disgrace' - as she spoke.

Marjory sought solace in reading, working her way through Mavis' modest library of classics within a year and moving on to join the local library. At first she read indiscriminately, glad to have any diversion for her cramped mind. But as the years past, she settled upon a love of lengthy, wordy, nineteenth century novels, so that she sometimes expressed herself like a Jane Austen heroine, much to the surprise of the Women's Guild when they came to visit.

When Alice was eleven years old, Reverend Band died quite suddenly. He had been home for just one other visit during Alice's first decade and had been entranced by his bright and beautiful granddaughter, tears in his eyes as he looked at her. His lugubrious sighs had depressed Marjory and irritated Mavis. They were both glad to see the back of him. Marjory tried dutifully to feel sorrow at his death, as she had genuinely done for her mother, but soon gave up and life simply went on in its familiar routine for a few months until the arrival of a lawyer's letter bidding her visit their chambers in the Lawnmarket in Edinburgh. Mavis received an identical summons.

The excitement of a trip to the capital would have been enough for the two of them without the intriguing prospect of the meeting at the lawyer's office. They planned it minutely: checking and re-checking train times; counting out the money they would need for tickets, taxis and lunches; changing their minds several times about what they would wear; arranging for Alice to go home from school with a friend to give them plenty of time.

Marjory would never forget the moment she heard the dry voice of the little bald solicitor naming the sum that she was to inherit: ten thousand pounds! It was a fortune. Mavis was left two thousand with thanks for her care of 'my unfortunate daughter'. For Alice, there was five thousand, to be left accruing interest in a trust until her twenty-first birthday.

'But where on earth did my father get all this money?'

The solicitor explained that Rev Band had been left some thirteen thousand pounds in his twenties, a bequest from a wealthy uncle in New Zealand whom he had never met, but who had had no children of his own to leave his New World money to. The Rev. had dutifully tithed thirteen hundred pounds to a worthy Christian cause and deposited the rest in the bank where it had lain untouched, gathering interest for thirty years. He had regarded the money as having no relevance to his own life which he had dedicated to God's work and for which he trusted that God would provide. Indeed, he had probably felt embarrassed by it, even a little ashamed. Certainly he had never mentioned it to anyone, not even his wife.

On his last trip home, however, he had made the trip to Edinburgh and consulted the Lawnmarket lawyer for the purpose of making his will. Marjory never understood why her father left so much to her, why he did not bypass her and leave it all to his granddaughter. But whatever the reason – perhaps, knowing his health was failing, he had felt some remorse and begun to grasp the doctrine of forgiveness – he had done it and it changed Marjory's life.

For one thing, Mavis immediately began to treat her quite differently: no more the disgraced schoolgirl who must be hemmed in and prevented from further indiscretions, Marjory found herself being treated as an adult, a woman of means, with the right to decide her own future. Mavis looked at her great-niece and saw, not the feckless teenager of ten years ago, but a woman of twenty-seven, the mother of a ten-year-old daughter. And Mavis also glimpsed beckoning freedom for herself: she could realise a long-held ambition and buy a cottage in the Highlands; she even had a recently widowed friend whom she was sure would come and live with her there.

The two women skipped down the Royal Mile and treated themselves to a slap-up lunch in a posh, touristy restaurant, all thoughts of their careful budget for the day banished. Before they left the smart establishment, it was settled that Marjory would buy herself a house in Dundee and Mavis would hand in her notice to her landlord and start looking at Highland cottages.

Within three months, Marjory had moved into the bungalow-with-upstairs-dormer on the Kingsway, perfect timing to ensure that Alice was in the catchment area for Morgan Academy, one of the best secondary schools in the town, just as she prepared to make the transition from primary school. The bungalow cost two thousand and there was plenty of money from the interest on the remaining eight thousand to cover living expenses. So Marjory had no real need to work, certainly not in the kind of job that her lack of qualifications would condemn her to. But she was desperate to find something meaningful to do at last and threw herself into a series of night classes, historical societies, film clubs and book groups.

It was not until tonight, however, five years down the line, that she had begun to think of gaining a qualification. The idea made her heart beat faster and she had a sense of prison gates opening to reveal a longed-for but rather frightening, big, wide world.

Alice does not appreciate the wonderful chance she has, she thought as she rose from her dressing-table stool. *She takes it all for granted, might even throw it away* ... She took a long time to fall asleep that night, her emotions swinging between irritation at her daughter's ingratitude and excitement at her own future.

CHAPTER SIX: MORAG AND JED

Pete shot the lights and reared up in the saddle to tackle the hill. A fine day: tufty clouds in a pale blue sky; buckets of greenhouse daffodils outside a florist shop; snowdrops in bloom, crocuses in bud. Navy-clad schoolboys and girls foamed around The Morgan, the impressive old building dominating the crossroads. It was quarter to four and the corner shop would soon be doing brisk business in Mars Bars and single cigarettes. His eyes ranged over the hordes until he spotted her walking slowly with two other girls, heading towards the Kingsway. He halted and fiddled with the saddle bag. When the trio was almost at the roundabout, he sped towards it, then stopped again just short.

The three girls lingered and Pete groaned as one of them opened her satchel, took out a book and began to show the other two a page. He had slipped out of his last lecture at half past three, fabricating a dentist appointment, and had been feeling pleased with his timing. But, at this rate, he would be late for milking and he had promised James that he would do his best to keep their father sweet this week.

Morag had wrought a minor miracle – or so it seemed to her sons who did not yet understand pillow-talk persuasion. Jed was not only agreeing to line their pockets and loan them the car for Friday's jaunt to St Andrews, but was going along with the plan for Jerry Dempsey to come over to Fintry Farm on Friday afternoon and stay till Saturday evening. James had asked around at the YF meeting, as instructed, and discovered that there was no need for money to change hands: a nice big bottle of twelve-year-old single malt would do the trick.

At last, the trio broke up and Alice turned left. A bus suddenly pulled out from its stop just behind him, incurring the wrath of a speeding white van, and Pete had to wheel his bike up to the roundabout on the pavement. Alice was at her gate as he raced up and leapt off the bike, landing almost on top of her. She whirled round with a cry of alarm.

'Sorry, sorry, sorry!' Pete's face was bright red with embarrassment and exertion. He rescued his bike, which was lying on its side in the gutter, and propped it against the gatepost. Alice had regained her composure and was half-leaning, half-sitting on the wall.

'What on earth did that poor bike ever do to you?' she wondered. 'Every time I see you, you're abusing it!'

He grinned. 'We have a tormented relationship.' A phrase from an essay about Macbeth and his Lady which he and Caroline had worked on for

Higher English. As the memory chased through his mind, he thought: *What am I doing here with this girl? What about Caroline?*

Alice called upon all her Garbo skills. 'Were you coming to see *us* or did you just feel the need to throw yourself on the pavement at this particular moment in time?' She emphasised *us*. *Me* might sound humiliatingly hopeful.

Pete struggled to remember what he had planned to say. His ruminations of the past three days had led to no conclusion. He did not want to lose contact with Alice, did not want her to think badly of him. But he did not want her to think he was *serious* about her either. Caroline was back in her old niche as best-pal-cum-very-attractive-girl. She had set his pulses racing with her invitation to Chattan Ball. Their relationship had taken a leap forward – or was it back?

'Well,' Alice was turning in the gate again, 'if you've nothing to say, I really must ...'

This was a different boy from the one who had chatted happily to her in the garage, the night he had come to pick up his bike, a few weeks ago. Clearly something was tying his tongue, but why had he chased after her and landed almost in her arms if he had nothing to say?

'Wait, Alice, please. I just wondered if you're going to that café - *The Hap* - on Friday? I've been meaning to go myself - been snowed under with work the last two weeks, but ...'

Alice mentally consigned Tom Morton and his career-building dinner engagement to the fiery pits. 'I'm afraid not.' She smiled sweetly. 'I have a previous engagement.'

Pete felt a fool. What had made him think that a *corker* like her would be sitting on her thumb waiting for him? *Some other lucky fellow.*

'But you said you didn't do dates! I mean,' he blushed, 'it's your own business, of course, I just thought maybe ... Maybe some other time,' he finished miserably and reached over to the handlebars of his bike.

'Mmm ... Maybe.' Then she relented. 'In fact,' - a teasing grin - 'pretty definitely *next* week, I should think.'

'But that's great! Actually, I was going to say I couldn't make it either this week – got to go to a thing in St Andrews on Friday.' He hesitated. *Best not mention The Ball. She might think I'm tied up with Caroline.* A flash of guilt flickered. Alice saw his grimace: *He's got some boring engagement he can't get out of, poor thing,* she surmised.

'Maybe next Friday then. *Au revoir.*' Her mother's car would be home any minute: Marjory went to a poetry appreciation group on Wednesday afternoons, had coffee in *Draffens* Tearoom afterwards and was always home by half past four. The last thing Alice wanted was her mother finding her chatting to Farmer Pete at the gate.

She marched up the short drive without looking back and Pete, fascinated, watched the long, shining ponytail swinging across her shoulder blades. He dug out what little French he had. *'A bientot!'*

She half-turned with the flicker of a smile and wave before disappearing into the house.

James watched as Pete finished his chores in the cowshed, stacked the rakes and pitchforks against the wall in the corner and began to *talk* to the cow nearest the door. No throwaway farewell remark: his brother was addressing the bemused animal at some length and even gesticulating with one hand. As the transistor radio in the other hand was still blaring out the latest chart-topper, James had no chance of hearing what was being explained to the cow. Pete finally ran out of words, gazed hopefully at the animal then shook his head and ran a hand through his hair, leaving a streak of smelly dirt on his forehead. He looked, James thought, like a man with worries on his mind.

Now, what's baby brother so fed up about? Haven't we got it all sorted for Friday and even Dad's quite happy to let him have a break for once? What else is he wanting?

Indeed, Morag had it all well in hand: their kilts and jackets had been pressed and aired; their white dress shirts freshly laundered, the handles of their *sgian dubhs* and the buckles of their sporrans and shoes polished; and a small suitcase packed with fresh clothes for the next day. She had even organised time off for haircuts on Thursday afternoon.

Jed had grumblingly agreed to start the milking alone that day. Morag had ear-bashed him unmercifully about the gap between Caroline's carefree student life and the draconian regime that Pete lived under. At first, Jed had shrugged and refused to make the connection; but persistence was winning the day. He was objecting less and less to the boys' trip to *this damned posh dance*. He knew his wife well enough to recognise a battle he was not going to win.

As Pete turned to open the barn door, he was startled to feel a heavy hand on his shoulder. James had been hidden behind the milking machinery in the far corner of the barn. He had returned in search of his pipe - his attempts to emulate his father's competence with the pipe had met with little success so far but, like Hugh, he was persevering.

'What the devil? I never saw you in here.' A slow flush was only just visible on Pete's dirty, streaked face as he realised he had been observed.

'What's bothering you, pal? You look like you've lost a shilling and found a sixpence! There's nothing to worry about: Mam's got it all sorted and Dad's eating out of her hand; so we're in the clear for a quick getaway on Friday afternoon as soon as you get home and we don't need to be back until …'

He stopped as Pete made a dismissive gesture and turned away to drag the barn door open. 'Is it something else then?' A sudden, horrified thought: 'You've not heard from Caroline, have you? She's not changed her mind about us going? She is still wanting us *both* there?'

'Oh, don't worry, you'll get your jaunt to the fancy dance in St Andrew's. Just bloody well make sure you behave yourself and don't embarrass me – and Caroline!'

'Is that what's on your mind? Is that what you were deavin' Bessie about?' James gestured to the cow who had lost interest and was now devoting her attention the straw in her manger.

But Pete had already passed through the big door and was striding off towards the henhouse to tackle the next job on his list. James caught up with him as he knelt down to begin mending a broken piece of the fence around the hen-run: A fox had been worrying at it. Jed had spotted the beginnings of a weak spot and had added the chore to Pete's list.

James began to assure him that there was no need to worry: he would do them proud at the Ball and be a model of decorum. He had already had several homilies from Morag and even a clipped reference from his father. Jed might pretend to scorn the *swanky carry-on* but he did not want his older son letting the family down in front of *a lot of toffs*. James had made enough assurances to both parents now to believe and mean them.

But Pete was not listening; the frown on his face had nothing to do with James' behaviour at the Ball. As Pete finished the task and rose, James barred his way. 'OK. Now tell me what's going on? We're both going to this Ball so, if there's a problem, I need to know. Come on, you can tell *me*.'

Growing up together, they had been good friends, competitive as boys will be but close confidants. But, in past four years, Pete had broken the mould and followed his star, to their father's disgust and James' bafflement. It had been some time since the brothers had confided their hopes and fears to each other.

Pete had thrashed the Caroline-Alice equation through his head as he cycled home and worked though his chores. The more he thought about it, the more confused he became. Each time his mathematical brain came up with a formula and reached a sensible conclusion, a flood of feelings would wash the sensible conclusion away. The thought of talking it out with someone – the cow had proved unhelpful – was extremely tempting.

'Ach, it's sort of women trouble. No, don't worry ...' as James looked alarmed, 'We're still on for the Ball. It's something else. I can't make up my mind. There's this other girl, ye see.'

'Ah! Women trouble, is it? *Another* girl! Well done, baby brother! You've come to the right place. I know all about playing two fiddles at the same time. I'll come up to your room after tea tonight. If you can spare half-an-hour from your precious books, I'll sort you out!' He strode off, laughing. *That daft wee bugger has got himself two girls at the same time and doesn't know what to do about it.*

Morag, smiled to herself as she set the table in the kitchen. It was good to hear the lads so happy together. This trip to the Ball was doing the whole family good. She hummed as she bent to extract the ham-and-egg pie from the oven.

James leaned back in the old basket chair in the window of Pete's bedroom. 'Let me see,' he intoned. He was mimicking his father: Jed would let Morag *rabbit on*, as he called it, till she ran out of words; then he would take his time recapping what she had said as he weighed his response. She would hang on his words, like a supplicant before a wise judge. James enhanced the comparison by taking his pipe out of his pocket and attempting to light it. The pile of matches grew in the saucer on the window sill while his face became redder with each attempt. He abandoned it and began to deliver his judgment.

'What you have here, Pete-me-lad, is a matter of working out your choices and deciding which one to go for.'

'I know. I've tried that, but ...'

'On the one hand, we have Caroline: there are two possibilities with her.'

'There are?'

'Possibility one: she fancies you again. She's had a wee sniff at all the pedigree pooches at her fancy university – thought she might prefer them to a working dog like yourself – but she's decided she prefers *you* after all.'

'D'ye think so?'

'Possibility two: she's got her eye on a varsity toff but he's not asked her to the Ball and she wants to make him jealous. So she's using you to do it.'

'I never thought of that. But – hang on - she wouldn't have to wait for him to ask her. It's the women's Ball – they ask the men.'

'Maybe she did and he turned her down. Maybe she's too shy or too scared to ask him. Or maybe another girl got in first.'

Pete groaned. 'It's even more complicated than I thought. Why can't people just be straight with each other and tell each other how they feel?'

'Och, where would be the fun in that?'

'Fun? Torture, more like!'

'So, it's up to you to decide which possibility you are going to go for.'

'How do I do that?'

'Do what?'

'Decide whether Caroline really wants me at the Ball or whether she's just using me to make some other bugger jealous.'

'Tsk, tsk! Language, baby brother. Now, on the other hand we have this new girl – what did you say her name was?'

'Alice. Alice Band.'

'You're joking! Is her father called *Brass* and her mother *Silver*?' James laughed at his own joke.

'She doesn't have a father - at least there's not one there. She said it was just her and her mother. I suppose he's dead. She didn't say.'

'Just Alice and Silver, then.' James tackled the pipe again. This time he was successful and the small room filled with the mellow scent of Golden Virginia tobacco.

Pete leaned across him to open the window. The afternoon's hint of spring had gone and a blast of icy air recalled James to his judicial duties. 'On the other hand, we have Miss Alice Band.' He sniggered. 'It would seem she is *quite* interested but playing hard-to-get. Not doing dates indeed! She'll do a date, all right, if she fancies you enough. But does she? And do you fancy her? That's what you have to decide. And, if so, do you fancy her more than Caroline?'

'God, James, I *know* all that. I've been over it a million times? I just can't make up my mind!' Pete paced round the small room.

'Well, let me put it this way: if it's possibility one – that Caroline wants to come back and be your lassie again – will you forget all about Alice? Is Caroline your first choice – if you can get her?'

'Yes … I think so.'

'But, if it's possibility two and she's just using you to make another fellow jealous, will you go for Alice?

'Maybe. But do you really think Caroline would do such a thing?'

'Women will do anything. They're not like us. They're devious devils.'

'Are they?' Pete was startled. 'Is mam like that?'

'She could give lessons. Look how she handles father.'

'Mmm. Point taken.'

'You've a lot to learn about women and you're out of your depth here. That's why you can't make up your mind. You're only just going on nineteen; you've a lot of damage to do yet before some bonnie lassie bats her eyelashes once too often and ties you down. Get yourself some experience – play the field, keep 'em both dangling.'

'You mean two-timing? I couldn't do that to Caroline.'

'What's to say she's not doing it to you? She's probably got half-a-dozen lads in Fife on the hook and you're just the one from back home, the comfy old shoe! And the Alice-Band, now, she'll have a string of them as well, if she's such a looker. Bet you get a surprise when you go to that café!'

'So what on earth will I do?' Pete was regretting the decision to confide in his brother. He was more confused that ever. He had been thinking it was all down to *him* to make a decision, to choose between one girl and the other. He saw now that it might not be up to him at all: that he might be no more than a pawn in a game at which he was a mere novice, an ill-equipped traveller in new and maze-like territory.

'Just go to the Ball and see what happens. Then go to the café the next week and see what happens there. And, if you end up with two lassies, then lucky you!' A happy thought struck James. 'I could always take one of them off your hands, if you like.' He leered and rose to pat his brother's shoulder. 'Cheer up, wee man. Ye never died a winter yet!'

He collected his pipe and saucer. 'Don't say I'm not good to you - spending a whole hour helping you with your problem!'

Jed was grumbling his way to bed as usual: this was always when he fretted over jobs not done, problems not solved and money not well spent; by the time he joined Morag in bed, he had laid his woes to rest for the night. They could then enjoy either a cheerful, cuddly blether or some leisurely love-making. He had never been one for rushing his fences and getting in a lather. After twenty-odd years of marriage, they had a comfortable routine that satisfied them both, even if it was never going to set the heather alight.

Morag, leaning back against her pillows, was not listening to his complaints about the price of seed, the re-appearance of that damned fox and his having to start the milking all on his own on Thursday evening. She simply gave a sympathetic half-sigh-cum-disapproving-*tut* and a sad little shake of her head from time to time. This saved wasting any real attention.

She ignored completely the moan about Thursday milking: that skirmish had been fought and won yesterday when she had noticed that the lads needed haircuts; she was not about to re-commence *that* battle. He was about to turn down the sheet and blankets on his side, when he paused and plunked himself down at the bottom of the bed, his back to her. She sighed. Clearly, he had not yet exhausted tonight's litany of woe.

'It's a thankless task, Morag, this bringin' up bairns. You do your best for them – bend over backwards to help them and let them enjoy themselves – but what thanks do you get? That's what I'd like to know!'

Was he harping on again about Pete's choice of career and persistence in the face of his father's opposition? Surely not? It had been nearly four years now and the lad was doing so well, so obviously doing exactly what he had been born to do. Surely even Jed now accepted that? Had James had got himself into another scrape? There had been a week of bedtime rants about the cost of fitting a new exhaust on the Zodiac after James had reversed into a concrete bollard in the car park of his favourite pub in Forfar.

'Oh, I don't know, Jed, love. I think the lads are very grateful for the money you've given them for their wee jaunt to St Andrews, not to mention the car, and their two days off from the farm. They're going to have a grand time. 'Just like a wee holiday,' James was saying only this morning. He's like a dog with two tails!' She smiled sweetly at her husband and patted his side of the bed.

'Aye, James is maybe grateful but what about that young pup, Pete?'

'Och, ye ken fine he's thrilled as well. It's high time he enjoyed some o' the fun that all the students get up to. Ye're only young once. Just because we never got the chance …'

'Thrilled, is it? He's a fine way o' showing it then! I've to do the milking on my own on Thursday night and then put up with some stranger, who probably doesn't know a cow's arse from his own, working alongside me for two days. And is the wee sponger happy? No' him! Face like a torn scone when I saw him in the kitchen half an hour ago. Could hardly give me a sideways look. That's all the thanks I get!' He had risen and was pacing up and down the rug that lay along the floor at the side of the bed.

Morag was not putting up with this. 'In the first place, Jed McCafferty, ye're *not* doing the milking all on your own tomorrow: the boys'll be back from the barber's in Forfar by quarter past five – half past at the very latest. Ye'll be a wee bit late in getting finished but that'll not kill you for once. In the second place, Jerry Dempsey is not a stranger, ye've known his folks for years, and if he doesn't know the difference between a cow's and a man's…' - she declined to use his coarse expression - 'then he's been asleep for the past twenty-four years. Ye ken fine he's been working

69

Inshaig farm with his father and brothers these past eight years since he left school. I hear he's a grand worker and has been doing night classes as well to keep up with all these new regulations that are coming in. And I won't have ye calling Pete a sponger – nobody works harder or complains less. You ken that fine or you wouldn't trust him with some of the jobs you give him these days. And what's all this tripe about the lad not being pleased? He's likely just dog-tired and his head full of stuff he's been studying all night. Maybe, if you didn't work him so hard in the mornings and expect so much of him when he gets back from college after that long bike ride from Dundee, then he might able to give you a big smile and some happy backchat at bedtime.'

Seeing her husband's look becoming blacker, she hastily changed tack. 'He's likely just starting to get nervous, thinking about this grand Ball. He's never even been to a proper dance. Yyou can't really count those school dances they had in the gym.' She chuckled. 'D'ye remember, Jed, the first time you took me to a real dance? It was a St. Andrew's night affair at the end of November, I mind, so it was all Scottish country dancing. We got on no' bad with the first two dances – the Gay Gordons and the Dashing White Sergeant, everybody kens them – but then it was Strip The Willow and you got a' mixed up and started birling with the men instead of the women. We had to give up and sit down – the mortification o' it!'

Jed's face lightened. He *did* remember: not just the ill-fated jig but the slow walk home after the dance and his bonnie Morag's blushing consent to be kissed for the first time. He had been a bag of nerves that night, anxious to please her and act the confident escort, so anxious that he had completely forgotten the dance formation of Strip the Willow. He relaxed and grinned.

'Och, ye're probably right, Morag, love. He's just a boy, after all, and a daft one at that. It's hard on him having to go to something so grand and strange for his first foray into the dancing. He'd have been better trying something smaller, more local, first.'

It was on the tip of Morag's tongue to point out that their son never had time to sample any small, local social opportunities. But Jed had finally got himself into bed so she held her peace. They spent quarter of an hour talking about *poor* Faye Dempsey, Caroline's mother, whom Morag had visited that afternoon. James had driven her over in the Landrover with Caroline's bike and the two women had had a happy hour discussing their children and speculating about the forthcoming Ball. Both mothers were delighted and hopeful at the turn of events. Faye had been only too happy to offer Jerry's services to facilitate Morag's plans at Fintry. Jed contributed a few sleepy remarks about the new combine harvester at Inshaig but he had worn himself out with his tirades and he soon lapsed into soft snores.

Morag lay awake, her mind turning over Jed's description of Pete. She had defended her son and deflected Jed's criticism but she too was concerned: Pete *had* been looking miserable most of the week and especially tonight at tea-time. Not at all like a boy about to get his first two days off his chores for four years and to embark on a delightful adventure at the invitation of his favourite girl. What on earth could be wrong with him?

Morag watched Pete as he wolfed down his porridge. 'All right, son?'

'Yeah. Smashing.' He scraped his bowl and rose. 'Best porridge-maker in the business!' He winked at her and went out whistling the latest Dave Clark Five number.

'I didn't mean the porridge. . .' But he was already at the top of the stairs, pushing down the straps of his dungarees and pulling off his thick jumper as he ran. A moment later she could hear him singing above the splashing in the bathroom.

Now, that's more like my Pete. He's fair back to his old self. I wonder what it's all been about? Maybe James will be able to tell me. I heard him coming out of Pete's bedroom at nine o'clock last night. The lads had been having a right good natter — about the Ball, I expect. It's brought them closer together again.

She rose to begin preparations for Jed's cooked breakfast. James would be in later in the morning for his three bacon rolls and two mugs of tea: he always had the first bowl out of the porridge pot at six-thirty then worked till nearly ten o'clock. Jed, on the other hand, took no more than a glass of hot water first thing and enjoyed a full breakfast about eight o'clock. Morag's breakfast duties lasted from Pete's first cup of hot, sweet tea at five to James' bacon rolls at ten. She had grown up watching her mother fitting similar breakfasting demands round all the other morning chores of a farmer's wife.

Unusually for him, Pete had found it difficult to get off to sleep last night. To James' analysis of the situation, he had himself added more possibilities and pitfalls. He had finally drifted into a dream: he was standing on a precipice; the wind was cold and the sky was full of black, lowering clouds. Looking down, he saw two small figures running through the sunlit valley. He leaned forward and focused on them: two little girls, hand-in-hand, skipping and singing. They stopped and looked up at him and waved. He leaned forward to see who they were. Caroline and Alice! But much younger, just kids. And then he was falling, falling, the ground hurtling towards him.

He had woken with the jolting gasp that ends a falling dream and had lain, heart pounding, for a few minutes. Then, he had shaken himself impatiently. As James said, he was not yet nineteen, he did not need to get embroiled with either of them, and he certainly did not need to be getting into such a lather about it.

In ten years time, I'll likely be married with two kids to some completely different woman and I'll have forgotten all about them both. On this comforting thought, he had drifted off again.

James had hit upon the right strategy to calm his brother's anxieties. Conscientious Pete would always stick at a problem as long as there was a solution to be had. But, if the problem was insoluble or lay outside *his* powers to affect, practical Pete would withdraw, hand it on to someone else if possible, and not waste any more time on it. Before his session with James last night, he had been seeing the Caroline-Alice dilemma like a dark tunnel with a couple of branches off. He had been attempting to find his way through, hoping that daylight would soon appear at the end. After Judge James' summing-up, it was now an impenetrable labyrinth.

He had woken with the sense of a burden lifted: it was all totally beyond him to fathom and beyond his powers to deal with. He had risen light-hearted and, released from the cloud of uncertain responsibility which had been plaguing him since Sunday, he had sung his way through pretty well the whole of the 'top twenty' by breakfast time.

He galloped down the stairs three at a time and almost landed on top of James who had come back into the house in search of some milk-yield paperwork. As his brother put out two arms to steady him, Pete caught him up in a waltzing embrace and whirled him happily up the lobby towards the kitchen, bellowing *I could have danced all night.* There he released him, blew his mother a kiss and raced out the back door.

'Well!' Morag smiled at her older son. 'He's full of the joys of spring, is he no'?' That wee chat the two of you had in his room last night has done him a power of good. Whatever it was about …' She left the statement hanging hopefully.

James tapped the side of his nose. 'Big brothers have their uses, you see, even if they're not fancy college boys. The lad was just needing some good advice from a man of the world. Affairs of the heart, you know. My specialty! I'll tell you all about it later, mam. See you at ten.'

Morag stared after him for a moment then burst out laughing. The idea of James as a man-of-the-world, specialising in affairs of the heart, was like imagining one of their smelly, old sheepdogs as a *Crufts* dandy, specialising in party tricks. But what on earth could Pete have been seeking his advice about? She was looking forward to her usual ten o'clock blether with her older son this morning.

'That's more like it!' Jed laid down his fork and beamed at his wife.

'Has there been something wrong with your breakfasts in the past?'

'What? Oh, I didn't mean the food..' He nodded his thanks for a third cup of tea. 'I meant that young son of yours. I was in Lower Field with the sheep when he went racing down the path on his bike. You know, I wouldn't be surprised if we get our first lambs this weekend. At least two of the ewes. . .'

'What were you going to say about Pete?'

'Mind, if it happens on Friday or Saturday, I'll have to manage working alongside a complete stranger.'

'Stranger, nothing! Ye've kent Jerry since he was a lad. And Inshaig has always had twice as many sheep as we have. The lad's been helping with lambing since he was knee high to a grasshopper. Now, what *was* that you were going to say about Pete, for any sake?'

'Pete? Oh aye.' He gave me a big smile and a right cheery wave as he passed. *And* he shouted out something about the ewe I was looking at - that he'd bet me it was going to be first past the post. He'll likely be proved right in a couple of days. We'll make a farmer of him yet!'

Ye ken fine ye're just kidding yourself there, thought Morag, but she did not spoil Jed's rare moment of satisfaction with his younger son.

For the first time in years, all her little brood seemed happy at the same time. She just needed to find out what James and Pete had been talking about last night. *Affairs of the heart,* James had said. Lugging the bucket of hen-mash over to the coop she paused: what affairs of the heart did Pete have other than Caroline? Pete must have been agonising over whether Caroline still fancied him, if her invitation to the Ball meant she preferred him to her new friends in St Andrews. James had obviously reassured him and put him back into exuberant good humour. She hummed a little tune as she emptied the mash into the feeding trough and scattered grain around the yard.

CHAPTER SEVEN: PATSY AND HUGH

Henry Castleton Forsyth rustled through the notes on the lectern then turned to assume his favourite position by the window looking on to Quad. He had been giving this same lecture for many years and required only a cursory reminder of its structure before launching into a word-perfect hour. 'We return to Descartes today and begin tracing his place in and contribution to the Platonic dynasty of thought.'

Hugh stretched his long legs and slackened his jaw into a wide yawn. Cassie swivelled his head and swept a piercing glance over the hundred-odd students. It came to rest upon Hugh who hastily clenched his teeth and tightened his jaw. The Dean's incomprehensible sentences did not falter as he transfixed the hapless Hugh until a single tear coursed down a painfully taut cheek.

As he picked up his pen in an attempt to appear attentive, Hugh felt a hand on his knee through the wool of his red gown. 'Just checking,' Cynthia murmured. 'Thought you might have been turned to stone.'

An hour later, as the lecture ended, Cassie handed a pile of paper slips to the last boy he passed on his way out. 'Pass them round,' he barked over his shoulder. 'This term's essay: due in by the Ides of March.'

Ritual groans deepened into genuine consternation: *Plato's dalliance with Socratic thought has a direct line to deviance in eighteenth century empiricism. Discuss.*

Hugh looked at the half-page of phrases and words in his lecture notebook: they bore no discernible relation to the essay topic. He stuck the slip of paper in the pocket of his gown and rose, sighing. He caught the back view of a short girl moving purposefully out the door into Quad. She had a thick plait of hair falling straight down the velvet yoke of her gown between her shoulder blades. Baffling essay topics forgotten, he grabbed his notebook and pen, thrust them into his tweed jacket pocket and hurried out the door after her.

'Well!' Belinda, sitting behind Hugh, leaning over to address Cynthia, had been almost knocked over. 'What's got into him, for heaven's sake?'

'Slumming it again, I wouldn't be surprised.' Cynthia's voice held a mixture of amusement and disdain. 'Poor Dorothea,' she added cryptically.

Eliza? No, Elsie? Oh, what is the dratted girl's name? Hugh pushed his way through the throng of red gowns around Quad tower and strode out into North Street. He could see the girl marching towards Chattan at the other end: for someone with such short legs, she was setting no mean pace. She had passed the cinema and was turning to cross the road towards the foot of Greyfriars Gardens when he caught up with her: 'I say, El … Els … *Elspeth!*' It came to him in the nick of time and he beamed at her in relief.

'Hugh! How are you? How lovely to see you!' They were right outside the Tudor Tearoom and, encouraged by his smile, she took the bull by the horns. 'Do you fancy afternoon tea? They do wonderful toasted teacakes in here.'

They settled in a table by the window. Elspeth was well aware that his interest was not in *her* but tea at the Tudor was vastly preferable to tea at Chattan; and being seen in the window of the Tudor with such an escort was not an opportunity to pass up. Through two rounds of teacakes and two pots of tea, they dwelt mournfully upon the philosophy assignment.

'I'm off to the library a.s.a.p.,' declared Elspeth. 'I'll throw myself on the mercy of that dishy librarian: he always seems to know just which books you need. He was great when I had this stinker of an essay recently for European History. Even knew which chapters from which books to use. And he *is* rather scrumptious. *He* can take me down to The Stacks anytime!'

'*He's* not interested in women. I wouldn't waste your time,' Hugh advised, flapping his wrist.

'You mean, he's … he' s …' She flushed. 'I never thought.' Hugh's southern sophistication had perceived what Elspeth's northern naiveté had missed. He regarded her confusion in amusement; then seized his advantage.

'Where is your friend, Caroline? She wasn't at lectures on Friday, I haven't seen her all weekend and she's still not here today. She's not ill, is she?' Elspeth blinked foolishly at him. 'What I want to know is this: is she going to Chattan Ball? Who with?'

But it was a mocking Irish voice that answered him from behind: 'Surely you mean *with whom*, don't ye? It's not like you to be forgetting your grammar, not a well-educated young man like yourself.'

Patsy, fresh from a two-hour practical in the lab and decidedly peckish, had seen the two philosophy students in the window of the Tudor. She had immediately revised her intention of heading to tea at Chattan, crossing the road instead and breezing into the Tudor, just in time to hear Hugh's barrage of questions.

Elspeth looked up with relief. Hugh was also pleased to see Patsy. With *two* of Caroline's chums, he must surely make some headway. Another chair was brought and a third round of teacakes ordered. 'With *lashings* of butter,' Patsy abjured the sour-faced waitress who went off muttering under her breath about pushy students. By the fourth round of teacakes, through much teasing and fencing, he had discovered that the object of his desire had been back on her home territory for the past four days and why. On the subject of the Ball, Patsy was particularly evasive, leaving him unsure whether he stood a chance or not.

Elspeth had almost wrecked Patsy's edifice of *could-be* and *you just never know* and *not that I know of* by starting to tell him about Caroline's promise to line up two Ball escorts from home. She had broken off abruptly at a prod on her knee from the toe of Patsy's boot. The white tablecloths in the Tudor were long enough to allow for such hidden hints but, in any case, Hugh suddenly looked at the expensive watch on his wrist and leapt up, throwing a pound note on the table.

'Must go! Excuse me ladies. Much enjoyed your company. That should cover it.' He gestured to the pound note.

'Well!' Elspeth caught a globule of butter running down her chin and licked her greasy finger. 'Where's *he* gone in such a hurry?'

'I'd have said the station, to meet a certain train,' Patsy peered out the window. 'But he's heading in the other direction. Curiouser and curiouser.'

Caroline sighed in relief as the train wound into St Andrews station. The usual five minute wait at Leuchars junction had lasted thirty-five, turning the thirty-minute journey into well over an hour. Coming out of the station, she saw that rain was lashing down, swept across the street by a gale. It was only a couple of minutes' walk from the station to Chattan but, even so, she would be drenched: her hair, which she had spent ages back-combing before leaving home, would be ruined. Still, there was nothing else for it. A *toot* arrested her and she turned to see an old sports car sidling up the kerb behind her. Peering through the gloom, she recognised it – who didn't know the battered trophy beloved of The Set? She glanced over her shoulder expecting to see one of them emerge from the station but the last passenger had gone. She turned her head back and collided with Hugh.

'Your chariot awaits.' He bowed. "It's no weather for a fair damsel to be abroad.'

'But how on earth did you know I was coming off this train? And it's half an hour late anyway.'

Hugh groaned. 'Don't I know it? Been sitting bent double in that tin can. Seriously considered abandoning it and waiting in Kate's' – he gestured to the welcoming windows of Kate Kennedy's café which could be seen just up the road – 'but I thought I might miss you.'

'But why? I mean, a lift *would* be welcome in this weather, even if it is just round the corner to Chattan – but what are you after?' The direness of the weather stripped away pretension or perhaps it was just the wholesome air of home still in her lungs. She could not be bothered playing word-games.

Hugh rose to the occasion: he could talk turkey too. 'Come and take tea in Kate's with me and I'll tell you.' He strode over to the little car and, with a squeal of the hinges, wrenched open the door. A howl of wind swept a sheet of freezing rain up the street and the sanctuary of the car was irresistible. She turned to lift her small suitcase but he was already throwing it into the car. He had to tie down the lid of the boot with the piece of string looped round the catch.

Five minutes later, they were ensconced in a corner of Kate's café and he was explaining that he had been wondering where she was and had sought information from her two friends who had explained about her mercy dash home. 'When I saw the weather, I thought such a ministering angel deserved better than struggling with a suitcase in lashing rain along the road to Chattan. So I raced along to Sally's and borrowed Colin's car.'

'But why? Why should you care if I get soaked? Or whether I was ill or not? What is it to you?'

He raised an eyebrow and drew once again upon Nanny Bodingham's tactics. 'Thank you very much, Hugh. That was so kind of you.'

She flushed, reminded of her high-handed behaviour on the stairs of The Younger at the Hop, aware of how ungracious she now sounded. 'Not that I'm not grateful ...' she tailed off and concentrated on heaping jam and cream on to a large scone. He was eating nothing, being already full of the Tudor's teacakes.

It's now or never while she's feeling contrite: 'Grateful enough to ask me to escort you to Chattan Ball?' He held his breath.

'Escort me to the Ball?' she spluttered scone crumbs and flecks of jam-and-cream on to the table. 'What on earth makes you think ...?'

It was Hugh's turn to flush. *Damn it all! Am I so undesirable as an escort?* 'Your friends didn't say you had anyone else lined up. And there are only four days to go.' He salvaged a vestige of pride. 'It's just an idea, you know. Thought you might like to get me before someone else does.'

'Queuing up are they?'

'I certainly could have at least one invitation if I wanted it.'

'Then I suggest you take it.' She recovered her composure, finished her scone and swilled the last of her tea down. 'I must go and get settled back into Chattan before dinner. Then it's a night of writing up borrowed lecture notes for me. Catching up, you know. Thanks for the tea and that lift will still be welcome.'

He said nothing more as he paid the bill, opened the car door for her and drove her to Chattan. An awkward silence fell once he had cut the engine.

'Caroline ...'

'Look, Hugh ...'

They both spoke at once then laughed.

'You first.'

'You first.'

Again they laughed.

'I like you and want to get to know you. What's so wrong in that?' These were possibly the most direct sentences Hugh had framed since he had come to St Andrews and found himself cloned into The Set.

'I'm flattered.' She was surprised to find she meant it. 'But I really don't think we have anything in common. You'd be much better with one of your own kind. One of that queue!' She finished on a teasing laugh.

'But who *will* you ask?' He could not quite accept his defeat.

'That's for me to know and for you to find out!' She tugged open the car door and jumped out. 'Thanks. I'll get my case out of the boot. Don't bother getting out.'

And this time, he did not.

Dorothea watched in consternation from the big bay window of Chattan's common room. She had gone there to scan the Financial Times, political economy being one of her classes and the FT being required reading. She had found an article annotated by a previous reader and had been happily cribbing from it, sole occupant of the enormous room, sitting on the hearth rug in front of a smoky fire, when the car announced its presence outside the window by a series of sharp retorts.

At first, she presumed that it was Colin driving past and ran over to the window to give him a wave but a shuddering crunch told her that the car had ground to a halt. She watched as the car remained outside Chattan's front door for some minutes. Then a strange girl extricated herself, leaned back into the car to say something to the driver and went to the boot to untie the string and remove a small suitcase before running up the four stone steps and into the Hall. The girl was one of those smirking C floor bejantines who had been irritating everyone in the dining room for the past week. Rumour had it that they were going to have the best room-party decorations.

What was going on? A horrified thought struck her. Could the girl have been collaring Colin for her escort. *Damn!* Dorothea had not yet plucked up the courage to ask Hugh, dreading the end of her hopes in a refusal, but she had been keeping Colin in mind as reserve. The idea of his being snaffled by a provincial nobody galvanised her. She marched out of the common room and along the corridor towards the front door, catching up with Caroline at the foot of the stairs.

'Well, what did he say?' she demanded.

Caroline, arrested with her foot on the first step, stared. 'Pardon? What did who say?'

'You were asking him to be your escort for the Ball, weren't you?'

Caroline recognised Dorothea as one of The Set and she saw how the land lay. *Miss Silky Drawers thinks I've snitched the bloke she was hoping to get!* She decided to exploit the situation and was already looking forward to telling Elspeth and Patsy all about it.

'Actually,' she mimicked the supercilious drawl of The Set, 'actually, it was quite the other way round, don't ye know? *He* was asking *me*. But, don't worry,' she grinned and delivered the *coup de grace*, 'I'm afraid he was rather out of luck. You're welcome to him. I already have an escort.'

She swept up the stairs, giving Dorothea a regal wave from the half-landing. Then she raced along the corridor of C floor and barged unannounced into Patsy's room. Elspeth and two other girls were on the floor in front of Patsy's fire, each holding a long-handled fork up to the blaze. The room smelt of toasting bread and within a minute was full of chuckles.

'Too cruel.' Patsy shook her head. 'You are without compassion, fair Caro.'

'Never mind that.' Elspeth had other things on her mind. 'What about *my* escort? Did you get me one as well? What is he like?'

'Fear not,' Caroline reassured. 'James is a fine figure of a man. He'll take your breath away in his kilt and full Highland dress. He's Pete's older brother and they'll both be here on Friday night.' She had a vision of Elspeth and James together, both stocky, sturdy and rosy-cheeked. Yes, it would do very nicely.

'Damn shame for old Apple-Pie Bed, though,' mourned Patsy. 'My money was on him for a touch of class at the room-party. I hope these lads-from-down-on-the-farm can cut the mustard. We don't want any country bumpkins lowering the tone.'

'And which classy fellow are you bringing, then? What's going to be your contribution to this glamorous gathering?'

But Patsy only tapped the side of her nose and gave a Mona Lisa smile.

..As the top table processed out of the dining-room, the C floor girls renewed their efforts to persuade Caroline to come and see how the room party decorations were progressing.

'But if I don't at least read the notes from Friday and Monday, I'll not understand a word of tomorrow's lectures.'

'No change there, then.' Patsy was firm. 'Get yourself along to Jennifer's room and see what's happening - it's amazing! The theme has just taken off. Everyone keeps coming up with more and more brilliant ways to use it.' She was delighted with the way her idea had developed but her smile was a trifle abstracted. As Caroline capitulated and was borne off by the others, Patsy quietly slipped away and made her way thoughtfully to the swot-room on B floor. She had no intentions of swotting tonight but it was a good place to get peace to think.

Her confident reply to Caroline's question about a Ball escort had not been quite honest: she had not yet asked anyone. This was not for lack of applicants for the job: a whole gaggle of medical students had been dangling for her favours for the past term-and-a-half and all would have jumped at the chance to be her Ball partner. But Patsy was wary of entanglements and of sending out falsely encouraging signals.

Everyone who knew her at St A's would have said she was light of heart, full of confidence and able to handle relationships easily. In fact, she had had her heart well and truly broken whilst still a schoolgirl. In a converse of the Caroline-Pete situation, she had given her heart and almost-but-not-quite her virginity to a boy a year older than her at school. Then he went off to Trinity College in Dublin. Within a few months, he stopped writing. At Christmas he mocked her and at Easter he ignored her. In the summer vacation, he went off to spend the summer on a kibbutz in Israel, sending her a platonic postcard that was worse than nothing. She learned the lesson hard but it had made her determined that nothing like that would happen to her at university. She had encased herself in a veneer of sarcastic disdain of the opposite sex. It made the other girls envious and drove the men wild. And she was – for the moment, at least – very happy with the situation. The last thing she wanted was for some man to get ideas above his station simply because she had invited him to be her Ball partner. Nor did she want anyone to get hurt. Despite her mocking façade, she understood heartbreak and rejection too well to inflict them on another.

But she needed a Ball partner – and quick! Someone who would understand that her invitation implied nothing more than one night but would not be hurt by the implication. But who? She had almost given up trying to think of someone and was rising to leave the swot-room when one of The Chelsea Set slipped in and settled herself at one of the desks. Patsy recognised her as the girl who had cannoned into her at the top of the stairs a fortnight ago. *Now there's an idea!*

She took her cigarettes out of her pocket but not her matches. Wandering up the room to the girl's desk, she casually asked her for a light and offered her a cigarette. After a moment's hesitation, the girl accepted and the two smoked for a moment companionably.

'Going to the Ball?' Patsy blew smoke rings up to the ceiling.

Dorothea hesitated.

'Still struggling to find a partner?'

'Of course not!'

'I know I am. Don't want to give the wrong chap encouragement. Men so easily get the wrong idea.'

Dorothea rather liked this view of things. 'Oh, there's one I can have easily – just a friend, you know – though there's another I'd prefer but I'm not sure if he's still free. That is, I haven't got round to asking him yet. And I've a horrible feeling I might be too late now, that someone else has bagged him.'

'Go for the friend,' advised Patsy, throwing her half-smoked cigarette into the grate. 'You can have fun without worrying about what you look like all night.' She slapped Dorothea cheerfully on the back and strode out of the room. She had found out what she wanted to know.

Old Fossil Forsyth had an uncomfortable feeling that there was a cuckoo-in-the-nest. Years of addressing his lectures out the window, appearing oblivious of the student body but, in fact, well aware of it, had given him a sixth sense. Hugh's aborted yawn of yesterday bore testimony to that. Today, he felt sure that there was someone in Lecture Room One who should not be there. As the clock began to toll the hour's welcome end, he paused before sweeping out. His piercing glance flicked over the students and settled on a girl sitting right at the end of the back row. Old and young eyes met and held; then the young ones wavered and fell as a flush crept over the pretty face. The Fossil allowed himself a satisfied smile as he billowed off to tea-and-crumpets in his study.

'Yoiks!' Patsy grimaced. 'The old boy must have reptile eyes - able to see out of the side of them.'

'Maybe he was a reptile before becoming a fossil,' suggested her neighbour. The nickname had become common coinage. 'Are you new to the class then? I've not seen you here before. Nor has The Fossil obviously!'

'Oh, just visiting, just visiting . . . well, gate-crashing really. I've heard so much about The Fossil that I wanted to see him with my own eyes.' These eyes were now ranging over the rows of student backs as she spoke. Then she rose quickly, slipping out the door before the neighbour had a chance to engage her in further conversation.

Patsy had to wait ten minutes, lurking in Cloisters and dodging in and out of Chapel to avoid being seen by her friends, before five members of The Set emerged. Then more dodging in and out of doorways as she followed them. For several minutes she thought all her efforts were going to be in vain, that the five would stick together and go off for tea somewhere. But, at last, just past The Buck on Union Street, there came a split: the two girls along with one of the boys set off; the other two boys began to make their way back towards Sally's. Patsy shot into the door of The Buck.

'Oh, come on, old chap. Let's go for a spin. It's the first day for weeks that it hasn't been raining. And I filled her up with juice this morning.'

'She a death-trap, Colin. The brakes squelch like mud, the clutch pedal flaps like a mongrel's tail and the gear stick nearly came off in my hand yesterday.'

'Monstrous ingrate! That's all the thanks I get for loaning you my precious old lady so you could go chasing some farm wench – and all to no avail, so you tell me now! Serves you right.'

'Oh, bugger off! I'm going to do some work on my French prose. Anything's better than shoehorning myself into your old rattle-trap.' Hugh wheeled round and stomped into the entrance-way of The Buck, almost knocking Patsy over. 'Gosh, I'm sorry! I didn't see you!'

'That's the second time ye've near done me grievous bodily harm.'

'Patsy! What are you doing here – you're medicine, are you not?'

'Oh, I like to keep my languages up, you know. Doesn't do to become one-sided. No-one ever said doctors can't speak a foreign language as well as healing the sick.'

Hugh laughed, his bad temper dissolving: Patsy often had that effect on people. 'Good for you!' He saw Colin still hovering on the pavement and waved to him: 'See you later, Col. Must concentrate on my linguistic studies. Can't be bested by a mere medic! Enjoy your spin.'

'So. Shall we apply ourselves to serious study or shall we fortify the body before the mind?' Patsy gestured towards Joe's café up on Market Street. Then, seeing him hesitate, 'My turn to pay! I can run to coffee and doughnuts.'

'Well . . . I suppose it would be better than not going at all.'

'Only marginally, of course!'

'I'm sorry, Patsy. You're an ace woman. I'm flattered. It's just that . . .'

'I know. Your heart belongs to another. But I shall bear up bravely and accept my place as a poor substitute.'

'Oh, get away with you!'

'Look, Hugh, I've told you why I am asking you. I don't want any of those sheep-eyed idiots in my class to get any ideas. I just want an escort for the night and nothing else – no strings attached, as they say. And I know you're not after *me*. No-one knows it better since you've been pumping me for info about Caroline this past fortnight. So, why not?'

'Well, maybe . . .'

'And, of course, I did tell Caroline that my escort would be adding a touch of class to the room party. God knows what these yokels she's bringing will be like - probably stink of the pigsty! Your chance to show her what she's missing, eh?'

'Quite a sales pitch! Never mind medicine or languages, you could have a career in advertising.'

'I'm right though, you have to agree. And what's the alternative – a room full of stuffy magistrands on A floor?'

Hugh groaned: he had been dodging Dorothea for the past two weeks ever since their walk on the sands that Wednesday afternoon. Not that he especially disliked her – she was just one of *The Set* girls, indistinguishable from each other in his book – but he had been saving himself for Caroline's invitation, unable to believe it would not come eventually.

'You need to go to Hell with me!' Patsy chuckled at his baffled stare. 'That's the theme of our room-party: Hell. You should see the decorations! We're the envy of the entire hall. It hasn't half wiped the smiles of those second-years' smug faces.' She bit into a sugary doughnut with a satisfied crunch.

'But what will Caroline say when you tell her I'm coming with you? I mean she knows I wanted *her* to ask me. Won't she mind?' He nibbled his own doughnut gloomily. 'No. I don't suppose she will, more's the pity.'

Patsy chewed thoughtfully for a moment. 'D'ye know what, me boy? I vote we don't tell her. If you want to know what she really feels about you, we need to surprise her - don't give her time to plan her reaction. Get it straight from the horse's mouth, no holds barred, caught on the hop.' She ran out of metaphors. 'What d'ye think?'

'But can *you* do that? Keep it a secret? You're seeing her all the time.'

'I've already hinted that I have a surprise escort up my sleeve and that he is going to stay up there till Friday night.'

'Well, if you're sure they won't prise it out of you.'

'My lips are sealed.'

It wasn't the entrée to Chattan Ball's most-talked about room party that he had hoped for, but it was better than nothing, and considerably better than an evening with Dorothea and the other A-floorers: Patsy was right about their air of terminal seriousness; they were altogether too near final degree exams. It would be torture to be in the same party as Caroline and to watch her with another man but, at least, he would be able to size up the competition and perhaps shine by comparison, as Patsy had suggested.

'Okay,' he said slowly. 'Okay. So what colour of orchids do you want? What colour is your ball gown?'

Cynthia regarded the girl sitting on her hearth-rug, arms wrapped tightly round expensive knee-length boots. Half an hour ago, the room had been full of students and cigarette smoke. The three from the philosophy lecture had picked up other members of *The Set* on their way to Cynthia's apartment. Her afternoon teas were famous, courtesy of regular hampers from Fortnum's or Harrod's. Invitations were rarely turned down. Only Colin, set on going for a run in his beloved car, and Hugh, too miserable to be in the mood for company, had missed out today. Now, everyone had taken themselves off and only Dorothea remained staring gloomily into the fire.

Cynthia frowned. She had been born and bred to play the society hostess but there were limits. She was way behind with a medieval history essay, due in the day after tomorrow, and she planned to get down to a full evening on it, starting as soon as possible. She had procrastinated when the essay subject was given out a month ago and had missed being able to borrow the requisite books from the library. She had only obtained them a couple of days ago and she needed to immerse herself in them – and fast.

'What am I going to do, Cyn? How can I find out if Hugh's still free for the Ball? I know Colin is because that dratted girl said she'd turned him down. She said she already had an escort: what if she meant Hugh? You know he's been fooling around, pretending he's interested in her. What if she's taken him seriously and asked him to the Ball and he's too much of a gentleman to say 'no'?'

'Well, he was in a foul mood today, certainly. I suppose that might account for it.'

'There you are then! If I ask him, he'll have to say 'no' and it will all be so embarrassing.'

They had already had this conversation several times and Cynthia was sick of it.

'And he'll never admit it's because he's been snitched by the milkmaid, hoist with his own petard. He'll have to pretend he *wants* to go with her. Or he might just say 'no' and not give me a reason and then I won't know if it's just because he doesn't like me. I absolutely *must* know before I ask him if *she*'s got in first. But how?' Dorothea ended on a wail.

'Oh, for God's sake, Dorrie! Just ask one of the milkmaid's friends. Who does she sit beside in the dining-room?'

'Oh, I couldn't speak to any of that lot. They're so full of themselves anyway at the moment. Seems they've got a really brilliant room-party theme. Everyone is talking about it. And the thought of any of them guessing why I was asking ... It would get straight back to *her!*'

'Get someone else to ask them, then.'

'That's brilliant, Cyn!' Dorothea leapt up. 'Thanks so much! You're a friend in a million, old thing. Come round to Chattan when dinner is finishing and I'll point them all out to you. I'm at the top table tonight so I'll be coming out before the rest. Be at the top of the stairs as we come up and I'll meet you there.' She snatched up her coat and headed out the door, clumping down the quaint little outside staircase, turning to give Cynthia a cheery wave before disappearing round the corner.

'Now how did that happen?' Cynthia demanded of the opulent Persian cat lying on a velvet cushion at the side of the fireplace. Solomon blinked at her. In his opinion, she talked too much and too loudly – and filled his house with others who did the same - frequently interrupting his slumbers. Really, she deserved all she got.

Colin started guiltily at the gentle knock. He was sprawled on his bed reading a Clifford Simak, one of his favourite sci-fi writers. He was two-thirds way through it and had been moaning at dinner that he could not put it down but really should pick up Copi's *Introduction to Logic* and tackle the truth-table exercises for tomorrow's tutorial. Hugh had been blunt: 'Get the work done first and keep the pleasure reading as a reward'

What a bore old Hugh is today. Just because he's in a bad mood over that country bumpkin woman. Colin had not taken his friend's advice: the Copi lay unopened on his desk amid the clutter. Now he jumped up, thrust the Simak under the pillow, sat down at his desk and opened the Copi at random.

'Mmmm?' He sounded vague, deep in concentration. The gentle knocking continued. 'Come in.' He had found the right page by now and had even opened a jotter. Still the knocking continued and, ostentatiously holding Copi open in his hand, he rose and went to open the door.

'What are you hanging about ...?' Not Hugh after all, but an older man in a navy uniform – one of Sally's porters who inhabited the small booth in the entrance hall.

'Excuse me, sir,' the man was impressed by the large book in Colin's hand. 'I am sorry to disturb your studies. There's a phone call for you.'

Cynthia's voice on the other end of the line was ingratiating. She had to go along to Chattan in a hurry. Would he be an absolute *love* and come and get her in his sweet little car and take her along? She had a history essay she desperately needed to get down to.

He stalled. He had logic exercises to prepare - hadn't even started on them yet.

'Those truth-table things? My tut. group did those last week. I'll let you have a copy of mine if you'll give me a lift to Chattan.'

'Mmmm ... It's a good offer. But what's so urgent at Chastity Hall?' The parsimonious male visiting times and the strict curfews had given rise to the nickname.

'Oh, I just need to get a book from a girl there, for my essay. She's due to hand it back to the library tomorrow – I checked today - so I'm hoping she'll give me it tonight. Please, Col, I'll throw in a quick drink at The Keys as well as the logic tables.'

Ten minutes later, they were bowling along a deserted North Street. With his mind on their destination, Colin asked: 'Going to Chattan Ball on Friday?'

Cynthia was going to gate-crash it, courtesy of a second cousin on B floor who was inviting her brother to be Cynthia's partner. 'I'll need to skulk in the room–party for the first half, same as at Abbotsford last month, not go down for the dinner, but there will be plenty of food in the room. Once the warden and any other staff have gone later on, I can go down and dance. It's the second half that's the most fun anyway, once everyone's had a few little drinkies.'

'Yeah,' Colin was gloomy. 'All right for some.'

'You're not going?'

'Not been asked! I thought old Dorrie might come up trumps but then I realised she was hanging out for Hugh. Then I thought I might be all right because Hugh was angling for an invitation from The Landgirl, but she's turned him down. Says she's already got an escort. Another country bumpkin, he seems to think. So that leaves him free for Dorrie to ask after all and poor old yours truly up the proverbial without a paddle.'

'Don't you know any other Chattan girls?'

'Nope. Well, I took a couple out of the Hop at the Younger a few weeks ago but I'd forgotten that I had no money that night – three damned days off allowance time – and they didn't fancy a romantic stroll down to the Castle Sands. Well, it was perishing cold and bloody raining as usual. So I didn't exactly make a hit with them.'

'You went to that scrum? And I thought Hugh was the one slumming it!'

'He was there as well. It was his damned idea to go. Come to think of it, I bet that was the start of his hot pursuit of the fair landgirl, though what he sees in her ... Hair like a chimney-sweep's brush.'

Cynthia chuckled. Then she banged her fist on the steering wheel, causing the car to slew dangerously close to the kerb.

'Steady on, old girl.' Colin straightened their course. 'What's up?'

'Let me get this straight: did you say the milkmaid turned *Hugh* down? I thought it was you who asked her and she turned *you* down.'

'I've never spoken to the woman.'

'But Dorothea said she saw your car outside Chattan yesterday evening, about six o'clock, and that girl got out of it. Dorrie pitched straight in and tackled her, thinking she'd been asking you to the Ball.'

'I can assure you ...' They had stopped outside Chattan and now regarded each other with puzzled frowns. Then Colin's brow cleared.

'Got it! Hugh borrowed the car yesterday to go and meet her off the train. He bribed her two friends with tea in the Tudor and got the gen. Seems The Landgirl – the milkmaid, as you call her – had been down on the farm for a few days – mother ill or something – and she came off the last train back. I think he took her to Kate's for tea and scones – I tell you he's spent some money on this escapade and he's always lecturing me about wasting money.'

'So, this girl hasn't asked *either* of you? Wait till I tell her! Come on, Col my darling, you deserve that drink. *Cross Keys* here we come!'

'But I thought you came here to get some book or other?'

'Oh, that. It doesn't matter now. I've got all the info I need!'

CHAPTER EIGHT: DOROTHEA AND COLIN

..Cynthia groaned: there was no mistaking the clip-clop of Dorothea's boots on the metal staircase outside. *Just when I was beginning to get somewhere!* She surveyed the open books and sheaves of lecture notes scattered around the room.   She had just composed an opening paragraph and was beginning to hope that she might turn in this essay by tomorrow morning at ten o'clock. This time, the long-suffering tutor had warned, there would be no mercy. Ten o'clock would be ten o'clock and not a minute – let alone hours or even days - later. The essay formed part of the term's assessment; if she missed it, she would have to re-sit in September. She did not fancy explaining *that* to her parents.

'Cyn! Cyn! Are you there? I can see your *Anglepoise* on, over your desk in the window.'

Cynthia groaned, her concentration shattered.

'I saw Belinda in Quad and she said you weren't at either of your morning lectures. You're not ill, are you? You *do* look pretty ghastly actually.' Dorothea peered at Cynthia's pasty face and red-rimmed eyes. Then she noticed the books and notes scattered around the room. 'Oh, you're working. Sorry …'

'Trying to.' Cynthia knew she must indeed look 'ghastly'. She had gone to bed late and had risen early, full of panic about the damned essay.

The session in *The Cross Keys* had gone on much longer than either of them intended, one drink borrowing another. Colin had spent a happy hour describing the plot of his Simak thriller; which Cynthia had read. This had led to a delicious books-we-have-both-read conversation, fuelled by Colin's pints of beer and Cynthia's gin-and-its . By the time they were ejected from the pub at ten o'clock, they were the best of friends, hanging on to each other as they made their unsteady way home. Colin abandoned his car outside *The Keys* and escorted Cynthia to her apartment on foot. Negotiating the outside staircase had posed a bit of a challenge as both felt that it would be fatal to let go of the other's waist. They had fallen into the apartment giggling and hiccupping at eleven o'clock. Many cups of black coffee later, with many more novels analysed, Colin had felt able to face the short walk to Sally's.

Cynthia had fallen into a drunken, dehydrated sleep, with no thought of the history essay. She had woken at nine with burning eyes and a mouth that tasted like the bottom of a bird-cage. Six large glasses of water and two aspirin later, she began to tackle the books and notes, sending the daily housekeeper away with a flea in her ear for daring to turn up to work and interrupt her. She made poor progress for the first hour, stopping to groan and lay her aching head down among the papers every so often. She forced herself to eat some toast and marmalade about half-past ten and began to achieve a little more.

Now it was twelve o'clock and her brain was just beginning to make sense of what she was reading. She had even begun to glimpse an argument which might form the premise for her essay. And now here was Dorrie. Again. Her mind groped through the effects of bubonic plague in fourteenth century England.

'Why didn't you come to Chattan last night? Will you be well enough to come tonight? How else will I find out if Hugh's going to the Ball with The Bumpkin? And there are only two damned days left. And what if Colin's not free either? I shall have no-one! I'll never get to the Ball! Everyone else will be there.'

'Oh dry up, Dorrie! You sound like a pantomime Cinderella.' The reason she had ended up getting blotto with Colin was coming back. *It's all her fault. If I hadn't had to go to Chattan, I'd never have asked Col for a lift and I'd have been here at home getting on with my essay – probably nearly finished by now – and I wouldn't be feeling like hell either.* She absolved her own weak will. 'I've really no time *or* inclination to get involved in your seedy little love-life - or lack of it.'

'What am I going to do?' wailed Dorothea.

But Cynthia had closed the door and gone back to the short but eventful life of Blanche, Duchess of Gaunt.

Dorothea clumped disconsolately down the stairs, her stiletto heels sparking off the metal rungs, and mounted her bike carefully. Riding it whilst wearing a calf-length skirt and long boots with buckles and high heels was a quite a feat. An indulgent aunt had bought her a smart new bicycle and delivered it to Chattan last October. But one look at it in the bike shed, among all the battered old models, had made her realise her *faux pas*. Even students from the wealthiest backgrounds did not ride new bikes in St A's: it was one of the many tyrannical traditions that bikes should be rusty old steeds. Dorothea had hastily done an exchange with a delighted dealer in a cycle shop in Cupar but she often thought with regret of the three-speed gears and comfortable saddle of the scorned new bike. She toiled up the hill from the harbour and dismounted to push the last fifty yards. *Bloody old heap of rust!*

By the time she had bumped along the cobbles of Market Street and down the short hill to Chattan, however, youthful vigour and determination had surfaced. A rainy morning was giving way to a fine afternoon, the wind light and teasing with a hint of spring. As she passed the top of the stairs on C floor, she could hear music and laughter drifting out of an open door at the end of the corridor. This was to be *the* room-party – everyone in Chattan knew that. Above the hilarity, she could hear *The Searchers*, suffering from *Needles and Pins*. Her good humour ebbed away on a jealous tide. On A floor, Wagner's *Valkyries* were competing with an aria from *Aida*. The PhD in German philosophy and the honours classics liked to work to appropriate background music.

Dorothea flung her bag on her bed, walked over to the window and gazed out at the wonderful view. A desperate plan was forming in her mind: it had begun as no more than a surge of anger as she passed C floor; it had flickered just at the edge of her thoughts as she climbed to B floor; and it had flared into life as she topped the stairs on A floor. Now she stoked it carefully, half-afraid of its fire. Did she have the nerve? Would it work?

Augusta Goldsmith glanced reprovingly across the dining-room. Caroline hissed: 'Shut-up, you lot. The Gusset's looking at us.'

The noisy group subsided but discussion persisted. A fortnight's planning and preparation was coming down to the wire. All the murals were done and ready to hang; the *hell-fire-hooch* ingredients were sitting in Jennifer's bay window; dozens of strips of red and orange crepe paper were ready to hang around the walls and from the ceiling; the *good intentions* crazy paving was ready to lay. Discussion now centred on finding time to put up all the decorations. It was going to take several people several hours – such was the wealth of material - and it was proving hard to evolve a workable plan. There were lectures and tutorials till late afternoon or hairdressing appointments; some girls had even managed to cram in a hair appointment after lectures (the hairdressers always stayed open late on Ball nights) and would only have time to rush back to Chattan and get into ball-gowns before the escorts began arriving.

'We'll just have to do it tomorrow evening.'

'No, that's not allowed. The maids complain they can't get in to clean and do the fires properly. My senior woman told me.'

'The Gusset won't have it. No putting up decorations until Friday afternoon.'

'I don't fancy sleeping in Hades, anyway.' Jennifer felt she'd already given up enough of her private space these past ten days.

'You will on Friday night, anyway. But you'll be too full of the hooch to care.'

'Maybe. But anyway, it's forbidden.'

Gloom descended on the table as they wrestled with some tough pork chops. 'Of course!' Elspeth clattered her fork against her water-glass, drawing another disapproving glance from the top table. 'Don't you remember, Caro? Logic 'n' Metafizz is cancelled this Friday afternoon. The Fossil told us about it weeks ago. He's got some meeting or other. I didn't connect it at the time with the Ball because, of course, the date got changed by The Gusset after The Fossil had told us. And we're doing each other's hair. So …'

The group considered these confusing sentences then heaved a sigh of relief. Elspeth began composing a brief. 'We'll need clear instructions about what goes where and how many flames you want where and …'

Dorothea, eavesdropping on her way to the serving hatch to collect desserts, stopped in her tracks. It had to be a sign! She had been mulling over her plan, worrying at it like a tongue finding its way to a toothache, but running up against the problem of timing. If The Milkmaid was going to be out of circulation, tied up in Chattan, on Friday afternoon, it *might* just be possible.

If Pete's dreams were of falling from a cliff onto two sweet little lasses, diminutive forms of the two girls who were leading him a merry dance, Dorothea's were of two lanky lads grown into large men. In one dream, she was playing bridge with them: both had enormous hands of cards which they had fanned out expertly and over which they were regarding her disdainfully; her partner, Cynthia, had a normal hand of thirteen cards; she herself seemed to have only three cards but they kept slipping out of her grasp until one finally tumbled under the table. As she groped on the floor for it, she saw *that girl*, the milkmaid, sitting under the table, dressed in a beautiful evening gown. As Dorothea straightened up, she saw that the other three round the table were now also wearing evening dress, Cynthia in a white and gold Grecian-goddess number, the men in frilled white shirts, black bow ties and maroon cummerbunds. Then, to her horror, she realised that she herself was wearing only her flimsy negligee – the one she had brought with her last October and had soon consigned to the bottom of her wardrobe in favour of a thick, candlewick dressing-gown – and that, horror of horrors, it was gaping open and her breasts were hanging out. She started awake briefly, hot with embarrassment, but soon plunged into the next dream: now she was standing in the doorway of Chattan common room; the carpet had been rolled up; bunches of balloons echoed the colours in the floral display on the grand piano; music was swelling around the room as the dancers circulated. She recognised none of them but could see one couple cutting a swathe through them. Gradually all the other dancers fell back, allowing space for an exhibition. She saw that it was *two men* dancing together – Hugh and Colin – and then she realised that she was watching the scene in the huge gilt-framed mirror above the fireplace. She saw herself in the mirror too, still wearing the flimsy wrap. It was gaping even further open and this time it was not only her breasts on show.

She woke up just before the twirling pair reached her, heart pounding with horrified shame. She pushed up her pillows and leaned back against them, pulling the covers up under her chin and humping up her knees. She sat for some time like this, watching a grey dawn edge round her curtains. A whole gamut of emotions flooded through her but by the time she turned to see the time on her bedside clock – twenty to seven – one had triumphed: *anger*. She leapt out of bed.

She was the first student in the dining-room when the breakfast gong sounded. She positioned herself for a good view of the C Floor bejantines' table. She finished her own breakfast and dawdled over a second cup of tea, half-listening to her neighbour complaining about the shopping deficiencies of St Andrews: seemingly, there was not a pair of size six gold dancing sandals to be found anywhere. There were only four small shoe shops.

Caroline, Elspeth and Patsy came in together on a tide of noisy banter. 'You'll have to possess your souls in patience – do you good!'

'Bet it's some grotty, spotty, swotty medic.'

'Yeah. Stinking of formaldehyde. We'll all need clothes pegs for our noses!'

'Now, how did you guess? And I thought it was *such* a grand idea: fish him out of his jar, bring him to life for the night and put him back into it in the morning. I was counting on a good belt of *Tweed* perfume to fool everyone, that smells a bit like formaldehyde, I always think.'

The three dissolved into giggles: *Tweed* was The Gusset's favourite. A waft of it often usefully signalled her approach.

Dorothea eyed them contemptuously, her gaze settling on Caroline. *She'll be laughing on the other side of her face soon.* She gathered her dishes together and crossed the room to the trolley for dirty dishes.

'You *can't* keep us in the dark right up to the last minute, Patsy. Come on, who is he? We've got a right to know who's coming to our own room-party. After all, Caroline and I have got all the work to do now, decorating the place.'

Dorothea did not know the Irish girl and had no interest in who was going to be *her* escort to the Ball. She glanced at Caroline: she felt more than ever convinced that the damned girl had snapped up Hugh.

'Just you two content yourself with getting on with the decorating. Never mind trying to speir the guts out of me about who I'm bringing.' Patsy rose and prepared to head off to a nine o' clock lecture.

'We must get plenty of drawing pins and sellotape, Caroline. Oh! - and a balloon pump.'

'Yeah. I'm really glad we're free tomorrow afternoon.' Caroline admitted defeat with Patsy and turned to Elspeth. 'I felt bad about doing nothing towards making all the decs - being away looking after mum and all that - so it's good to be able to do my bit.'

Patsy gathered her breakfast dishes into a precarious pile. Balancing them in one hand, she pointed a Kitchener-like finger: 'We've all got to do our bit – Your Room-Party Needs You!' The precarious pile lost its cutlery. Their laughter was drowned out by the crash but revived by a loud blasphemous yelp from a startled kitchen maid.

Dorothea's irritation and isolation deepened. But one thing was for sure: the milkmaid and her yokel friend would definitely not be abroad on Friday afternoon. Her plan was looking better and better.

She was normally the most diligent of students, attentive during lectures, prompt with assignments. But, today, political economy, modern history and German literature had lost their appeal. From force of habit, she scribbled at breakneck speed, trying to capture every word that fell from the lecturers' lips, but she had no idea what she was writing. It was going to be hard job deciphering the notes.

What had seemed like a crazy idea – no more than a wishful-thinking flash of spite – was crystallising into a real possibility. Every time she thought of Hugh and The Milkmaid together, every time she looked at the damned girl – what on earth did he see in her? - and every time she encountered the excited anticipation of the C floor group, she felt a miserable sense of exclusion and a powerful surge of jealousy.

She had never wanted to be part of their set before. Educated at Roedean, she had gravitated immediately towards the 'Oxbridge Rejects' at matriculation, glad to be taken on as one of *The Chelsea Set*. But now, she felt like a child with her nose pressed up against a window, looking in on a wonderful party to which she was not invited. She stoked the fire of her resentment through lectures on economic graphs, social reformers and Goethe's poetry.

By three o'clock, she had reached a decision and worked out what information she needed to implement it. She could see the Logic and Metaphysics students filing into Lecture Room One and she watched both Hugh and Caroline with narrowed eyes, though they were nowhere near each other in the line nor attempting to communicate with each other. The last student disappeared and peace descended upon Quad for another hour. There had been no sign of Cynthia. *She must be really unwell and still in her flat. Good! That means I can get her on her own right now.* With no sense of the callousness of this thought, Dorothea wheeled the rattling old bike out of Quad and headed towards the harbour.

'Care for a spin, old bean?' Colin sniffed the afternoon air: another hint-of-spring day. After the stuffy confines of the lecture room, the idea of breezing, open-topped, along the East Neuk coast was appealing. 'Shall we do tea at *The Crows Nest* in Anstruther?'

'Can't, sorry. Got to meet someone.' Hugh looked at his watch. 'Now, actually. See you later.'

Where's he off to? What is he up to? He's been acting really strangely these past few days. If we were a married couple, I'd say he had another woman! Colin chuckled, then, shrugging off all thoughts of Hugh, strode happily off to the little car park area at the back of Sally's. He threw his red gown and lecture notes folder into the boot and retied its string.

'I say, Col … Col …' Dorothea tripped across the yard, heedless of the cobbles. She *almost* made it but a deep rut between two of the ancient stones caught a stiletto heel just as she reached the car and she jerked forward, falling across the bonnet with a scream.

'Lawks A'mighty, Miss Dorrie!' Colin borrowed a phrase from dear old Nanny Carruthers. 'No need to throw yourself at me, dear girl. I am always at your service.' He twinkled at her as he set her on her feet again.

Dorothea blushed. She wished she wouldn't: it was one of her most hated deficiencies. 'That's good to know. I mean, I've got something to ask you. I mean … It doesn't matter if you're engaged already. Or if you don't fancy it.'

'Spit it out, Dorrie dear. There's a good girl.' Colin could see his window of time, before darkness fell, beginning to vanish.

'Well, it's Chattan Ball. Tomorrow night, actually.'

'I know.' He grimaced. Not one Chattan girl had asked him – or Hugh. It beggared belief, really.

Dorothea saw the grimace. 'Oh, have you been cornered by someone you don't want to go with?'

'Not cornered at all.'

'Not at all? You're not going?'

'Don't rub it in. And Hugh …'

The last thing she wanted to hear was how Hugh had been invited by The Milkmaid to the most talked-about room-party. She cut in: 'Look,

94

Col, I know it's desperately short notice but I wonder if you'd like to come with me. I've been putting off asking anyone ...' She remembered Patsy's approach. 'I didn't want to give any man the wrong idea. It's so easy to do that, you know. I just want a man to be my escort for the night, as a friend, nothing else. No offence. If you wouldn't mind ...' She petered out in confusion. This seemingly simple approach was more difficult to implement that she had realised.

It suited Colin down to the ground. Dorothea came from the classic upper-class English stable: face long and equine, bosom tiny, hips large, thighs thunderous. She was what Colin's sister, Miranda, called, 'a hefty horse humper'. Miranda herself was petite, slim and shapely, like their French mother who had captivated their father during the war. Thus Colin's taste in women leaned towards the slim and shapely rather than the equine and thunderous. 'That's sporting of you, Dorrie. What's your room-party like?' He had a moment of misgiving: 'It's not all those stuffy seniors on A Floor is it?'

'Oh, they're not that bad, really.'

'What's the theme?'

'What? Oh, for the room? I don't really know.' She had not been party to any of the high-minded discussions of the four PhDs and five magistrands. 'I'm sure it will be fun, though.'

'Well, it's better than ...' Colin almost committed Hugh's blunder with Patsy. Dorothea's blush deepened and her eyes filled with tears.

'Better than anything I'd hoped for!' declared Colin hastily. 'I'd given up hoping for an invitation and the word on the street is that Chattan Ball's the best – unmissable and all that!' Dorothea's red face lit up. *Like a Christmas candle*, thought Colin. *Poor old thing.* On impulse, he waved his hand towards the car.

'I was just going for a spin. Fancy joining me? Tea at *The Crows Nest*?'

Dorothea accepted with alacrity. Not only was she almost dizzy with relief at having finally secured a Ball partner, she was badly in need of cheering up. She had cycled down to Cynthia's flat to find it empty. No lamplight over the desk in the window today. She had run up the stairs intending at least to ring the bell just in case, but had been met by a note pinned to the front door: *Gone away for the day. Don't need you till tomorrow. C de Vere* - clearly intended for the daily housekeeper. Where could Cynthia have gone? It was just the worst luck in the world: she would have to try and find out from someone else which lectures Hugh would be at tomorrow morning. Maybe Colin could help if she could think of an excuse for asking him.

..He had moved round to the passenger door and was holding it open. She manoeuvred her bottom into the tiny seat, her large thighs completely filling the space. She turned to beam at him and he felt a rush of brotherly affection. She was a good sort, old Dorrie, a bit intense maybe. He wondered why she had not asked Hugh to the ball, now that The Landgirl had turned him down. Perhaps she did not realise Hugh was still free? Everyone knew she had been mooning over Hugh ever since they came up to St A's. If he told her, he might shoot himself in the foot and end up sitting in his room doing truth tables tomorrow night – or nursing a lonely pint in *The Keys* - instead of dancing with the glitterati at Chattan Ball. Colin held his peace and concentrated on feeding the old lady just enough and not too much choke: she had a tendency to gobble up the extra fuel and stall, engine flooded, like a greedy child stuffing its mouth with sweets and then being sick all over you.

Hugh watched the medical students pouring out of classes and thronging around the courtyard outside the medical faculty buildings. He spotted Patsy and began to cross the yard towards her. She did not see him but suddenly turned on her heel and ran back into the building.

'Damn!' He waited impatiently whilst the yard slowly emptied. Twenty minutes later she re-appeared. He was now quite alone apart from an interested squirrel on a low branch of the enormous tree in the middle of the yard. Hugh levered himself up from the bench encircling the venerable tree and strolled over to her, cutting her exit off as she made for the little lane which led out of the courtyard and on to South Street. She was rummaging in her book bag which was bumping against her side and did not immediately see him.

'God! It's you!' She fetched up inches from him, almost bumping her head against his. 'What in the name of all that's holy are you playing at? What is it with you *Rejects*? Every time I see you, you try to mug me!'

Hugh burst out laughing. It was true. This was the third time they had collided, the third time she had almost sustained an injury at his hands. 'It must be fate. We can't gainsay it. Our paths are destined to cross in destruction – like stars or planets.' He looked up towards the sky dramatically and his attention was caught and held by the splendid coat of arms above the arch, bearing the inscription: *In Principio Erat Verbum.* 'Here, hang on a minute!'

Patsy was striding away under the arch leaving him gaping up. He caught up with her in the street. 'Damn it, Patsy! You might wait for me. I've been waiting for you for the best part of an hour.'

She stopped. 'Whatever for?'

'It's about your corsage for the Ball. Thing is, by the time I got to the shop yesterday, there wasn't much left to choose from - no orchids left, only roses and fuschias, white and yellow ones. I'm so sorry. I would have gone earlier if I'd realised they run out. Mind you, it was Tuesday by the time you asked me and I think all the orchids had already been booked by then anyway.'

'What are you wittering about? What does it matter what flowers you get? They'll probably fall off as soon as we start dancing anyway. Daft nonsense!'

'Are you sure?' Hugh had been going on memories of Belinda and Cynthia's's fuss over the colour, size and design of their corsages for the last two Balls. It had been more than his life was worth to get it wrong. Patsy's cavalier attitude amazed him. 'Well, if you're really sure.'

'Look, I don't care if you send me a bunch of dandelions. Now, I've got to go – got an appointment at the hairdressers.' She shook her mane of shining hair at him. 'Time to deal with my split ends! See you tomorrow night!'

Dorothea slipped thankfully into one of Chattan's back doors opposite the bike shed. The old car had refused to release its hood from its moorings and the wet, windswept ride home from *The Crow's Nest* had left her cold and dishevelled. She had not managed to extract the information from Colin about Hugh's lecture timetable. Cynthia would have been a much better source. She could have been frank with Cynthia about why she needed the information whereas she had had to try and slip in artless little questions to Colin, most of which he had answered in a very unsatisfactory manner. Without arousing his suspicion, however, it had been impossible to persist. But even if Dorothea had found out for certain about Hugh, there was still the problem of ascertaining the milkmaid's timetable. Unless she could be sure that Hugh and the bumpkin would not meet up tomorrow before the Ball, she could not hope to put her plan into action. She sighed as she turned to walk along the sub-basement corridor: all this indecision was giving her a headache – or maybe it had just been the cold wind and that damned noisy car.

She could hear voices coming from a half-open door. This was the territory of laundry, heating system, property maintenance and storage. She remembered that the domestic bursar had made one of her twittery announcements last night at the end of dinner: a lot of old sheets, rolls of wallpaper, curtains, etc. were to be piled up in one of the storage rooms and this would be left open for the next few days; the girls were welcome to borrow anything they could make use of for their room parties.

'Look at these, Caroline! These cushions will be perfect for the floor. Great colours!'

'Yeah. And that red and orange stuff up on that top shelf - what's that? We need something to cover the bed and drape over the bureau before we lay the glasses out on it for the hooch. Anne's hiring two dozen from the off-license, you know.'

'What a great idea. Much better than us all just bringing our tooth-mugs. I think it's sheets or curtains. Shall we get those two boxes over and climb up?'

Dorothea lifted her noisy boot-heels off the ground and tiptoed towards the open door. There came the sound of a heavy box being dragged across the concrete floor then some puffing and grunting as a second box was lifted on top.

'I'll give you a leg up. You're taller than me. You've more chance of reaching the stuff.'

A moment later, Dorothea heard Caroline's exultant: 'Perfect, Els! Curtains, orangey background with great whorls of red and black — hideous, actually. In fact, *hellish!*'

For some reason that Dorothea did not comprehend, both C floor girls burst out laughing. She continued to eavesdrop as Caroline and Elspeth manhandled the heavy bolts of material down to the floor, her teeth set on edge by their excited giggling.

'We'd better begin carrying all this stuff upstairs. We'll need to wash and get tidied up for dinner. My hands are filthy and your face is all streaked.'

'Hang on, Els. Look at that stuff in the corner. White woodchip paper, a whole roll of it.'

'But we don't need any more wall-paper. The murals are all done and the lining paper for the background has all been painted. Besides, woodchip's awful stuff to paint - you need tons of emulsion, at least two coats - we'd never have time to let it dry.'

'No, but it would be perfect for snow. We can scrunch up big handfuls of it, make a pile of snowballs and make a big sign above saying *No Chance.*'

'What's that got to do with ...? Oh, I see! You *are* clever, Caro. A snowball's chance in *Hell!* Brilliant! Now come on, we really must get going.'

Dorothea was about to resume her soft-footed progress to get out of their way quickly when, once again, she was arrested by Caroline's voice.

'You know, Elspeth, even with the afternoon off, we are going to be pushed to get it all done. There's still the last minute painting of the border round all the background paper – Jennifer's got the design for that all drawn out but it's fiddly and will take ages. Then we'll really need to put some tacking stitches in these curtains once we've got them draped over the bed and bureau, otherwise they'll just keep falling off. Then there's all that crepe paper to untangle from the boxes and hang up; and the murals to position; and we've to fix lots of crepe paper flames coming up under the murals; and all those balloons to blow up; and ...'

'Well, it's a big job but we can only do our best. Maybe one or two of the others will get a wee bit of time to come and help later on if we've not finished. Let us get away to start doing our hair.' Elspeth sounded dubious.

'Only one thing for it.' Caroline made up her mind. 'We take the *whole* day off lectures. Then we can just get straight into old clothes first thing after breakfast and we can be preparing as much as possible in the morning down here. We can bring the boxes of flames down and get them all sorted out, start painting some of the borders before we put them up. Then, as soon as lunch is over, we can get started on the room. We can even get some of the balloons blown up in the morning. Use the bathroom on C Floor once the maids have finished cleaning it.'

'You mean skip *all* our lectures?' Elspeth sounded as if Caroline had suggested robbing the collection plate in Chapel.

'Well, it's no big deal.' Caroline drew upon her recent experience. 'It's surprising how quickly you can catch up. Other people's lecture notes are just as good as your own – better sometimes. And I'm sure Anne and a couple of the others who do English and History will oblige – after all, it's their room-party too.'

'But aren't we *supposed* to go to lectures? Unless we're sick or something? And won't the lecturers be suspicious? I mean everyone knows tomorrow is Chattan Ball.'

'It's not like school. I don't think the lecturers notice - or care - and this *is* a special case. I'm not advocating we do it regularly or anything.'

'Well, if you think so.' Elspeth battled with her strong work-ethic upbringing. Then, sounding extremely daring, 'OK, then! Let's do it! Oh, it's all so exciting! Tell me again, is my escort really nice, is he good-looking?'

'A fine upstanding figure of a man!' Caroline lifted two large cushions and turned to back out the door. 'Get the light, Els. Mind you, he's not nearly as handsome as *my* man, of course!'

Dorothea, pressed into a shallow cupboard on the opposite wall, ground her teeth. *Damn that self-satisfied bitch! She deserves everything that's coming to her!* She waited until the sound of their voices and footsteps had faded. Then she wriggled out of the cupboard and stretched her cramped muscles with a groan. But the physical discomfort of the past ten minutes – even coming after the ordeal of the bone-shaking jaunt to Anstruther - had been a small price to pay. It was all falling beautifully into place: she had a partner for the Ball; she had a clear field tomorrow with the certainty that Caroline would not be venturing out of Chattan the whole day; and she had even – what a bonus! – discovered the best-kept secret in Chattan, the theme of the most talked-about room party. It was a priceless snippet of information. *Operation Sabotage!* she thought gleefully. *Death to all country bumpkins!*

That night at dinner she watched the giggling C Floorers as a cat watches an unwary mouse, letting it have just a little more time, just a little more life, before snuffing it out.

CHAPTER NINE: MORAG AND MARJORY

Morag regarded James incredulously. 'Are you trying to tell me …? I just don't believe you! Pete with another girlfriend - as well as Caroline?' She rose and, with agitated movements, began to clear his dishes away - he only just managed to hang on to his mug which still had half a cup of tea in it. 'You must have picked him up wrong, James. What chance does he have to even meet girls, let alone turn them into *girlfriends?'*

'Well …' It was a pity to spoil a good story with the truth but James had to admit he had over-embellished Pete's dilemma. 'Well, she's not exactly his girlfriend *yet* but he definitely fancies her.'

Morag faced James coldly like a policeman interrogating a suspect. 'How did he meet her? Where?'

'You mind that night he came home from Dundee late for milking – he'd run all the way from the Kingsway 'cause his bike got a puncture?'

'Mmm, and he took the Landrover in later to pick it up. Aye, I remember. That was about a couple of weeks ago. What of it?'

'Well, he'd left the bike at this house, one of those bungalows on the Kingsway.'

'Aye, he told me someone had been kind enough to look after it for him.'

'Did he tell you who the *someone* was?'

Morag screwed up her face. 'No, I don't think so. I'd definitely have remembered if he'd said anything about a *girl.'*

'There you are then! He didn't want to talk about it. Is that not proof in itself?'

'Proof of what?'

'That he had something to hide!' James was triumphant. Colin and Hugh would have said *Q.E.D.*

Morag poured herself the last dregs from the teapot and added a large spoonful of sugar for fortitude. 'And you've discovered what this something is, then? That's what he was telling you last night when the two of you were up in his room for so long?'

'Her name's Alice.'

'How far has it gone?' All her relief that Pete and Caroline were back on track, all her hopes for a rosy future, drained away. 'How often has he been out with her?' Even as she asked the question, it seemed ridiculous. Pete's tight schedule of college, home-study and farm-work, without time or space for other activities, was an open book. His relationship with Caroline was part of it. But this … this *clandestine* affair? *How? When?*

101

Where? It seemed as likely as discovering that Jed had another wife somewhere. 'How did it start? Tell me more about this girl. What's her name?'

'Alice.'

'Alice what?'

James sniggered. 'Alice Band!'

'I meant her real name not some kind of nickname. Stop fooling about, James. Tell me the lassie's right name and how Pete got in tow with her.'

'It *is* her right name – honest. It's a scream, isn't it? The night he went back for his bike, she was all on her own at the house. Her mother goes out to evening classes or some such. So he had The Alice Band all to himself and the two of them had a right good chinwag. Mind how long he was gone? Near an hour and a half. It doesn't take all that time to drive to the Kingsway and back.'

'I never noticed.' Morag had been tucked up in her snug, with a shovel of hot coals in the tiny grate and this month's *Good Housekeeping*. 'But what about her father? Where was *he*?'

'Seems there's not one. Silver's a widow, Pete thinks.'

'Silver? Her mother's called *Silver*?' Morag was momentarily diverted.

James guffawed. 'Naw! I made *that* one up. Thought the dad could be called *Brass*.'

'You said there isn't a father. Alive anyway.'

'There's not. I just meant that if there had been …'

'Enough!' Morag shook her head in irritation. 'What happened that night? When the two of them had all this time to talk? Did he ask her out?'

'Aye, he tried, that is. But she turned him down.'

Morag heaved a sigh of relief then felt a flash of anger. *Who does this Alice Band girl think she is, turning my handsome son down?*

'She's just playing hard-to-get, if you ask me. And Pete's fallen hook-line-and-sinker for it. It's made him all the more desperate to see her.'

'But how could he? What about Caroline? How could he even look at another girl when he'd just agreed to be her partner at this lovely ball you're off to tomorrow?'

'Thing is, mam, he met The Alice Band and fell for her *before* Miss Varsity came home for the weekend and asked us to the Ball. He thought she didn't want anything more to do with him after she'd given him the brush-off at Christmas. But then she came over all pally again and invited him to the Ball so he started fancying her again as well.'

'As well?'

'As well as The Alice Band.'

Morag passed a distracted hand over her brow. 'Well, he'll have to make up his mind. He can't have them both. And he's known Caroline for a lot longer. This Alice girl is just a flash in the pan. *And* she's turned him down anyway.' It galled her to say it even though she was glad of the fact.

'Well, she has and she hasn't.'

'What the devil does that mean?'

'She said she wouldn't go on a date with him but then she told him she goes regularly – every Friday night, I think - to a café in Dundee. So Pete's been trying to get time to go there and see her.'

'And has he?'

'No, not yet. He's hoping to, soon. But he managed to catch her coming out of school on Tuesday and spoke to her again.'

'You mean, he's seen her again? He went to see her even *after* he'd seen Caroline again and agreed to go to the Ball with her?'

James grinned proudly. 'He did! There's hope for the lad yet. But then he started brooding over the two lassies and getting his knickers in a twist. Sorry, mam!' Morag might be a farmer's wife – and a farmer's daughter, able from childhood to describe and discuss the mechanics of animal copulation and reproduction – but, when it came to human beings' intimate functions and garments, she was a prim Presbyterian. James corrected himself: 'I mean getting himself in a fair old lather.'

'So that's what's been bothering him and giving him such a fiddle-face the past few days? Even your father noticed. But Pete's got over it. I could see that at breakfast time. He's as happy as a sand-boy again. So what cheered Pete up? What did you say to him last night when the two of you were in his room?'

'I told him to stop taking it all so serious. He's barely nineteen. He's got a lot of damage to do yet before he settles down with one lassie. He's far too young tobe …'

'Your father and I were only eighteen when we met.'

'I told him just to string the two of them along together. Likely they'll be doing the same. Miss Caroline'll have a few toffs on the hook at St Andrews and The Alice Band'll likely have a wee gang of admirers at this cafe, if she's as stunning as Pete says. Main thing is just to stop them finding out about each other but that should be easy enough with Caroline away most of the time and Alice living in Dundee.'

'You told him to do *what*? Deceive Caroline? Have this other girl – this Alice-Band creature as well - and keep it a secret? Pete would never do anything like that. I'm ashamed of you, James! What did he say when you suggested it?'

'You can see for yourself how he feels. You were just saying how he's cheered up. He just needed a bit of worldly-wise advice from his big brother.'

'You're saying *that's* what's made him so happy again? I think that's disgusting. To think a son of mine would suggest such a thing and the other one go along with it – *and* be delighted about it! Your father and I would never have behaved like that. Nor would any of the boys and girls when we were young.'

'Ach, mam, that was the old days. Times have changed. This is the sixties.' He borrowed a phrase from Pete's tranny. 'It's the *swinging* sixties, man!' He tossed off a final gulp of cold tea and rose. 'Must get back to work. Got tons to do. Dad's getting his pound of flesh.' He lowered his voice in imitation of his father's growl. '*Damned swanky dance . . . leaving me all on my own to do the milking and the lambing.*'

'Stop that!' Morag boiled over. After the shock of his disclosure about Pete and the affront to her moral values, this was the last straw. 'Yer father's quite happy for you to go. I've told you that. He just likes to have a wee moan now and then. Now get away out of here – I've had enough of your tripe!'

James held up his hands. 'Whoa, mam, don't ...' But she advanced towards him, almost baring her teeth, and he fled.

She finished her evening tasks, opened the door of the stove and thrust the shovel into the hot coals. The heat flamed her face as she carried the shovelful through to her snug and her heart was beating uncomfortably fast. She knew that what she was considering was unforgivable meddling.

She had been so delighted to see Caroline and Pete reconciled, sure that they were meant for each other, just as she had surmised last summer. That Pete should have another girl, lurking secretly in the background, had knocked the complacency out of her. Like one of their Jack Russells in the barn with a half-dead rat, she had worried at the news all afternoon. By tea-time, she had reached a decision: meddling or not, she was going to try and nip this new connection in the bud. Pete belonged with Caroline and Morag was going to see that no other girl – least of all one with such a stupid name - got in the way.

She had a few pieces of information to build her strategy on: she knew the girl's name; she knew the street where she lived; she knew that there was no father on the scene; and she knew that the mother's name was *not* Silver. She shook her head, smiling, despite herself, at James' witticism.

He had not mentioned any brothers or sisters in the Kingsway bungalow. Morag knew those houses: she had been driven along that road and admired the heavily-swathed bay windows and the antique-brass carriage-lamps hanging over freshly painted doors. Alice could be the precious only child of a wealthy widow; and the girl was still at school, innocent and inexperienced. It could well be that the mother was as anxious as Morag to rein in this budding romance. Perhaps she did not even know of it? There could be mileage in playing the mothers' solidarity card - protecting feckless youngsters from unsuitable relationships. *Silver and I need to become allies.*

She tiptoed through to the tiny office, next door to the parlour. She rarely went in here except to answer the phone. It was chronically chaotic with piles of letters, charts, scribbled notes, advertisements and books, even sometimes the odd vegetable lying about. She could see a sprouting seed potato lying on top of a pile of farm machinery catalogues in a corner. Jed was having forty winks as usual after his evening meal, pretending to be 'taming the paperwork', slumped in the big swivel desk-chair. She tiptoed over and extricated a big blue book from the bottom of the pile: the telephone directory. She almost dropped it as she shot out a hand to stop the potato landing on Jed's foot. Holding her breath, she got the big book and her buxom figure out of the tiny room without waking her husband.

Morag never phoned anyone and only answered it if there was no-one else in the house. It made her nervous. She found herself saying things into the mouthpiece that she later regretted, or coming off the phone without saying half of what she had meant to. Jed would be very surprised at the sight of his wife with the directory and would ask questions she did not want to answer.

She bore her trophy back to her den, shutting the adjoining door to the kitchen firmly. She was safe here: none of her menfolk ever dared to intrude upon 'Mam's snug time' of an evening unless there was a dire emergency. She settled down into her rocking chair, opened the directory and began to scan the names listed under *B*.

There were only three Bands: A&S, C&J, and M. Morag considered these: her first feverish thought was that A&S could be Alice and Silver; but that was ridiculous. It was unlikely a seventeen year old girl would be listed and, of course, the mother's name was *not* Silver. No, these &s would be married couples: Alec and Sylvia or Andrew and Sally; Charlie and Janice or Colin and Jemima. She procrastinated, putting off the moment when this girl and her mother would become real people, entries in the phone book.

Finally, she did the obvious: she looked at the matching addresses beside each set of initials. And there it was: it seemed as if the tiny one-line entry stood out in huge, bold capitals:

M. Band, 155 Kingsway, Dundee -- 66454.

With a shaking hand, Morag took up a small notebook and pencil and copied down the address and telephone number. Returning the directory would have to wait. She couldn't face the pile of catalogues and the potato again. Jed would never miss it and she could return it in the morning.

She stared at the words and figures in the little notebook and contemplated the phone call. She would leave it till mid-morning, once James had had his bacon rolls and gone back to work. There were always a good two hours between that and dinner-time at half past twelve. What would she say? How would she broach the subject of Pete and Alice? She must make no mention of Caroline, of course. Silver would not take kindly to the idea that another girl was being preferred over her daughter. The thing was simply to make Silver - Morag wished she could stop thinking of her by this name: if she wasn't careful, she'd be calling her that on the phone – to make *Mrs. Band* think that her daughter must be stopped from a disastrous liaison with Pete and to encourage her to take action to prevent it.

The problem was – Morag jabbed the poker into the tiny fire – how to put this over without blackening Pete's name? However annoyed she was with her younger son, she drew the line at making him seem an undesirable boyfriend. In any case, it would look extremely strange for a mother bad-mouth her own son. Hearing Jed coming through to the kitchen, she gave up and went to join him for the pot of tea they liked to share before bed. This was usually an oasis of closeness in their busy lives but tonight both were self-absorbed. He did not notice her abstracted air and his bedtime grumbles received even less attention than usual.

The clock on the kitchen wall ticked on: almost quarter to twelve. She had only half an hour left. Jed had been known to come in quarter of an hour early and wander off to the office to 'putter about' till dinner was ready at half past. Since James had gone off at half past ten, she had been spinning out one task after another, promising herself that each would be the last before she made the phone call.

Do it now! she ordered herself, and started resolutely towards the office. Then she doubled back and moved the kettle on top of the stove from the warm burner to the hot one: she needed a fortifying cup to take with her. She took the tiny one-cup pot down from the shelf, setting it on the warm burner. The three brown Derby teapots, large, middle-sized and small, had been their wedding present from Jed's sister, Alison: 'like the three bears', she had said gaily. Morag thought sadly of her as she waited for the water to come to the boil. The thought of that tragic waste of young life stiffened her resolution.

The big, black telephone looked as forbidding as ever as she plumped herself down in the swivel chair, almost knocking over the tea-tray as the chair swung round. She drew the sheet of paper from her apron pocket and smoothed it out on the desk. She eyed the numbers on the sheet and the holes on the dial, matching them up. She poured out the tea slowly. The grandfather clock in the parlour struck noon, echoing through the house. Only fifteen minutes left! *If I dial a wrong number, that'll be a sign that I shouldn't do it at all.*

But there was no chance she would do that, so painstakingly did she mouth each number before putting her finger in the correct hole in the dial. She listened to the phone on the other end ringing: five, six, seven times. *She not in! Thank God! It's a sign. I won't try again.*

'Hello. Dundee 66454.' The voice was crisp, cultured, no trace of a Dundee accent.

I was right. Morag thought. *They are toffs.* 'Is that Mrs Band?' she whispered.

'Hello? Is there anyone there? I'm afraid I can't hear you.'

Morag took a large gulp of tea and tried again: a strangled croak came out.

'I'm afraid I can't make you out. There must be something wrong with the line. Do you want to hang up and try again?'

It was like one of those dreams, she thought, when you are screaming, positively bellowing in fact, and then you wake up to find you are making only a mouse-like squeak. Her third attempt produced a mere squawk.

'Hello. This is Marjory Band speaking. Can I help you? My goodness, what's the matter? Are you in some kind of trouble?' Morag had let out a terrified yelp at the sound of the name. The line went dead: she had thrown the heavy receiver down on to its cradle as if it was scalding her.

When Jed came into the kitchen ten minutes later, whistling *I could have danced all night* – James had been humming it all morning as they worked together - his wife was sitting at the table with her head in her hands.

'What is it, love? Have we had some bad news? What's happened?'

She did not answer for several seconds. Then she shook herself like a dog coming out of water and leapt up. 'I've been a daft bitch, that's what's happened, Jed. A daft, meddlin' bitch! And I've had my comeuppance: I'm no use at it and maybe that's just as well. Things'll just have to take their own course without me sticking my oar in. But, mark my words, it'll be a crying shame if he throws away his best chance of happiness.'

Jed was bewildered. 'What's happened? Who are you talking about?'

But James could be heard shucking off his boots in the back porch and she simply shook her head and turned to the oven to take out the shepherd's pie.

Marjory stared at the phone, nonplussed. *Who on earth was that? It sounded like whoever it was needed help. But who could it be?* Her thoughts flew to old Mavis up in her cottage in the Highlands. *I must find out.*

There was a way, she felt sure, to track a caller. One of the members of her writing group had written a story recently – a sort of 'whodunit' - in which this had featured. If it was Mavis in need of help, she must hurry. There was not a telephone in the cottage or she would have phoned her old aunt. She dialed the operator anxiously.

A deadpan voice assured her that he could certainly trace the call. It might take a few minutes. Would it be all right to call her back with the information?

'Yes, yes, but hurry up!'

Marjory prowled around her sitting room waiting for the call. Her eye fell upon a book: it was the one to be read before the next meeting of the *Prizewinners* book group which she had recently joined. The group was working its way through all the Pulitzer Prize–winning novels of the past ten years. This month's book was *To Kill a Mocking Bird*, an American novel, the 1960 winner. Restlessly she picked it up and began to read the synopsis on the inside of the sleeve: *A young black man is on trial for raping a white woman …*

She felt sick. Memories of that ridiculously happy summer in Africa and its terrible, shameful ending came flooding back. She saw the ignorant, foolish girl she had been, the pathetic, pregnant refugee, and then the hidden years as the pitied, too-young, half-wit mother of a half cast, illegitimate child. She saw the long road she had travelled towards the independent, confident adult she had become since her father's death and the purchase of her own house and her own life.

The phone rang shrilly. She stared at it in confusion; then she remembered the operator and the strange call. Moments later she was looking at a number written down at the operator's dictation. It meant nothing to her: it was certainly not a number in Mavis' neck of the woods – that was a relief. It was a local number, in fact. Who could it be? And why on earth had they called her? She reached out for the phone: there was one sure way to find out. Before she could pick up the receiver, however, it rang. *It's them again! Good! Let's hope we can clear this mystery up.*

But, confusingly, it was Aunt Mavis herself, with a shilling's worth of chat from the phone box in her village. With memories still drumming through her head, Marjory found herself thinking of the old, anxious Aunt Mavis who had confined her for years rather than the good-hearted and encouraging friend she had become once they were both released from Rev. Band's regime. Mavis prattled on, as she always did, about life in her happy Highland village, only running out of prattle when she became aware of Marjory's unresponsiveness.

'Is everything all right, dear? How's Alice? Are you both well? You seem very quiet.'

'I'm reading a book, Aunt Mavis. At least, I'm just about to start it ...'

'That's nice, dear. I know how you love your reading. What's it called?'

'*To Kill a Mocking Bird.* It's American. It won a prize – the Pulitzer, actually - four years ago.'

'It must be very good, then. I'm sure you'll enjoy that. What's it about?'

'About a trial. A black man is accused of raping a white woman.'

Now it was Mavis who did not respond. Marjory waited, twisting the telephone cord round her fingers.

'I don't think that's the kind of book you should be reading, dear.'

'Why not?' Marjory was belligerent. 'In fact: why *the hell* not?'

'There you are, you see, dear. It's upsetting you already. It was all a long time ago. Least said, soonest mended. And Alice must never know, she thinks her father died just after you were married out in Africa, that you and he were childhood sweethearts, that he was dying of a dreadful disease and you married him to make him happy before he died. And then she was born after you came back here to live with me, you kept your maiden name and gave it to her because his name was too hard to say, that you were too sad to put his name on her birth certificate . . .' Mavis was once again the jailer, dinning the old cover-story into her again.

The mention of Alice brought Marjory's rebellion to an abrupt end. Mavis was right, of course: she must not destroy seventeen years of careful pretence just for the sake of a sudden selfish need to revisit her shameful past. Alice must never know: Alice *would* never know.

'You're right, Aunty. I'm sorry. I can't think what got into me. Don't worry - I won't read the book,' she lied. 'Let's forget about it, dear. Let me tell you about how well Alice is doing at school this year: she's really working so hard, I'm sure she'll get enough Highers for university. Oh, and I'm thinking of doing some real studying myself. One of my evening class tutors says I should try and get some Highers. Well, start with O levels, of course. Maybe even go to university myself one day. Imagine that!'

'Aren't you a little old for that sort of thing, dear?'

'No! It seems that mature students are really welcome now. Or there may be a new thing called the University of the Air starting up in a few years. I could study at home through the wireless and get a television as well ...'

The call lasted another fifteen minutes and, by the time it ended, the two women had moved into calmer waters and affectionate goodbyes. She sat for a long moment when the call was over, looking at the book, dwelling upon the safe and spotless life of her daughter, thanking God that *she* would never know the misery of making one life-wrecking mistake.

Then she remembered the strange caller she had been just about to chase up when Aunt Mavis phoned. Was it still worth it? Whoever had been in such dire need would surely have found help elsewhere by now? Probably a wrong number anyway; still, it would be good to know for certain. She decided to have her usual lunchtime sandwich first – it could hardly be urgent any more, it was more than half an hour since the call. Plenty of time this afternoon.

Morag started awake. Was that a bell ringing? The little clock on her bedside table said almost three but she had not set its alarm. She often slipped upstairs for a little lie down after dinner nowadays. Usually she dropped off quickly enough for a comfortable half an hour or so and was up and about again shortly after two. Today, enervated by the debacle over the phone call, she had puttered about, accomplishing nothing, finally trailing upstairs at five past two. She had wriggled about on top of the eiderdown for some twenty minutes, finally falling into a fitful doze which had carried her to this late hour.

'Morag! Are you still up there?' Jed's voice from the foot of the stairs.

'Coming! Coming! Just ... Just doing some tidying up.' She swung her legs off the bed and straightened her crumpled clothes. He was waiting for her as she descended.

'I'm off out again. Got to go to the pigs. That sow I was telling you about - I decided to phone the vet and he'll be here soon. Probably a waste of money but I can't take the risk when she's so near term. We should get ten or twelve off her this time.'

'Right.' She wondered why he had waited to tell her this. Normally he came and went about the day's business, only stopping to explain his movements if they involved her.

'There was a phone call just now. I wondered if you knew anything about it,' Jed lingered doubtfully. Morag had been mighty strange throughout dinner, jumpy and defensive, shoo-ing him away when he had attempted again to ask her if anything was wrong. Thinking that she didn't want to talk about it while James was there, he had waited till the boy had gone back to work. But, even with just the two of them left in the kitchen, Morag had not been forthcoming. He had given up and gone off to spend an hour in the office, catching up on the paperwork which seemed to multiply daily as the long arm of the Common Market reached into the age-old habits and methods of farmers.

It must have been the telephone ringing which had woken her: 'Who was it?'

'I'm not really sure. It was a woman. She said she'd had a call from our number this morning – well, about twelve, I think she said – but it had been a bad line and got cut off. She seemed to think maybe whoever phoned was in some kind of trouble so she'd gone to the bother of getting our number traced with the operator and she was just phoning back to see if everything was all right and to find out what it was we wanted. Did *you* phone anyone at twelve? I know *I* didn't. I didn't come in till about twenty past. Hey! Are you all right, love?' Morag had gasped and clapped a hand to her mouth.

'Did she say her name?' she croaked.

He eyed her. 'This is to do with the way you were going on at dinner time, isn't it? What *is* this all about? Who ... ?' A loud *toot* sounded in the yard outside the kitchen door. 'Blast! That's the vet. I'll have to go. We'll talk about this later, love. Don't you be worrying now, we'll sort it out, whatever it is.' He strode away along the hallway, towards the kitchen.

'What name did she say?' She ran along the lobby and caught his arm. 'What name?'

'Name? Mmm ... I think it was Bond, something like that. Mrs - definitely, yes - *Mrs* Bond.'

'Band.' Morag's voice was flat and despairing.

'Yes, it could have been. Do you know her? *Did* you phone her? She seemed quite concerned ... Oh, yes, hello, Hamish, come in. We'll just get over to the sty right now.' The vet had stuck his head round the porch door. 'I have to go, dear. Tell me all about it later.'

She subsided on to a chair at the kitchen table and groaned. It had never occurred to her that Silver – no, *Marjory* – Band could trace her call.

Morag had no idea how the technology of telephones worked and such a refinement had never crossed her mind. It had been hard enough dealing with the shame of her inadequacy on the phone. She had decided that it was a sign from God, that what she had been planning to do was sinful, that she must put it behind her and keep her meddling nose out of it. She had accepted that her hopes for Pete and Caroline might be futile.

But now, it was all starting up again: she had unleashed a force she could not control. *Stop that!* She took herself in hand. *Ye're makin' a mountain out o' a molehill.* If the woman had spoken to Jed and been reassured that there was nothing to worry about, she would be unlikely to call again. The whole business would peter out..

The telephone bell cut cruelly through these comforting thoughts. Morag leapt up as if she had been shot. *It's her again! What am I going to say?* Without pausing to put on a jacket or change into her boots, she hurried out of the house.

Marjory doodled thoughtfully on the notepad that lay beside the telephone. The mystery was not cleared up at all. She had finally called the strange number at ten to three. She had started reading *that book* while eating her lunch and had quickly become engrossed in it, time running away with her. The brisk male voice, *Fintry Farm, Jed McCa... speaking,* had borne no relation to the strangled squawks of the earlier caller. She had explained the reason for her call but the man had been mystified. He knew nothing about it. But he would ask his wife. If *she* knew anything about it, she would phone Marjory back. He had taken Marjory's name and number and hung up.

She looked again at the number written on the pad and her scribbles underneath it; then she gave up. She had never heard of Fintry Farm and she had not fully caught the man's name. *I've done all I can*, she decided. *We'll see if his wife phones back – if not, well ...* She went through to the kitchen to begin preparing an early evening meal for Alice and herself Tonight was the monthly meeting of the local history society and she always met up with another local lady in a nice little ladies bar for a discreet little sherry before the lecture in the Marryat Hall.

The fish pie made and ready to be put in the oven at half past four, she settled down again with the book, instantly immersed, only acknowledging Alice's homecoming with a quick smile and the usual unanswered question about homework.

Alice, trailing down the stairs at nine o'clock, after hours of homework, bent on cheering herself up by baking a batch of cherry scones, paused to read the scribbled note left on the telephone table. Her eyes almost fell out of her head: *Fintry Farm. Jed McKa.* She did not know the telephone number but the name of the farm rang terrifyingly loud bells. On the first night of their acquaintance, during their chat in the garage as he reclaimed his damaged bike, Pete had teased her about her name. *Got a brother called Rubber?* She had assured him that, in the twelve years since she had first gone to school, she had heard every possible witticism about her name. *I suppose you've got a dead ordinary name, no chance of having jokes made about it? How boring!* He had saluted like a soldier on parade: *Peter McCafferty of Fintry Farm at your service.*

She stared at her mother's writing. Had her mother been phoning Fintry Farm? What on earth for? Or had someone at the farm phoned her? *Maybe it was Pete looking for me* – a happy thought, but quickly quashed by the name on the pad: *Jed* McKa...

One thing she felt sure about: this did not bode well for her hopes of getting to know the handsome Farmer Pete better. Her mother would be down on her like a ton of bricks. Higher exams were only two months away, the pressure was on, and Marjory was determined that Alice would not fall at the last fence.

Hearing her mother's car in the drive, Alice tore the sheet out of the notepad, slipped it into the pocket of her school skirt and went through to turn on the oven. Marjory breezed in full of excitement about a forthcoming field trip to Killiecrankie – where the famous 'Bonnie Dundee' had fought and died. She made no mention of the note on the telephone table: she had quite forgotten about it and went off to get ready for bed singing softly: *To the Lairds o' Convention, 'Twas Claverhouse spoke ...*

CHAPTER TEN: COLIN AND THE OLD LADY

Dorothea grimaced as she laid down her pen and scanned the page of history lecture notes she had just written up. Even an optimistic assessment could not describe it as anything more than scanty and disjointed. The other two lectures had not fared much better.

She looked round the swot room at the other occupants: wasn't that one of *them* over there in that corner. She had not noticed Elspeth slipping into the swot-room an hour ago. She watched the long, thick pigtail move on the girl's shoulders as she turned her head from side to side to copy chunks of text into her jotter from the pile of opened books on her table. She seemed to be using a prepared list and was working confidently. Dorothea's lip curled. After her own frustrating attempts to make sense of her notes, the sight of such organised diligence only served to hammer another nail in the C Floor gang's coffin.

The swot-room door opened to admit another one of the hated mob - that Irish girl. She made her way over to the pigtail's table and leaned down to whisper to her, pulling at her arm. Pigtail put up some resistance, gesturing at the open books, but she soon gave in. Dorothea could hear them start to chatter and giggle in the corridor. She waited till the noise of their happy conversation had faded towards the head of the stairs; then she snatched up her jotter and hurried out of the room. She could hear them clearly on their way down to C Floor.

'We've been havin' such a laugh, Elso, trying out make-up on each other. Caroline ended up looking like a Zulu warrior! And even Anne ...'

'I'm allergic to all that stuff. I never wear it.'

'Rubbish! Jennifer's got a great range for sensitive skin. You'll be all right. And we all tried on our party-frocks and had a catwalk parade up and down the corridor. You missed yourself!'

'I wish I'd seen that.'

'Still can! Most of them are still in theirs. I just changed to come and get you. We want to see you in yours. Come on!'

Dorothea caught a burst of loud pop music mingled with noisy laughter as a door was opened and closed. She mounted the stair up to A Floor with trailing footsteps. The morgue-like silence here was punctuated only by an occasional cough from the studious inhabitants of the rooms – or perhaps it was just the rustle of papers. Going into her room, she went over to the wardrobe. Her beautiful ball gown hung there – pale greenish-grey silk with a scalloped low-cut neckline and full, billowing skirt. It had been Daddy's Christmas present, so sumptuous it had had to be boxed and sent separately from her luggage when she had returned to St A's after the festive season. Thinking morosely of the C Floor set and their 'catwalk', she gave in to a sudden urge and quickly stripped down to bra and pants. Then she threw the gorgeous gown over her head and settled it on to her figure. She lifted the lid of her desk and looked at her top half in the small mirror affixed to its underside.

Very satisfactory. Her creamy, voluptuous shoulders were her best feature and the dress showed them off to perfection. The tiny half sleeves nicely concealed the fleshy upper arms which she did *not* consider one of her better features. The padded front even made it look like she had a real bosom. It was all quite miraculous. She glowed but she wanted more. There was a full-length mirror on the wall at the end of the corridor. She cautiously opened her door and peeked out: silence and emptiness. She slipped out into the corridor and looked towards the mirror; then she began to walk slowly towards the mesmerising image of the beautiful creature she saw there. *Is that really me?*

The dress had worked its expensive magic and transformed her pear-shaped figure into a beguiling hour-glass: gone were the large backside, the tree-trunk thighs and the despised flat chest. She preened, twirling and pouting. The door nearest the mirror opened and a little mousey woman emerged, yawning, with a kettle in her hand and spectacles in her hair.

'Wow! Is that what you're wearing tomorrow night?'

Dorothea beamed. 'Yes it is. Do you like it? Will it do?'

The woman looked bemused. After six years at St A's – she was now doing a PhD in geology – she had seen too many over-priced ball gowns and been to too many over-excited balls. She herself would be wearing a dress that had already graced several balls over the years and had not been very interesting or flattering to begin with. She tossed a discouraging reply over her shoulder and made for the bathroom to fill the kettle for her bedtime cocoa. Then, remembering that Dorothea was only a bejantine, she paused outside the bathroom door and called more kindly: 'You look very nice, dear. Don't worry, balls are vastly overrated events. You'll be absolutely fine in that dress. None of us up here will be wearing anything too fancy anyway.' Then she yawned once more and disappeared.

Dorothea's confidence drained away. She bolted back to her room, terrified that another door would open and expose her to more patronising pity. She tugged the dress over her head and flung it on the bed. Then she burst into tears

115

'You're sure you don't mind, old chap? I mean, really?' Colin wished Hugh would slow down. Trying to explain why he had accepted Dorothea's ball invitation was hard enough - everyone in The Set knew that she wanted Hugh and would have jumped at the chance if she had known he was free. Colin had been feeling uncomfortable since last night. He had avoided Hugh after dinner, sloping off with excuses of *lots of work to do*. If Hugh had thought such an excuse unlikely, he had made no comment. Nursing his own secret, he had been glad of the solitude.

Now it was after midday. They had caught up with each other in Quad and were drifting towards Sally's for lunch. As soon as Colin had raised the topic of Chattan Ball with a tentative *I suppose you've still had no luck with a partner for the shindig at Old Chastity tonight*, Hugh had accelerated his pace, grunting something inaudible.

'Poor old Dorrie. I mean, it just seemed too rude to tell her to ask someone else. I know she'd rather have you, of course, old bean. She must think you're going with someone else. Maybe she thinks it's The Landgirl, though you'd think she'd be in the know being in Chattan herself - she only has to ask her, after all. Anyway, it was just sort of done before I knew what was happening and I didn't have the heart to tell her.' He ran out of breath as well as excuses: Hugh was keeping up the punishing pace and they were now running up the stone steps into Sally's. He tugged at the trailing sleeve of Hugh's gown. 'For heaven's sake, say something! Am I cast into outer darkness and consigned to the fiery pit or not?'

Hugh checked. 'It's fine, Col,' he said flatly. 'No, really,' as Colin looked set to begin regurgitating his garbled excuses, '*really!* I'm glad, honestly. If I can't go with Caroline, I don't want to go with anyone else, especially ' - he could not resist punishing Colin just a little - 'especially Dorothea and the senior swots. You'll be pushed to stay awake all night in *that* room party'. He thought smugly of where *he* would be and what a shock Col was in for. *Serves him right!*

'Well, that's jolly sporting of you.' Colin was too relieved to resent the mild punishment. 'Jolly sporting. My God, what's that ghastly smell?'

A disgusting stench was emanating from the dining-room. Even for Sally's, whose culinary offerings were legendary, it was remarkable. The current cook, new in post, was attempting to redeem his reputation by a combination of experimentation and flamboyance: last night's *devilled pear and parsnip puree* had been foul. But, obviously, today's lunchtime soup had gone badly wrong.

116

'Tell you what!' Colin made a snap decision. 'Let me take you out to lunch, old pal. You deserve a treat. Make up for the Ball and you being such a brick about me going with dumpling Dorrie. I got a postal order from dear old Aunt Kitty this morning; so, I'm in funds. Let's go to Kate's and try her haggis pies - whatever *they* are!'

Hugh hesitated. He had intended to avoid Colin as much as possible today until just before the ball. Then, if Colin was around in Sally's in the early evening, he would probably *have* to let him know he was going as his preparations to get ready for it would become obvious. But that had been when Colin was not going himself. Now, he was wrapped up in his own invitation and guilt at having accepted Dorothea. He was trying so hard to excuse his own disloyalty and make atonement to Hugh that he would not see what was under his nose. It all felt much safer.

'Good idea! Let's get out of here before we asphyxiate. Haggis pies can't be any worse!'

Dorothea pedalled slowly along Market Street, deep in thought. This morning's lecture notes had fared no better, as she cudgelled her brains for a way to get access to Hugh some time this afternoon. Ideas for excuses to approach him, ranging from the feasible to the ridiculous, had been flitting though her mind for the past five hours since early morning. She had cried herself to sleep last night, leaving the ball gown lying in a heap on the floor, and had awoken more vengeful than ever. The contrast between the excited anticipation on C Floor and the cynical indifference on her own floor had been the last straw. However crazy her plan, however awful the repercussions, it now seemed like the only possible course of action.

As she slowed down towards the junction at the end of the street, her eyes widened. *Colin's car! Outside Kate's! What's he doing here? Why isn't he in Sally's for lunch?* Then she saw two boys uncurling their lanky bodies out of the car: Colin *and* Hugh. She slewed hastily into the gutter behind a parked van and watched them go into the café. Then she parked the bike and followed them.

The café was busy and noisy, with a queue at the self-service counter and all the tables occupied. She slipped to the back of the queue, craning her neck to see Colin's dark head - of Hugh's blond mop, there was no sign. She watched Colin keenly, following his progress with a laden tray across the room. He disappeared through a beaded curtain to the back area and, as he pushed the curtain apart, she caught a glimpse of Hugh guarding a two-seat table in the far corner. Her heart leapt. *It's now or never! I'll not get a better chance. It doesn't matter if Col's there as well.*

117

'Yes! What are you having? Hello-oh …'

The hot-cheeked girl behind the counter was waving a serving spoon along the range of bubbling metal troughs like a conductor in front of an orchestra. 'Are ye eatin', Miss, or are ye just here to take a photo?'

Bloody cheek! Some of these local, Scottish types, honestly.

'I'll take the macaroni cheese and a pot of Earl Grey tea.'

The baton was wielded over the glutinous yellow mess. 'Wot kinda tea?' The conductor puffed to blow her hair off her sweaty forehead. 'We've only got Lipton's or Tetley's.'

'Earr-ll Grrr-ey.' Dorothea enunciated elaborately, as if for a child or imbecile.

'Never heard o' it, dearie. Ye sure that's the name?' The queue was becoming fractious and she cast an anxious glance over Dorothea's shoulder. 'I'll just give you a cup out of the pot. OK?' Without waiting for an answer, she poured a cup of tar-black tea into a thick mug and handed it to Dorothea. 'Milk 'n' sugar at the end o' the counter. One and ninepence, love.' Dorothea paid up and bore her tray across to the beaded curtain. She poked her head through it, as if in search of nothing more than an empty seat. It was a small ante-room and Hugh, facing the curtained opening, saw her at once.

She saw how his eyes widened in horror and his gaze fell. *He can't even bear to look at me.* Her vindictive purpose sharpened. She pushed through the curtain and with three strides was in their corner.

'What's up, old man? You look like you've seen a ghost?' Colin had his back to Dorothea.

'Mind if I join you, fellows? There's not another seat in the place. I can sit here.' She indicated a tiny shelf covering hot pipes in the corner.

Both boys sprang up to offer her a chair, insisting that one of them would take the shelf. She did not protest.

Oh, damn! She's bound to discover that Hugh's doesn't have a partner and change her mind about me. Colin groaned inwardly.

I hope to God she doesn't ask me who I am going with. Col thinks I'm not going and if he says so to her she might decide to throw him over and ask me after all. I promised Patsy I wouldn't tell a soul. Hell's teeth! It's rotten luck her coming in here just now. Hugh tried to smile blandly at Dorothea as he squeezed his bottom on to the corner shelf. The wood was rather hot from the pipes below and the discomfort of toasted thighs added to his anxiety.

For a few moments there was silence round the tiny table as all three ate. Each would have been surprised if they could have been privy to the thoughts of the other two. At last, Dorothea opened the batting:

'There's been such a to-do in Chattan this morning.'

'Can I get you another cup of tea, Dorrie?'

'I'm going to have an ice cream for afters. Would you like one?'

At the dreaded word *Chattan*, both boys had jumped up as if their pants were on fire – which was not far from the case for poor Hugh. She declined both offers and waited impatiently till they returned to the table.

'You'll never guess what's happened at Chattan,' she recommenced doggedly. Unable to think of another way to forestall her, they waited apprehensively. 'The Gusset – Miss Goldsmith, the warden – has *forbidden* one of the room parties. She says the theme is blasphemous, that it's offensive to the Christian religion. She is *so* sanctimonious. It's such a shame, the girls concerned don't have a room-party to go to now. It's much too late to do any other decorations and anyway they're all too fed up about it. They're just cancelling the whole thing and having a girls' night out instead. They were asking us all to spread the word in case any of the escorts hadn't heard.' She flicked a glance at Hugh and saw his gaze sharpen.

Colin sucked in a sympathetic breath. 'My God! That's jolly hard luck. What an old prig! It's well named Chastity Hall. But what on earth *was* the theme that upset her so much? I mean, what could have been so bad?'

'The Gusset said it glorified the devil and outraged propriety - or something.'

'Really.' Colin whistled. 'So what was it?'

'The theme was *Hell*.'

'Hell? You mean, Hades? The fiery pit? What a great idea! I wish I'd seen the decorations – I bet they had horned beasts and hideous monsters – I saw a great fresco in the cathedral in Florence last summer. What a damned shame it's been squashed.'

'Yes, well ...' Dorothea sneaked a glance at Hugh. He had gone very pale and was scoring lines in the tablecloth with an unused fork. 'Luckily, it doesn't affect us, Col. Did you manage to get me anything decent for my corsage tonight?'

'Did my best, old girl,' he muttered uneasily, glancing at Hugh. Really the old chap seemed to be taking it quite badly. He had definitely said he didn't mind, but now that Dorothea was here, rubbing his nose in it, he was clearly finding it unpalatable. To Colin's relief, Dorothea pushed away the untouched tea and rose.

'I must be off. Tons to do before the big event.' Now that she had delivered her bombshell, she wanted nothing more than to get away from them. Her heart was hammering so hard she felt sure they must hear. Her voice came out as little more than a squeak. 'See you tonight, Col.' She bolted out, sending the beaded curtain rattling.

'Well, that's a turn-up for the book!' Colin stared after her. 'Fancy the warden actually cancelling a room-party like that! I tell you, that place is more like a convent than a hall of residence. If you ask me, that woman needs dragged kicking and screaming into the twentieth century. I wonder if anyone we know was going to it.'

Hugh trudged along Market Street silently, hands in pockets, shoulders hunched. Colin tried to initiate conversation on a range of subjects but each met a stone wall. Finally he made his best offer: 'Fancy a spin in the old lady? Weather's getting better and we don't have Lost 'n' Found this afternoon, remember? Old Fossil's got to go to some meeting. Some *fossils' forum!*' This comic gem was wasted on his dismal friend. 'We can take a few hours and explore a bit, if you like. I've got enough money left off the postal order to put some more juice in her. You won't even have to lend me money for petrol!'

But even this rare inducement failed. Hugh looked vaguely at Colin then turned away to cross the road, his throwaway farewell only just audible. Something about the library and the philosophy assignment. Colin sighed. There was no doubt about it: Hugh had been very odd all week. Hugh suddenly retraced his steps and called across the street to Colin: 'If anyone comes to Sally's this afternoon looking for me, tell them I'll be in the upstairs reading room of the Library.'

'Are you expecting anyone?'

But Hugh was striding away again, heading for the University Library on South Street. His head was a jumble of half-formed thoughts and he needed a place of sanctuary to sort them out. Dorothea's rapid exit after her startling announcement had precluded all possibility of finding out more. By the time he turned into South Street, he had decided that he must go round to Chattan and try to speak to Patsy; then, as he neared the Library, he decided that was a bad idea – Caroline might see him and wonder what he was doing there, what the cancellation of the room party had to do with *him*.

Patsy had been adamant that no-one was to know until he turned up on the night. But if the room-party was cancelled, did it matter any more? Or would Patsy prefer to keep it a secret forever – a secret that came to nothing? Surely she would get in touch to tell him about the cancellation? Perhaps not. Hugh thought of her off-hand approach to the corsage question, quite unlike any other girl he knew. She might just drop the whole thing and rely on the grapevine.

120

And what of Caroline's escort from down-on-the-farm? Indeed *two* escorts, two yokels coming to squire Caroline and her pigtailed pal. Presumably, Caroline would telephone home and break the bad news to them. Hugh felt a small glow of glee: at least *that* wasn't going to happen. He would have another six weeks till the end of term before she would be seeing any brawny farming lads again.

He found himself in the entrance hall of the old building and hesitated. His exit line to Colin about the philosophy assignment had been no more than a cover: he could not imagine concentrating on anything so abstract when there were so many pressing real concerns.

'Can I help you, sir?' The voice was light and breathy, though the young man was tall and muscular. Hugh remembered his conversation with Elspeth earlier in the week. This must be her *dishy librarian*, he who *always seems to know just which books you need, even which chapters from which books to use.* Half an hour later, he was ensconced in the upper reading room with five books and a list of recommended extracts.

As the afternoon wore away, he alternated between forcing himself to copy reams from the books and sloping off outside to struggle with his pipe and grapple with his anxieties. The medical faculty labs and lecture rooms were quite close and twice – at four and five o'clock – he slipped up to the courtyard with the grand old tree and looked for Patsy among the students coming out of lectures and tutorials. But she was nowhere to be seen. He considered phoning Chattan but was afraid this might betray their secret. If Patsy was not in, one of her friends might take the call.

He packed up his notes and wandered dejectedly out on to South Street at six o'clock when the Library closed. He thought of going back to Sally's to watch Colin, and all the other chaps who were going to the Ball, getting ready. There was always a charged air of excitement on Ball nights. As he came out on to North Street, he glanced over at the tiny cinema opposite Quad tower. It was advertising the latest James Bond.

And so it was that, while the C Floor bejantines were putting the finishing touches to a spectacular room-party, bodies were being bathed and perfumed, hair was being curled and straightened, faces were being powdered and painted, girlish dreams were being dreamed and Patsy was looking forward with mischievous pleasure to the moment when her escort would be revealed: so it was, that Hugh Appleby–Bodington, The Apple-Pie himself, for whom a starring role was lined up, was sitting in the back row of the cinema, feeling sorry for himself and settling down to spend his evening with a box of *Maltesers* and two showings of *From Russia with Love*.

Weighed down by *Kate's* haggis pies, Colin plopped himself down in his armchair and contemplated the pile of books on his desk. Of course, he *meant* to take up either the Descartes or the Locke, spurred on by Hugh's reminder of the metaphysics assignment. But somehow it was an Isaac Asimov – another of his favourite sci-fi writers - that ended up in his lap. Two hours slipped away while he ventured into unknown galaxies with unimaginable life forms. A burst of winter sunshine through the astragal window created a dappled diamond on the wall beside him. It broke his concentration briefly but he plunged back into the last chapter of the short book, racing greedily towards the ending.

As the enchantment of the story subsided, he felt restless. He looked out of the window, down to *the old lady* in the car park. He consulted his watch: a good two hours till he needed to start getting ready. He snatched his duffle coat off the bed, checked for car keys in its pockets, then bounded down the two flights of stairs and out into the chilly, bright afternoon.

Where to? He looked up and saw black clouds to the east: not the coast road then. The sky was definitely lighter in the north and west. He had no map, no idea what lay in that direction, but he did have the soul of an adventurer and the confidence of the inexperienced. Thinking to see if Hugh had got over his hump and wanted to join him, he drove up to the library and ran up the stairs to the reading room whistling – to the disapproval of the senior librarian and the admiring interest of the junior one. But there was only a large, pasty-faced girl in one corner and five open books lying on a table in another. The clock on the reading-room mantelpiece gave out four tinkling chimes and a sad little sigh at the end of them. Colin hurried to recoup what was left of his afternoon.

He headed out of town towards Leuchars, thinking to skirt the airfield and see if anything interesting was happening, but there were roadworks at the turning, with a stationary line of traffic, so he raced past and on towards Cupar, a small town he had never been in. He had only acquired his beloved car in November – a nineteenth birthday present from his doting mother. So far his jaunts had been all round the *East Neuk of Fife* coastline; this inland expedition was uncharted territory. He felt his adrenaline surge as the old lady rose to the occasion and reached her top speed of sixty-five. Cupar was upon them in a flash, the little streets quiet in the darkening late afternoon, shopkeepers beginning to pull in awnings, a few office-workers dawdling home towards the weekend. He passed quarter of an hour idling round the little town, noting only two points of interest: a very old pub purporting to brew its own beer and a car body-repair workshop with a yard full of old cars, not unlike the old lady. *Could be useful – must remember that if any bits fall off her.* The violent shudders that accompanied her starting-up and switching-off performances must be putting considerable strain on the rusty bodywork. *Such a responsibility!* Colin sighed happily. He relished the burden even if he did nothing about its demands.

He was tempted and fell as he passed the promising pub again. *In the interests of geographic exploration,* he murmured as he parked the old lady. The beer was wonderful and the conversation he eavesdropped on, as he leaned against the bar, was quite entertaining, despite the Fife accents. Two young bank-clerks were celebrating a big win at the bookie's and debating how to keep it from their wives. One favoured simply giving it all to the slate here in the pub – it would buy their drinks for the next year at least. The other felt they needed a bit more flexibility: may be they could set up a secret account in another bank in another town. On one thing they were agreed: it would go to fund a reminder of happier, freer times; it was not to be swallowed up by the baby's piggy bank or the wife's new spring outfit. As he came out into the almost dark street, Colin made a mental note not to get married and shackled for many years to come. He glanced at his watch – almost five. He really should head back soon, but the beer had given him a rush of energy and a desire to flex his driving skills. As long as he was at Chattan by seven-fifteen. Dorrie wouldn't mind his being a *little* late.

The car roared out of Cupar and seemed to take the road towards Perth of its own volition. Colin had been once in the Highlands as a child, accompanying his parents to a grouse-shooting house-party, but he had only vague memories of it. The very word *Perth* was exotic, conjuring up *The Monarch of the Glen*, that iconic painting of a stag at bay. Singing *The Happy Wanderer* at the top of his voice, he swept through another small place, its streets almost deserted: Newberry? New-something? He was through it too fast to read the signs. The old lady was loving it, roaring gleefully at every touch of the accelerator, swinging round corners like a dancer only just in control of her legs. It was quite dark now and the swoop of the headlights added to the sense of being in a bubble of excitement, like a fairground ride.

He was on the razor sharp bend before he had time to register the Z warning sign. As he plunged into it, he swore and braked desperately. The car checked and made it out of the first bend but the second one, twisting away in the opposite direction, was too much for her. Her back wheels broke away into a shrieking skid. He had no experience of skids and could only slam the brake pedal to the floor, close his eyes and scream, hanging on to the steering wheel like a lifeline. Every nerve in his body was tensed for the crash and he could barely believe it when he realised that the car was stationary and – except for a slight tinkling of glass – silent, the engine stalled. He opened a terrified eye and saw a gate inches away from the bonnet. Opening the other eye, he saw the lights of a small lodge at the side of a wide drive and read the sign on the impressive wrought iron gate: *Pitcurran House*.

It was only by means of the lodge lights that he could see anything. The sound of breaking glass had been the old lady's protruding headlights crushing against the gate: the car was sitting right across the middle of the road in complete darkness apart from one flickering back-light. Even as this horrifying fact dawned on him, he saw the headlights of a car coming out of Abernethy village and heading towards the Z-bend at a steady speed. He swung his legs over the driver's door and leapt out, running down the grass verge towards the oncoming car, desperate to attract its attention before it came round the bend. His black duffle coat and dark grey trousers barely showed up in the gloom. The driver, slowing into the bend, caught a glimpse of the pale moon that was Colin's terrified face, realised that there must be a hazard ahead and braked even more strongly. But it was never going to be enough: a gut-wrenching crash resounded over the quiet countryside and, once again, the sound of glass breaking – this time much more violently.

CHAPTER ELEVEN: ALICE AND MARJORY

Morag carefully unpacked the little suitcase which lay on James' bed. She surveyed the contents and came to a decision: if she repacked them differently, there would be room. She was worried about her boys going hungry. They might be too busy enjoying themselves to eat properly at the Ball and she did not trust hotel breakfasts, never having had one. She had baked a batch of large fruit scones and thought she might make room in the case for a couple. She glanced at the bedside clock: five past four. Pete intended running out of his last class the minute the lecturer stopped speaking and cycling as if the hounds of hell were on his heels, breaking all his own records and being home by quarter to five at the latest. James was out in the field with Jed, keeping an eye on two ewes in labour. Jed and Pete had both been right: they would have their first lambs this weekend though whether Pete's hot tip or the other ewe would win was not yet known. Jerry Dempsey was expected at half past four to relieve James who would have his bath first, giving Morag time to stoke the fire and heat up more hot water for Pete.

As she headed downstairs to the kitchen for the scones, the telephone shrilled, startling her horribly: it was one of the things she hated about the damned device. She had a moment of fear, remembering yesterday's shenanigans; then her brow cleared. *Of course! It will be Faye Dempsey. She promised to phone when Jerry was setting off. That's good – he's goin' to be early. I'll just have time to put the scones in the case and go and run the bath.* She picked up the receiver almost confidently and announced their number, adding helpfully: 'It's Morag here.'

There was a moment's silence, then she thought she heard an exclamation that sounded like - surely not, right out loud on the telephone! It had definitely sounded like *'Bugger!'* What was the world coming to? She remembered Caroline coming out with the same crudity in the parlour, that Sunday she had come over to tell them about the Ball – but, at least, *she* had had the grace to apologise. There was to be no chance of that this time: the receiver at the other end had already been slammed down.

Some twenty-odd miles away, Alice was berating herself. *What was I thinking of? Of course, he wouldn't be home from college yet.* She had been so keen to make the call while there was time. There had been a note from her mother, lying on the kitchen table, when she had come home from school. *Will be a little later than usual. Having a meeting with my tutor after the class!!*

The two exclamation marks were a sign of Marjory's excitement about the meeting. She had told Alice all about her high hopes. *We haven't all had your opportunities, Alice. It's all been so easy for you.* Alice wished she could hand these 'easy opportunities' over to her mother and get on with what *she* wanted to do with her life.

Today she was less interested in Marjory's career plans than in her late return. Ever since she had found the note with the Fintry Farm telephone number yesterday evening, Alice had been pondering what it could mean. She had expected her mother to bring up the subject of Farmer Pete – why else would her mother have been talking to his father? – but Marjory had not mentioned it.

By the end of a very unproductive school day – both Dorothea's and Alice's studies were suffering from lack of concentration – she had made up her mind to phone Fintry Farm herself and ask to speak to Pete, see if he knew what was going on between their parents. He was not living under the same draconian rule as she was: there could be no harm in his receiving a phone call from a girl. He probably got lots of them – a depressing thought.

But as soon as she had heard Morag's motherly voice, she had realised her mistake. *What an idiot!* She glared at the telephone and tried to think when her next opportunity might be. Maybe she could use a public phone box sometime over the weekend. Then she remembered her baby-sitting duties tonight. She could use the Mortons' phone, once the children were settled down for the night.

'Hello, dear. Was that someone on the phone? Was it for me?'

Alice had not heard the car coming into the drive or her mother entering the house. She moved away from the telephone table and hurried through into the kitchen, calling over her shoulder; 'Just Millie, confirming the time for tonight.'

Marjory might have accepted this but, unfortunately for Alice, a telltale scrap of paper fluttered out of the pocket of her school skirt as she whirled round towards the kitchen. Marjory bent tidily to pick it up and saw her own handwriting: it was the note she had made yesterday after her call to Fintry Farm. Now, what was *that* doing in Alice's pocket?

'Fancy a slice of that banana loaf I made yesterday, mum?'

'Thank you, dear.' Marjory's face was grim as she came slowly into the kitchen. 'I think you and I need to have a little chat.'

My goodness, but didn't they look splendid! Morag wiped a tear away. Pete, tall and dashing, the romantic Highland hero; James, muscled and sturdy, the clansman warrior. Even Jed was beaming, catching the glamour of the moment as he put his arm round her waist to accompany the lads out to the car. The three men had had a grand car cleaning session last night, bonding happily in the torch-lit task, and now the Zodiac was gleaming, a fitting chariot to take the two Princes Charming to the Ball. The well-cared-for engine purred into life, James at the wheel, Pete with the map and Caroline's instructions on his knee, grinning at his mother as she called last-minute instructions about the contents of the suitcase.

'… and have a wonderful time … and give my love to Caroline … and don't forget to …'

They were gone, cruising regally down the farm track and out into the road. 'Well, that's that then.' Jed gave her waist a squeeze. 'They'll be back tomorrow, love. Not to worry.'

They stood for a moment in the falling darkness, strangely bereft, as if they had just waved farewell to emigrants bound for the Antipodes. Then Morag gave a brisk nod. 'You'd best get back over to the barn and make sure Jerry's coping with the milking.' Jed, a last-minute convert to the glamorous expedition, was now reluctant to end the magic moment of the departure. She laughed and gave him a little push.

It was strange cooking the evening meal just for two and stranger still to sit, just the two of them, at the big table eating it. Jerry had declined to join them and had driven off, once all the work was done, back to Inshaig to get spruced up for his usual Friday night date with his girlfriend, promising to be back at five-thirty tomorrow morning.

It felt like being the only customers in a big restaurant. There was a tendency to whisper and the cutlery seemed to make a terrible noise. When Jed let out his usual belch at the end of the meal, he blushed. It was a relief when it was over and he could take himself off to the office.

There seemed no point in lighting the fire in the snug since there was no-one to disturb her in the kitchen. Evening tasks complete, she settled down in the old armchair at the side of the stove and took up her knitting. She glanced at the clock: half past seven. The Ball would have started; the boys would have made their debut, stealing the show in their beautiful Highland dress regalia. Caroline would be bowled over, no doubt looking gorgeous herself. It would be a glittering occasion and Pete would be swept off his feet. Silly schoolgirls with silly names would be no threat. Everything was going to work out just fine. She thought no more of the strange phone call earlier and its rude ending. She dozed a little in the heat until the telephone aroused her, followed almost immediately by Jed's shout.

'Morag! Are ye there, love? It's that woman again – that Mrs Bond. Can you come through? She's asking to speak to you.'

..Alice slammed the front door and made a great deal of noise bringing her bike out of the garage. Watching her out the window, Marjory shook her head. Really, it was too bad of Alice to start behaving like this so near to her exams. Marjory had been congratulating herself that the firm line she had taken this year had paid off and that Alice herself realised that it would be worth it. But now, here she was, throwing a positive tantrum and all over some boy she barely knew.

As soon as she had seen what the slip of paper falling out of Alice's pocket was, Marjory had surmised that the weird phone call from Fintry Farm yesterday had something to do with Alice. She soon winkled out the truth. An ugly scene had ensued.

'So, you've been seeing the boy from this farm? The one who left his bike here a few weeks ago?'

'I've seen him twice, both times here!'

'Here? You've had him in the house!'

'No, of course not. I spoke to him for a wee while in the garage the night he fetched his bike. And then, he was passing on his way home from college a few days ago and we just chatted for a few minutes at the gate. That's all, for heaven's sake!'

Unfortunately for Alice, Millie had chosen that moment to phone and ask if Alice could come over as soon as possible and help with the children's teatime and bath. That Alice had lied earlier about the phone call was immediately obvious.

'What are you up to, Alice? Why did you lie to me? Were you phoning this farm-boy? Why?'

'Oh, for God's sake, Mum. Nothing's going on. I told you. I just found your note with the phone number on it and I was just …'

'You're sure? Tell me you've not broken your promise and been out with him?'

'Fat chance of that with you as my jailer!'

Alice had stomped upstairs to change out of school uniform. The banana bread had remained untouched and they had not spoken again before she had flounced off to babysit the Morton brood.

Marjory replayed the scene in the kitchen in her mind as she stood at the bay window. When she came to Alice's last angry retort, calling her a 'jailer', she felt a sudden, sick clutch in her stomach, exactly like yesterday when she had read the flyleaf of the Pulitzer book. Once again, she was catapulted back into her miserable youth.

My God! Is that what I am doing to Alice? Just as Mavis did to me? Except, of course, that Alice was not the cowed captive she had been, so racked with guilt about her mother, so browbeaten by her father and so pathetically grateful to Aunt Mavis, that she had accepted every rule and shackle. Alice was fighting back. Indeed Alice was ahead of the game: she had analysed her mother's motives and, in the heat of their argument, had thrown them in Marjory's face.

'I don't care about getting these blasted Highers anyway. It's you who's so keen on them – just because you don't have any yourself. For God's sake, go and be a 'mature student' and get a degree for yourself. Stop trying to make me do it for you!'

'But you can't just throw away your chances like this. It's downright sinful, you ungrateful little brat.'

'I'm not throwing away any chances. I won't get the damned things anyway. I hate all that stuff and I'm useless at it. I want to learn to cook - really cook, I mean. Become a chef, maybe, or run my own catering business.'

'But only men are chefs.'

'That's rubbish. Women are getting in on all the male professions nowadays. There are some women chefs - why not? You're so hopelessly old-fashioned, mother!'

Marjory stood for a long time, seeing in the darkening window images of her blighted youth and, behind them, the adult she had become, as described by her daughter less than an hour ago: trying to live her life through her child, imposing her own ambitions. And she saw what Alice could not, being ignorant of the true story of her birth: she was recreating her own life, as it had been at Alice's age. She had told herself she was just making sure that Alice concentrated on her studies *for her own good* but was it something more like revenge? That unlovely trait in human nature which gets satisfaction from seeing someone else go through the same suffering, even someone innocent, even someone loved? Had she been letting a long backward shadow from that fateful night in the African bush reach across eighteen years?

She wandered into the kitchen, opened and closed a few cupboards, but could not think of anything she wanted to cook for her meal. In the end, she just stood leaning against the sink, drinking tea and eating the two slices of banana bread. Even in her distracted state of mind, she could not help noticing that it tasted delicious and the texture was perfect. She thought of all the cooking and baking Alice did. She had never really paid much attention to it, dismissing it as a hobby or a ploy to avoid studying. But, considering it now, she acknowledged that her daughter had a talent. She visualised Alice in charge of the kitchen of a big hotel, chef's hat topping her dark hair, dozen's of minions scurrying at her bidding as she prepared amazing dishes; or maybe the director of a successful company, catering banquets and select business dinners in The City. It wasn't quite the career she had planned for her daughter but … if it was what she wanted …

She was beginning herself to taste the sweet freedom of pursuing a career path that beckoned invitingly. The fracas with Alice had swept away the excitement of her meeting with her tutor this afternoon but now she let it re-surface. She would be enrolling for O-level courses in September and a study plan was in place to make sure she would be ready. The tutor was as keen as she was herself: *Time to stop playing at it, Mrs Band, with all these odds and ends of groups and classes: time to get yourself a real education. I know you can do it!* Alice was right: she did not need to live her life through her child; she was going to have a life of her own – at last.

For the next hour and a half, she mulled over these realisations, finally reaching a conclusion. A feeling of liberty and anticipation swept through her. She felt as if she and Alice were poised on side-by-side springboards in a swimming race, straining for the starter's pistol. She went back into the lounge and crossed to the cocktail cabinet. Alcohol had occasionally been her solace over the lonely years, and Mavis had not been averse to a consoling sherry now and then. But Marjory had rarely drunk in celebration except for frugal festivities at Christmas and New Year. Now she poured herself a large brandy and ginger, recklessly tipping in two cocktail cherries.

'Cheers!' she toasted her reflection in the mirror. 'Let the games begin!'

The second drink fired her with the need to do something to celebrate her decision, to declare it publicly. She thought of phoning Alice at the Morton's. They had parted on such bad terms: would Alice believe her - or even speak to her? *How can I prove to her that I really mean it? That her sentence is over and the jail is open?*

Wandering restlessly through to the kitchen again, she saw the note still lying among the cake crumbs on the table. Now, that was an idea. He had seemed a perfectly nice boy, after all.

Jed held out the phone to Morag as she hesitantly entered the office. 'It won't bite!' he mouthed. Then, 'Oh, all right,' as she took it from him and flapped her hand in dismissal. He was well aware that she hated anyone watching or listening to her while she struggled with the phone.

'Yes.' Her voice was cracked and anxious. She swallowed and made a huge effort. 'It's Morag McCaff...' Despite the swallow and the effort, it was still little more than a nervous squawk.

At the other end of the line, Marjory frowned. *Here we go again! What is wrong with their phone?* Then it dawned on her: there had been nothing wrong with the phone line when the man had been speaking; perhaps the wife had a speech impediment or a throat infection. Marjory spoke slowly and kindly, as if to a child: 'This is Marjory Band here, Mrs McCa...' She realised she still hadn't fully caught the name from either the man or the woman and she hurried on. 'I know you tried to phone me yesterday and I think I know why now. I've been speaking to my daughter and I gather that she and your son are becoming friends. I was wondering how you felt about that.

'F-f-felt about it?' stuttered Morag, confirming Marjory's suspicions of a speech problem. *Tell her! Now's your chance!*

In her head, it all seemed perfectly simple: she wouldn't even mention Caroline; Pete was a dedicated young lad, too focused on his studies and his career to have time for girls at the moment; she wanted to protect Marjory's daughter from getting hurt, in case the lass was setting store by a chance meeting; no-one knew better than she how charming her son was and how easy it would be for a girl to read too much into a brief encounter – yes, she had seen it happen before – and she wanted to save young Alice from this.

But, while the sentences rolled through her mind, she continued to open and shut her mouth like a fish on a hook and with about as much sound coming out. The receiver was slippery in her sweaty palms.

Marjory tried a few more times to coax the strange woman into intelligible speech. Then, she had an idea.

'Look, Mrs McCa.... How would it be if I came to visit and we talked it over, woman-to-woman, as it were? If something is happening between Alice and your son, then I'd like to meet you and talk about it. Alice is only seventeen, you know, and ...'

'Yes!' Morag almost blasted Marjory's eardrum. 'Yes! That's exactly what I think. 'You see ...' she lapsed once more into incoherent mumbles.

'Right.' Marjory was beginning to wonder if this woman was quite normal. Maybe she had better go up to this farm and check the situation out. Her original intention had been simply to smooth the path for Alice and encourage the friendship with the lad - a way of making it up to Alice for the past year and proof that she really had had a change of heart. Now she was wondering if she might be a little hasty. After all, she knew nothing of this boy or his family: perhaps it would be best to check them out first before saying anything to Alice. Certainly, the mother was rather odd.

'I'll find your farm on the map, I'm sure, but it's too dark now to try. How would it be if I came over mid morning? Tomorrow, I mean?'

'Tomorrow? You're coming here?' The yelp reminded Marjory of a dog whose paw has been trodden on.

131

'Is that not convenient?'

Morag nodded vigorously. Although she could not communicate her thoughts over the phone, her brain was now working quite clearly. There could be a lot of mileage in this woman-to-woman chat. She would have to try and get Jed out of the way. She didn't want him knowing about her meddling, but it could be possible. The boys were not expected home till dinner-time or later.

'That's fine,' she managed. 'C-come at half past t-ten. Are you sure you'll f-f-find us? You take the road out of F-Forfar. Well …well … it's the one …'

Marjory cut in swiftly. The idea of this woman attempting to give directions was alarming. 'Don't worry at all. I have a very good map and' - she remembered one of Mavis' favourite sayings – 'a good Scots tongue in my head! I'll see you tomorrow at half past ten. Thank you. Goodbye.'

Morag listened to the click as the phone went down at the other end; then jumped as the dialing tone buzzed loudly in her ear. She returned the receiver to the cradle slowly. *Well! Fancy that! The Silver Band coming here. A chance to talk to her face-to-face.* It was better than she could have hoped. She had no qualms about the visit. Meeting a real person on home territory held no terrors. She just needed to find a reason to get Jed out of the way tomorrow morning. She would bake a nice cake and put the parlour fire on first thing to make sure the room was nice and warm by half-past ten. Jed never went into the parlour in the morning so he would not notice.

She was mulling over ideas for getting rid of Jed, when the man himself came though to the kitchen and wrinkled his nose appreciatively. 'I smell somethin' awfy good! Are we having company tomorrow?'

'No, no. I just thought to bake something a wee bit special to welcome the lads home.'

'They'll no' have been gone twenty-four hours. It's no' exactly the prodigal son.'

'No, but so much will have happened to them. They'll have so much to tell us.'

'True.' He sat down with her to their last-thing-at-night pot of tea, chatting about the four new lambs that had made their appearance within minutes of each other. 'And Pete was right – wait till I tell him – his ewe was first! Only by four minutes though! Jerry and I had a good laugh about it.'

'You're getting on fine with Jerry, then? He's easy to work with?'

'Oh, aye, a fine lad. Kens what's what and just gets on with it. Oh, that reminds me. I forgot to tell you. He's invited me over to Inshaig tomorrow morning to see their new combine harvester. It's one of the ones James and I are thinking about. Jerry says I can have a good look at it, even have a shot at driving it. So, once we're finished up here for the morning, I'll go over with him. I'll just get a ride over with him and walk back – it'll give me a chance to have a good look at the boundary field before we start ploughing next month.'

'That's a great idea, love.' Her enthusiasm was out of proportion to her usual interest in combine harvesters, but he was too glad to see her back on form to notice. She had irritably turned aside all his efforts last night to find out what was bothering her. But now, it looked like the disturbing matter of the Bond woman had been cleared up and his Morag was herself again. He beamed back.

'Ye got that funny woman on the phone sorted out, then, whatever her problem was.'

'Oh, aye. It was nothing to worry about. Just a wee misunderstandin', a wrong number and a bad line.'

Alice laughed out loud at the final gag, as the credits for the comedy show rolled up the television screen. She looked at the neat piles of unopened books and jotters on the Mortons' coffee table; then she picked up the *Radio Times*. The next programme was a news discussion – well, anything was better than the accusing piles on the table.

The first two hours of babysitting had gone by in a blur: a messy eating session with three under-fives, snatching no more than a few mouthfuls of the bland boiled fish and mashed potatoes herself, mentally adding herbs and a béchamel sauce with a cheese-and-breadcrumb topping; an even messier bathing session; catching and confining all three of them into their cots; reading bedtime stories, finding precious scraps of dirty, soggy blanket and priceless chewed-up old teddies, kissing them good-night, switching on subdued overnight lights, leaving their room, then returning several times with increasing firmness that finally brought a result. Three demanding little monsters were transformed into sweet-smelling, softly-snuffling angels.

Once the children were settled, she unpacked her school satchel mechanically and had almost begun her *eeny-meeny-miny-mo routine* when she recalled her idea to phone Pete. She was halfway across the room to the phone when she remembered his plans for tonight: some occasion in St Andrews, he had said, sounding unenthusiastic. Some tie-up between his college and the university there, a special lecture perhaps, which he could not get out of. Now that her mother had found out about him, the whole thing was doomed anyway. It had been the one light on Alice's horizon these past few weeks, one distraction from the looming horror of the Highers exams and the even greater horror when the results came out. Even if, by some miracle, she did manage to get in to a university, she knew that she would have clawed her way to the pinnacle – and beyond - of her academic ability: the chances of her getting through the first year of a university course, let alone ever achieving a degree, were laughably slim. The very thought of trying filled her with the depressing certainty of failure.

At the sound of a car drawing into the drive, she leapt up, switched off the television and hastily opened several books and jotters at random. The farewell white dot on the TV screen only just faded in time.

'Look at you!' marvelled Millie. 'Still at it at this time of night. Your mother was just telling me how well you're doing this year. She says you're bound to get into St Andrews or Edinburgh, though we favour Aberdeen, don't we, Tom?' She and Tom had met in Aberdeen when she was doing her nursing training and he was a pharmacology student. 'Goodness! What's the matter, dear?'

Alice was stuffing books and jotters into the satchel but they were buckling and catching on each other, refusing to pack in properly; her eyes had filled with tears and a sob escaped. Millie put an arm round her shoulder. 'Pre-exam nerves, dear. They say it's a good sign. People who are going to do well always have them.'

Alice jerked out of her embrace and whisked through to the lobby to collect her coat. Millie caught Tom's eye as she re-packed the satchel and snapped the lock shut. 'Best walk Alice home, dear. I know she's got her bike but it's late - *and* it's foggy now. Just wheel the bike. I don't think she should ride it home.'

Alice's would much rather have been alone to recover from Millie's suffocating assumptions, but she found herself walking along the foggy street beside Tom who was pushing her bike. Thankfully, *he* was not disposed to analyse her state of mind or make predictions about her academic future. They said nothing until they reached the Bands' gate when he pressed a pound note into her hand. 'Have a wee treat with that. Keep your pecker up. It'll be all over soon.' She demurred: Millie had already paid her for baby-sitting. But he just patted her shoulder and winked at her, before striding off into the fog.

The outside light flared and the door opened. Marjory came out with the garage key in her hand and a smile on her face. 'Let me see to the bike, darling. You go in and get warm. Brrr! What a horrid night! I'm just heating some milk. Let's have hot chocolate by the fire, maybe even a wee swirl of cream on top.' Her voice was light and guileless but Alice was instantly on the alert. *Now what's she up to? Can't she just let me get away to bed in peace without starting on me at this time of night? God, I'm so fed up of bloody adults!*

But half an hour later, as the two women sat by the dying embers of the fire, she was very glad that she had agreed to the hot drink. At first, it seemed incredible, like the answer to some crazy prayer – except that Alice had never prayed for such a miracle, never envisaged such a *volte-face* from her mother. There was much that Marjory did *not* say: she explained that her education in Africa had been of a poor standard, curtailed by her early marriage and pregnancy but she did *not* divulge – or even hint at - the real reason for her flight to Scotland; she explained Mavis' restrictive regime as only to be expected from a churchy old maid landed with the care of a young girl and her newborn baby but she did *not* describe the spectre of her father's disapproval which had lived with them, a watchful presence, for eleven years.

'So, you see darling, when you reached the age I was, when I had you, and I saw you with all these wonderful chances for an education and a career ...'

'But there are other careers, Mum.' *It's just another tirade, another guilt trip.*

Marjory held up her hand. 'I know, dear, I know. That's what I've been thinking about all evening. You were right: I *have* been trying to live my life through you, to make you do all the things I never got a chance to do. I couldn't believe you would just throw it all away ...'

'But you can do them yourself now, Mum.'

'I know! I *am* going to do it. I had a meeting with one of the tutors at the college and he has it all planned for me. I'm going to start studying for my O-levels in September, then on to Highers and maybe even university.'

'I know – you told me about it - be a 'mature student.'

'Oh, Alice, I am so excited about it!

'I'm glad for you, really I am, Mum. I just wish I felt about it the way you do.' Alice drained her cup and began wearily to rise. She *was* glad for her mother but it made no difference to her own woes. Her mother pushed her gently back down on to the hearth-rug.

'I understand – better than anyone – what it's like to want to do something with your life and have it frustrated by older people who mean well but just don't understand. I see now that your cooking and baking are more than just a hobby for you. You're really good at it and you love doing it. It's ...' She remembered a French word she had heard at her writing class from a man who had spent time working abroad. 'It's your *métier!*'

135

'What are you saying, Mum?' Alice was afraid to breathe, afraid to believe what she was hearing.

'I'm saying that, if you want to train to become a chef, then I'll support you. I won't force you to go to university. Maybe it'll have to be me that does that in this family, eh?'

'I can go to Dough School?'

'Well, dear, I'm wondering if we can't aim a bit higher than that. You don't want to be a Domestic Science teacher, surely? No? Well, there you are!' Alice had shuddered. 'There's a man in my writing class who's a chef. He's got this idea to write a novel situated in a restaurant with each chapter revolving round a particular dish on its menu. What do you think of that?' It was from him that she had learned the word, *métier*.

'It sounds brilliant but what's it got to do with me?'

'Well, I think he trained to be a chef somewhere in England, then he worked in hotels and restaurants in France. Oh, and he talked of doing a … a … "Gordon Blue Course". Something like that, in London. Have you heard of such a thing, dear?'

'*Cordon Bleu!* You bet I have!' Alice was breathing again, but with difficulty. *I'm going to wake up soon. This can't be happening.* 'It's the best of the best of French *cuisine* – that's the term you use for different types of food from different parts of the world', as her mother looked blank.

'Another gap in my education, obviously.' But Marjory was grinning, not only because she was going to get the chance at last to fill so many of these sad gaps, but because she had it in her power to make her beloved child as happy as she was herself. 'What do you think, then, Alice? Shall I ask this chap's advice about the best way for you to get started on your chosen profession?' She felt a thrill: her daughter, with a *profession*, and an unusual one – at least for a woman. Already she was rehearsing how she would describe it to her various groups and classes, employing these new expressions: *métier, cordon bleu, cuisine*.

'But what about my Highers? Do I still have to do them?' Alice felt the need to shed the cold light of reality over the rosy scene her mother was laying out, to check it would not vanish like dreams upon awakening.

'I suppose you might as well sit them, since you've worked so hard this year. You must be going to do really well.'

Marjory recoiled from Alice's bark of harsh laughter. 'I haven't a chance, mum. Oh, I've tried, I really have, But I can't make head nor tail of the maths, my French proses are hopeless and, if I have to re-write another blasted critical appreciation of another boring poem or play, I think I'll kill myself!'

'I see,' said her mother slowly. 'I see. So you won't shed too many tears if you don't sit the exams? You'll not be too disappointed if I tell the head at The Morgan that we've agreed on a different career path for you and ...' Her teasing was smothered in an enormous hug.

Alice took herself off to bed, tripping lightly up the stairs, singing, in a way that made Marjory realise how different had been the dragging or stomping of the past months. *I've done the right thing. Thank God I saw it before the Highers. Who knows what Alice might have done?* Of course, her dramatic 'I'll kill myself' had been just youthful exaggeration; but, all the same, the force of Alice's feelings had shocked Marjory.

Of the boy from Fintry Farm they had not spoken. All thoughts of him had been driven out for Alice's head. As she took herself off to bed, it was filled instead with visions of gleaming kitchens, wonderfully equipped, their surfaces groaning with amazing ingredients. Tenuous romantic possibilities with handsome young farmers were eclipsed.

Marjory smiled as she thought of her proposed trip tomorrow. She was enjoying playing fairy godmother to her daughter, after a year of being the dragon at the gate. She was looking forward to seeing Alice's face when she gave her this extra gift.

CHAPTER TWELVE: PETE AND JAMES

Old Chattan was like a beehive anticipating the advent of the queen. Girls buzzed from room to room, calling out unfinished sentences, wheedling to borrow everything from lipsticks to lingerie, from emery boards to eyelash curlers. There was a complex pall of coal tar soap, musky perfume, Bostik glue, chicken casserole and treacle tart.

On B and C floors, girls in various stages of undress darted in and out the bathrooms and each others' bedrooms or posed in full fig up and down the corridors, jostling to get a look at themselves in the full-length mirrors on the landings. On D Floor, the warden and the domestic bursar were having a quiet little sherry in Miss Goldsmith's sitting-room and dwelling contentedly on how wonderful the common room looked with a blazing fire, two fine floral displays and the four-piece band just arriving and beginning to tune up in the corner beside the grand piano. In the basement, cook was congratulating her staff on a long hard day's work, preparing the food, decorating the tables and sprucing themselves up to look like real waitresses. Even on A Floor there was a low hum of dignified activity and the ladylike scent of Yardley's lavender was losing out to the astringent aroma of Balmain's *Vent Vert*. The Honours French magistrand had topped up her duty-free supply on the cross-channel ferry last summer.

'How do I look, Caro?' Caroline grinned. Elspeth's parents' idea of a ball-gown was a white dress and tartan sash, exactly like the one her mother wore for country dancing. Her rotund waist was buttressed by the broad sash, creating an illusion of voluptuous curves; her abundant hair had been released from its plait and Anne – whose own *gamin* hairstyle took only a couple of minutes to dry and fluff up – had spent hours piling Elspeth's tresses into elaborate loops on top of her head; the deep green eye-shadow matched the hues of the tartan; the ruby red lipstick echoed the roses of her corsage; and her blue eyes were snapping with excitement. She looked, thought Caroline, like a sonsie Scottish dolly in a Royal Mile tourist shop. She visualised James' stocky physique in full Highland dress.

'You and James are going to look absolutely perfect together!'

Elspeth dimpled happily and went off to see if there were any last minute touches to be put to the room party. Jennifer was re-gluing some of the lower paper flames which she had tripped over and pulled off the wall and the sharp smell of the glue mingled with the fruity, boozy smell coming from the hell-fire hooch which Patsy was stirring and sniffing.

138

Jennifer had made herself a stunning backless number in shimmering gold; Anne had followed up on her Audrey Hepburn look with a sleeveless shift in pale lilac silk; Patsy wore a creation, picked up in a second-hand shop in Belfast: a miniscule, A-line, black tunic with silver edging on the neck and skirt hem. A rope of chunky glass beads hung down lower than the tunic and her legs in glittering fishnet tights seemed to go all the way up to her freshly-shaved armpits.

'Your flowers are still lying on the hall table, Patsy. They're the only ones left.' One of other girls involved in the room party had come in, holding her own spray of purple fuchsias to her bosom and fiddling with the pin to attach it.

'Oh, yeah. I forgot about that carry-on.'

'Better hurry, then. It's nearly seven. Some of the men are arriving already. You don't want your chap to see the corsage he's paid a fortune for still lying there.'

'Not the best start to the evening, I suppose.' Patsy relinquished the punch ladle to Elspeth. 'See what you think, Elso. I'd favour a bit more vodka myself.'

There were several well-dressed young men at the foot of the stairs on D Floor, looking up hopefully for a first sighting of their ball partners. Two of the younger room-maids were running up and down the stairs, alerting the girls to the arrival of their escorts, and chattering excitedly. 'It's just like *Gone with the Wind*. Remember when Vivien Leigh came sweeping down the staircase and Clark Gable was standing at the bottom.'

Patsy breezed down, affording the waiting men a delightful view. Under the tiny black tunic and on top of the silver fishnet tights she wore gorgeous-Gussie frilly knickers. Sure enough, on the large table which had been specially set up for the corsages, there lay only one forlorn specimen. In the absence of any instructions from her, Hugh had played safe and ordered two large white rosebuds on a cloud of silvery foliage. Perfect for her outfit. 'Well done, little apple-pie,' she murmured as she lifted it out of its box, and held it against her flat front.

She leaned forward across the broad table towards the mirror and fiddled with the tiny gold safety pin, giving the fascinated young men a good back view of the white frilly knickers. 'That bunny has a fine scut!' exclaimed one wag. The group burst into laughter, hastily stifled as a knot of ball-gowned girls descended upon them.

Patsy slipped quickly past them, turning on the landing for a final glance down, to check that Hugh had not arrived. No sign of any farming men in kilts either. She stuck her head in at Caroline's room door: 'No sign of them yet. Jeez, don't you look good enough to eat!'

Caroline was putting the finishing touches to a hairstyle that had taken hours of effort: half an hour with a disgusting mess of egg-yolks and olive oil on it; then shampooed twice and conditioned with a bottle of brown ale – the bathroom still smelt like a brewery; left to dry naturally which had taken almost two hours; skilfully ironed by Elspeth; and finally set in four large rollers to create a flick at the ends. She had been sporting strips of sellotape on her brow for the past two hours and she was now peeling these off and contemplating the beautifully straight fringe in her desk mirror with great satisfaction.

'What do you think, Patso? It's almost as good as yours.'

'Not a frizzy curl in sight.' Patsy's eyes widened as Caroline rose and came out from behind the desk. Faye Dempsey was a fine seamstress with an interest in fashion rare in farming circles and, much as she loved her three rowdy sons, she specially loved having a daughter. Ever since she had been a baby, Caroline had always had pretty clothes, lovingly made by her mother. The challenge of dressing her daughter for her first Ball had been, for Faye, one of the most exciting aspects of Caroline going up to St Andrews University. She had spent months looking through magazines, adapting ideas and choosing the style. Red was Caroline's colour, especially in winter, so the choice of rich red velvet came easily. The dress had been completed at Christmas and Jerry, Matt and Jack had whistled and stamped in YF-type appreciation when Caroline had paraded round the parlour at Inshaig. It was smooth and fitting over the bosom, high at the neck, slashing straight across to her shoulders; the back had a deep cowl that hung open and low, almost to the waist, exposing shadowy glimpses of shoulder blades and below; the skirt hung straight and sleek and only when she walked did you realise that it was split all the way to mid-thigh at one side. It was utterly stunning.

'Yoiks!'

'Is it too much? Mum sometimes gets carried away.'

'It's fab! Told you so last night when we were trying them on. It's just, now you've done your hair an' your make-up an' all, are you sure it won't be too much for this poor, innocent farmer lad?'

'Let's hope so! What's the point, otherwise! No sign of them yet? It's nearly ten past seven.'

The tinkling demise of the old lady's headlamps had caused no more than a short puzzled glance between Arthur and Jean Menzies as they sat over the remains of their evening meal in Pitcurran Lodge; but the loud crunch of metal on metal a minute later, followed instantly by the smash of shattering glass, had them both leaping to their feet wide-eyed. Arthur strode across the small kitchen and yanked the curtain open. He could see nothing: all was in darkness. 'That was two cars crashing into each other right on the bend, Jean, or I'm a Dutchman. We'd better get down there and see if anyone's hurt.'

He was lifting his coat from the peg on the back of the door as he spoke. Jean glanced anxiously round the kitchen. There were dirty dishes on the table, pots and utensils in the sink and on the cooker. She had been just about to start clearing up.

'Come on, Jean. Don't start worryin' about tidyin' up the kitchen. If anyone needs to be brought in here that's just been in a car crash, it's no' dirty dishes they'll be thinkin' about!'

Jean conceded reluctantly and, taking the other torch from the shelf beside the door, followed him out and down the track. As they neared the gate, they could make out three figures standing in the middle of the road. Then, as their eyes accustomed to the darkness, two cars at right angles to each other: an open-top sports car sitting right across the road and a heavy, coach-built saloon – Arthur recognised a Zodiac - rammed into the side of the driver's door. The headlights of the Zodiac had been smashed on impact and the back lights had now gone as well, plunging the wreckage into darkness.

Arthur had been groundsman at Pitcurran for many years and he knew the dangers of this bend. He wrenched open the gate and ran towards the three figures. He saw that they were all young men, two in smart kilt outfits and one in a duffle coat. Without preamble, he thrust his torch at the duffle coat: 'Get yourself round to the start of the bend and warn any oncoming traffic that the road's blocked. And here,' he snatched Jean's torch from her and thrust it at one of the kilts, 'you take this one and get to the other side and do the same. We don't want any more stuff beltin' round here and causin' a pile-up!'

The shorter kilted man at once took the torch and ran briskly off with it towards the village: the headlights of a car could be seen approaching and he would be just in time to stop it. The duffle coat stared blankly at Arthur as if he had spoken in an unknown language.

'For God's sake, man, are ye daft?' Headlights could be seen approaching from the other side of the bend. Arthur thrust the second torch at the taller kilted lad who seized it and sprinted off towards the oncoming vehicle, flashing the torch vigorously. The duffle coat began to speak, agitated and indistinct, but with enough of a *posh* London accent to confirm Arthur's private belief that one Scotsman was worth ten Englishmen. This was further reinforced when the idiot fumbled in the pocket of the duffle coat, took out a cigarette, stuck it shakily in his mouth and began to raise a lighter to it.

Arthur knocked lighter and cigarette out of his hand, the lighter skittering on the ground and disappearing under the Zodiac. 'Do ye no' ken there could be petrol leakin' from one o' the cars? Ye could blow us all to kingdom come! Have ye no sense at all?'

Arthur peered at the lad in the darkness and saw that he was trembling, teeth beginning to chatter. *He's just a bairn! He's in shock.* 'Jean, you take this laddie back up to the house and give him some hot sweet tea.'

'Och aye, wi' a wee drop o' brandy in it, I'm thinkin',' Jean had a soft spot for handsome young men. She and Jed had not been blessed with children and she would have so liked a son.

'I'd ca' canny wi' that.' Arthur had caught the beery fumes. 'He's got a wee bit o' a start in that direction already – likely what caused the crash in the first place. It's high time they did something about drinking and driving.'

He left Jean to her work of mercy and went to speak to the kilts stationed at opposite ends of the Z-bend, explaining he would now go up to the big house and telephone the police to alert them that the road was blocked by an accident. The lodge did not yet have its own telephone but he had keys to the big house which was the country retreat of a wealthy Edinburgh family and uninhabited at the moment. He and Jean looked after it in the family's absence and acted as housekeepers when they were in residence.

The shorter lad had been driving. 'I wasn't going that fast. I'd already started to brake for the bend - 'cause I'd seen the Z sign - and I just caught sight of the lad that was driving it at the last minute He was running down the road towards us. So I slammed my foot to the floor and that slewed me across the road right into the driver's door. Bloody good job he'd got himself out of the car. I'd no chance of not running into him. He must have skidded and lost control. I couldn't get any sense out of him before you arrived.'

'No, and I canna get any out o' him yet. He's away up to the house with Jean – she'll take care of him. I don't think he's hurt, though. What about yerselves?'

'We're all right. Can't say the same for the car, though. My father's not going to be best pleased.'

'Well, it wasn't your fault, lad. I can vouch for that and so can the English laddie once he comes to his senses. Your father will just be glad you're in one piece – that's the main thing.' Arthur took himself off to the other side of the *Z* bend and conveyed the same messages of comfort to the taller kilted lad.

This boy seemed more affected by the crash, but he brushed aside Arthur's enquiry about injuries.

'We're on our way to St Andrews, to a Ball there.' He had to stop to flag down a car and tell them the bad news and deal with the occupants' disgust at the inconvenience. Then he turned back to Arthur. 'We're supposed to be there by seven o'clock.'

Arthur glanced at his watch: quarter to seven. 'Ye've no chance o' that now, lad, I'm afraid.'

'Oh God! What a disaster!'

Arthur began to reiterate that their lucky escape with no damage to life or limb was the most important thing, but the tall lad cut across him: 'If you're going to a telephone, can you try and phone Chattan Hall in St Andrews and tell them what's happened - why we're not there. Tell them we're really sorry. We'll come as soon as …'

'What name did you say?'

'Chattan Hall. Ask for Caroline Dempsey. Please. She'll be wondering what on earth's happened to us.'

'I'll see what I can do. Chatting Hall.'

'Don't forget - Caroline Demp . . .'

But Arthur had stridden off towards the gate and the lights of another vehicle were now bearing down on the corner.

The *Hell* room-party was well underway with six couples consuming the hell-fire hooch, nibbling savouries and batting the usual banter to and fro. As the hands of the clock crept past eight, Caroline, Elspeth and Patsy found it harder and harder to join in the jokes. The other six girls did their best to pretend that nothing was wrong, that they hadn't noticed the time, that the missing three men would be here any minute. But that too was becoming harder. An awkward silence fell as the record stack was being changed and, when the first disc turned out to be *You'll Never Walk Alone*, Jennifer leapt up.

'Come on, let's go down to the common room and see what's happening. I fancy some dancing before it gets too crowded.' She was a devotee of *The Twist* and liked plenty of space. The others sprang to their feet with relief: the atmosphere in *Hell* was becoming uncomfortable.

'Never mind, you three. I'm sure your men will be along soon. You all look really nice. I'm sure they'll turn up.' One of the boys was gabbling in embarrassment. He was yanked out of the room by his partner and told in a loud whisper not to ' make matters worse, you idiot!'

When the twelve had gone, the room seemed enormous as the notorious characters in the murals above the crepe-paper flames sneered down at them. No-one spoke for few moments, then Elspeth rose. 'I'm going over to the Ardgowan to see if they've arrived or sent a message there or something. Caro, why don't you come down with me and wait beside the phone in the hall, in case they phone here. Something must have happened to them. It must be some sort of hold-up, maybe an accident has caused a traffic jam and they're stuck somewhere and can't get to a call box.' She did not state the obvious fear: that their escorts might *be* the accident..

'Well, I suppose anything's better than hanging about here.' Caroline glanced at Patsy who was helping herself to her fourth glass of hooch. 'But what about *your* man, Patsy? Why hasn't he turned up either? He's not coming from far away as well and maybe caught up in the same accident or traffic jam, is he? You still haven't told us who he is.'

Patsy hesitated. She was furious with Hugh. If something had come up to stop him coming, surely he could have sent a message? There were loads of Sally's men here who could have brought her a note. She had thought him rather sweet in a puppy-dog way and had been amused by his polished manners. That he would let her down like this had never crossed her mind.

'Well, you're going to think I'm daft, but I just didn't want to ask any of those doe-eyed dopes in any of my classes. They'd have thought I was giving them the come-on. And they all look the same to me! I'd never have remembered which one I'd asked. It could have been embarrassing if I'd gone off with the wrong one. If, like, one of the others was here as well. If … if another girl had asked him, I mean.'

Caroline and Elspeth stared, hardly recognising their full-of-the-blarney friend in this stuttering girl. 'What on earth's wrong?' said Caroline eventually. 'Who *is* this man you've asked? Why are we going to think you're daft? And where is he now?'

But she was not destined to have these perfectly reasonable questions answered because, just at that very moment, one of the young maids stuck her head round the half-open door.

'Is there a Miss Dempsey in here? Oh! In the name o' God! Just look at *this* place!' The girl was staring round the room. 'That's Brigitte Bardot is it no'? An' there's that Jayne Mansfield. Would ye look at the bazookies on her! An' there's that mannie that murdered a' they lassies - Jack the

Ripper. An' they're a' in the flames o' hell. My, but it's awfy clever.' She moved further into the room.

Caroline grabbed her by the elbow and steered her out. '*I'm* Caroline Dempsey. What did you want me for? Has there been a phone call?'

'Oh, aye.' The maid was recalled to her station in life. 'Aye, that's it, miss, there's a man on the phone for you downstairs. He said to hurry up. He's in a call box.'

'Hello.'

'Is that you, Caroline?'

'Pete! Where on earth are you? What's happened? I was going to phone home and find out if you'd left, then I thought that you'd surely have phoned if you'd been held up or couldn't get away. And I didn't want to worry your mother and father. They might think you'd had an accident.'

'We have, that's the thing.'

'My God! Where? What happened? Are you all right?'

'We're OK. It happened on that Z-bend just outside Abernethy.'

'Abernethy? What were you doing there, for heaven's sake? I thought you'd get the ferry over to Newport and just drive through Fife.'

'Aye, but Dad says the queue of cars for *The Fifie* is terrible in the evening after work these days. Lots of Dundee people moving to live over in Newport, buying up houses now 'cause the price'll go up in a couple of years once the new Tay Road Bridge is built. So we thought we'd better drive round by Perth instead. We left in plenty of time. It wasn't much past six o'clock when the accident happened. We'd have been in St Andrews in half an hour, forty minutes at least.'

'What about the folk in the other car? Are any of them hurt?'

'There's only the driver. He's a funny fellow -one of your lot.'

'*My* lot?'

'Student from St Andrews. Driving this old sports car, open-top job, an MG-TF. They were great machines in their day. But the driver's door just crumpled like *paper-mashey*! The Zodiac's such a heavy brute.

'Hang on! Did you say a student from here? Driving an old sports car?'

'Yeah. And a right *nob* he is too, real posh London accent. Not much good in a crisis though. Went to pieces and had to be taken away up to the lodge by the woman who lives there.'

'What does he look like? Is he hurt?'

'Look like? Does it matter? You won't know him, I'm sure. Not your type at all. Public-school, yah-yah, marbles-in-the-mouth.'

'Did you get his name?'

'Yeah, eventually. James has it written down and the name of his insurance company. There'll have to be a police report because we had to call them to get the road blocks set up: it was too dangerous trying to stop the traffic ourselves. Anyway, we couldn't get the Zodiac reversed out of the side of the sports car because our radiator's jammed under his steering wheel. The police called the fire brigade and they're cutting out the steering wheel now. It's taking ages. But once they get it off, we should manage to back the Zodiac out and take off radiator grid. So we're going to need …'

'What *is* his name?'

'Who?'

'The man who was driving the sports car?'

'I think it's Colin something. What does it matter?'

'And you're quite sure he was alone. No-one in the passenger side? No-one got hurt?'

'No, we're all right, don't worry. We just have to …'

'No-one in the other car got hurt either?'

'No, there was just this one guy. He was pretty shocked and in a state, but he's better now and no harm done.'

'And you're sure there was no-one else in the sports-car?'

'I've already told you. Caroline, what *is* all this? You seem more bothered about the other guy than me and James! Don't you want to hear what we're going to have to do, what's going to happen now?'

'What? Oh, yes, of course. When can you get here, then? The Ball's well underway. But if you hurry, you might still be in time for the meal. And I can hear the music from the common room where the dancing is. They're playing *Batchelor Boy*, the new Cliff Richard one. Do hurry!'

'We can't. Have you not heard what I've been saying about the car? I'm awfully sorry, Caroline. All three of us are going to have to stay in Abernethy and see to the cars in the morning. We're going to push them through the gate onto the track up to the big house, and Arthur and Jean – that's the lodge-keeper and his wife, a lovely couple – have said the three of us can stay here with them for the night. James is going to phone Dad and tell him – ask him to come over with the Landrover in the morning to tow the Zodiac home. The other car's going to need a pick-up truck to transport it – no steering wheel any more, of course, so can't be towed. Arthur's going to help the guy sort out what to do. There's a garage in Abernethy will help him to …'

'You're staying in Abernethy? But what about the Ardgowan? What about the Ball?'

146

'I've said I'm sorry, Caroline. We're bloody disappointed ourselves. And it wasn't our fault. If you want to blame anyone, blame this gormless English idiot that you seem so concerned about. He must be some rotten driver to end up...'

Pete's four pennies ran out to the sound of *Peep! Peep! Peep!*

Caroline replaced the receiver and came slowly out from under the large protective shell in the phone alcove. She looked blankly at Elspeth and Patsy.

'Who was it? What's happened? *Is* it an accident?' Elspeth leapt in.

'Yes. That was Pete. A car crash.'

'My God! Where are they? Is he hurt?' Patsy chimed in.

'No. It's all right. He wasn't there.'

'Wasn't there?' Both girls stared at her mystified.

'How could he not be there if he's just phoned to tell you?' Elspeth frowned. Caroline did not answer. She passed a hand over her hot face and glared at a group of noisy ball-goers who had come down the stairs and were passing them on the way to the common room. The singer in the band could be heard giving a fair imitation of Cliff Richard prophesying that he would be '*a batchelor boy until his dying day*'.

'For God's sake, let's get out of here!' Caroline began to march towards the front door.

'Hang on!' Patsy grabbed her arm 'It's perishing cold out there and we're all in bare arms and daft party frocks. Let's at least go up and get our coats.'

But Caroline broke away from her. The other two caught up with her in the small porch between the inner and outer front doors. With an effort they persuaded her to sit down on the wooden bench.

'You're in shock,' diagnosed Doctor Patsy. 'Elspeth, nip down to the dining room and get a glass of water for her. No' - as Caroline made to rise - 'you sit still. Take it easy. Do you feel faint or sick?'

'I'm OK. I'm just . . .' Caroline took a deep breath. She was beginning to realise what she had said to Pete on the phone and to Elspeth and Caroline in the hall.

As soon as Pete had mentioned the old sports car and said the driver was a student from St Andrews, she had had a vision of sitting in the car beside Hugh outside Chattan on Monday evening after he had unexpectedly met her at the station. But, of course, the car was not his: she remembered Hugh saying that he had 'raced along to Sally's and borrowed Colin's car'. Then she had had another vision of Hugh in the car as a passenger and her anxieties had shifted focus. But why was she thinking of *him* when she should be concerned about Pete and James? She shook her head and groaned.

'Steady on!' Patsy put an arm round her. 'Tell me what your Pete said on the phone.'

'Right. Yes. They've had a crash in Abernethy.'

'Where's that?'

'It's on the road from here to Perth.'

'What happened? How bad is it? Has anyone got themselves hurt?'

'No, I don't think anyone's hurt. It seems their car ran into the side of a sports car and their radiator is stuck under its steering wheel. Something like that. The fire brigade's there cutting them apart, I think. Then they'll all have to stay in Abernethy tonight.'

'All?'

'Pete and James and the guy with the sports car. Colin. It's *that* car, the one The Oxbridge Rejects drive about in. You know.'

'*That car!!* Great God!' Patsy digested this with saucer eyes. Then a thought dawned. 'Is his pal, Hugh, you know, your apple-pie that's always chasing after you. Is *he* there?'

'No. It's all right. *He wasn't there.*' The disjointed sentences echoed round the small porch.

'Wasn't he, then?' said Patsy, raising an eyebrow. Caroline felt a blush creep up her cheeks. 'Where on earth's Elspeth with my glass of water,' she demanded, avoiding Patsy's gaze.

'Well,' Patsy sighed. 'I just thought that might be why he hasn't turned up.'

'Turned up? Why would he have? Did someone else invite him? Oh my God, Patsy! *You* did! *He's* your secret escort to the Ball! I can't believe you actually did that! I thought you were just joking.'

'Did what?' Elspeth arrived, flushed with her efforts to fight her way into the busy kitchen, find a tumbler and get to a tap. It was almost time for the dinner recess. She had narrowly missed having treacle sauce poured all over her white dress.

'Patsy asked The Apple-Pie to the Ball!'

'You didn't! The gorgeous Hugh! Wish I'd had the nerve. Did he say "yes"?'

Much good it's done me! Do you see him here? He's stood me up, bloody posh *Brit!* I thought he was maybe in this car crash with his pal, but it seems not. So you tell me: where the hell is he?' She glared at Elspeth, who shook her head bewildered.

'I'm lost! Why would *he* have been in the Pete-and-James car crash? What's been happening, Caroline?'

Once the story had been relayed to her, she sat down on the bench and began to wrench hairpins out of the edifice on top of her head. 'Every cloud has a silver lining! I was wondering how much longer I could stand these damned things sticking into my scalp.' Her abundant gold hair was tumbling down her back and over her face.

'Geez, Els, you look like Lady Godiva in the mural upstairs. Take you clothes off and you could pass for her!'

The three dissolved into hysterical giggles. The din of inebriated students thronging down the stairs to the dining-room was drowning out the dying chords of *The Wayward Wind,* the band's last number before the interval.

'Let's get the hell out of here and go to the bloody pub. It's turning out a *shite* night and I've had enough of it,' declared Patsy, her language deteriorating with her spirits. 'Once all these numpties have gone down to stuff their faces, we'll nip upstairs, ditch this get-up, stick on some proper clothes and make a break for it. I'll buy the first round.'

You've crashed the car?'

'Yeah. Look, Dad, it really wasn't my fault.'

'Are you boys all right? Are you hurt? What about Pete? The passenger usually gets the worst of it. Maybe you'd better go to the nearest Casualty Department and see.'

Arthur was right, thought James, with a rush of affection for his father. Jed was more concerned about their welfare than about damage to the car. James relaxed and leaned back in the phone box.

'We're fine, honestly. I was braking anyway into the corner and I saw the guy from the other car running towards us at the last minute so I braked even harder. I couldn't stop the Zod hitting the sports car but we were braced for it, sliding to a halt anyway.'

'Sports car?'

James embarked on the tale, emphasising that the fault lay entirely with the other driver. 'So best thing is for you to come over with the Landrover tomorrow and tow us home. As I say, this lovely couple, Arthur and Jean – they've been great! – are giving us beds for the night.'

'Aye, that's best son. I don't fancy towing the Zodiac home in the dark if its lights have gone. We'll need to see if the steering's up to it as well. Let's hope so, I'd rather get it seen to back here than use some garage away over in Fife. What about the other car?'

'It'll have to be fixed here – if it can be. Might be a write-off. The bloke's in a real state about it. Keeps going on about *the poor old lady*. I thought at first he meant a pedestrian had been hurt, then I realised he was talking about the car.' James chuckled. 'These posh London types!'

'Well, as long as he's insured and admits liability.'

'Oh, aye, he keeps telling us how sorry he is and he says his father paid for "top-notch insurance to cover all eventualities". Sounds to me like his father kens him only too well and expects him to have accidents. He'd been drinking as well, you could smell the beer off him. Said he'd had a couple of pints in Cupar, but it was strong stuff.'

'It's high time people realised how dangerous drinking and driving is.' Jed was echoing Arthur. 'Well, I'll get off then and tell your mother. You're quite sure you're not hurt? She'll be right worried about you. And what about the dance? Have you let Jock Dempsey's lassie ken that you'll no' make it?'

'Oh, aye. Pete phoned her a minute ago. He tried to get Arthur to phone her earlier, when it first happened, but Arthur couldn't find the number of the place in the phone book. Seems it has two names and the one Pete told him isn't the one in the book.'

'Well, as long as she knows. I'll head over tomorrow morning once Jerry and I finish things here. I was going to go over with him to have a look at their new combine but that'll have to wait now. I should get away from here by half nine or ten and get to you within an hour or so. What's the name of the big house?'

'*Pitcurran* – name's on the gate – right on the bend coming out of Abernethy. We'll be in the lodge. But you'll see the car. Thanks, Dad. And mind and tell mam we're OK – no bones broken. Shame about the Ball, though. And the car, of course.'

'There'll be other Balls, son, and cars can be fixed – or replaced. People can't. Just thank God you're both all right.'

James came out of the phone box and gave Pete a thumbs-up. 'Cheer up, wee brother, it's been a shock but we're OK. Dad said that's the main thing.'

Pete said nothing as he plodded back up the road from the phone box.

'Are you awful fed up about missing the Ball? It's a right bugger, I admit, but never mind. There'll likely be other chances. Caroline's here for three or four years isn't she?' James gave his brother a consoling pat on the shoulder.

'Caroline!' Pete spat the name out. 'She doesn't care about me. She was more interested in this English *yah* who was driving the sports car – or in some other bloke who might have been with him. Kept asking if *he* was all right, or if he'd had anyone else in the car and were *they* hurt. She didn't even listen to what I was saying about the crash and the state of the car. Thought we could just hurry up and get to the damned Ball and not spoil her night!'

'So,' James digested this tirade. 'Miss Varsity's more interested in some other bloke who might have been in the sports car, is she? Well, you know what this means, don't you?'

'What?'

'It's possibility two.'

'What the hell are you talking about?'

'Remember what I told you when you asked me whether you should go for her or the other lassie? Possibility one: she fancies you. Possibility two: she's got her eye on someone else and she's using you to make him jealous. It's clear as the nose on your face, Pete. Whoever it is that she's so worried about getting hurt in the sports car, *that's* the other fellow she's after.'

Pete stopped and turned to face James. It was a bright, frosty night now and, in the light of the moon and a million stars, the brothers could see each other clearly. The raw disappointment on Pete's face tugged at James' heart. 'Don't you bother with her! Bloody women! Lucky you've got The Alice Band waiting in the wings, eh? Let Miss Fancy Varsity-Knickers go after her toff. Who needs her?'

151

CHAPTER THIRTEEN:
DOROTHEA AND CYNTHIA

Cynthia curled her legs under her and leant against the second cousin's shoulder in the sagging old armchair they were sharing. The room-party had emptied at the sound of the dinner-gong, leaving them to enjoy a picnic, thoughtfully provided by his sister, whose room this was on B Floor, and augmented from the remains of Cynthia's last 'mercy parcel' from Harrods Food Hall. Once she had seen that Rupert bore no relation to the spotty fourteen-year-old she remembered from their last encounter at a family wedding, she had been looking forward to this time in the evening when she would have him to herself.

'Fancy another glass of bubbly, old thing?' He was leaning across her to reach the bottle in its ice-bucket. She pouted and slicked her tongue over her lips ... he was turning his head towards her ...

'I thought you'd be hiding in here during dinner.' The door had opened and there stood Dorothea.

'Dorrie. How ... how nice to see you. Why aren't you down at ...?'

'Do *you* know where he is? He's not here!'

'Do I know where who is? Do you mean ...? Oh, sorry!' Cynthia found her manners. 'Sorry. Rupert – Dorothea: Dorothea – Rupert. He's my second cousin, up from the LSE for the weekend for the Ball.' She favoured Rupert with an approving smile then turned back to Dorothea. 'I presume you mean Hugh? No, I haven't seen him tonight. In fact, not for a few days. I think he was at the logic lecture yesterday afternoon but I didn't see him around afterwards.'

'Of course I don't mean Hugh! He's here with that blasted bumpkin-milkmaid girl. You know that.'

'He is? You sure? Colin said she had someone else.' She wrinkled her forehead. 'Wasn't it some farming fellow? Yes, I'm sure of it. Another bumpkin.'

Dorothea stared at her. 'You *knew* she'd asked someone else – that Hugh was free – and you didn't tell me? You *bitch*! How could you?' Her voice was rising.

'I say! Steady on!' Rupert had no idea what all this was about but he sensed that the beautiful ball-gown in the doorway was trouble.

Dorothea ignored him. 'When did you find that out? You didn't come here after dinner on Tuesday – as you promised – and you wouldn't speak to me when I went round to your place on Wednesday morning. And then you were damned well out yesterday afternoon with that bloody stupid note on your door. How did you find out? Why didn't you tell me?' The voice was heading for hysteria.

'Calm down, Dorrie. I'm sorry I didn't get time to tell you about Hugh. I had this hellish med. hist. essay to do for yesterday morning – ten o'clock deadline. I wasn't ... wasn't feeling too well on Wednesday. You remember. And it took me ages to get going on it; so then I was up all night finishing it. I only just got it all copied out by quarter to ten and had to race up to the tutor's office. He was actually just shutting his damned briefcase when I went in and I thought, for one ghastly moment, he was going to say I was too late. I think I would have thrown the blasted thing at him! Anyway, he relented and took it but I was so exhausted, darling, after all that, I just went home and battened down the hatches, stuck a note out for the housekeeper and went underground. I must have been dead to the world when you came round in the afternoon.' Cynthia felt the tiny clutch at the heart, that even the most brazen liar feels. She *had* heard the clip-clop of Dorothea's boots on the stairs but she had pulled the bedcovers over her head and dismissed the thought of getting up to face Dorothea.

She rose, sighing. She could see the precious half-hour alone with Rupert evaporating. God, but Dorrie was a bore! 'What does it matter? You've obviously got someone else anyway. Lovely dress, by the way. Dior, isn't it? Or is that one of Givenchy's?'

'Chanel, actually. But I'm *not* with someone else! He hasn't bloody well turned up! I hate him! And to think I could have had Hugh. I hate you. I hate you all!' Dorothea's eyes were bulging, bright with tears, her face was fiery red and the veins on her neck stood out in cords. She looked, thought Rupert, like that children's game where cardboard bodies are cut up into three parts and the fun is in mismatching the parts so that a pirate's head has a ballerina's torso and a footballer's legs. The ugly red face seemed unrelated to the creamy, voluptuous shoulders and the sumptuous gown.

'Your man hasn't turned up? Who on earth is it? What kind of rat does that?' Cynthia rolled her eyes at Rupert, implying that *he* would never behave like that. He looked suitably shocked and nodded smugly.

'It's Colin – Colin Carruthers. I was sure Hugh had been asked by that swine of a girl, so I asked Colin yesterday.'

'And you're sure he agreed?' Cynthia was beginning to doubt if Dorothea was quite right in the head. Perhaps she had imagined – or hallucinated – the whole thing. Maybe she'd got hold of some magic mushrooms.

'Of course I'm sure.' Dorothea stamped her foot. 'We went out afterwards in his car, to that place down the coast, *The Crow's Nest*, and had tea.'

'Oh, that's a charming place. They do super lunches, great view over the sweetest little fishing harbour.' Cynthia smiled at Rupert. He was getting the Edinburgh-London night sleeper, so did not have to leave St Andrews till early evening, next day. 'There's a bus, I believe. Or maybe Colin would lend us his car.' Rupert grinned back encouragingly.

'But where *is* he, Cyn? I'm the laughing stock up on A Floor. All those fourth-years and PhDs, wearing the most awful frumpy stuff with their stuck-up partners. One's even a junior lecturer now, over in Dundee. All trying to be so damned kind, admiring my dress over and over again and saying "I'm sure he'll be here soon", patting my arm as if I was a fractious child in the nursery.'

Cynthia felt some sympathy with this view. She could hear some diners coming back up the stairs and her patience was running out as fast as her time alone with Rupert. 'Look, Dorrie, obviously something's happened to Colin - if you're *sure* he really agreed to come?'

'Of course, I'm bloody well sure. He asked me what flowers I wanted for my corsage and I saw him at lunchtime.' She suddenly remembered what she had said to the two men in *Kate's* café. She began to clutch at the skirt of her gown with shaking hands.

'There you are, then.' Cynthia soothed. Was the girl really on some kind of weird drug? Back home in London, it was becoming all the rage, but here, in this backwater, there was little sign of it as yet. 'I'm sure there will be a perfectly simple explanation. Why don't you go down and phone Sally's?'

'But why hasn't *he* phoned *me*? Oh, I could kill him. And Hugh. And you!'

'Steady on.' It was Rupert again, 'Try this Sally woman. Maybe he's at her house, as Cynthia says.'

Cynthia's laugh jarred in the tense atmosphere. 'Oh, Rupie, you silly old thing. Sally's is the men's hall of residence – St Salvator's – Colin has a room there.' They both giggled.

Dorothea erupted. 'You're laughing at me too, I suppose! Stupid old dumpling Dorrie does it again! Thought she had an escort all lined up, even if it wasn't the one she really wanted - *and* could have had if *someone* hadn't let her down and not told her he was free. And now even Mr Second Best hasn't bothered to turn up. The dumpling is dumped!' She *was* hysterical now, shrieking, attracting attention from couples returning to another room- party down the corridor.

'Steady on.' Rupert had a limited response to histrionic females. 'Cynthia's right. Just go and phone this Sally place and find out what's happened to him. Perhaps he's been taken ill, too ill to phone you. You never know. I'm sure he won't have just *stood you up*, as they say.' In a burst of inspiration, he added gallantly: 'Not a smashing girl like you!'

'I can't. It looks so desperate. I wouldn't know what to say.'

'Then get someone else to …' Cynthia stopped, remembering the last time she had been caught this way.

'Would you, Cynthia? Oh, please!'

'Can't,' said Cynthia firmly. 'Can't leave the room till after ten. Gate-crashing, remember? Got to wait till the warden and the bursar have gone to bed.' A cast-iron excuse this time, thank God.

'What about you, then?' Dorothea turned on Rupert. 'You could do it. No-one will stop you. You could be anyone's escort. In fact, I'll come down with you and it'll look like you're mine.'

'Me?' Rupert was horrified. 'But I don't know the chap. Never spoken to him in my life? I can't do that!'

Dorothea ground her teeth. 'No-one ever does anything to help me!' The sound of the band beginning to tune up again, ready for the second half of the evening, drifted up the stairs. She began to cry in earnest now, the beautiful shoulders shaking, the boned front of the dress jerking up and down.

'For God's sake!' Cynthia's patience ran out. She had to get this embarrassing girl out of here. God knows what Rupert was thinking. It was his first visit to St Andrews and, at this rate, it would definitely be his last. 'Here!' she grabbed a bottle of gin off the drinks table and thrust it at Dorothea. 'If I were you, I'd just accept that this is not your night, old thing. Bloody men and all that!' She winked at Rupert to reassure him that present company was excepted. 'Go and drown your sorrows, have a little party all to yourself, get tucked up in bed and just ignore all this.' She waved a hand vaguely. 'It's too bad of Colin, I'd not have thought it of him, actually. He's a desperate scatterbrain, it's true, but forgetting to come to Chattan Ball. It's the best one of the year.' A smile to Rupert to remind him how lucky he was.

Dorothea cast one last venomous glance at them both, whirled round and pushed her way through knots of students in the corridor. Her sobs could be heard as she ran up the stairs, the gin bottle clutched to the bosom of the ball-gown.

'What a drama queen!' Cynthia closed the door firmly, picked up a couple of plates and returned to the armchair. Within a few moments, amorously feeding each other quails' eggs and slivers of smoked salmon, they had dismissed callous Colin and disappointed Dorothea from their mind.

To Jean's relief, neither Colin, being soothed with hot, sweet tea and sympathy, nor Pete and James, tramping wearily into her kitchen at half past nine, noticed the dirty dishes on the table and the clutter of pots and utensils around the sink and cooker. When two policemen arrived, however, she hastily put two electric fires and a tray of tea and biscuits in the ice-cold, pin-neat sitting room and ushered them all – Arthur included – into it. As she whirled round her kitchen, reducing it to order, she could hear the policemen's Fife accents mingling with the drawl of the English boy and the north-east voices of the kilted lads. She fetched bacon, sausages and eggs from her cold store, greased her big frying pan and set the table for three. They had had some night, the poor laddies, a good feed was what they needed.

At last, with the clock leaving ten, the door opened and Arthur came through. 'Nearly done. The lad's lucky. I thought they'd take him to the station and make him walk the white line. But it's been four hours since he was at the pub and all that tea you gave him has taken the smell off his breath. They haven't mentioned drinking. But he'll be charged with dangerous driving, for sure. The other two are in the clear. In fact, they did well to slow down as much as they did. Otherwise, the damage could have been a lot worse: they could be lying in Perth Royal right now - or in the mortuary.'

Jean shuddered as she lit the gas and moved the frying pan on to the flame. 'We can put the two kilties in the spare room – they're brothers, so they'll not mind sharing a bed. Colin can have your sleeping bag on the couch in the sitting-room. Not quite what he's used to, of course.'

'Damn lucky to get it. Beggars can't be choosers. If he doesn't like it, he can go into the village and get a room in the hotel.'

'That won't be necessary.' Jean spoke firmly. 'I'm sure the lad'll be quite happy to stay here. He's just a bairn, really, an awfy nice lad when you get talking to him.'

'Aye, well, bairns shouldn't be drivin' fast cars,' said Arthur repressively. He was well aware that any nicely-mannered young lad could wind himself round his wife's heart. He softened: 'D'ye want me to make some toast to go with that for them?'

The kitchen door opened and all three lads trouped in followed by the policemen. The older policeman nodded courteously to Jean. 'Thanks for the tea. We won't take up any more of your evening.' He turned to

James. 'I'll let you have a copy of the report for your insurers. 'You too,' he added curtly to Colin.

The smell and crackle of frying bacon did much to dispel the gloom, as Jean invited the three lads to table. None of them had thought about food for hours. Colin had had only the beer in the Cupar pub since Kate's haggis pies; James and Pete only a quick swill of tea and a few bites of scone before leaving home. All three fell upon the food and silence reigned round the table. Jean surveyed them. Colin was looking a bit better, she thought, still deathly pale, eyes bloodshot, but his mouth and hands had stopped trembling. She had listened for the best part of an hour to his ramblings. She knew that his panic was a combination of fear of what his father would say and anxiety about *the old lady* –she had finally realised he meant his car and not his mother or a passing pedestrian. Shock, added to the panic, had made his teeth chatter, his hands shake and his speech verge on incoherence.

The brothers were another matter altogether. Their years of living on a farm, among animals, mud and machinery, had shown in the way they had dealt calmly with the crisis. True, their beautiful Highland dress outfits were now the worse for wear: Morag's snowy white shirts were grubby and crumpled; the black patent shoes and shiny buckles were caked with mud; the white stockings were splattered; James had lost his *sgian dubh* from its sheath; and Pete's jacket sleeve had split at the elbow. Their faces were grimy and their hands black.

Arthur turned out round after round of toast, while Jean sat at the table sipping her tea and watching the three lads. Colin and Pete were just the age that the twin babies she had miscarried would have been. It had been her first and last pregnancy. She closed her eyes and allowed herself to imagine that these were her twin sons having supper with a pal a couple of years older.

'That was smashing, Mrs M!'

She opened her eyes and basked in James' beaming smile.

'Delicious!' Pete wiped the egg yolk off his plate with a toast crust. 'I thought our mam was queen of the breakfasts in Scotland, but you could give her a run for her money.'

'Och, I'm sorry it was breakfast fare. I just thought it would be quick.'

'Don't be sorry! I only get time for a cooked breakfast at weekends so they're always a treat for me.'

'How's that, son?'

'Too much to do in the mornings on the farm before I head off on my bike into Dundee. I'm at college there.'

'I see. And what brought you all the way over here tonight, then?'

157

'We're going … we *were* going to a ball at the university in St Andrews. An old school friend of mine is studying there now and she asked us to come through for it.'

'Ach, that's a right shame, you missing it. But did you manage to phone and tell her. She'll be wondering what on earth's happened to you.'

Arthur chimed in. 'I couldn't find anything called Chatting Hall in the phone book. But then Pete remembered there's another name over the door of the place and he looked that up in the book when he and James went down to the village to phone their father.'

'And you got through?' Jean turned back to Pete.

'Yeah. It's really *MacIntosh Hall*. I spoke to Caroline.' His face clouded.

Colin had not said a word throughout the meal but now, spluttering through a mouthful of tea and toast, he demanded of Pete: 'Do you mean to tell me that *you're* her partner? You're the one she passed over Hugh for?'

Pete eyed him warily. Colin's behaviour, ever since Pete and James had first encountered him on the bend, had been very strange and he had been largely incomprehensible, not least because of his posh public-school accent. Now Pete considered his words and began to fit them into James' '*possibility two*' analysis.

Colin was continuing: 'Of course, Hugh found out from one of her cronies that she'd asked some fellow from down on the farm.' For the first time, he looked at what the brothers were wearing. 'That's Scottish evening dress, isn't it?'

'It's called Highland Dress,' James sniggered

A horrified look suddenly swept over Colin's pasty face. 'Oh my God! Oh, bloody hell!'

'Mind your language, young man.' Arthur frowned.

'What's wrong now, son?' Jean hastened to save the lad from further reproof.

'Chattan bloody Ball, that's what wrong!' Colin was not for saving and Arthur cleared his throat warningly. Colin burbled on, impervious. 'I forgot all about it. What with the skid and then the crash. And all this damned palaver with policemen and firemen and …'

'Ye'd have been in a sorry state without them, my lad, let me tell you.' Arthur was liking this fellow less and less in comparison to the sensible lads from the farm.

'Poor old Dorrie!' Colin stared gloomily at the eggy remains on his plate. 'Damned shame! Bet she's all done up like a dog's dinner too; *and* that corsage cost me a fortune.'

Silence fell as the other four tried to make sense of this. Then Jean said hesitantly, 'Who is Dorrie, son? Is she your girlfriend? Were you supposed to be meeting her?'

Colin groaned. 'She asked me to be her partner yesterday. But it went out of my head after the crash. All I could think about was the old lady.'

'Partner? Do you mean at Chattan Ball?' Pete was piecing information together. 'You mean there's a girl there expecting you to turn up and be her partner at the Ball and you haven't yet let her know what's happened to you?' Pete could not keep the disgust out of his voice.

'I forgot,' wailed Colin. 'It all happened so quickly. All I could think about was the old lady and what the pater is going to say and whether she'll be able to be repaired and if I can drive her again.'

'Well, thanks for your concern.' James shook his head. 'You could have killed us. Nice of you to worry about whether *we* were all right.'

Colin flushed. An uncomfortable silence fell for a few moments. Then his distress resurfaced. 'I should have phoned Chattan to tell Dorrie. What will the others think of me? And she could have had Hugh if I'd told her that I knew Caroline had asked someone else – well *you*, actually' - glancing at Pete.

'Never mind,' Jean sought to console. 'Pete's phoned the Hall and told *his* girl – Caroline, is it? – so she'll likely have told your girl.'

'But they don't know each other. Did you tell the Landgirl that it was my car you'd crashed into? Did you mention my name?'

'The Landgirl?'

'It's just a nickname. I mean Caroline.'

Did you get his name? What is his name? You're quite sure he was alone? 'Yes, she got your name all right,' said Pete, sourly.

'There you are, then. Nothing to worry about. The lassies will have told each other. It'll likely be all over the place, everyone at the Ball will be talking about it. Your lassie will have heard and she'll understand.' Jean leaned across the table and patted Colin's hand. 'Now, stop worrying about it. It's time we got you lads organised for bed. I'll show you where the bathroom is and we'll get Arthur's old sleeping bag down from the loft for you. It'll be nice and warm because the hot tank's up there and it's a right cosy one. Arthur had it when he used to go climbing and camping in the fifties.' Jean kept up a cheerful flow of chatter as she directed operations over the next half an hour.

By quarter past eleven, the lodge was settling down for the night: Arthur and Jean were drifting out on a sleepy tide of questions half-started, answers half-finished; Pete and James were already asleep in the spare room, their Highland dress ensembles a muddy heap in one corner,

159

Morag's overnight bag a jumble in another; Colin lay wide awake on the couch in the sitting-room, re-living the scene played out here a couple of hours ago as the police questioned him about the cause of the accident. He had not even had his driving license with him and, of course, the farm-boys had both had theirs, all smartly preserved in little leather wallets. Everything had conspired to make him seem an incompetent idiot and a bad driver, unfit to be let loose on the roads, and to make *them* seem pillars of good sense and skilful, reliable drivers.

He ground his teeth remembering the policeman's withering: 'I'd stick tae a bike, sonny, if I were you. A machine like that's for those that *ken how to handle* a car – no' for silly wee laddies. You go tae the shows an' have a ride on the waltzers, if it's a wee thrill ye're after!'

The conversation at supper had made matters worse. Once again, he had been shown up by the lads from the country. *They* had thought to phone Chattan; *he* had behaved like a thoughtless, selfish idiot. Again.

Hugh would be wondering where on earth he was. He would go down to the phone box in the village first thing in the morning and phone Sally's; *then* he would phone Chattan and apologise to Dorrie; *then* he would have to phone his father; and the insurance company; *then* he and Arthur would have to go down to the local garage and start finding out what was to be done about the poor old lady.

He dreamt he was a child again, riding Dixie, his docile, old pony, but she kept turning into a racehorse and trying to jump hurdles. He tossed and turned, sweating and swearing in his sleep.

She was still sobbing, eyes and nose streaming, as she struggled up to the top of the stairs and turned into the corridor of A Floor. Monica Baxter, coming out of the bathroom and preparing to head back into the soft music, low lights and conversational hum of the room-party, glanced behind her. Dorothea thrust the gin bottle into her voluminous skirt as the magistrand turned towards her.

'Are you all right, my dear? You seem upset.' Monica's tone was cool She was simply doing her duty as Head of House.

Dorothea struggled for composure. 'It's all right, really. Just … rather unfortunate. My partner for the Ball, he's …he hasn't …'

'Oh, yes, of course. Is there still no sign of him? Have you heard what's happened? He hasn't had an accident, or been taken ill, has he? Is that what's upsetting you?'

'I don't know! I bloody well just don't know!' Dorothea's short-lived control snapped. 'The rat hasn't even phoned. And I could have had

Hugh after all. That bitch, Cynthia, didn't bother to tell me the milkmaid had asked someone else.' She was crying again.

'I see,' said Monica, who did not. 'Well, perhaps you should go into your own room and have a little rest.'

'I'm going to bed and I don't care what's happened to him. I'll never speak to him – or Cynthia – again!' The voice was rising towards a yell.

'Good idea.' Monica was relieved. 'That's probably for the best. Get a good night's sleep. Forget all about him. We're just going to listen to a new recording of Beethoven's *Pastoral* – one of the men brought it with him - so it'll not be noisy up here. Not like some of the room-parties down there.'

Dorothea let out a furious wail and kicked open the door into her room. She left it lying open and began to pace around it, sobbing hysterically. The Head of House thought quickly: this situation had to be contained and this mad girl calmed down. She followed Dorothea into the room and closed the door. The girl had subsided on to the bed, babbling incoherently. Monica did not see the bottle of gin which had sunk into the quilt under folds of skirt.

'I'm going to get you a couple of my magic pills,' she decided. 'I get terribly nervous before exams and my doctor gave me them to get me through the mocks for the finals, before Christmas. They have a wonderfully relaxing effect. Just what you need. Back in a jiffy.'

When she returned, Dorothea was beginning to undress, trying to wrench down the top of the ball-gown without undoing the zip at the back. The sound of a seam ripping sent her into a new paroxysm of fury.

'Careful,' said Monica. 'Shame to spoil such a beautiful creation. There will be other balls.' This was the wrong thing to say: it brought on a fresh bout of sobs.

'Here.' Monica produced the magic pills. 'Come on. Let's get you calmed down. This really won't do at all. Oh, blast these new childproof caps! 'Her black evening gloves were hindering her attempts to open the little bottle.

'Monica! Are you coming? We're ready to start the record now. Do hurry up.' It was her ball-partner outside in the corridor, tapping discreetly on the bathroom door. 'Are you all right? You've been such a long time.'

'Oh, drat the thing. Here!' She thrust the bottle at Dorothea. 'Just take one of these. If you're not asleep within half an hour you can take another one. Just give me the bottle back tomorrow. Get yourself a good night's sleep and I'm sure it'll all seem better in the morning. No man's worth it, you know!' This woman-to-woman jocularity was met with a glare and a huge, unsavoury sniff.

Monica closed the door and stepped thankfully into the corridor.

'There you are!' Her partner turned in surprise from the bathroom door. 'What on earth have you been doing? We're all waiting for you. Come *on*!'

Bejantines! thought Monica, as she followed him along the corridor. If they weren't careering down corridors, almost knocking one off one's feet, or spoiling formal dinner with their giggling, they were having *une crise de nerves* right in the middle of the Ball – and on A Floor too! *We were never like that in our day.*

Hugh had fallen asleep during the last twenty minutes of the second showing of *From Russia with Love*, waking just in time to see the final love scene. The icy, damp night air brought him to his senses. He was starving. The Maltesers seemed a long time ago. *Fish and chips*, he decided, and turned up the narrow, cobbled lane towards *Joe's* café. The sight of the *Star and Garter* pub on Market Street changed his mind. He would have a pint first - he was thirsty after his nap.

The *Star* was quiet, as always on a Ball night, heading towards closing in twenty minutes time He placed his order at the bar and watched the brown liquid begin to create a creamy foam head in the tilted glass. He turned to look around the bar. Over in the corner were three girls, huddled over a small table. Three heads in close confab: dark and sleek, flicked at the ends; golden-fair, tied back in a thick pony-tail; and a mane of black curls. He remembered Dorothea's saying that the disappointed girls from the aborted room-party were going to have a 'girls' night out'. *Damned shame! Bugger Chastity Hall and its killjoy warden! I'll go and cheer them up.*

He was halfway to their table when Patsy looked up and saw him. Her face froze. She said something to her two companions and immediately he was subjected to three frosty stares. He checked: what were they looking so frozen-faced about? Surely, he was the one who should be annoyed: Patsy hadn't even bothered to make sure he knew the room-party was off.

'Well, what have we here? Girls, do you detect a terrible smell? Would you say *rat* or *skunk*?' Caroline and Elspeth tittered like a Greek chorus.

Hugh recoiled from her contempt. Then he rallied. 'You don't smell so sweet yourself, m'dear. You could have at least sent a message. Luckily I found out the room-party was cancelled from someone else. No thanks to you!'

162

There was a moment's bewildered silence. The noise of the barman washing up glasses seemed strangely loud. The occupants of two other tables fell silent, staring at the foursome.

'What are you talking about, Hugh?' Caroline spoke first.

It took only a minute for Hugh to recount Dorothea's story of the fate of the *Hell* room-party and for the three girls to put him right that no such thing had happened.

'But why? Why did she say that to you?' Elspeth was out of her depth.

'Did you really think I would just not bother letting you know if such a thing had happened? It's little you think of me!' Patsy was indignant. 'And here's me calling *you* for everything, thinking you'd just given me the old heave-ho!'

'I'd never do that. Not to any girl.' Hugh flicked a glance at Caroline.

'I think,' Caroline spoke slowly, twirling the dregs of her vodka and lime, 'I think she was jealous. She thought *I'd* asked you. She wanted to spoil it for us. She didn't know that there isn't an *us*.'

'But she asked Colin. They'd been out in his car, down to *The Crows' Nest* yesterday. She seemed quite happy about going with him when we saw her at lunchtime today in *Kate's*, when she told us that the *Hell* room-party was cancelled. When she lied, that is. What a mess! I'm so sorry, Patsy.'

He turned to Caroline and Elspeth. 'But what about you two? Why aren't *you* at the Ball? I thought you had escorts from back home? Where are they?' He glanced round the empty bar as if expecting to see two strapping farmers lurking in a corner.

'There's been an accident. Pete and James, that's the boys who were coming to be our partners, they've been in a car crash.' Elspeth moved the story on. 'Oh, and you'll never guess who they crashed into?'

Hugh groaned. He was having a dreadful premonition.

'It was your friend in his flashy car! But don't worry' - as Hugh's eyes widened in horror -'it's all right. No-one is hurt. But they're all stranded at a wee place called Abernethy 'cause the cars are too damaged to be driven any more.'

Hugh put his head in his hands. The shocks were coming thick and fast. When he raised his eyes, he looked straight in two sad, grey ones.

'It's such a mess.' Caroline spoke very quietly. '*She* won't have a partner either, now. And it was going to be such a splendid night.' Tears quivered on her lashes.

Hugh set his pint of beer down on the table: he had lost the appetite for it. He looked at the three glum faces.

'Come on, girls! Let me buy you all the best fish suppers that *Joe's* can provide. If we can't have a Ball, at least let's have a feast!'

'Now, that's more like it.' Patsy was first on her feet, shrugging on her red duffle coat. 'Let's drown our sorrows in chip-fat!'

It was after eleven o'clock when the four of them wandered back towards Chattan. His breezy banter and genuine gallantry had won over even the cynical Patsy. They were all feeling much better, ready to dismiss the disastrous evening as best-forgotten. Patsy yanked Elspeth ahead on the narrow pavement, leaving Caroline behind with Hugh. What they talked about she had no idea but she was satisfied to hear a buzz of conversation, peppered with shouts of laughter from Hugh and giggles from Caroline.

They were in surprisingly good spirits as they neared Chattan, but the sight that met their eyes stilled their laughter. An ambulance was sitting outside the front door and, as they watched, two ambulance men bore a stretcher down the stone steps and began to load it in to the back of the vehicle. The figure on the stretcher still wore her ball-gown, the skirts trailing in the muddy gutter. There was a blanket over the body and an oxygen mask over the face but Hugh, running forward with his second premonition of the night, saw at once who it was.

'That's Dorrie!' He turned back to Caroline and grasped her arm. Then, seeing her blank look, 'The girl who said the room-party was off. My God! What can have happened?'

'I don't understand. Has she been taken ill?'

'She's taken an overdose.' Elspeth had moved among the crowd. She had not even had to ask - the clutch of students round the steps and ambulance was talking feverishly about it. 'A whole bottle of tranquillisers and most of a bottle of gin. One of the magistrands on A Floor went into her room half an hour ago and found her. Rushed down and told The Gusset. *She* sent for the ambulance. Can you believe it? What is that girl going to do next?'

Her words were plain and practical but her tone was hollow and her face forlorn. Instinctively, Hugh put his arm round her and then somehow all three girls were in his embrace. He was aware of Caroline's head on his shoulder and her tears on his coat.

CHAPTER FOURTEEN: AUGUSTA AND MONICA

Morag and Jed lingered over their last-thing-at-night cup of tea. For the umpteenth time, they re-hashed the meagre information they had about the accident. They had been down the *'what if?'* road many times, thanking the Good Lord that none of these *what ifs?* had happened. They had speculated on reasons for the sports car being stranded in the middle of the road on a bend: failing brakes; a tyre blow-out; driver speeding and losing control; driver being taken suddenly ill; driver drunk. Now Jed was worrying his way through the practicalities of fetching the car home, getting it repaired and managing without it; Morag was regretting the deeply disappointing end to a promising evening.

'What a waste!' She shuffled their dirty cups and saucers together.

'Aye. All the effort you put into getting their kilt outfits perfect and organising Jerry to come and do their work.'

Morag was not giving any of that a thought, nor even all the effort she had put into persuading Jed. She was thinking of the lost opportunity for Caroline and Pete to spend a romantic evening together. But she did not enlighten Jed. She knew he would dismiss her attempts to facilitate the romance as meddling, tell her to mind her own business. And he certainly would not attach any importance to Pete's love life. *The lad doesn't know his own mind. All this racing back and forward to Dundee every day when his place is here on the farm.*

At least there was no problem about getting Jed away from the farm tomorrow morning to leave the coast clear for Marjory Band's visit. He would be gone several hours, driving to Abernethy in the Landrover, getting the Zodiac coupled on to the tow-bar, then towing it all the way back home. It was much better than the tight timeframe she had expected to work within while he went over to Inshaig to see the combine harvester. But where did all this leave her interfering strategies? If Caroline and Pete had not seen each other at all last night, then things were no further forward between them. Was she still justified in closing the door on the Band girl? What if nothing more ever happened between Caroline and Pete and she had spoiled things for him with Alice? He would have neither girl then.

Morag sighed as she turned out the kitchen light and prepared to follow Jed up to the bedroom. Of course, Caroline would be around from time to time during holidays; the families would still be neighbours. There might be other chances to encourage their relationship in the future. But

Pete might – surely *would* – meet and court other lassies. She could hardly spend the next ten years scaring off every girl he fancied.

'If only you hadn't left her with the whole bottle.'

Monica Baxter was not even sure if Miss Goldsmith had actually uttered these words or whether they were just reverberating in her panic-stricken mind. The relatives' waiting room in the cottage hospital was so tiny that their knees were almost touching and she could feel the waves of reproach coming from the warden.

'How many tablets were in it?'

It was the same question that the nurse had thrown at her in the back of the ambulance as they had jolted through the empty streets and it had been repeated by the frowning, white-coated doctor who had taken charge of the unconscious Dorothea. Monica tried to think exactly what the contents of the bottle had been: the label said 30 tablets and was dated 22nd November 1963 – *the day President Kennedy was shot*, the doctor commented. She remembered the world-shattering news breaking in Chattan just after dinner that night. She had barely registered it, so exhausted had she been from a week of sleepless nights pacing the floor of the swot room. She had worried herself into a cycle of wasting so much time panicking that she then panicked even more at the thought of all the time she had wasted. In desperation, she had gone that day to her doctor who had diagnosed acute pre-exam tension and prescribed the tranquilliser.

Miss Goldsmith peered at Monica. In the haste of their exit from Chattan, she had forgotten her spectacles. Monica cudgelled her brains trying to remember how many of the pills she had taken herself but gave up with a defeated shake of her head. The silence in the tiny room contrasted with the bustle in the emergency room down the corridor and relegated them to impotent bystanders.

Miss G shifted on the hard seat. In the brief interlude as Dorothea was being loaded into the ambulance, there had only been time to rush back to her room, throw off her chenille dressing gown and pull her tweed suit on quickly over her nightdress. Monica could see its lacy hem hanging down below the herringbone skirt.

A plump, rustic face appeared round the door.

'Is there any news? Has she come round? Is she going to be all right? Can we see her? When . . ?'

'Hang on.' The body, also plump and rustic, appeared as the nurse toddled into the room, filling the remaining space. 'I just came to see if you two ladies fancied a cup of tea. I might even be able to find a chocolate biscuit to go with it,' she added, noting their strained faces and absorbing the air of fear and self-recrimination in the cramped room.

Miss Goldsmith looked at her watch: almost midnight. She thought of the scene she had left back at Chattan an hour ago: the Ball abandoned; the musicians silenced; room-party doors lying wide open as students, both male and female, thronged the corridors, passing titbits of information up and down the stairs. When Monica had first banged on the D Floor door of her small suite of rooms, she had been just about to carry a mug of cocoa from the little pantry through to the bedroom.

She immediately caught Monica's urgency, knowing her Head of House to be normally calm and pragmatic. The two raced up to A Floor, pushing past surprised couples and sowing the first seeds of scandal. After one look at the comatose Dorothea slumped on the floor and at the empty pill bottle on the bed and almost empty gin bottle on the desk, Miss Goldsmith raced down to the telephone in her suite. The bursar greeted her at the bottom of the stairs, her anxious face framed by plastic rollers netted in yellow chiffon. Miss Goldsmith waved her away but the bursar followed. Monica appeared a moment later, barging in without knocking, leaving the door ajar. As Miss Goldsmith was dialling 999, demanding an ambulance, Monica tossed a few frantic sentences to the bursar which wafted out to a knot of curious students.

The news had spread like wildfire and within minutes Chattan was buzzing. If someone had rung the fire alarm, there could not have been a better response. Room-parties emptied and students poured down towards the front hall, hampering the ambulance-men's ascent to A Floor when they arrived quarter of an hour later and forming a guard of honour down all three flights of stairs as the stretcher was carried down.

The grandfather clock out in the lobby of the cottage hospital struck twelve. Miss G leapt up. 'I must go back to the Ball. The girls will all be worrying. And the bursar. Yes, definitely, I must get back.' She rose and tugged at her skirt trying to hide the nightdress hem. 'Besides, I need to get to my files and find a telephone number for the girl's parents.'

'You're going to phone her parents!' Monica's looked at the warden in horror. 'But, surely, we should wait and see. I mean, she may be all right. No need to worry them yet, surely?' *Her mother and father will blame it on me. The whole world will know what I did.*

She had been looking forward to putting *Head of House at Mackintosh Hall, St Andrews University* in her *curriculum vitae* when she started out on her career. It would make a nice accompaniment to a first class honours degree in classics and moral philosophy. But head of a house at the centre of a tragic scandal, exposed as the irresponsible magistrand who had given a depressed, hysterical bejantine a whole bottle of tranquillisers and left her alone with a bottle of gin? That would *not* be an asset to any C.V.

'Whatever happens, they need to know that their daughter is in a very unstable frame of mind.' Miss G had enough experience of graduating girls to know exactly what was going through Monica's mind. She was also dreading the opprobrium that would attach to Chattan – and to herself as warden - if this night ended in tragedy. 'I don't think that young lady is fit to be living so far away from home just yet.'

'But she's bound to have been at boarding school. She should be used to it. Roedean, I should say, or Cheltenham.'

'I've seen this sort of thing before, Monica. These girls have been in a very regimented environment. Girls from the state school system adapt better to the freedom and independence here. I often think ...'

She stopped herself from launching into one of her favourite hypotheses, born of years of observing girls from all kinds of backgrounds. 'You stay here. I shall go and phone a taxi. Call me at once if there is any news. I'll come back once I've seen to things at Chattan.'

She patted Monica's arm. 'Keep your head, my dear. I know I can rely on you.' She tugged once more at the hem of her skirt and hurried out into the corridor. Monica heard her exchanging a word with the nurse who was bringing the tea and biscuits.

Chattan should have been quietening down, lights going out, male escorts all gone, girls either trailing sleepily off to bed or lingering in messy, dimly-lit room-parties to re-hash the evening's events and finish off any remaining food and drink. The scene that met Miss Goldsmith was quite different.

For a start, most of the men were still there. The front door was still open, lights were blazing everywhere and anxious knots of students were clustered all along the entrance hall and up the stairs. She had no money with her and had to ask the taxi-driver to wait while she went in to get her purse. She found the bursar in her sitting-room with three senior girls. Miss Goldsmith sighed. The bursar was excellent at her administrative job but she had no talent for dealing with the emergencies that a hundred girls under one roof threw up on a daily basis. As soon as she saw Miss Goldsmith, she leapt up and latched on to the warden's arm.

'For goodness sake, Felicity! Let me pay off the taxi. I'll tell you what's happening once I've done that.' Miss G shook off the bursar and gestured to the girls to take charge of her. When she returned a few

168

moments later, the bursar was back on the sofa being soothed with brandy-and-hot-water.

'I wouldn't mind one of those myself.' She sank down on the sofa beside the bursar. She felt chilled. After the hot little room in the hospital, coming out into the freezing night air had felt like jumping into a cold bath. 'Once I've had that, we must deal with the students and get the gentlemen out of the Hall and the young ladies off to their beds. This is a ridiculous state of affairs. No good can come of everyone hanging about like this. Oh, thank you, my dear.' She drank gratefully.

'But, what's happening? Is the poor girl going to be all right? She not … not …? She hasn't …?' Felicity Campbell launched into one of her twitters.

'She's in good hands and I'm sure everything will be all right.' Augusta Goldsmith wondered if saying it often enough could make it true. Just at the moment, however, what mattered most was making it *sound* true. Hysteria must be quenched and order restored. She finished the drink and rose briskly. 'Can you girls see that Felicity - I mean Miss Campbell - gets to her room and settles down? Then, please come and help me to get the Hall calmed down and settled for the night.'

The three girls, all fellow A floor residents with Dorothea, began to manhandle the wretched bursar out of the warden's sitting-room and along the corridor to her own suite. Augusta could hear them exchanging soothing words with enquiring students as they went. *Good girls.*

Within half-an-hour, word had been passed around that the suicidal bejantine, who had so dramatically brought the festivities to a sorry end, was in hospital and being cared for, that nothing more could be done at the moment, that she was in good hands, in the best place, and so on. Optimistic platitudes had been repeated over and over again; the men had taken themselves off at last; and the girls had repaired to their rooms, if not to sleep, at least to talk in hushed tones over cups of cocoa.

The exhausted warden finally returned to her sitting-room and contemplated the thought of calling another taxi and returning, as she had promised, to the cottage hospital. At least Monica had not phoned with any bad news. First, however, she must phone the parents: she had dug out Dorothea's file and had the number. She stretched out a weary hand to the receiver.

The *Hell* room-party was in disarray. The larger-than-life characters in the murals still leered down from the walls but the crepe-paper flames were mostly in tatters, lying in sad bundles on the floor; the hell-fire hooch bucket was empty and sticky glasses with pungent dregs were scattered everywhere; overflowing ashtrays lay around on side tables with greasy bowls of peanut and potato crisp crumbs. Jennifer had given up all hope of reclaiming her bedroom and gone off to collapse on Anne's floor for what remained of the night. One by one, the other girls had drifted off to bed and now only Caroline, Elspeth and Patsy remained – and Hugh. Of course he should not be there: all male presence had been shooed out of Chattan more than an hour ago. He had slipped in during the commotion that had followed the departure of the ambulance and had somehow ended up staying.

In the first wave of shock, there was a tendency to wallow in guilt. 'I should have let her ask me. I kept avoiding her even though I knew she wanted to ask me.' Thus Hugh.

'I should never have teased her that I had an escort already when she saw me coming out of the car on Monday.' Thus Caroline. 'She must have thought I meant you, Hugh.'

'And if I hadn't jumped in and snapped you up for myself, she might have found out that you were still free.' That was Patsy.

'But it's only a ball. It's only one night. Can it really be that important? I mean, to do something like that.' Elspeth's world was rocking under her feet.

'It was obviously pretty important to her.' Hugh was sombre.

'But surely it's only a bit of fun, isn't it? Not real, just a sort of ... *game?* ' Her homely face was earnest.

Brows cleared and consciences lightened. 'You're right, Elso. It's just all part of this hoity-toity St Andrews muck. Fancy frocks, wasting good money on silly wee flowers, who's got the best-looking fellow. It's all a load of candyfloss!' Patsy had no trouble with this view.

'It was great fun decorating the room,' conceded Caroline, 'but the rest of it *is* the most awful rubbish really. Us girls carrying on like daft debutantes and the boys prancing about like fops.'

'It's supposed to be preparing us for future social occasions. Part of our university education.' Hugh had experience of parents and other family members who moved in social circles where such events took place. His female cousins had been among the last 'daft debutantes', presented at court seven years ago.

'Well, I suppose once we're grown up. .I mean graduated with jobs …' Caroline considered enlarging her horizons.

'But I want to be a teacher - history, I think. My old teacher in Forres Academy is retiring in a few years time and there'll be a vacancy. She thinks I'll stand a good chance. They always favour former pupils.' Elspeth had a very definite horizon. 'There's the school dance, but it's nothing like all this Ball nonsense. Mum and dad occasionally go to the dinner-dance at the golf club but I can just see mum's face if dad started wasting good money getting wee boxes of flowers sent before it. They grumbled for days about the cost of the wreath for Granddad's funeral last year.'

'You'll not get me plastering about with all this pretentious tripe.' Patsy was firm. 'I want to go and work abroad. I mean in some of the really poor countries where they don't have any decent hospitals and people get ill for lack of stuff we take for granted here. Babies and kids dying all the time.' Patsy revealed a serious underside. 'I can't see much call for ball-gowns and fancy manners in the African bush, though maybe,' her incorrigible sense of humour broke through, 'maybe I could put on a *Mud-Hut Madness* Ball!'

For the next half-hour, they distracted themselves from fear and guilt by debating how useful the etiquette of formal functions was as part of their education.

'My God!' Hugh caught sight of the time and became aware of the wee-small-hours silence outside. 'What am I doing still here? It's nearly half past two!' He stood up, uncurling his long legs from the floor cushion. His flick of corn-coloured hair flopped over his brow and brushed a few straggling paper flames still clinging to the ceiling. Caroline looked up at him from the end of Jennifer's bed. Since Hugh had accosted them in the Star and Garter, she had barely given Pete and his unfortunate adventures in Abernethy another thought.

The girls put their minds to the problem of spiriting Hugh out of Chattan. Patsy's suggestion of a knotted sheet ladder out the window was disallowed: Hugh could end up impaled on the railings under Jennifer's window. Elspeth came up with a practical proposition. 'If we get him down into the sub-basement – you know, where we were yesterday getting all that stuff to decorate the room, Caroline – I think we can let him out the back door. It looked to me as if it only gets bolted on the inside at night, not locked up like the front door. If we're dead quiet going down the stairs to D Floor – just in case The Gusset is still around – then there won't be a soul in the dining room or kitchen and we can get down to the sub no bother.'

But the need to preserve complete silence often induces the urge to giggle hysterically. So it was with them as they crept down the stairs. They staggered to the door of the dining-room, clutching at each other, squeaking like a nest of baby mice, and collapsed in a heap. Hugh slid down the wall with his hand over his mouth, his eyes popping; Patsy and Elspeth sank to the floor; and Caroline ended up in Hugh's lap.

The dining-room door opened cautiously, with a slight whine of its hinges. The four conspirators froze. Their hysteria left as sharply as if a bucket of cold water had been thrown over them. The door swung wide to reveal a white and gold Grecian goddess.

'I thought I caught a glimpse of you earlier, Hugh, just after Dorrie went off in the ambulance.' Cynthia stared at her fellow member of *The Set* in the dim light. 'But what on earth are you doing still here? And who are *these* people?'

She peered at Patsy and Elspeth who were now struggling to their feet; then she swivelled her gaze to Caroline who was still sitting on top of Hugh. 'For heavens' sake, isn't that the country bumpkin that all the fuss has been about? But Colin said she'd turned you down. And, come to think of it, where the devil *is* Colin? This is all *his* fault - if he'd bothered to show up and be Dorrie's escort, none of this would have happened.'

Neither Monica nor Miss Goldsmith spoke as the taxi bore them home. Both were exhausted. Augusta had made it back to the hospital shortly after two. To Monica's anxious enquiry about Dorothea's parents, she had replied curtly that they would both be travelling up from London in morning.

That had been a most unpleasant phone call. The delicate task of imparting the news to them had paled before her disgust at their reaction. The father was brusque at first – perhaps pardonable since she had disturbed his sleep – but then, as he came fully awake and took in Augusta's story, increasingly irritable. She could almost see him pursing his lips and shaking his head. *What has the foolish girl done this time?* was the burden of his response, with a subtext of: *and why are you bothering me with it in the middle of the night?* The mother sounded hazy, speech slurring, questions and responses barely comprehensible. When she finally grasped that her daughter had tried to take her own life, she wailed: 'But what on earth made her do that? What can be wrong with her *now*?' The whine set Augusta's teeth on edge. At last, after a few minutes of confab together, the parents agreed that they would try and get seats on a north-bound train in the morning.

'It's very last minute, of course. May not be any first class seats available. I'll have to cancel my lunch party. And miss a bridge match. Still, I suppose it can't be helped.' Then, belatedly, 'Well, give Dorothea our love and tell her we'll see her tomorrow evening.'

Miss G tried to impress on them that their daughter was in no fit state to be given any messages but they lapsed into a fretful discussion about cancelling a dinner party and she gave up. The best she could do was make sure they had the telephone number of the cottage hospital. 'And, of course, I shall give *your* telephone number to the hospital so that they can contact you as soon as there is any news.'

'Well, I suppose we're awake now. Might as well ring for some tea. Yes, yes, we've written down that number. Goodnight Miss Goldfish … Goldhammer …'

'Goldsmith. And I really am sorry to be the bearer of such news but please try not to worry. The little hospital is very good; I'm sure that Dorothea …' But the line had gone dead.

Augusta sat for several minutes after the call, replaying the conversation in her head, sifting the evidence. The girl's deranged mental state was becoming less of a mystery: there was fertile ground here for deep insecurity. Now she needed to find out what had brought the girl to the edge and tipped her over it.

'Aren't they furious with me?' Monica interrupted her thoughts as the taxi swept down Hope Street towards Chattan.

'Furious? Who? About what?'

'The parents. Are they blaming me for giving her the pills?'

'They didn't ask where she got the pills from and I never mentioned your name.' Now that she came to consider it, this was a glaring omission. Unless their daughter had had such drugs before - or perhaps they used them themselves. Had there been some trouble like this before? She recalled the father's *What has that foolish girl done this time?* This time? And the mother's *What can be wrong now?* No hint of surprise that Dorothea had been in possession of the tranquillisers.

The entrance corridor – D Floor – was deserted. Or so it seemed. As they made their way past the top of the stairs down to the dining-room, a girl suddenly ran very fast up towards them. This was startling enough but the sight of a young *man* following her was downright shocking. Then a second girl appeared from below, this one still in Ball finery: she halted on the half landing. 'Oh, let her go, Hugh. What does it matter if she takes offence? She *is* a damned country bumpkin. You've said so yourself.'

The first girl rounded the newel post and began to run up towards C Floor. The boy looked set to follow her, but the warden recovered her wits. 'Where do you think you're going, young man. Those are the ladies' *bedrooms* up there! And what are you doing in Chattan at this time of night?'

On cue, the grandfather clock in the corridor struck three.

It was a subdued trio that trouped into Miss Goldsmith's sitting-room. Monica's grim countenance, as she ushered them in, did nothing to alleviate their fear. Caroline and Cynthia had frozen horrified on their half-landings, staring respectively down and up at the tableau of Warden, Head of House and Hugh. Only Patsy and Elspeth, arrested by the sound of The Gusset's voice, remained out of sight below: they listened in horror as the warden ordered the three into her sitting-room.

Augusta Goldsmith had never had a more trying night in her fifteen years as warden. Usually Ball night was an evening of two halves: the first half, amused, as she watched the young people pretending to grown-up elegance, whilst their youthful high spirits simmered below the surface; the second half, indulgent, as she prepared for bed, listening to soft music in the common-room and subsiding revelry in the room-parties. Then, at midnight, the young men would leave and the bursar would lock up the daughters of Chattan.

But this night seemed to be going on forever, with frightening experiences and responsibilities – not to mention stuffy mini-cabs and over-heated hospital waiting-rooms. She cursed this irrelevant postscript to the wearisome night. Despite her distracted state of mind, she had immediately recognised that the first girl, fleeing up the stairs to C Floor, was a resident: her instinctive knowledge of those under her roof was faultless. By the same token, she had known at once that the second girl in the white-and-gold Ball dress was *not*: she was a gate-crasher.

As for the young man, his presence here at three in the morning was even more shocking. Guarding a hundred young unmarried ladies – each someone's precious, virginal daughter – was a responsibility Miss G took seriously and discharged with inflexible rules about men visiting the residence. Now here was this fellow charging up the stairs after one of her young ladies in the middle of the night.

There had been intense relief when the senior doctor had come into the waiting room, shortly after her return there at two-thirty, to tell them that Dorothea was regaining consciousness. Her stomach had been pumped out and he was pleased to report that a significant quantity of the drug had been evacuated. Now it was a question of keeping the patient under close observation for the next twenty-four hours but she *should* make a full physical recovery.

'You have the parents' number? I shall phone them now and tell them. They are coming soon? Good! I shall talk to them about treatment for her mental state – recommend she be referred to a psychiatrist. Perhaps some time at home, away from university, to recover. She's just a child.

Plenty of time to pick up her education again, eh? I'm sure her mother and father will agree. I shall go and set their minds at rest.

'And good luck to you,' Augusta thought ruefully, as she went to call for yet another taxi.

Now she was aching to get to bed, to lay her throbbing head on a cool pillow and let the waves of exhaustion and relief engulf her. She dragged her mind away from thoughts of depressed young ladies with self-absorbed parents, doctors with life-and-death pronouncements and the siren call of her bed. She glared at the three who sat in a stiff row on her sofa and began her interrogation.

'*You* are not a Chattan lady but you have obviously been at our Ball? Which room-party were you hiding in? Why are you still here?' Cynthia squirmed.

'What were *you* doing in the basement at this time in the morning? You obviously have *not* been at the ball. When did you arrive? Where else in the Hall have you been? And for how long? What have you been doing?' Hugh flinched as he realised that Miss Goldsmith was questioning whether his intentions – or even his actions – in Chattan that night had been honourable.

'And you: you *are* a Chattan lady. This is your first year with us, I believe. What is the meaning of this? What are you doing with these' - Miss Goldsmith waved a hand - 'these intruders?' Caroline bit her lip, unable to meet the warden's eyes.

Silence fell: with her legal training and court-room experience, Augusta was not afraid to let silence do its work. Hugh glanced from side to side and registered Cynthia's discomfiture and Caroline's dismay. He squared his shoulders.

'We're here, Miss Goldsmith, because of our concern for Dorothea. We've all been quite involved with her lately and now we feel that … that maybe we should have taken more care of her. We didn't realise she was so unhappy. We do apologise for being here at this time of night,' he included Cynthia with a sideways glance, ' and for keeping Caroline up so late, but we simply couldn't leave without finding out what has happened to Dorrie. Can you put our minds at rest? Is she going to be all right?'

Augusta stared at him. Whatever she had expected by way of explanation it was not this. She thought of her telephone call to the dreadful parents; of her insight into a deeply unhappy girl; and the need to find out what had tipped her over the edge of reason. She sat down in her favourite armchair by the fire. Some thoughtful person had stirred up the embers and replenished the coal – one of those sensible senior girls, no doubt.

'I think you'd better tell me all about it.' Her tone was still firm but had lost its accusing sharpness.

Hugh glanced at the girls on either side of him, raising his eyebrows, seeking permission. Cynthia shrugged and glanced away. Caroline met his eyes and nodded. She spoke for the first time.

'Let me start, Hugh. I should, really, shouldn't I, Miss Goldsmith?'

The warden nodded. 'You *are* the Chattan resident here.' Then she sat back and listened intently.

CHAPTER FIFTEEN: ARTHUR AND JEAN

Marjory drew into the lay-by and consulted the map. Yes, there it was, just as the woman in the garage, where she had stopped for petrol, had said. Any minute now, according to this helpful lady, the road would reach the top of an incline and drop down to a dip. She would see the sign, pointing up a farm track: she couldn't miss it. She glanced over her shoulder and pulled out into the road, her hands at ten-to-two on the steering wheel, the watch on her wrist at twenty-five past ten.

Morag surveyed the parlour with satisfaction: the fire would be a welcome sight to her visitor on this raw February morning; the cushions were plumped up; the firelight twinkled in the brass fender; the old rosewood furniture shone from years of beeswax polish; and the dainty tray of home-made scones and cake looked inviting. The scones were not the muckle mouthfuls that she made for her hungry menfolk. These were what she called 'ladies' scones', the ones she made when it was her turn to entertain The Rural, perfect fluffy discs, a third of the size of her everyday variety. The cherry and sultana cake she had been making when Jed noticed the aroma in the kitchen last night had been sliced thinly and four neat slices were arranged on a small china plate, leaving plenty in the tin for the lads' homecoming.

Jed had finally taken himself off after two false starts. He came back into the porch outside the kitchen the first time for the map which he had left on the bench by mistake and she hastily closed the lid of the cake tin and bustled through to the porch as if to fetch vegetables from the rack for the dinnertime stew, nonchalantly bidding him a second farewell. The second time had been a closer shave: he actually drove off down the track and had been gone a full two minutes so the parlour door was lying open. She was standing at the kitchen table laying a pretty embroidered cloth on the tea-tray when she heard the crunch of the Landrover's wheels in the yard outside. She threw the tray into the cool oven of the stove out of sight and rushed to close the parlour door. He collected his pipe and tobacco from the mantelpiece, murmuring about never knowing *how long all this carry-on'll take*: then, with a wink and a wave, he was gone again. This time, she waited a full five minutes before fetching the rather warm tray out of the bottom oven and resuming her task.

She glanced at the kitchen clock, as she laid out the teapot and checked the water in the kettle. Two minutes before half past ten. Would Mrs Band be late? She had sounded more like the sort of person who would always be bang on time, with everything about her in perfect order.

Morag was not intimidated. She was on her home ground and her mind was clear and focused.

She had allowed herself a good half hour's mourning last night over the demise of her Pete-and-Caroline dream and the failure of her plans. As she lay sleepless beside a softly snoring Jed, she revisited her plans and strategies, acknowledging that each had met with failure. Morag had been brought up by strict Presbyterian parents whose theology had a backbone of Calvinist predestination. *What's fur ye'll no' go past ye* had been one of her mother's favourite sayings.

She had reviewed the series of setbacks: Pete finding another lassie he fancied; Pete finding *time* to find another lassie; her own bungling attempts to stop that relationship developing; and now, even a road accident to prevent Caroline and Pete getting together at the Ball. She would have to be blind and stupid not to read the signs, she had concluded, as sleep finally claimed her.

By the morning, her feelings had moved on and she found herself thinking quite differently about the Alice girl. It was good, she reflected as she enjoyed a leisurely late start at six o'clock, that she and the girl's mother were going to get to know each other. She would be able to assess if this was the right kind of family for her darling son to get involved with and, if so, to be in a position to encourage him. If not, she would be forewarned and ready to *dis*courage.

She might have conceded to predestined fate as far as Caroline was concerned, but this was not going to stop her trying again. The new challenge energised her: she sang and joked as she dealt with morning chores and Jed's breakfast, helped him to find the tow-bar, whisked up the batch of ladies' scones without him noticing and generally smoothed his path as he prepared to mount the Abernethy rescue operation. If he had not been so preoccupied with what lay ahead, he might have found her high spirits suspicious.

The sound of a car engine coming up the track broke into her musings and she watched out the kitchen window as a grey Hillman Minx cruised past the kitchen yard and came to a stop at the side of the house outside the main front door. This was an entrance rarely used by visitors and never by family and friends. It often lay, door bolted, vestibule dusty, for months on end: it had last been opened on Christmas Eve to let in carol-singers for mince pies. But Morag had anticipated this eventuality and had already swept and washed out the vestibule, destroying cobwebs and dislodging spiders. The front door now stood slightly ajar, allowing a glimpse of a winter-flowering cactus, spilling its showy red flowers over a corner shelf.

Marjory stepped out of the car and looked around. She had half expected a cross between a tinkers' settlement and a scrap-yard: the woman of the house had sounded like a half-wit on the phone. She saw, instead, a well-ordered farm, a well-maintained farmhouse, a neat back yard with a well-tended vegetable plot, an overall air of care and competence. The impression was strengthened by the appearance of her hostess.

Morag had not quite gone the whole hog and treated her guest to the royal blue Sunday outfit but she had done the nearest thing and dressed in her second best, which had been her Sunday-best a couple of years ago: a sage green twinset and pale grey tweed skirt. Without Pete to see to first thing in the morning, she had had time to do her hair, fix in her favourite pearl earrings and even to put on some powder and rouge. Earlier on, she had covered up her finery with a wrap-around pinafore and Jed, absorbed in his preparations and plans, had not noticed anything different about her.

'You must be Mrs Band. Welcome to Fintry Farm. I hope you didn't have too much difficulty finding us?'

Marjory blinked. 'Are you the lady I spoke to on the telephone?'

Morag laughed. 'I'm afraid so. I don't know what it is about that dratted instrument, but as soon as I take that receiver in my hand, I lose my wits.

'That must be very inconvenient for you.'

'Och, I just let Jed or one of the boys answer it.'

'But what if you need to make a call yourself?'

'I managed all my life without a telephone in the house until three years ago. I just do what I've always done. Nothing's changed. The world doesn't revolve round telephones.' Morag beamed at her. 'But never mind that! Come away in. You'll be needing a cup of tea and a wee warm at the fire after driving all this way.' She opened the front door wide and Marjory felt waves of warmth drawing her in.

Morag took her coat in the tidy hall and hung it up on a polished coat-stand. Marjory wondered where the muddy boots, torn old jerseys, dirty jackets and piles of unidentifiable bits of machinery were. This was not like any farm she had ever known – not that she had actually known any, but she had driven past a few and had formed an impression of muddiness and untidiness, overlaid with extreme smelliness. Fintry Farm seemed more like a country manor. Morag saw her visitor's eyes darting around and smiled to herself. Her early-morning efforts had not been wasted. Fintry was putting its best foot forward and Mrs Marjory was falling for it beautifully.

'Would you care to sit in here by the fire while I make us a nice pot of tea?' Morag led her guest to the parlour. 'Or would you prefer coffee?'

'Tea will be just lovely, Mrs McCafferty.' She had learned the full name at last from the woman in the garage. *Fintry Farm? You'll be wanting the McCafferty place?*

Marjory sat in the armchair beside the shining brass fender and looked into the blazing fire. Morning had brought doubts. She had been seriously doubting the wisdom of the excursion. But her welcome by this sensible, *articulate* woman reassured her. This was a woman she could do business with.

Jed had never been in Abernethy. It surprised him: he had imagined a hamlet, no more than a straggle of cottages. On this Saturday morning, it seemed full of life. He saw a primary school, two churches, a library, a village hall - its environs jumping with excited, dressed-up children clearly winding up to some kind of performance - and a clutch of shops, all busy with chattering customers. People bustled up and down the pavements, calling out to one another or stopping to gossip. As he paused at a Belisha beacon to allow three pram-pushing mums and two dog-walkers to cross, he glanced down a side street and saw a garage purporting to do a bit of everything – sell petrol, service vehicles, buy and sell used cars, change tyres, patch up bodywork and repair accidental damage. *Maybe the other lad will manage to get his car fixed there,* he thought. *Mind, if it's an old MG sports, that could be a specialist job.* The toot of an impatient horn from behind made him jump. *Is everyone in this part of the country in a fleein' hurry all the time?*

He saw the Z-bend sign as soon as the main street through the village petered out into a row of large, detached houses. It *was* a vicious bend, he acknowledged, as he guided his big vehicle gently round it, meeting the local bus at the sharpest angle and passing so close he could see the tobacco stains on the bus driver's front teeth. By the time the bus had lumbered by, he could just see the Pitcurran gate on the other side of the road, receding behind him. Not that he would have stopped on this bend anyway or risked driving across the road to park at the gate. Some road-hog might come tearing round: one smash on this bend was enough for the moment. He drove on through the second bend of the Z and waited till the road straightened out and provided a lane to reverse into and turn the Landrover. He saw the Zodiac sitting behind the gate as he drew up in the shallow bay in front of it. The big car's radiator grid had been removed and lay in a twisted heap on the grass verge beside it; one of the headlights was completely smashed, the other one was crumpled with the bulb dangling loose; and the front number plate hung at a drunken angle, one corner resting on the path. Jed sucked in his breath and shook his head as he turned off the Landrover's ignition.

'Dad!' It was Pete, running down the path, pulling open the gate.

'Pete, lad! Are you all right? How's James? Your mother and I have been that worried.'

'It's just so good to see you. Everything went wrong. We never got to St Andrews. And the car … It wasn't our fault. I'm so sorry.' Pete was through the gate now and, for a moment, Jed fancied that the boy would throw himself into his arms and demand comfort as he had done when he was a wee lad with a scraped knee or a bumped head.

'We'll sort the car. Don't worry about that.' Jed was gruff, close to giving in to his own need for a hug. He contented himself with reaching up to pat Pete's shoulder and nodding his head several times.

They walked past the battered Zodiac without giving it a second glance. Jed strode up the path, intent on setting eyes now on his older son and getting the same reassurance that seeing Pete hail and hearty had given him. He met James in the doorway of the lodge and the two shook hands happily, like two businessmen concluding a satisfactory deal. Then Jed turned round to draw Pete into the circle and the three of them stood grinning at one another.

'Come away in, Mr McCafferty. Your boys have been fair lookin' forward to you coming. And two fine sons you have: you're a lucky man.'

'You must be the lady of the house. I have a lot to thank you for, being so kind to my sons, taking them in overnight and helping them.'

'It's been a pleasure, Mr McCafferty, a real pleasure. I don't know when I've met two nicer, more mannerly boys, and so sensible and well-brought-up. They're a credit to you, both of them. You must be right proud of them.'

Morag need not have worried about not having plenty of time alone with Marjory. Jean Menzies was not about to cut short this delightful interlude in her childless, middle-aged life. James and Pete had both risen early – although half past seven felt like a lie-in to them – and wolfed their way through a breakfast of porridge and cream, followed by kippers, poached eggs and crunchy, buttery toast. She left them alone to finish their meal while she went upstairs to make her bed, returning to find Pete up to his elbows in soapsuds in the sink, with James drying dishes and stacking them on the table, which had been cleared and wiped clean. She tutted and insisted they had no need to be doing such a thing but in her heart she was impressed. Of Colin there was no sign: she peeped into the

181

sitting-room as she passed on her way upstairs but he was still fast asleep, worn out from a night of sleepless episodes and nightmares.

Arthur had come in then from his usual morning check-up of the big house and invited the boys for a walk round the estate. James responded keenly but Pete shook his head. 'I'm afraid land use and horticulture are not my things, Mr Menzies. Now, if you would let me have a look at that old Morris Minor I see peeping out of the garage. It looks like a quite a vintage specimen.'

Jean laughed. 'That old thing! That's *my* car – or it was. I can't get it to go at all any more. It broke down on me a few times last year and then one day - last October I think it was - it just refused to start at all. I've given up on it. It's so old it doesn't seem worth spending good money on. So it's just lying in the garage. I should get rid of it really.'

'Can I have a look at it? I might be able to work out what's wrong. And if you have any tools ...?'

'Do you ken about cars, then, lad? About engines and the like?' Arthur was wary but ready to be impressed.

James gave a shout of laughter. 'Ken about them? He practically *is* an engine! He's been interested in nothing else since he was a bairn. And nowadays, he spends all his time either at college in Dundee learning about them or stuck upstairs in his bedroom with his nose in a book studying about them.'

So Pete had spent a happy hour and a half, tinkering under the bonnet, finding tools in the garage and wriggling underneath the car, whistling happily and giving Jean a cheery wave whenever she appeared at the kitchen window or crossed the back yard. At last, she heard the engine roar into life and a moment later he drove the Minor slowly out of the garage and leaned out its window to ask if he could try it out on the track to the big house. She watched as the little car chugged up the path, all round the big house and back to the lodge.

'There you are! Nothing too difficult – just needed some tweaking, adjustments to the points, a bit of tuning, oiling and so forth. And the battery had gone flat, of course, with sitting so long. Old Minors can be bad for that. She should be fine now.' Pete had held out his hands. 'But I'll need something to get this oil off. I can't see any *Swarfega* in the garage.'

'It's here, under the sink. Thank you, son. That was fair miraculous. Ye're a clever laddie: you've a real talent there. Your mother and father must be very proud of you.'

'Oh, I don't know so much about that. Well, Mum's OK about it, she understands. But Dad's another matter altogether.' Pete looked glum for a moment.

Jean sat the lad down at the kitchen table while she finished cutting out her batch of scones. 'Tell me about that, lad.'

So he told her. It was the first time he had ever really dwelt upon how much his father's attitude gnawed away at his pleasure in his studies, how hard it was to keep going and believe that one day his father would relent. 'He's so proud of James and so damned pally with him – farmers together, all that stuff – interested in everything he does. It never seems to matter how much I do on the farm as well – *and* fit in college and studying – nothing's ever good enough. Oh, I'm sorry, Mrs Menzies, what must you think of me? I think it must be delayed shock from the accident. Just ignore me. It's fine really, I don't mind, I'm going to do my course and become a mechanical engineer no matter what Dad says. I guess he knows that too. He'll come round to accepting it one day.'

Jean was lifting the baked scones out of the oven and turning them on to a cooling rack: Pete had been talking for almost quarter of an hour. 'He doesn't know how lucky he is' was all she said.

Then Arthur and James had come breezing back in, sharing a joke, full of gardening projects and plans, and she turned away to fill the kettle. Pete had risen and wandered over to the window where he had spied the arrival of the Landrover.

If Jed thought to couple up the two vehicles and simply drive off with a cursory, if heartfelt, expression of gratitude to the kindly couple, he soon realised his mistake. Within minutes of setting foot in the lodge, he found himself sitting round the kitchen table eating scones that rivalled any that his wife could produce – not that he would tell Morag that. He also found himself listening to a litany of his sons' good qualities.

'You'll be giving the lads big heads, if you don't stop, Mrs Menzies. They're just ordinary boys, you know.'

'I *don't* know, Mr McCafferty. There was nothing ordinary about what your Pete did with my old banger there. Arthur couldn't make head nor tail of it and I didn't want to be spending a fortune in that garage in the village. They just think of a number and double it down there. And you never know what they've done – or not done. I don't trust garages! That's a grand asset to have in any family – someone that kens how to mend cars and save you garage bills. He's one clever laddie. You must be very proud of him.'

There was a short silence. Pete stared down at the half-eaten scone on his plate. Arthur frowned, puzzled at the suddenly tense atmosphere.

183

James looked across at Jean thoughtfully. Jed cleared his throat. 'Yes, of course,' he managed at last. 'Yes, of course I am.'

At last it was time to get down to business. Pete and James stood sentry at opposite ends of the Z-bend to stop the traffic, as they had done the night before, while Jed pulled the Landrover out into the middle of the road then reversed through the gate so that the crippled Zodiac could be hitched on to the tow-bar with a stout rope and the battered radiator grid loaded into the back of the Landrover. 'We'll need that to show the insurance boys. And tell that lay-abed in there I'll be in touch about that. We've got all his details,' said Jed. 'Now, you boys go back to your posts and stop any traffic until I pull out and get round the bend and on to the straight stretch into the village. Then I'll stop and wait for you.'

'No need for that, Jed.' Arthur was a first-name sort of man. 'Jean and I will do that and you can all three of you just get straight off.' Jean nodded in agreement.

Pete protested. 'Oh, but surely, Mrs M, *you* shouldn't be doing that. It's not right, it might not be safe.'

Every woman likes a little chivalry. 'Bless you, lad,' she murmured, 'but I've been doing it for years. I'll be just fine.' She reached up and patted his cheek.

'Thank you. For *everything*,' he said and stooped to kiss hers.

Colin had woken to the sound of voices in the kitchen, men's laughter, a woman's softer tones, the rattle of crockery. There was a delicious smell, something freshly-baked: his stomach rumbled and his bladder twinged. He slipped out of the sleeping bag and, hopping into his trousers, made his way secretly along the passage to the bathroom. He intended to seek the smell and promise of breakfast, but the sound of an older man's voice arrested him outside the kitchen door. Not the man of the house, Mr Manners-or-whatever-his-name-was. This was another voice, another accent, but the same age bracket. It must be the father of the two brothers – the owner of the Zodiac!

Colin scuttled back into the sitting-room and bolted into the security of the sleeping bag. He was definitely not strong enough to face the scorn and blame he felt sure would be waiting for him in the kitchen, not before he had even had breakfast. He lay wide awake, watching the door-handle, dreading that he would be summoned to face judge and jury. The tea-party in the kitchen seemed to go on forever.

At last, he heard them going out into the yard. He crept towards the kitchen but shot back into the sitting room when he heard Jean coming back in, calling over her shoulder: 'I'll just check the bedroom and the bathroom – make sure they've got everything.' She returned a few moments later, bearing Pete's sporran, one of James' dress shoes and a toothbrush. She bore her spoils out to the group of men who were busy with more important things like ropes, tow-bars and rival football team banter.

Colin waited a few more hungry minutes to be certain, then he fell upon the remaining three scones, washing them down with a slug straight from the milk jug. He hid behind the curtains and watched out the kitchen window as farewells were said. He saw manly handshakes being exchanged and the tender moment between Pete and Jean. He groaned. Those farm lads surely knew how to put him in the shade. If he had hoped to make up some ground this morning and improve the prevailing opinion of his character, he had failed signally. Still, they were out of the way now: he had a clear field to shine in.

He returned to the sitting-room, collected the rest of his clothes and made for the bathroom. Without any accoutrements of his own, it was not easy to achieve his objective but he was able to scrape his stubbly chin with Arthur's razor and splash on some *Old Spice* aftershave. It was not his preferred scent but it would have to do. He washed with the suspiciously bright-yellow bar of soap, wrinkling his nose at the plebeian smell, and tamed his thick hair with Jean's hairbrush. He practised his most winning smile in the tiny mirror, trying out a few opening lines, before making his way through to the kitchen.

'Hello, there, Mrs M, Mr M. How are you both this fine morning?' The winsome smile and hesitant flick of shining black hair was usually a killer combination. Colin had several doting aunts and had learned how to play them when he was a mere toddler.

Arthur and Jean had not exactly forgotten about the third young man in their house but, caught up with the McCafferty family all morning, they had given little thought to Colin beyond a cursory reply to Jed's enquiry about his whereabouts.

'Still asleep – worn out, I expect. We'll just let him be for now. The boys have all the stuff about his insurance an' that.' Jean had been indulgent.

'Skulking in his bed, keeping a low profile. Kens what he'll get if he shows his face.' Arthur and Jed had exchanged middle-aged glances.

Now, the couple stared at Colin blankly.

'I seem to have missed the two boys from the farm. Dead to the world. Had a bad night. Nothing to do with your excellent facilities, of course.'

He flashed a smile at Jean. 'Just the old mind churning, don't ye know? It *was* quite a night, last night! Finally dropped off in the early hours. Missed the father coming for the big car. Damned pity!'

'Oh aye.' Arthur recovered his wits. 'A terrible pity,' he added sardonically.

Colin ignored him and pitched his best effort at Jean. 'I have so much to thank you for, Mrs M. That lovely meal last night, such a beautiful room to sleep in, such a comfortable couch, so much kindness to a mere troublesome stranger. You shall have the best bouquet of flowers I can find in St A's, delivered straight to your door!'

Jean knew that this was all *soft soap*, as Arthur called it. But she had never in her life had flowers delivered to her door – indeed her last bouquet had been her wedding one, twenty-odd years ago – and she was not proof against such seduction. 'You must be starving, lad. Let me get this table cleared and I'll get you some breakfast. Well,' - casting an eye at the clock - 'dinner, lunch, whatever you want to call it. What's that new word they use nowadays?'

'*Brunch!* That's the one. Bless you! That would be simply wonderful.' The stolen scones-and-milk were long forgotten.

Arthur harrumphed and stomped out of the room. It was never any good trying to stop Jean in this mood. 'I'll be back to take you up to the big house as soon as you've eaten,' he threw over his shoulder. 'We'll get those phone calls made. Time marches on!'

Colin flinched feeling his confidence and appetite drain away. But ten minutes later, the appearance of a hearty ham-and-tomato omelette did much to restore them.

'… and the rain was getting heavier every minute but the more we pulled and tugged, the more it seemed stuck. In the end, we just had to drive back to Sally's with the dashed thing down. I kept trying to tell Dorrie just to pretend she was Grace Kelly with a Hermes headscarf, and I was Prince Rainier, and the sun was shining, and we were heading for the casino in Monte Carlo.'

'Did it work?'

'Not quite, I'm afraid. She certainly didn't look much like a film star by the time we got back to St A's. Poor old Dorrie! More like my old Uncle Barnabus after a second bottle of port. And her hair was like a wet haystack.'

'That's not very gallant of you.' But Jean was laughing. Colin had finished his *brunch* and was sitting back, chair tilting, his long legs resting on the box of kindling beside the stove. He had been regaling her with *tales of the old lady*, employing all his wit and harum-scarum charm.

'How right you are, Mrs M! Not gallant at all. But we do have such times in the old lady. There's always an adventure when we take her out for a spin. At least, there *was*. God! I hope we can get her fixed!' His voice changed and Jean saw again the frightened lad of last night.

Art hur barged back in. It had begun to rain, a fine, icy sleet, and he brought with him a blast of the wintry real world. 'Right, lad. Let's get you up to the big house to make those phone calls.'

'Let him finish his cup of tea,' protested Jean as Colin leapt up.

'Just let me get my coat, *sir*. Shan't keep you a moment.' Colin's tone was deferential and his head gave a respectful nod. It was a tactic that worked well with the uncles attached to the doting aunts: they were usually good for a fiver. But Arthur was made of sterner stuff: he was already out in the yard, jingling a large bunch of keys.

They exchanged no words as they hunched into the sleety wind on the path to the big house. Arthur undid locks and bolts on one half of the enormous double doors and then on the glass-panelled inner door. This was not an entrance he ever used, normally slipping in through one of the back doors whenever he came up to do any work in the house or check its security. But the telephone stood on a big oak table in the front hall. Arthur never failed to be impressed by the stately fireplace, sweeping staircase and the view all the way up to the beautiful cupola at the very top of the house. He threw open the door with a flourish but Colin did not notice either the house or the gesture: impressive country homes were a familiar environment for him. In any case he had other things on his mind. He crept towards the telephone and hesitated, one hand on the receiver.

'I take it you know your own home number?'

Colin ignored him and spoke to himself. 'I think I'd better talk to Mother first. Then get her to tell the pater. Yes, that's by far the best idea. Well, here goes.'

But this strategy failed immediately. 'Hello, Knightsbridge 8326. The Carruthers residence.'

'Betsy? It's me, Colin, here. I need to speak to mother. Can you fetch her quickly?'

'Oh, hello, Master Colin. Nice to hear your voice. I'm afraid your mother's not in at the moment but I can get your father. In fact, here he is, coming out of the drawing room right now. Excuse me, sir, it's Master Colin on the telephone.' Before Colin could stop her, she had handed him over to the enemy.

Left to himself, he would have passed it off as no more than a social call, made some small talk and phoned again later to ask for his mother. But with Arthur standing shotgun behind him, listening to every word, there was no chance of that. Colin stuttered his way through the miserable story. He stressed how brutal the bend was, how bad the light had been, how the road had been greasy with a slick of rain. He made no mention of the beer in Cupar.

'You lost control of the car? What speed were you doing? Had you been drinking? Did you have a gaggle of other idiots in the car with you?'

Colin bluffed his way through the speed question, lied outright about the beer but was, at least, able to tell the truth on the last point. 'I was on my own in the car.'

'Is this man, this lodge-keeper, there? What sort of fellow is he? I'd better speak to him.' Colin was only too glad to relinquish the receiver – it felt red-hot in his hand – though he hopped about anxiously as the two older men despatched the business. Arthur handed the phone back to Colin.

'Right. That's settled. Mr Menzies tells me you have the name, address and telephone of the owner of the car which crashed into the MG? I have pen and paper ready. Yes, yes, I've got all that. I shall take care of this. I shall telephone this Mr McCafferty and talk to him and I shall speak to the insurance company. There will be no problem. Mr Menzies will arrange to have the MG taken down to a local garage where it can be assessed and possibly repaired. He tells me there's a place not far away that specialises in parts for old sports cars.'

'Yes, yes, I saw it on my way through. It's in Cupar. I could ...'

'All *you* have to do is get yourself back to St Andrews and concentrate on your studies. I told your mother that it would be a disaster, giving you that car. Thank God, I got the best insurance. If it can't be repaired and sold, at least we'll get a decent write-off value.'

'But, if she *can* be repaired, why on earth would we sell her?'

'I think you know the answer to that one, my boy. You've had a lucky escape, thank God.' And that was as near to an expression of concern as Brian Carruthers was going to let slip.

Colin was dazed and despondent. He would have headed out of the house, strongly in need for a fortifying fag, but Arthur recalled him to his duties. 'Now, phone that girl in St Andrews. The one you let down last night at the Ball. And what about your own residence? People there will be wondering where you've got to.'

Colin shied from the thought of speaking to a reproachful Dorrie. He was too fragile after the encounter with his father, overwhelmed at the prospect of *the old lady* being either sold into slavery or flung on the scrapheap. The humiliation of standing by, like a mere child, while Arthur and his father did the business, had reinforced the sense of inferiority that had plagued him since the moment he had clapped eyes on those damned McCafferty fellows.

He grasped at a crumb of comfort: he would phone Sally's, speak to Hugh, get some reassurance, ask *him* to speak to Dorrie and explain. Yes, that would be better.

CHAPTER SIXTEEN: CAROLINE AND COLIN

Hugh struggled towards consciousness. The gentle knocking on his door intensified. There could be no ignoring it. Only one person knocked like that.

The porter was polite and apologetic. 'Pardon for disturbing you, sir, but there's a friend of yours on the phone. He seems very anxious to talk to you.'

Hugh shook the hair out of his eyes and blinked. 'A friend?'

'Yes, sir. Colin, I think he said his name was. Would that be Mr. Carruthers? That's his room along the corridor, isn't it? I took a call for him one evening earlier in the week, I remember.'

The events of the night flooded back as sleep ebbed away. 'My God! Colin! Yes. Where is he? What is he doing? What time is it?'

'It's half past twelve, sir. He didn't really say where he is or what he's doing, I'm afraid. Just seemed very anxious to talk to you.'

Hugh threw on his dressing gown and, bare-footed, followed the porter down into Sally's entrance hall and over to the porter's booth.

'Colin? Where are you? We heard about the accident. Caroline got a call from her farming friend who was supposed to be coming to the Ball.'

Colin barely heard. Arthur had gone off somewhere else in the big house, losing interest now that arrangements for removal of the sports car had been confirmed, and leaving him to get on with this other business to do with girls and balls. This gave Colin a clear field and he made the most of it.

'I've had the most ghastly night. I'm stuck in some God-forsaken Scottish village. I had to sleep in their sitting-room. They sent for the bloody police *and* the fire brigade. They hacked the God-damned *steering wheel* off the old lady. This damned, lumbering great car came round the corner and just rammed straight into her. Then the police blamed me for everything. Told me I wasn't fit to be driving if I couldn't control the car. Bloody cheek! The road was wet and the bend was like something out of a nightmare - went on forever. It shouldn't be allowed - bends like that.'

'Hang on, Colin. Slow down. Tell me exactly what happened.'

'And those bloody farming bumpkins! Everyone made out like they were God's gift to driving. Even had their licences in dicky little leather wallets. Made me look like a proper idiot. *And* they got up at the bloody crack of dawn and started sweet-talking the old couple, had them eating out of their hands. Then they all sat about for hours with the bumpkins' father when he came, proper little tea-party it was. I thought they'd never go and let me get up.'

'Look, Colin, you're not making much sense. When are you coming back? Are you all right? You didn't get hurt in the accident, did you? And what about your car? What's happening to that?'

'Oh, the big grown-up boys have sorted all that out. Nothing to do with me. *I'm* only the owner.'

'What grown-up boys?' Had Colin suffered a bang on the head? Was this delayed shock?

'All I've got to do is "get myself back to St Andrews and concentrate on my studies", he says. And he's going to sell the old lady if she can be mended – *sell* her, Hugh! - or scrap her if she can't.'

'Who is going to sell her? Or scrap her? You're not making any sense, Colin.'

'Goddammit!' Colin's oath echoed through the big house and Arthur, checking window-catches upstairs, shook his head. 'Who do you think? The pater, of course. He never wanted me to have the car in the first place, been just waiting for me to foul up. All the fault of that stupid girl, Betsy, handing him the phone. She'll get no more mistletoe kisses from me at Christmas.'

'Right.' Hugh took command. Clearly, Colin was raving and might be dangerous. 'Tell me exactly where you are. I'm going to come and get you.'

'But how can you do that? I mean, you don't have a car.' But Colin's voice was lowering and his breathing slowing, at the thought of rescue.

'I'll get a bus.'

'But that'll take ages. I've got to get away from here. You don't know what it's like - there's this dragon of a guy, Arthur, treats me like I'm a half-wit.'

Hugh spared a commiserating thought for this unknown man. 'Just get yourself down into the village – Abernethy, is it? – and find the pub. There's bound to be one. Wait in there. I'll be with you as soon as I can.'

'Oh, well done, old chap! That's a great idea. I've still got some dosh and I could do with a fortifying beverage, I can tell you. You're the best of fellows. I'll have a pint waiting for you.'

Hugh mounted the stairs wearily. *Just what I need,* he thought. *What a drag! And I still have to tell him about Dorrie. That'll probably send him right over the top.* He contemplated the difficult task ahead, the lonely journey into unknown territory. *Wonder what Caroline is doing this afternoon. Wonder if she fancies a little excursion.*

'Well, Morag,' Marjory saw with surprise that it was after half past twelve. 'I'd better go and let you get lunch ready for your husband and sons. They should be home soon.'

'Aye, and right glad I will be to see the lads again, Marjory.' They had now been on first name terms for over an hour. 'It was quite a shock when we first heard they'd had the accident, I can tell you. But they've not been hurt themselves, thanks be to God, and the car can be sorted. Pete'll probably know just what's needed. He's a wonder with anything to do with cars and the like, as I was telling you.'

'Yes, I'm looking forward to getting to know him better. He sounds a fine boy. Perhaps he'll have a look under the bonnet of my Hillman. It's been making a funny ticking sort of noise lately when the car is stationary and the engine is running.'

'Oh, yes. Idling. Pinking.'

'Pardon me?'

'Pinking while the engine is idling - or idling while the engine is pinking, something like that. I've heard Pete talking about it. Don't ask me what it means, though!'

The two women laughed. It had been a most enjoyable morning. The first hour had been given over to sniffing each other out. At the end of it, Marjory was satisfied that the McCaffertys were a respectable, church-going family with a long pedigree in the farming community of north-east Scotland. Morag had satisfied herself that Alice and Marjory were a small but suitable family unit for Pete to become involved with.

Morag was impressed by Marjory's plans to pursue her education as a mature student: she had no idea you could do such a thing. Marjory had skirted round her early widowhood in Africa and dwelt instead upon her parents' missionary endeavours and her ladylike aunt in Dundee. Alice's dead father was touched upon lightly. *We were very young and a little foolish. Things are very different out there. It was all rather tragic.*

Morag conceived a hazy picture of blighted young love and admired this woman who had brought up her daughter single-handed. Of course, Jed would need careful handling: Morag could imagine his reaction to one of his sons going out with a *half-cast*, but she would think about that later.

In the second hour, the talk had turned to the young folk. Marjory described her daughter's ambitions to become a chef. Morag had no idea what *metier* and *cuisine* meant but she was suitably impressed. Like mother, like daughter, she thought, both ambitious, both moving into new worlds. She told Marjory all about Pete's career plans. Not for him the obvious route of a farming life - he too was moving into a new world.

'He tells me it's the coming thing – 'the technological era' he calls it, whatever that means. Things called computers that will soon be doing in ten minutes what it takes twenty people all day to do.'

'Goodness! Won't that put a lot of people out of a job?'

'Maybe, but I suppose there'll be other jobs, working the computers and such. It's progress, he says. You'll have to ask him.'

'I will. It sounds fascinating.'

And so, as the clock crept round to half past twelve, the two women reached agreement: Alice and Pete sounded a good combination and the two mothers would be doing everything in their power to encourage it.

Marjory helped Morag to carry their crockery through to the kitchen and they lingered as Marjory admired the view of rolling hills from its window. They laughed together over a childhood photograph of Pete and James in the hall – James' baby front teeth had just come out the week before it was taken, and Pete was trying much too hard to obey the command to *smile*. Marjory cooed over the sight of two newborn lambs as they walked out to the car, which led to Morag telling her about Pete's winning prediction as to which ewe would be first past the post this year. That reminded Marjory of the bets she and Alice used to have on which of Aunt Mavis' Women's Guild friends would be first to arrive at church with their new spring hat on.

All in all, it was past one o'clock when the Hillman Minx finally tooted off the track. Morag sang as she began to set the table for dinner. *Now that was a good morning's work.*

It had been well past four in the morning when they had finally been released from The Gusset's sitting-room. The story of Dorothea had been painstakingly pieced together under relentless questioning. Hugh and Caroline explained their parts in rejecting and confusing the poor girl. Cynthia grudgingly admitted her failure to tell Dorothea what she had found out several days ago: that Caroline was going with neither Hugh nor Colin to the Ball.

'I was working so hard on my med. hist. essay that day. You know, head down, absolutely immersed in the stuff. I could barely remember what it was she wanted to know. If I'd realised it was so important to her - it's only a silly Ball, after all.'

'I thought she was quite happy going with Colin. She certainly seemed OK when we saw her in *Kate's* at lunchtime - when she told us that Caroline's room-party was cancelled. I mean it wasn't, of course. We know that now.' Hugh weighed in with another strand in the strange story.

Miss Goldsmith was astonished. 'Cancel a room-party? I've never done such a thing! I always enjoy seeing the decorations – if I am invited to do so. What on earth was the theme? What could possibly have been so bad?'

'It's wonderful, honestly, Miss G,' said Caroline. 'Really artistic and witty. There was nothing about it you would have disapproved of. The murals are still up. You can come and see them if you like.'

'Perhaps I shall, Caroline, tomorrow, before you take them down. It sounds very inventive. What on earth possessed the girl to tell such a lie?'

'She wanted to spoil it, to stop it happening. She thought *I* was going to the room-party with Caroline. But I had another partner, actually.' Hugh explained about Patsy. 'Then, when Dorrie told us that the room-party was off, I didn't come, which left Patsy high and dry. But, of course, she had company because the farm boys didn't make it either, which left Caroline and Elspeth without escorts as well. There's been an accident, you see. No-one's injured but the cars are smashed. Can you believe the coincidence? It was Colin's car they hit. So that left Dorrie without an escort as well.'

Miss Goldsmith began to think it was quite surprising that *anyone* had had an escort at the Ball that night.

'Did anyone speak to Dorothea at the Ball? When did she realise that this boy - this Colin - wasn't coming, that he'd had an accident?'

Cynthia admitted that she had seen and spoken to Dorothea at the dinner-time recess. 'She was in such a state. Going on and on about Colin not turning up.'

'He hadn't phoned to tell her? How did you know he had been involved in this accident then?' The Gusset turned to the other two. Caroline explained about her own phone call with Pete but no, as far as anyone knew, there had been no such call to Dorothea from Colin.

Monica chimed in. 'She definitely had no idea what had happened to him when I saw her upstairs after dinner. She wasn't really making much sense but I did pick that up.'

'We know where she got the bottle of pills from' - Monica squirmed - 'but what about the bottle of gin? Surely she didn't have that in her room?'

There was an uncomfortable silence.

'Oh, all right!' Cynthia said truculently. 'I gave her it. She was making such a to-do, getting herself so wound up, I thought we'd never get rid of her. I told her to go and drown her sorrows. Well ...' she faced three pairs of accusing eyes – Monica kept hers on the ground, not feeling that the pot should call the kettle black – 'How was I to know she'd get hold

194

of a bottle of knockouts as well and half-kill herself? I mean, she's always been a bit heavy going, but this is the limit! It's not my fault.'

And there was the rub. Whose fault was it? They had all had a part to play: thoughtless, insensitive perhaps, but none with malice aforethought; none aware of the accumulation of pinpricks that had been driving an unstable mind towards breakdown.

'Why did she do it, Mrs G?' Caroline whispered miserably.

'She was unhappy before all this started, my dear. There are causes we know nothing about. Perhaps if she had had more friends here in Chattan ...' She blamed herself for giving in to her brother's request and agreeing to give Dorothea a room on A Floor. The girl would have been much better on a lower floor with the other bejantines. And this other girl – the gate-crasher – had obviously been a poor friend to her, even if she did come from the same set.

The telephone rang: the cottage hospital doctor wanting Miss Goldsmith to know that he had been in touch with Dorothea's parents and had been able to reassure them that the girl was now out of danger.

'Well, we shall say no more about this. You three have all suffered enough worry and guilt, I think, and I hope you are all sadder and wiser. It's never amusing to play with other people's feelings and I hope you have learned an important lesson tonight. Compassion, consideration for others, humility, honesty: these are the hallmarks of a true lady - and gentleman. We expect nothing less from alumni of this ancient university. Therefore, strive to be worthy in the future of graduation not only in academic matters.'

The Gusset's homily might have stretched on for several more minutes if Hugh had not given an enormous yawn, recalling the warden to the late hour. 'You had better get off upstairs to bed, Caroline. And I shall call a taxi for you two. Go and wait out in the front porch. Good night.' She closed the door firmly and their ordeal was over at last.

They congratulated each other on a narrow escape from serious retribution. Then Caroline and Hugh wanted to know how on earth Cynthia had ended up in the kitchen. She had come running down to the front hall when the dramatic news about Dorothea had percolated up to B Floor; then she had seen the warden coming back in once the ambulance had arrived and been terrified Miss Goldsmith would see her. She had tried to get back upstairs but the press of students coming down had been too great and she had fled downstairs. She had tried several times to come back up: once she had almost run into the bursar and some magistrands, as she crept to the top of the stairs.

She had been starving. Foraging, she had found half a bowl of treacle sponge and a jug of cold custard. The kitchen had been warm, redolent of the surprisingly good dinner, and the old armchair by the stove, in which Chattan's cook took her afternoon nap, had been inviting. Food, warmth and weariness had proved an irresistible cocktail: she had fallen asleep promising herself that this was would be the last ball she gate-crashed. She had been jerked awake some two hours later by the sound of people giggling and falling about outside the kitchen door.

When the taxi arrived, Cynthia ran thankfully out of Chattan. Just at that moment, she hoped she would never set foot in it again.

Caroline was woken from an exhausted sleep some eight and-a-half hours later by a summons to the telephone. 'Miss Dempsey!' The little maid stuck her head round Caroline's door. 'There's a gentleman on the phone for you. Name of Hugh. Maybe I'd better tell him to call back later,' she added, as she took in the sight of the bleary-eyed girl in the bed. 'Are you ill, Miss? Or was it just one too many wee drinkies at the Ball last night, eh?'

'Neither,' said Caroline shortly, swinging her legs out of bed and reaching for a robe. 'Hugh, did you say?' She pushed her feet into slippers and crossed the room. Then she stopped and backtracked over to her desk, lifted the lid and peered in the mirror. She groaned. 'Thank God he's only on the phone.' She had fallen into bed without washing her face which was now streaked with mascara and – even worse – without putting in her large rollers. Her hair was a disaster!

It had seemed a good idea to invite Caroline along on this rescue trip to the wilds of Perthshire – apart from the pleasure of her company, her local knowledge would be useful. But now, as he waited for her to come to the phone, Hugh felt his confidence draining away. Had he imagined the sense of closeness as they parted?

It had been such a roller-coaster of a night: the gloomy hours alone in the cinema; the shock of the three girls' animosity in the *Star*; the thawing as explanations were pieced together; the bonding as they wandered back towards Chattan, eating fish and chips out of greasy newspaper; the sudden horror of seeing the ambulance and Dorrie, comatose on a stretcher, being loaded into it; the recriminations in the remains of the *Hell* room-party; the giggling creep down to the basement of Chattan; the hysterical collapse outside the kitchen door; the wonder of Caroline actually lying on top of him, sobbing with laughter on to his chest; the abrupt end to such delight by the appearance of Cynthia and her thunderously tactless exclamation about *The Country Bumpkin*. Caroline's

196

reaction and immediate flight had seemed like the end to his run of luck. But – of all people – The Gusset herself had saved the day.

In the little drama played out in her sitting-room, something seismic had happened to his relationship with Caroline, he felt sure. In the face of the warden's hostile questions, they had bonded as comrades-in-arms. As the atmosphere changed and became less of an angry interrogation and more of a sharing of insight, they had drawn still closer together. They had laughed over Cynthia's tale of her sorry career as a Ball-gatecrasher, while waiting in the front porch for the taxi. The squeeze he gave her hand as the taxi arrived and Miss G reappeared, back in her chenille dressing-gown, to unlock the front door and pay the taxi, had been returned. His farewell wink and wave had been answered with a smile.

But it was almost nine hours later and they had both slept on it. He felt a lot less certain. There was still the question of that disastrous epithet ringing from Cynthia's lips as Caroline had fled up the stairs from Chattan kitchen. Cynthia's voice rang in his head: *Let her go, Hugh. What does it matter if she takes offence? She* is *a damned country bumpkin. I'm sure you've said so yourself.*

'Hugh? Is that you? God, how *are* you this morning? I mean afternoon. What a night! I feel like *I'm* the one that's been in a car crash.'

A tide of optimism washed over him. 'I'm OK, Caro. Well, sort of.' He laughed. 'It was a night and a half, you're right. Remind me to be out of town next time Chattan Ball comes round!'

'Me too! Though, you never know, we may feel differently next year.'

Was that a hint of promise? His heart lurched. Then he remembered his mission of mercy. 'Got a favour to ask of you, Caroline. Are you feeling like doing an old friend a favour? Especially such a charming one as me?'

'Modest, too! Go on, then, ask. If nothing else, I owe you for that fabulous fish supper.'

He explained.

'Mmm. Yes, I do know Abernethy -well, I been driven through it once or twice. The bus'll take at least an hour, I should think from here. And I've no idea how frequent they are. Why don't I nip up the road to the bus station and find out? Then I'll ring you back at Sally's once we know when we need to leave. It sounds like someone had better go and get your pal. Honestly, you *Rejects*, what's wrong with you all – gormless, or what?' But the gibe, though reminiscent of her past treatment of him, had an affectionate ring to it.

'Hey! Watch it! Don't class me with them. And they're not *all* like that.' Hugh felt stirrings of loyalty to his old cronies. 'Colin's all right really, heaps of fun and very kind, just a bit …'

'Gormless? Right! I'm off to get dressed and head up to the bus station. I'll phone Sally's as soon as I get back. Give me about quarter of an hour.'

'I'll be waiting. And Caroline . . .'

'What?'

'I'm rather looking forward to our trip together. Are you?'

'A wee bus run to Abernethy, eh? Now there's a thrill! But, of course, we *bumpkins* do like our simple pleasures.'

Hugh was grinning as he put down the receiver.

It was a long, slow journey through Abernethy, Perth, Dundee, Forfar and a string of villages in between. Jed concentrated on driving the Landrover at a steady pace, allowing time for Pete, who was steering the Zodiac at the end of the tow-bar to control the swaying of the big car and reduce its tendency to zigzag, especially on some of the tight bends and narrow village streets crowded with parked cars and families meandering through a bit of Saturday shopping. Jed had not hesitated in his choice of son for this tricky task: Pete was the man for such a job and James did not question it.

James and Jed were in the Landrover. James had offered to accompany Pete in the Zodiac but Pete had shaken his head. 'I'll need to have my mind on the job. If we start chatting about things, you know, with all that's been happening …'

Jed agreed. 'I ken what you two are like when you get together. He'll need all his wits about him. It's no easy job. We're no' sure just how good the steering is after the crash but he'll manage fine if he gets peace to concentrate.' James heard a new note of respect for Pete in his father's voice.

Pete sure knows how to get the old women on his side, he thought, as they bowled along the Kingsway towards the Forfar Road roundabout. *Mum always takes his part and Mrs M back at the lodge obviously thinks the sun shines out of his bum. She did quite a number on Dad.* It occurred to him that his halcyon days might be coming to an end.

'Do you think Caroline Dempsey's the lassie for Pete, Dad?' he asked as they edged cautiously on to the big roundabout. Jed did not answer at first, absorbed in watching the Zodiac in the rear-view mirror and admiring the way Pete was controlling it between a motorbike-and-sidecar on the outside and a police car on the inside. As they came off the roundabout, he gave Pete a wave in the mirror and received a thumbs-up back. Then he replied with surprising thoughtfulness to James' question.

'Your brother's more interested in his cars and engines and learning about them. Girls are no' that important to him right now. He'll get round to them later, I expect. He's got his sights set on other things.'

'But, what about Caroline?' persisted James, finding such a concept hard to grasp. He personally spent most of his waking hours thinking about one girl or another, sometimes about two or three at the same time. 'If he *is* going to have a girl, is she the one for him? Do you think she wants him?'

'I think,' said Jed, as he slowed down to let a grey Hillman Minx sidle past their convoy on the narrowing road, 'that it's none of our business. Let your mother worry about things like that. Women like to play these wee games, moving folk about like draughts on a board. We men just let them get on with it. We've more important things to do.' James rather liked this worldview and he especially liked the sound of 'we men'. He let the subject drop – at least for the moment. He would pick it up again with Pete later, of course. He was his mother's son.

Pete almost lost control of the Zodiac as they speeded up again and headed into a long slow bend. As the Hillman had slipped past, the driver had turned her head and looked straight at him. Then she had smiled and waved a friendly hand before accelerating away. There could be no mistake: it was Mrs Band, Alice's mother.

It was past two o'clock when Marjory returned home. She found Alice in the kitchen, still in her pyjamas.

'Oh hi, mum. I've just woken up. What time is it? Gosh! I've missed the morning altogether! It was so great to have a long lie without worrying about weekend homework. Where have you been? Library? Shopping?'

'I've been to Fintry Farm.'

Alice turned saucer eyes on her mother. 'You've been *where*? Oh, heck!' The kettle she had been filling had overflowed, soaking her pyjama sleeve.

'I'm going to change.' Marjory's was tranquil. 'Why don't you make us one of your lovely brunches? Then I can tell you all about it over that.'

'But did you really go there? Why? What's it like? Did you meet his mother and father? Was *he* there? Do you think …?'

'I think you should dry off your sleeve and get on with that brunch.'

Later, over perfect poached eggs, succulent stuffed mushrooms and feather-light pancakes, Marjory revealed phase two of Alice's wonderland. As she floated upstairs, Alice thought *my cup runneth over*.

The late midday dinner at Fintry Farm drew at last to a close. There had been so much to talk over, so many experiences to recount, so many *what ifs* and *thank Gods* to be exchanged.

'Want to come and have a look at the new lambs with James and me, Pete? Your ewe won the bet, by the way!'

'I knew it! That's great. I'd like to come, but I really must get on with the weekend's work upstairs. I've not opened a book since Friday afternoon and I've tons to get through before tomorrow.'

There was short silence: then Jed nodded. 'Fair enough. You'd best be getting on with it then.'

Morag blinked: was that Jed sounding positively amiable about Pete's studies? She was further astonished when, after tramping out of the kitchen in James' wake, her husband returned a few moments later to stick his head round the door and say: 'Don't worry about your evening chores, son. If you can just give James and me a hand with the milking, we'll see to everything else. Jerry Dempsey did such a good job – he's a grand, fast worker – we're well ahead with everything. You need all your time to catch up with your books.'

'I'll take some coals from the stove upstairs with me, Mam.' Pete made for the door out to the porch to fetch the big shovel.

'No need, son. I lit a wee fire up there before you came home. I knew you'd be needing to get right into your books this afternoon.'

'Thanks, Mam. You're a pal.' He turned to make for the other door out into the passage. Morag crossed the room and blocked his way, as if by accident. There had been very little said about Caroline beyond the bald fact that Pete had phoned Chattan and told her they would not be coming to the Ball. When Morag had asked if the lassie was *awful disappointed*, Pete had merely shrugged without reply. James had started to say something but had been silenced by an under-the-table kick from his brother, which had not gone unnoticed by Morag.

'*Was* Caroline very disappointed, then, that you didn't make it to St Andrews? Faye was telling me about the beautiful frock she made for her. What a shame.'

'Caroline's got other things on her mind. She has another fellow up there that she's keen on. I'm sure she's sorry about missing the Ball, but I don't think she's bothered about seeing me.' Pete spoke flatly, without a trace of self-pity. His initial sense of rejection and disappointment had been swallowed up in the demands of the post-crash scenario. By the time he had fallen asleep beside James, in Jean's spare bed, his mind had already moved on to an acceptance of James' analysis: *possibility two* was falling into place, strengthened by the English boy's vague references to some fellow called Hugh. As he had tinkered with Jean's Morris Minor, his brain had sifted through to a simple solution: let Caroline have her Hugh; he would have Alice. Or at least, he would try.

Morag heaved a sigh of relief. It was the one remaining worry. It felt like betrayal – or, at the very least, disregard for the feelings of a girl she knew and liked – to encourage Pete with Alice. But, if Caroline did not want Pete, if she preferred another boy …Morag's own feelings towards the girl cooled abruptly. She had not, of course, explained in any depth to Marjory why Pete had been going to St Andrews: the implication had simply been of a neighbour's daughter who needed a partner for the night. Of Caroline and Pete's close friendship over the past two years, she had said nothing.

'Well, never mind, son,' she said brightly. 'There's plenty of other fish in the sea. Have you any other lassie in mind at the moment?'

'Well, there *is* this girl …' Pete stopped and regarded his mother's air of innocence. In the excitement of arriving home, telling their story and answering Morag's many questions, he had forgotten the sight of Mrs Band in her Hillman Minx passing them on the Forfar road.

'Have you been up to something, Mam?'

'Up to something, son? What *would* I be up to? Tell me about this lassie you're interested in. What is she like?'

'She's really nice, Mam, very pretty and fun to talk to, I really like her,' he finished, after describing Alice, explaining how they had met, what they had talked about, how he hoped to get to know her. A long speech for her Pete, Morag thought smiling to herself. 'It's not that easy, though.'

'How's that, son? What's stopping you?'

'Well, she seems to want to meet me but then she says she can't - or won't - I don't know. I think there something else she hasn't told me. Something stopping her. I've a funny feeling her mother doesn't like her having boyfriends. *She's* a bit frosty.' He remembered again the Forfar Road encounter. 'But I'm sure I saw Mrs Band, passing us just outside Forfar.'

'I don't think you have to worry about the mother.'

'I don't?'

'Sit down again, son, for a wee minute. There something I need to tell you.'

It was another hour before Pete finally got his books out. The little fire had died of neglect and he needed a shovelful of red-hot coals from the stove after all. *Good job Dad's let me off with tonight's chores – there's hours of work here.* A little smile played around his lips as he settled down to his studies. He allowed his mind a delicious flick towards Friday night at *The Hap* cafe. Then he opened a book and immersed himself in Quantum Theory.

Colin's cup was not running over. The local garage duly sent a pick-up truck and removed the old lady: he watched as she was pushed up the ramp and chained down. *Like an old horse being taken off to the knacker's yard,* he thought mournfully. Then he had taken his leave of Arthur and Jean.

There were two pubs in the village at either end of the main street. Colin spent some two hours shuttling back and forward between them, in case Hugh turned up in one or other. This meant buying a new drink each time, and his funds were drying up at an alarming rate. On his fifth trip up the street, he spotted a bus stop. He had no idea what the hieroglyphics on the poster in the shelter meant – he had not been on a bus since the days when Nanny Carruthers used to take him on the top of a London red bus for a treat - so he accosted a middle-aged couple who informed him that this was indeed the stop for the hourly bus from St Andrews and there was one due any minute. He waited hopefully but the bus came and went with no sign of Hugh. He repaired to the pub and slumped in a corner.

'What can I get you, sir?' The barmaid, a middle-aged woman, was not a welcome sight. Not that he wouldn't like another half pint of McEwen's ale: but the final dregs of Aunt Kitty's postal order had gone on the last one in the other pub.

'Can I take your order?'

'There isn't a damned order. I'm skint.' He realised that some charm was in order. He smiled bravely and explained his plight: the terrible accident; the danger he had escaped by a hairsbreadth; the sad plight of his beautiful car; and now his destitute state as he waited for his friend who had insisted on coming to make sure he was really fit to be travelling after his terrible ordeal. She patted his arm and brought him, not only a full pint, but a bag of crisps and a packet of cigarettes as well – *on the house, you poor lad – and just you sit there, as long as you like, till your friend comes.*

Full of beer, exhausted by the mental anguish of the past eighteen hours and tired from tramping up and down the street for the past two, he was soon snoring. The barmaid removed the dangling cigarette from his lips and stubbed it out in the ashtray. Then she cleared away the empty pint glass and left him to sleep.

The bus was beginning to rev up. *Where the devil is he?* Caroline had felt sure he would be waiting for her. She had been relieved to find that the next bus was not for over an hour, giving her time to do something about her appearance. She had mercilessly turfed Elspeth and Patsy out of their beds, recruiting their unwilling service as ladies-of-the-bedchamber. They had somehow found themselves, still sleep-befogged, both holding hairdryers pointed at Caroline's roller-covered head. She herself had been holding a third with one hand and trying to put on make-up with the other.

'But where are you going?' Elspeth came to and managed to frame a question.

'Abernethy. On the bus. It leaves in quarter of an hour. Hold that hairdryer nearer. It'll never be dry at this rate.'

'To see Pete? Can *I* come? I'd like to meet James even if I'll never get to dance with him now.'

'Nope. They'll be long gone, I should think. Their dad will have been over to fetch them this morning.'

'Then why . . ?'

'Hugh and I are going to get Colin – the one whose car ...'

'Yeah, I know. But why? I mean, why does Colin need you to do that? Can't he get the bus back here on his own? Why can't Hugh go on his own?'

Patsy came awake. 'Elspeth, Elspeth, have ye no imagination? Why you think she's wanting to be rushing off on a long bus trip with the gorgeous Apple Pie f? Did we not see the sheep's eyes they were making at each other last night?' She began to sing: 'As beeeyootifool Kitty, one mornin' was trippin'...'

'Caroline ignored her. 'It's a mission of mercy. The poor boy is in such a state after last night that Hugh thinks it would be better if someone was with him on the bus back to St A's. Hugh doesn't know the countryside at all round here so he asked me to help – be a sort of guide – that's all there is to it. And that's fine: you can turn off the dryers now. I need to get going – if it's not dry enough: too bad!'

'Guide, indeed,' Patsy murmured to Elspeth as they watched her hastily brush out the straightened hair and throw on her sheepskin coat. 'Is that what she's calling it?' They watched her go, like fond duennas seeing their charges suitably mated at last.

Hugh raced round the corner and they boarded the bus with no time to spare. 'Where were you? I thought you weren't coming!'

'Breakfast! I haven't had time for anything and I guessed you probably didn't either.' He produced a vacuum flask and a paper bag from which the delicious smell of fried bacon burst forth. Caroline's mouth watered.

'But where did you get all this?' she marvelled as she sunk her teeth into a warm bacon roll.

'Ran up to that ironmonger's on Market Street and bought a flask. Then I threw myself on the mercy of *Joe's Café* and asked them to fill it. They bagged up the bacon rolls for me as well.' Like Colin, Hugh knew how to sweet-talk older ladies and it had not taken him a minute to persuade the assistant behind the counter in *Joe's* to let him have the little picnic.

By the time they had eaten the impromptu meal and dusted the crumbs of flaky roll and scraps of crispy bacon off each other's' coats, their conversation had moved on from teasing and sparring.

Caroline told him all about life on the farm; her three brothers; her schooldays; her coaching of Pete for Higher English and her friendship with him; Pete's obsession with all things mechanical; her enjoyment of student life in St A's; and the wonderful new experience of a having a circle of girlfriends.

He told her of his schooldays at Harrow; failing to get into Cambridge; his parents indifference to St Andrews as a second best option, being Cambridge alumni themselves; his arrival at St A's last October, trailing the weight of their disappointment; the relief at finding there were others in the same boat who understood; the natural progression thereafter into *The Chelsea Set*.

'So you didn't know them all before you came up?'

'No. None of us knew each other. We'd all been at different schools.'

'But you all seem so close, so *exclusive*. As if you'd been a *Set* for years. '

'Not at all. I guess we just gravitated towards each other because we were all coming from the same situation - with our parents disappointed in us, ending up here.'

Caroline thought of her own parents' pride in her gaining a place at St Andrews. She remembered Morag's envious fascination with its traditions and customs.

'But St A's is the oldest university in Scotland – and it's known all over the world.'

'Yeah, but it's not Oxford or Cambridge, is it? That's what matters to the parents.' He sighed.

'So I suppose that's why your Set look down on the rest of us and act like there's a bad smell under your noses all the time? If you have to be here and not there, then at least you can act like you know *here* is a poor second to *there*?

'Something like that.'

'So you wish you were *there* then?'

He turned his head and looked at her. He looped a stray strand of glossy, straight hair back over her ears. 'I would be mad to wish myself anywhere else but here, with you, right now, on this old bus.'

The bus, as if delighted to be given a part in this tender drama, lurched round a bend, throwing them together, driving Caroline's head on to his shoulder. She did not remove it from there once the road had straightened out. Content with the results of its manoeuvre, the bus chugged happily on.

Hugh was not surprised to find Colin sunk in inebriated sleep. They could see him lolling against the window of the pub as the bus passed it, slowing down towards the stop. Colin started awake at Hugh's touch and stared groggily at his rescue party.

'What's *she* doing here? I'm glad to see *you*, old chap, but why the hell did you bring The Land …'

'This is Caroline. Caroline Dempsey. She very kindly agreed to come with me because she knows this part of the country. It was very good of her.' Hugh fixed Colin with a meaningful eye.

'What? Oh, all right. I *see*.' Colin made an effort and turned a pale shadow of his legendary charm upon Caroline. 'Nice to see you, m'dear. Very good of you to come. Can I offer you some refreshment?' He had totally forgotten his lack of funds.

'Yes, please, Colin. I'll have a coke, thanks.'

'Hugh?'

'I'll have the same. And so will you. Looks like – and smells like – you've had enough beer already.'

'Ah, my better half. I am Pinocchio, he is my Jiminy Cricket - you see how it is.' He laughed and Caroline could not help smiling back.

Once the cokes had been brought – and Hugh had found himself paying for them – Caroline cut into Colin's flood of invective against the Zodiac and self-pity over the fate of the old lady. 'There's something else you need to know. It's about the girl you were taking to the Ball.'

'Dorrie? Oh, I know. I should have phoned her to tell her. I just didn't think of it till too late. Shock, you know. Have you seen her? Is she blazing mad at me?' He pulled down the corners of his mouth and hunched his shoulders, fending off shadow punches. This time, Caroline did not smile.

'It's a bit more serious than that.' She glanced at Hugh who nodded for her to continue. 'I'm afraid she was very, very upset about a lot of things. Your not turning up for the Ball was just the last straw. She … she had a bit of a breakdown. She took too many sleeping pills and drank a lot of gin with them.'

'What did she do that for? That could be dangerous. She could have killed herself!'

'Well, we think … we think she meant to do just that. Or perhaps to make us all *think* she meant to do it. A sort of cry for help.'

'Bloody hell!' Colin stared at his bottle of coke as if he'd never seen it before. 'Bloody hell! That's a bit serious, isn't it?'

'You bet it's serious!' Hugh rose. 'And it'll be more serious if we miss the bus back and end up hanging about here. I haven't got enough money to sub you for another couple of hours. It's due in five minutes. Drink up. Let's get you back to Sally's.'

There was time on the long journey home for Colin to be brought up to speed with the causes and effects of Dorothea's breakdown – as far as they knew them. 'And Miss G hinted at stuff we don't know about. I mean it wasn't all just our fault. I think what we all did to her just tipped her over the edge.'

'But …' Colin sought to comprehend the tragic story. 'Is she going to be all right, for heavens' sake? What's going to happen to her?'

'I think her parents are going to send her away for a while. I met Miss Goldsmith – Chattan warden, *you* know – on my way out to the bus. She said they had phoned to say they're on their way up here from London and that they are going to take her home and then send her to an aunt in America for a while. I just hope that'll help her get back on track. I don't think Miss G's too impressed with the parents. I got the impression she thinks they might be partly to blame. Let's hope the American aunt's a better spec. With any luck, she might be able to come back next year and start again – or maybe get a place at some other university.'

Colin grappled uncomfortably with his own part in the near-catastrophe. 'But why did she have to take it all so seriously? It's all just a bit of fun. Balls, corsages, escorts, gate-crashing. I mean what's wrong with the woman?'

'When is a game not a game?' said Hugh sombrely. His eyes met Caroline's.

'I guess' she whispered 'when it's serious.'

Colin blinked owlishly at them. 'There's something going on between you two,' he declared pettishly. Then he grinned. 'I say, Hugh, old chap.

You've done it, haven't you? You've captured the Landgirl? You've scooped The Milkmaid! Well done!'

Hugh turned horrified eyes on him. 'Shut up, you fool! Caroline, please don't think …'

'I think,' she said, rising to her feet, 'I think this is our stop. We're here. Back in jolly old St A's.' She turned thoughtful eyes on Colin. 'You know, I *have* milked a few cows in my time and I did spend a lot of my childhood up on the tractor beside my father and brothers, which makes me a landgirl, I guess. And my home *is* in the country But, as far as getting on with life goes, I do believe it is you who are the *Bumpkin*!'

Hugh caught up with her on the open platform of the bus just before it stopped. 'Take no notice of him, Caro, please. It was just their silly game. All those ridiculous names. I never …'

'You don't have a monopoly on nicknames, you know. We call *you* 'The Apple Pie.'

'Aaah! Flaky and stodgy, eh?'

'Could be sweet and fruity.'

'And best with fresh cream from the farm?'

They held hands and jumped off the bus as it cruised to a stop.

THE END